"We're in position, Captain," Kelso called out from the helm.

Nodding at the report, the captain activated the intercom pickup affixed to the flexible arm on the right side of his chair. "Kirk to engineering. Scotty, start the power transfer."

There was a momentary pause before the chief engineer replied, *"Transfer under way now."*

From the science station, Spock reported, "The connection is not stable. It's being affected by the pulsar's emissions."

"Aye, I was afraid of that," came Scott's aggravated voice from the intercom. *"Too much interference, Captain. I cannot recommend taking us any closer, though."*

Kirk looked up to see Spock stepping down into the command well, moving to stand next to him. "Doing so is the only way to stabilize the connection, sir."

The captain nodded, not seeing any choice in the matter. Things only had to hold together for a minute, two at most. Surely the *Enterprise*, which already had performed admirably to this point, could take that limited amount of additional abuse? The people of Mestiko certainly deserved everything that could be done on their behalf, did they not?

STAR TREK®
MERE
ANARCHY

Mike W. Barr, Christopher L. Bennett,
Margaret Wander Bonanno, Dave Galanter,
Dayton Ward & Kevin Dilmore, Howard Weinstein

Based upon STAR TREK®
created by Gene Roddenberry

POCKET BOOKS
New York   London   Toronto   Sydney   Mestiko

Pocket Books
A Division of Simon & Schuster, Inc.
1230 Avenue of the Americas
New York, NY 10020

First Pocket Books trade paperback edition March 2009

POCKET and colophon are registered trademarks of Simon & Schuster, Inc.

For information about special discounts for bulk purchases,
please contact Simon & Schuster Special Sales at
1-800-456-6798 or business@simonandschuster.com.

Cover art and design by Alan Dingman

Manufactured in the United States of America

10 9 8 7 6 5 4 3 2 1

ISBN-13: 978-1-4165-9494-9
ISBN-10:   1-4165-9494-9

CONTENTS

INTRODUCTION

by Keith R.A. DeCandido

Mere Anarchy came about from such a simple event: the 40th anniversary of the debut of *Star Trek*. In 2006, Pocket Books was publishing several books that tied into that anniversary: the anthology *Constellations*, which featured stories set during the five-year mission of the TV show; the trilogy *Crucible* by David R. George III, which focused on the "big three" of McCoy, Spock, and Kirk; *Burning Dreams* by Margaret Wander Bonanno, the life story of Kirk's predecessor, Christopher Pike; *The Empty Chair*, with which Diane Duane finally brings her *Rihannsu* epic to a close; and Dayton Ward and Kevin Dilmore's *Summon the Thunder*, continuing the *Vanguard* series.

At the time, Pocket also had a monthly eBook program, for which I was the editor, and I wanted the eBook line to celebrate the anniversary as well. The one thing that none of the above did was look at the in-story *history* of *Star Trek*. Unlike any of its spinoffs, the original *Star Trek* has many distinctive eras, by virtue of two pilots that take place significantly prior to the main series and six-plus movies that also span a lengthy period of time.

And so I set out to do a six-part story that would cover each of those time periods: just prior to "Where No Man Has Gone Before"; during the five-year mission; during the "lost years" between the end of the TV show and the first movie; between *The Motion Picture* and *The Wrath of Khan;* between *The Final Frontier* and *The Undiscovered Country;* and after Kirk's apparent death in the prelude to *Generations*. I wanted there to be a planet that the *Enterprise* and/or its crew would find itself visiting many times over the course of the thirty years covered by those time periods.

It was Dayton Ward and Kevin Dilmore who came up with the notion of how to get the *Enterprise* to that planet: a natural disaster. And then we worked out what the disaster would be.

I say "we" there with good reason. I assembled a group of authors from the git-go on this, and while there are separate bylines for each of the six stories, it was truly a collaboration among the eight of us. Literally hundreds of e-mails were exchanged at a fast and furious rate as we tossed ideas at one another, about the nature of the disaster, about the culture of the different nations on Mestiko, about which *Star Trek* characters would be used, about the original characters (particularly Raya elMora), and so much more. (We also would wind up going on multiple digressions—especially about monkeys. I blame Galanter . . .)

The authors I put together were all chosen very carefully, and they all came through brilliantly.

First we have Dayton and Kevin. They've written a couple of eBooks in the *S.C.E.* series that took place just prior to "Where No Man Has Gone Before," and they perfectly captured the unique feel of that period (slightly, subtly different from what we got in the TV show proper), and so they were the obvious choice to kick off the miniseries with a story that featured Kelso, Mitchell, Alden, and Piper alongside Kirk, Spock, Scotty, and Sulu.

After that came Mike W. Barr. Mike has the distinction of writing comic books for five companies (Marvel, DC, Malibu, TokyoPop, and IDW), and he has a knack for the characters of the original series that is hard to match. He was a natural to do the story that would take place in the midst of the five-year mission that we observed for three years on TV (and again in the movie that's coming out shortly after this book).

For the "lost years," I specifically wanted a story that focused on Kirk as an admiral and McCoy as a civilian—a buddy movie, as it were—and Dave Galanter was the ideal choice. I knew Dave had been itching to write a good Kirk story for a long time, and his McCoy is just as spot-on. I also wanted to actually show Kirk *as an admiral*. Every story after Kirk's promotion seemed to focus on his wanting to get back into the center seat, and I wanted to see him using his flag rank for once. Dave ran with the notion with both feet.

The Motion Picture and its aftermath is not the most popular time frame for authors to work in these days, but Christopher L. Bennett did some wonderful work in that period in his novel *Ex Machina*, really exploring the texture of that first feature film. So he was a natural to do the story that took place between the first two films (and his wound up being the single story that covered the most time).

For years, Howard Weinstein wrote the monthly *Star Trek* comic book for DC, and those issues all took place between the fifth and sixth movies. He created some great stories, so I figured he'd take to doing another like a duck to water. And he did! (It turns out that his contribution is a variation on a story he'd originally pitched as a novel, then later pitched as a comic book to DC/WildStorm, and finally got to write in this storyline. Let this be a lesson to you aspiring writers out there: Ideas don't go bad.)

The concluding story is by Margaret Wander Bonanno. I remember reading *Dwellers in the Crucible* when it first came out, and thinking how cool it was. I didn't know that a *Star Trek* book could do that. Throughout the years she's shown an amazing ability to write in this world we've all loved for forty-plus years, and I simply had to include her. We both agreed that it would be fun to do this after Kirk's presumed death, showing the repercussions to Mestiko (as well as the main characters) of his loss.

(This, by the way, means that there's no one of the seven main characters who appears in all six stories. McCoy isn't in the first part; Kirk isn't in the final part; and *only* Kirk and McCoy are in the third part. That wasn't planned, it just worked out that way.)

It was truly a privilege to put this together. All the writers in this volume have been people whose work I've admired as a reader, and are also all people I'm proud to consider friends and colleagues. And the spirit of collaboration that this story-line was created with was truly a wonder to behold. We all worked together to make the story better, and I think the results speak for themselves.

But don't take my word for it. This was originally released as six eBooks to celebrate the 40th anniversary, and now we give it to you in a single print volume as part of the celebration of the release of the new *Star Trek* movie.

Enjoy!

—Keith R.A. DeCandido
somewhere in New York City

2265
THINGS FALL APART

Dayton Ward & Kevin Dilmore

IN TRIBUTE
Paul Carr
February 1, 1934–February 17, 2006

SIX MONTHS AGO

CHAPTER
1

"First Consul, believe me when I tell you that every living thing on this planet is going to die."

Mino orDresha felt frustration mounting even as she delivered the blunt, harsh statement. Despite that, she still was satisfied at finally getting the reaction she sought from Flen etHamwora, watching as his pale, withered features tightened for the first time into a mask of genuine concern.

"You are absolutely certain, my friend?" the first consul asked, his faint and raspy voice one of the more overt symptoms of *neplatrenu*, the degenerative disease with which he had been diagnosed during the previous season. Acting on the directions of his advisors, Flen had chosen to keep his affliction concealed from the public he had been elected to serve, a course of action that only would have become harder as time passed and his condition worsened.

Not that any of that matters now, Mino mused with only a slight degree of bitterness as she regarded Flen, the first consul's aged, diminutive body seeming even paler than normal and all but swallowed by his high-back chair as he sat behind the simple, uncluttered desk that was his spacious office's prominent piece of furniture. While *neplatrenu* was not fatal in all cases, it was a virtual certainty that Flen would not survive long enough to see the disease run its course.

"I have checked my findings three times, First Consul," Mino replied. "There is no error. I remained silent while I verified the data, as you directed, but now that it is confirmed we must take action."

"I do not understand," Flen said after a moment, turning in his seat in order to take in the breathtaking view of Yabapmat, the sprawling city that had served as the capital of the Gelta nation-state for thirty-eight generations. "How can something so far away present such an enormous threat?"

Mino sighed. Though she had attempted to describe the scope of what the planet faced, she knew that Flen's impatience and inability to grasp the finer aspects of the sciences would only serve to prolong this discussion. "Yes, it is true that the object we detected is a great distance away, and in fact will never actually collide with or pass very close to Mestiko. That is not the issue here, First Consul."

Deep-space telescopes had detected the object three lunar cycles ago, and it had taken nearly every waking moment since then to corroborate what Mino had feared upon her initial analysis of the telescopes' collected data telemetry: The rogue phenomenon—essentially a compact star moving through space—was emitting lethal levels of radiation. While the object's path would not bring it into proximity with Mestiko, that did not matter, as the radiation it emitted would wash over the surface of the planet, destroying its atmosphere and inflicting a death sentence upon all life harbored by it.

Those most fortunate would perish quickly as the event occurred, rather than survive a brief aftermath characterized by immense, unremitting suffering from which there would be no escape.

Flen swiveled his seat so that he could see Mino again, his expression still retaining a large measure of doubt. "You will have to forgive me, my friend, but this prediction of yours is a bit much to take in all at once. It does at first sound quite outlandish, would you not agree?"

Once more Mino felt frustration as well as the first hint of anger as she listened to Flen's continued denial. "First Consul, I have been your chief science advisor since you took office. You know that I am not disposed to alarmist theories or reckless, uncorroborated declarations. I stand before you today and tell you without any doubt or reservation that our world is doomed, and that we must act if we are to have any hope of preserving anything of our people or our culture." Indeed, Mino's entire career had been devoted to the sciences and the pursuit of knowledge, to say nothing of the careful weighing and investigation of each new piece of information. Working alongside some of the greatest minds in history, she labored to understand not only the origins of the Payav but also their place among the other worlds and peoples that must inhabit the universe.

And it was that part of my work which was just beginning to show such promise.

Flen placed his frail, withered hands atop the polished surface of his desk. "You misunderstand me, my dear friend. It is not that I doubt you, for you have served not only the people of Gelta but me personally with unflagging loyalty and integrity." He paused to release a small cough, as though the act of speaking at such length was becoming a strain. "The problem I face is my own, for I find myself unable to decide how best to proceed in the face of what you tell me is an inalterable fate for our civilization."

Not for the first time, Mino felt the impulse to simply shout that which she had been keeping contained within herself. It was a struggle that had grown ever more difficult with the dawn of each new day that itself was but one of a dwindling number left to her people. The answer to Flen's question and perhaps even the dire fate that apparently had been levied on Mestiko might well be within her grasp. She had only to speak the words.

I cannot, she reminded herself yet again.

Instead, Mino said to the first consul, "Based on the technology available and the time remaining to us, we have nothing that might be employed to destroy the object, alter its path, or protect against its effects. However, there is something else we can consider."

She paused, stepping around Flen's desk so that she might study the expansive Yabapmat cityscape, which she had called home for nearly her entire adult life. For a brief moment, she imagined it scorched by fire, enveloped in dust and smoke, drenched in acidic rain, with millions of its inhabitants lying dead in the streets or huddled inside their homes, fearfully waiting for a merciful end.

Enough!

Forcing away the gruesome imagery, she returned her attention to Flen. "We have developed the ability to propel a spacecraft faster than light. We can increase its scope to accommodate one or more larger craft, capable of supporting a representative sample of our people. They would be a group who might carry forth our heritage, perhaps to begin anew on another world somewhere far from here."

Flen's eyes grew wide as he listened to Mino's proposition. "That is quite poetic, my friend, but is it practical? How are we to select such a sample of survivors to carry on our name and culture? How do we ensure that an equal representation of all the peoples of our planet is created? Most important, how do we go about such a venture without inciting a global panic?"

"I do not know," Mino said. "That is not my area of expertise. I can only provide you with facts and my opinions on how best to proceed. The rest is up to you."

Remaining silent for a moment, the first consul rose from his chair, using an ornately carved wooden cane to support his aged body as he moved closer to the window. He placed his hand on the thick, ovoid glass of the portal, and Mino saw him close his eyes as though attempting to commune with the city and landscape beyond. After several moments, he turned back to Mino.

"The answer, my friend, is that we cannot."

Mino did not respond at first, unsure that she had heard Flen correctly. Shaking her head, she said, "I do not understand."

"We cannot proceed as you have recommended," the first consul replied, "not without causing worldwide calamity."

Frowning, Mino asked, "You are suggesting we remain

silent, even now?" She held up a hand. "No, it is more than that. You actually believe we should take active steps to ensure the public remains uninformed about this."

Flen nodded. "I do not see that we have a choice." Waving toward the window, he indicated the city. "Once the people learn of what is to come, our entire civilization will likely crumble and descend into chaos and terror. People will turn on one another, perhaps even sacrificing their fellow Payav in the hopes of securing their own safety, which of course will be a futile effort. We essentially will see to our own fate before it can be visited upon us."

"How do you propose to keep such an enormous secret?" Mino asked.

Making his way back to his desk, Flen lowered himself into his chair before replying, "There are only two other nations that currently possess the technology to detect the object's approach as we have. It would be best to alert those leaders, so that we might coordinate how best to proceed. I imagine they will feel similarly with regards to informing their respective peoples. After that, we shall also need to alert the other members of the *Zamestaad*."

Mino nodded in agreement. Given the information and options currently at his disposal, there was of course no faulting Flen for what he was contemplating. Notifying the global security council—created nearly three generations ago in the aftermath of the last great worldwide conflict and which to this day served as a body whose sole mission was to prevent future wars—was a prudent course of action. Once more, Mino felt herself longing to provide her friend and leader with another option, one he likely would not consider even in the most desperate of times.

No! The command echoed in her mind, seeming as though she had shouted it aloud to herself. *I gave my word that I would not divulge what I know.*

Drawing a deep, calming breath, she instead asked, "First Consul, what will you do when the people learn not only what is happening but also that their leaders chose to keep that information secret?"

Flen offered a small, wizened sigh. "We will address that

issue when it presents itself, my friend." Releasing a small, tired smile, he added, "For now, and as odd as it might seem, I must tend to the normal business of the Gelta people. I trust I can depend on you to do as you have already done, to keep this information to yourself, in the interests of preserving the peace so long as we are able?"

"You have my word, First Consul," Mino replied. "I and those I have already entrusted with this information will obey your directive."

Knowing that she likely would be spending an increasing amount of time in these chambers in the days to come, Mino took her leave of the first consul. Her body seemed to move toward her offices of its own volition, leaving her mind free to reflect on her world and the inability of anyone currently living upon it to do anything about the crisis it confronted. She wanted to believe that it was how the people of Mestiko faced what was to come that would define them as a people for all time and in the eyes of those who one day would learn of what was to happen here.

It was also something she feared, never more than as she entered her office and beheld the lone figure standing there, waiting for her.

"Thank you for coming," she said, turning to close her heavy, soundproofed door and ensuring its lock was engaged, thereby concealing from anyone who might happen by the presence in her office of the being from another world.

CHAPTER
2

"I thought you might want to talk," said Dr. Nathan Apo-hatsu as he watched Mino secure the door. Though he had met with the Payav scientist on several occasions in recent months, this was the first time she had summoned him. In keeping with the protocols he had established at their first meeting, all contact was to be initiated by him or a member of his team, which at Starfleet direction had been in place on Mestiko and observing the people of this planet for nearly a year. The controls were enacted as much for the protection of Apohatsu and his team as the local population, who of course had no inkling that visitors from space walked among them.

"I know I should not contact you," Mino said as she moved toward her desk, which appeared on the verge of overflowing with uneven stacks of papers, folders, and various other as-sorted office-related detritus, "but given the circumstances I thought this warranted the deviation from procedure."

Watching her settle herself into her old yet still comfortable-looking chair, Apohatsu could not help but notice that she appeared to have aged considerably since he had seen her, less than a month previously. He saw the new lines around her eyes and mouth, and that her skin seemed even more ashen than the already pale pigmentation that was normal for her race.

Fate truly is a cruel bastard, Apohatsu considered, and not for the first time. The Payav had been of interest to the Federation from the moment they had learned of Mestiko's progression to faster-than-light technology, thanks to a passing Andorian passenger transport's sheer chance detection of the unrecognized—and decidedly primitive—warp signature while traveling in proximity to the planet's star system. As it was the nation-state of Gelta that had developed the successful prototype warp ship, Federation officials decided it was their culture that merited closer observation, bringing about Apohatsu's assignment—along with two other cultural observation specialists—to study the society as well as the dozens of other independent states that formed the planet's sociopolitical landscape. In Apohatsu's opinion, the Payav showed great potential to one day be a valuable member of the Federation. As such, he had been transmitting promising status reports for months, and had been prepared to recommend that formal first contact with Mestiko be initiated.

Then, the pulsar had been detected.

As part of their ongoing cultural observation of the Payav—itself an exercise in preparation for formal first contact proceedings to be initiated by the Federation—Apohatsu and his team had learned of the approaching pulsar as part of their continuous monitoring of all planetary communications. Studying the data collected by the Gelta space agency's telescopes, the Starfleet team had come to the same staggering initial conclusions about the rogue space body and its lethal effects as those reached by Payav scientists. Even as Mino and the Gelta government's science ministry worked to corroborate their findings, Apohatsu himself had been transmitting information back to Starfleet Command in the hopes of getting a more refined analysis of the telemetry. Once that verification had come, it had been with a heavy heart that he met with Mino to confirm her worst fears.

He watched as Mino reached up to caress her smooth, bare scalp, the six digits of her right hand brushing over the small, intricate pattern rendered in dark maroon ink along the top of her skull. Not for the first time, he found his eyes drawn to her neck, thin and longer than that of most other humanoid species with which Apohatsu was familiar but which was normal for the Payav. It always had struck him as one of Mino's more alluring physical characteristics.

"I find myself in the unfamiliar position of not knowing what to do next, my friend," she said, gesturing Apohatsu to the only other chair in her office, which featured a sloped backrest but was still not altogether different from an over-stuffed recliner with which he might furnish his study in his Okinawan home on Earth.

"So," she said after recounting her meeting with First Consul Flen, finishing with Flen's decision to withhold knowledge of the pulsar from the public, "those who do or will know about the Pulse will say nothing. Every discussion will be uttered in hushed whispers; every report from this time forward will be couched in code and cipher. No one will know anything until it is too late, and after that, nothing will matter."

"Flen's reaction isn't unexpected," Apohatsu replied. "In fact, there are plenty of arguments that keeping the Pulse secret is for the best."

He paused, blinking at his own use of the colloquial—if largely inaccurate—term by which Mino had taken to calling the approaching pulsar and its anticipated effects. In the months since he had begun secretly meeting with Mino, he had picked up a good bit of the language used by the majority of Gelta citizens, but he still relied upon the universal translator he wore on his belt to help him. Because of that, he occasionally caught himself employing various idioms and other shorthand used by Mino in their periodic conversations.

"Better to die ignorant and happy rather than informed and terrified?" Mino said, the words sharp as she spoke them. She shook her head. "Given a choice, I do not know if that is the option I would want." Looking across her desk at Apohatsu, she then smiled. "Of course, if I had chosen the career my parents wished for me and become a musician, I would be much happier this evening, yes?"

Apohatsu felt a new pang of sorrow. To see the reality of the current situation weighing so heavily on Mino was all but unbearable. Not only did she carry the burden of knowing what would soon befall all of her people, there were precious few others with whom she could share that knowledge and perhaps seek comfort, and now that isolation had been cemented by consular decree.

"Nathan," Mino said after a moment, her smile fading even as the universal translator produced the slight mispronunciation of his name that was the closest the Payav woman could manage, "we have spoken before of your people and the laws you have against interfering with civilizations that are not as advanced as yours."

Apohatsu nodded. "Just one law, actually. Our Prime Directive. Generally speaking, it applies to civilizations that have not yet discovered faster-than-light travel." In Mestiko's case, while the government of the Gelta nation had successfully broken the warp barrier, the technology remained untried in regular use and, more important, unshared with other governments and leaderships across the planet. It was a leading factor that had prevented him from advocating first contact earlier than he had. Only after prolonged observation, during which it had become apparent that Gelta's ultimate goal was to use the capabilities of warp travel for the betterment of the entire world, had Apohatsu been led to his final recommendation.

"I admire the spirit inherent in the law," Mino said, "that you are unwilling to risk cultural contamination by introducing societies to technology and concepts for which they might not be prepared." She leaned forward in her chair, placing her hands atop one of the shorter piles of papers on her desk. "Given your overtures to me and my select circle of peers, it would seem the directive no longer applies."

"I don't know if it's that simple, Mino," Apohatsu replied. Using standard pre–first contact protocols, he and his team approached targeted members of Mestiko's scientific community, employing a series of burst transmissions on low-band radio frequencies that when interpreted would translate to mathematical theorems. Once those broadcasts were received and returned, the team began a dialogue with that small cadre of scientists, eventually leading to face-to-face introductions.

In particular, Apohatsu's first meeting with Mino orDresha, held months ago, resonated in his memory as if it had happened earlier in the day. Since that initial encounter—which she had taken with great aplomb and poise considering she was among the first of her people to meet with an extraterrestrial—they had forged a fast friendship. In their coded transmissions and during their rare personal meetings, they had spoken of family, of history, of art, and of ambition. The bond he had developed with Mino was unlike any he had experienced among his friends or colleagues.

Realizing he was staring at Mino's small hands—something he had done on several occasions—Apohatsu cast his gaze downward to discover that he was absently fidgeting with the sixth finger of his left hand. Essentially an opposable thumb opposite the one he already possessed, the extra digit had been reproduced via a biomechanical prosthetic he wore on each hand, concealed beneath artificial skin colored to mimic indigenous pigmentation. While the mock-ups did not possess the full functionality of actual Payav hands, and would not pass muster if subjected to close examination, the prosthetics, working in concert with other skin coloring and a hair-hiding skullcap, allowed him to move casually through the city disguised as a local inhabitant.

"While you and the others we have approached know about the Federation," he continued after a moment, "and my superiors are aware of our contact with you, there are still issues to consider. We can't simply announce our presence here. That would likely do as much damage as informing the public about the pulsar."

"But there is so much you could do!" Mino exclaimed, pointing at him with a gesture made all the more odd due to the extra digit on her right hand. "You have the ability to evacuate an untold number of our people, ensure they are taken to a world that can support our species. Even if our planet is doomed, you can make certain that our civilization and our culture is not lost."

With renewed anguish, Apohatsu shook his head. "You know that we couldn't evacuate the entire planet in time, and as your first consul said, there would be no way to enable a program of selection for potential evacuees without causing global alarm."

Whatever he was going to say next was forgotten at the sound of the lock on Mino's office door disengaging before the door itself swung open to admit a trio of armed guards, each wearing dark body armor and helmets with visors that concealed their faces. Apohatsu saw that all three carried ominous-looking rifles, the barrels of which were aimed at him and Mino.

Oh no. The words echoed in Apohatsu's mind. *They know! How?*

"What is the meaning of this?" Mino shouted, rising from her chair. "How dare you barge into my private office!"

Another shadow fell across the threshold of the door, and Apohatsu watched as the small, hunched form of an elderly Payav male walking with a cane entered the room.

"I hope you will forgive me, my dear friend," First Consul Flen etHamwora said as he stepped toward Mino's desk. "The guards are of course acting on my order." Apohatsu saw that the aged leader of Gelta was not looking at Mino as he spoke, but instead was scrutinizing him with a piercing gaze.

"With all due respect, First Consul," Mino said as she stepped around her desk, "would you kindly tell me what this is about?"

Finally turning to face his science advisor, Flen replied, "Considering the gravity of what we face, I suspected you might seek counsel from other parties." He shifted his weight, using his cane to maintain his balance as he regarded Apohatsu once more. "Though I admit I never expected what the true nature of that counsel might be. What manner of being are you, sir?"

Doing his best to feign an expression of surprise and confusion, "Forgive me, First Consul, but I do not—"

Flen held up his free hand, prompting Apohatsu to silence. "Let us not waste time with false pretenses." To Mino, he said, "I have had your offices—as well as those of your associates— monitored for quite some time now. There was some concern that you might attempt to inform the public about the Pulse."

"You would accuse me of insurrection?" Mino said, her

voice rising an octave. "I gave you my word that I would remain silent, and so far as our people are concerned, I have
done just that."

Nodding, Flen replied, "An interesting choice of words,
given your present company." To Apohatsu, he said, "There
will be time to discuss the historic aspects of our first meeting
at another time, sir. For now, I have but a single question: Is
there anything you can do for the people of my world?"

Swallowing the lump he felt forming in his throat, Apohatsu shook his head. "First Consul, I honestly do not know."

NOW

CHAPTER
3

Jim Kirk hated meetings.

It was not that he failed to see their occasional usefulness, at least when information of importance was conveyed. Still, he always had been impatient when it came to such proceedings, discussing the merits and potential pitfalls surrounding a particular course of action rather than actually getting on with whatever tasks needed accomplishing. Despite what he recognized as a personal foible, Kirk was no fool. There obviously were times when meeting to hash out the details prior to undertaking a complicated, hazardous mission was a prudent strategy.

Acting to prevent the extinction of every living thing on a planet definitely qualified in that regard.

Kirk forced away the casual, even flippant thought, annoyed with himself even for harboring it as he looked around the oval-shaped conference table to the other people assembled in the *Enterprise*'s main briefing lounge. While Lieutenant Commander Spock, his science officer as well as his second-in-command, displayed his usual implacable Vulcan demeanor, the other members of his senior staff—

Dr. Mark Piper, ship's physician; Lieutenant Commander Montgomery Scott, the *Enterprise*'s chief engineer; and Lieutenant Hikaru Sulu, leader of the ship's astro-sciences department—each wore expressions of concern and doubt that Kirk was certain matched his own.

"A rogue pulsar," he said. Seated at one end of the conference table, the captain leaned forward until he could rest his forearms atop its polished surface as he regarded the image in the viewer at the far end of the table. He took an extra moment to study the computer-enhanced image of the pulsar as collected by the *Enterprise*'s sensor array. "I've heard of them, but I never thought I'd actually get to see one."

"They are a rather rare form of stellar phenomena, Captain," said Professor Lindsey Cameron from where she sat just to the left of the viewer. A human woman perhaps forty years of age, Cameron wore her blond hair cut in a style short enough to expose the tanned skin of her neck. Dressed in a contemporary one-piece jumpsuit that flattered her trim, athletic figure, the professor presented the appearance of someone far more accustomed to outdoor activity than spending long hours huddled in a windowless research laboratory. "I was most surprised when I received the report about it from Starfleet Command." Offering a demure smile, she added, "I never expected to actually see one myself, let alone get very close to one."

Though he had been captain of the *Enterprise* only for a short time, Kirk could appreciate Cameron's excitement at facing the "unknown." Indeed, it was that aspect of his ship's forthcoming mission—a long-duration assignment that would take him and his crew into an uncharted region of the galaxy with the primary task of discovering and establishing peaceful contact with other intelligent space-faring civilizations—that filled him with a sense of anticipation unlike anything he ever had experienced.

Before he and the *Enterprise* could set out on that mission, however, they first would have to complete the task currently facing them.

"The object was discovered almost six months ago," Cameron said as she rose from her chair and moved closer to the viewer. Using the stylus from her data slate as a pointer, she indicated the pulsar centered on the screen. "Astronomers on Mestiko became aware of it thanks to telemetry received from orbital telescopes, and its presence was later confirmed by additional data transmitted by a long-range probe currently traversing the outer boundary of their solar system. Long-range sensor scans from a Starfleet science vessel removed any lingering doubt."

"It's headed for Mestiko?" Kirk asked.

Cameron nodded. "In a manner of speaking." Stepping away from the viewer, she clasped her hands behind her back as she began to pace the perimeter of the briefing lounge. "Though its projected course will bring it no closer than five hundred and twenty million kilometers from the planet, the pulsar still poses a tremendous threat."

Seated next to Scott, Sulu said, "Captain, a pulsar emits X-ray radiation from its magnetic poles while spinning at high rates of speed. Think of it as a lighthouse, its search beams rotating dozens of times per second. In this case, those beams will intersect with Mestiko as the pulsar moves through the system."

"What kind of damage are we talking about?" asked Dr. Piper, leaning forward in his chair, his frown acting to deepen the already prominent lines etched into his aged face.

Turning to face Piper, Spock replied, "The event will be sufficient to wipe out all life on the planet, Doctor. While that portion of Mestiko facing away from the pulsar will be spared from direct exposure, the damage to the entire planet will be catastrophic.

"The X-ray emissions will also have detrimental effects on the atmosphere, completely destroying the planet's ozone layer and allowing lethal levels of ultraviolet radiation to reach the surface. Within forty-eight hours, the heat buildup resulting from radiation saturation will trigger innumerable severe weather events. Over time, that radiation also will inflict widespread ecological damage."

"The Payav have also deployed a network of satellites and three staffed orbital facilities," Sulu added, "some of which were utilized as part of their research into faster-than-light travel. Those exposed to the pulsar will have their guidance systems fused. Eventually, the heating of the atmosphere will increase drag on the satellites, slowing their velocities to the point that their orbits decay and they plunge back to the planet." The astrophysicist shook his head. "There's also a permanent research base located on one of Mestiko's two moons. No evacuations have been ordered as of yet. Anyone at that colony or aboard one of those space stations doesn't stand a chance."

His own expression one of dread, Scott said, "Sounds to me like the lucky ones are those killed right away."

"You'd be correct, Commander," Cameron replied. "Those who survive the pulsar's immediate effects will be doomed to eventual extinction, either by prolonged radiation exposure or by an atmosphere saturated with toxic pollutants."

Shaking his head, Piper whispered, "Dear God."

Kirk saw the anguish in the doctor's eyes even as the older man released a sigh of resignation. His brown hair, thinning on top, was graying at the temples. There were bags under his eyes and the skin along his jawline was sagging and wrinkled. Kirk knew the man had seen his fair share of suffering and death during his career, and he wore the strain of more than four decades in service to Starfleet for all to see. Though he recently had put in his paperwork for retirement, Piper had agreed to remain aboard the *Enterprise* until the ship's return to Earth, currently scheduled for three months from now. Perhaps he believed those final weeks would be uneventful, but instead he faced the possibility of watching an entire planet die while he stood by, powerless to prevent it.

Well, Kirk mused, *not if we have anything to say about that.*

As though reading his mind, Cameron halted her pacing and turned to face the group of assembled officers. "Of course, the reason we're here is to make an attempt at preventing this catastrophe. At first, we discussed the possibility of building a larger version of the old Verteron Array on one of the system's uninhabited planets, but eventually we decided that was not a practical approach."

Frowning, Kirk leaned forward in his seat. "Verteron Array? Why does that sound familiar?"

"It was a mechanism constructed on Mars in the mid-twenty-second century, Captain," Sulu replied. "Essentially, it was a massive emitter, using verteron pulses to direct comets to the planet as part of the then-ongoing terraforming efforts."

"Aye," Scott said, "but creating an emitter capable of moving a pulsar would be something else entirely."

Spock nodded. "Indeed. The mass of such an object would be far beyond the capabilities of anything we could construct in such a short period of time."

"Which brings us to our current plan," Cameron said. Returning to her place at the conference table, the professor tapped a series of controls on the portable computer terminal Spock had placed there for her use. In response to her actions, the image on the viewer shifted to that of a technical schematic, albeit one for a device Kirk was not sure he recognized.

"This is a Series Alpha sensor probe," Cameron said, "although it's been substantially modified from its original configuration. As you know, this design is intended for investigation of spatial areas where it's considered too dangerous to send a starship."

From the opposite end of the table, Scott said, "Those beasties carry some heavy-duty shielding." He indicated the viewer with a wave of his hand. "That looks to have had some enhancements, though."

Cameron nodded. "Quite right, Mr. Scott. We've taken six of these probes and modified them with increased shielding, and replaced their sensor arrays with enhanced deflector emitters and power transfer relays. We've upgraded their auto-navigation and remote-controlled course correction components, and they each now feature a networking interface so that they can operate in concert with one another." She pressed another control on the computer terminal, calling up another image to the viewscreen depicting six of the probes arranged in a hexagonal formation, with a pale yellow field filling in the space between them.

"Once deployed," the professor continued, "the probes will assume a course parallel to that of the pulsar, traveling so that they are positioned between it and Mestiko. The emitters we installed will deploy a single field designed to act as a moving shield, deflecting the pulsar's X-ray emissions away from the planet. Based on the pulsar's current speed, the shield will only have to perform this function for the duration of time its emission cones are intersecting with Mestiko's trajectory." She shrugged. "Perhaps five minutes, ten at the outside, and it'll all be over."

Scott offered an appreciative nod. "A fine bit of engineering, Professor."

"Extraordinary circumstances, Mr. Scott," Cameron replied, once more offering a small smile. "As an engineer, I'm sure you know and appreciate that any attempt to help these people would be of similar scope and mindset."

Scott nodded. "Aye, Professor. Indeed I do."

"Assuming it works, of course," Spock countered. "It is worth noting that not only is this technology experimental, but this would also be the first known attempt to deflect or divert the radioactive emissions of a stellar body."

Taking her seat at the table once again, Cameron replied, "If you're saying that we don't know whether this will work, Mr. Spock, well of course you're right. However, it's not as though we're graced with a number of options here."

Clasping his hands on the table in front of him, Kirk frowned. Untested technology usually meant all manner of unexpected complications. While he was not in the habit of shirking from a course of action simply because it had never been attempted, he also preferred to examine a problem from all possible angles in the hopes of reducing head-on collisions with the unforeseen. "It's a valid observation, Professor. Suppose this deflector screen doesn't work; what are the alternatives? What about evacuation?"

"All but impossible," Spock replied matter-of-factly. "Mestiko's space travel capability is equivalent to that of mid-twenty-first-century Earth. The Payav have completed automated exploratory missions to four of their system's other six planets as well as several of those worlds' respective moons. They're incapable of evacuating themselves, and there is insufficient time for any Federation effort to succeed in rescuing more than a fraction of the planet's population. Indeed, it would not have been possible to complete an evacuation even if we had begun the process six months ago."

Cameron said, "A large portion of our task is covert in nature. If knowledge of the pulsar reaches the populace—which we have to assume it will at some point if it hasn't already—we have to make sure our diversion of its X-ray emissions cannot conclusively be connected to extraterrestrial action."

Looking to Spock, Kirk asked, "What about our team on the surface? Where are they now?" He had seen the reports about Dr. Nathan Apohatsu and his people being discovered by Payav government leaders.

"According to Apohatsu's reports, which Starfleet continues to receive," the first officer replied, "they remain with the leaders of the Gelta nation-state, who have taken measures to ensure their secrecy as well as that of the pulsar and the existence of beings from other worlds. Such knowledge would likely result in widespread panic among the populace."

When Spock paused, Kirk noticed the slight, almost imperceptible tightening of his jaw. Though the captain was still learning how to read his normally unflappable first officer—a task made all the more difficult by Spock's strict observance of his father's people's cultural mandate to keep their emotions suppressed beneath a veneer of logic—he recognized uncertainty when he saw it.

"Something else on your mind, Mr. Spock?" Kirk asked.

Folding his arms across his chest, the science officer turned to regard Kirk. "I was merely considering the implications of our mission here with respect to the Prime Directive, sir."

"Seems to me," Piper said, "that went out the window the minute our people on Mestiko contacted the Payav scientists."

Kirk had read the transcripts of the messages received from the team of Federation pre–first contact specialists, embedded on Mestiko for nearly a year at that point, in the days and weeks following the discovery of the pulsar. He was struck by how the world's leaders had elected to conceal that information. Realizing that nothing could prevent the catastrophe, they evidently had decided that a swift end to their civilization was preferable to the months of chaos and anarchy that certainly would result when the reality of looming disaster became public knowledge.

That might well have been the way of it, save for the actions of the cultural observation team.

Starfleet Command had received an urgent message from them, requesting assistance for the Payav in dealing with the pending crisis. The team, already in close contact with a cadre of trusted scientists and other high-ranking officials from the planet's largest provincial state as well as a handful of that nation's allies, had revealed much knowledge regarding the Federation and its dozens of member worlds, each of them possessing technology far beyond that of the Payav, and had held out the possibility that aid in dealing with the coming calamity might be available.

"The Payav achieved warp drive, Mr. Spock," Kirk added. "According to the observation team's reports, they were recommending an accelerated timetable for formal first contact protocols even before the discovery of the pulsar."

Spock nodded. "That is true, of course, but the fact remains that according to regulations, the observation team undertook considerable risk by divulging to Payav leaders that we might be able to render assistance."

"I can't believe what I'm hearing," Scott said, his brow furrowing in irritation as he leaned across the table. "Are you actually suggesting we leave these people to their fate and go about our merry way?"

Though the engineer's tone and expression conveyed his rising ire, Spock's features in contrast remained composed. "I was simply attempting to convey the complete context of the situation we face, Mr. Scott."

Because formal first contact protocols had not been enacted with the planet, lawyers had argued that revealing the Federation's presence to the population at large and attempting to render aid would also be in violation of the Prime Directive. While the policy was intended to protect societies that had not yet ascended to a level of technology allowing them to travel to other worlds and interact with other space-faring races, more cynical minds tended to view the decree as a means of allowing the Federation to soothe its conscience while remaining blissfully unengaged in the affairs of those who might genuinely benefit from so-called "interference."

For weeks after the receipt of the observation team's message, the semantics of the situation with the Payav—the letter of the law versus the spirit it was meant to foster—had consumed legal experts. A number of other factors had also been considered, not the least of which was the Mestiko system's proximity to territory claimed by the Klingon Empire. Given that reality, having an ally in this part of space would be of no small value.

Assuming the Payav survived the coming days, of course.

Ultimately, it was determined that the Federation could not in good conscience stand by and do nothing while Mestiko faced certain annihilation, a decision for which Kirk was thankful. While he understood and respected the purpose of the Prime Directive as a means of preventing the contamination of a fledgling civilization, debating the policy's merits in a classroom setting and applying its principles in situations when real lives hung in the balance were two entirely different matters.

"The Prime Directive still applies to the balance of the planet's population," Kirk said, "and Dr. Apohatsu and his team are upholding it by ensuring their presence remains a secret except to the parties they approached as part of the normal pre–first contact protocols. It's too late for second-guessing those decisions, and now we've got a job to do." To Cameron, he added, "I've no illusions that this is a simple task, Professor. What do we do next?"

Apparently satisfied at the direction the discussion had taken, Cameron said, "The effectiveness of the deflector field will be dependent on getting accurate sensor readings of the pulsar. The only information we've gotten to this point was taken from long-range scans. I'll require more detailed readings—the intensity of its X-ray emissions, rate of rotation, and so on. The probes will need that information as a baseline in order to more effectively make automated course-corrections while in flight. I'll also be able to better estimate how long the shield will need to be active."

Kirk frowned. "That means we need to get close enough for

Enterprise sensors to make an intensive sweep." He turned to Spock. "Can we do that safely?"

"We will have to take precautions, sir," the Vulcan replied. "Our own deflector shields will provide some measure of protection, and we should remain free of danger so long as the ship avoids the pulsar's X-ray emissions."

"That's why I have a top-flight helmsman," Kirk said, offering a smile. Then he asked Cameron, "How much time do we have?"

Pausing to look at her data slate and review her notes, the professor replied, "The pulsar entered the Mestiko system about five days ago. Its trajectory will take it past the planet in twelve days, sixteen hours."

"If we proceed at our maximum safe cruising speed," Spock added, "we can be in a position to conduct the requisite scans in approximately sixty-five hours."

Kirk nodded in approval. There would be plenty of time to study the pulsar and allow Cameron to complete her work in preparation for deploying the deflector drones. "Flash the bridge, Spock. Order Mr. Mitchell to lay in an intercept course and engage at warp six." He already could anticipate the reaction his navigator and close friend would have when he learned of the potential danger they faced in bringing the ship so close to the pulsar and its hazardous effects. Gary Mitchell thrived on the thrill of the unexpected, and this mission promised to deliver that in no small portion.

After dismissing his officers and making his way from the briefing room into the corridor, Kirk could not help feeling the same way. With no more questions or items to consider—for the moment, at least—and with orders issued, it was time for action. If good fortune chose to smile upon him and his crew, that action would result in the salvation of an entire world.

A damn sight better than sitting in a meeting.

CHAPTER
4

Her mind still clouded from a half-day session on changes to regulations governing the construction of public housing, Raya elMora groaned aloud as she pushed past the doorway of her small office. Her first act upon entering her private workspace was to relinquish the weight of assorted binders and folders she carried onto her already overburdened desktop. Letting her lithe arms drop to her sides, she sighed and turned back to her door to swing it closed, only to hear a loud, ruffling clatter behind her, a sound that could be only that of once neatly stacked and sorted papers cascading from the desk to a significantly less orderly state on the floor.

Raya brought one hand to her bare forehead and let her thumbs lightly massage her temples as she squeezed her eyes shut, hoping the pressure might scrub away her memories of the last few moments or, better yet, the entire morning.

Despite all of the advances made in communications and electronic data storage, why does the Convocation still insist on committing the bulk of its information to print?

She entertained the thought of proposing the elimination of hard-copy records for the entire national government of

Larenda, until it occurred to her that she would likely be put in charge of an entire subcommittee to research the idea.

"And print the whole cursed proposal onto more stacks of paper," Raya finished her thought aloud.

"Servant?"

Raya's eyes snapped open at the sound of the voice, and she looked up to see her aide, Blee elTorno, standing in the now-open doorway, the sounds and sights of a bustling hive of interconnected office spaces spilling around her small form. Blee's soft features carried a look of puzzlement and some concern as she peered inside.

"Is something wrong?" the young woman asked. "I thought I heard a crash."

Raya allowed her aide a small smile, knowing she should have expected the typically overfunctioning Blee to follow her into her office despite anything the aide might have overheard. "Just making more work for myself," she said as she turned to her desk to survey the damage. "Apparently, someone thinks I do not have enough to do already."

Blee stepped into the office and bent to the task of collecting the spilled folders and scattered papers. "Perhaps they simply observed the lone area of your office not otherwise occupied with documents, and wished to alleviate that oversight."

Laughing as she moved to assist with the cleanup, Raya smiled not only at her aide's zealous enthusiasm to help but also at her sense of humor. The younger woman displayed the typical energy of a recent graduate from schooling for governmental service, particularly those students fortunate enough to receive appointments as Convocation aides.

As for herself, Raya admitted that her seven seasons as a Servant—one selected by the people of her province to join the three-hundred-member Larendan Convocation—had been long enough to allow the reality of the governmental process to dull some of the shine from the allure of national politics.

"So, what happened in the meeting?" Blee asked. "Did they really think we might fail to notice such a severe relaxation of the codes for construction materials?"

The comment elicited a small laugh from Raya as she returned some of the spilled papers to her desk. "*We?* Blee, you were the one who read through that huge proposal and wrote the brief to oppose it. To be honest, except for my showing up at the meeting, the only 'we' this time around was you."

She noticed a grayish cast begin to spread across Blee's pale features. It seemed obvious that the remarks had begun to embarrass her aide.

"I was only doing my duty, Servant," Blee said, and Raya noted the humility in her voice. "So," she added as she straightened a handful of folders, "what *did* happen at the meeting?"

Raya shrugged as she made her way back to her chair. "That depends on whom you ask. Either I once again raised my voice against the threats of profiteering and greed to speak for the unsuspecting masses, or I provided yet another example of my reactionary whining to demonstrate once more just how uninformed I really am."

"It could not be both?" Blee asked, keeping her expression neutral as she collected the last of the scattered papers.

Chuckling at the remark, Raya replied, "In any event, I said just enough to get the proposal pushed back into review. We won't have to worry about code changes again anytime soon. So, you did good this time but *we* will do even better next time."

Blee smiled as she placed the final collection of papers atop Raya's desk. "Yes, we will, Servant."

Glancing toward the ornate timepiece positioned above her office door, Raya realized for the first time that she had missed her morning meal. Given her appointment calendar for the remainder of the day, she knew it was unlikely that she would have a chance to eat anytime soon, and her stomach already was beginning to announce its annoyance at this fact.

Ignoring the protests, Raya instead looked to the schedule on her handheld computer interface. "As far as doing better goes, did we ever hear back from Umeen on those air-quality reports?"

"I connected with the Atmospheric and Astronomic Council office three times this morning," Blee said. "I left two voice messages for Councillor Umeen personally, and a third with the council clerk. I am sorry, Servant."

Raya knit her brow. "He is late with that data we need, and he is *never* late. Something else must be going on. Try him again this afternoon, and if he has not connected by the end of the day, you will have to go to the AAC to meet with him personally. I cannot let the pollution proposal slip past me like I did with the construction codes." Tapping a control on her portable keypad, she asked, "What is next on the agenda?"

Looking to her own personal computer interface, Blee replied, "Con orStapa with the Convocation news feed wants your comments on the poll—"

"The pollution proposal, yes," Raya finished. "That can wait until after I review Umeen's reports. Anything else?"

"Yes," Blee said, her mouth fighting a smirk. "Two connects from your *elor*."

Raya felt a pang of guilt as she realized that she could not easily recall when she had last spoken with her father's mother, the woman whom she had affectionately addressed as Elee for as long as she could remember.

"I hope she was not too short with you," Raya said, "and kept any editorial comments about my lack of communication to herself."

Typically, not even a full schedule of Convocation duties could keep Raya from taking a few minutes to contact her, even if only by mobile link as she made the commute to and from the Convocation complex. Despite that, for uncounted reasons—none of which sounded valid to her at this moment—Raya had forsaken that routine, and now she would have to answer to her *elor*, who of course would take no small amount of amusement from that act.

"She was polite as usual," Blee replied, "and I told her you happened to mention to me just today that you intended to sit down to a nice long talk with her this evening."

"Oh, nicely done," Raya said, nodding in appreciation at her aide's deft handling of the situation. "And with that settled, I suppose I need to—"

"Servant Matthi stopped by to invite you to midday meal," Blee said, tapping her keypad.

Raya sighed, her stomach again rumbling with the thought of food as she consulted her schedule for the remainder of the day. "As much as I enjoy his company, I just don't have the time to meet with him."

"You'll be of no help to me at the review meeting if your mind is on your grumbling belly," a deep voice echoed through the small office.

Looking up, Raya smiled as Matthi orJurbes strolled into the room, his richly colored robes of blue and red—a display of wardrobe other Servants cited as much too casual for the atmosphere of the Convocation—adding a warm hue to his pallid skin. After sixty seasons of public work, Raya figured, the man had earned the right to wear anything he pleased, and he had said as much to anyone risking an audible comment about his apparel in his presence. His adherence to his convictions despite any resulting clash with long-standing convention, and his vocal defense of anyone else willing to shake up the status quo in similar fashion, warmed the two to each other almost instantly upon their initial meeting, when Matthi was assigned as a mentor during Raya's first season as a Servant. She found herself particularly pleased that he had chosen today to call on her.

Noting the small bundle he carried in his left hand, Raya asked, "Dare I ask what gifts you have brought me this day?"

The elder statesman craned his thin and quite wrinkled neck in an evident expression of pride, offering the paper-wrapped parcel with a dramatic wave. "Spiced curd spread and greens, just the way you like it."

"And that is my cue to go . . . somewhere. Anywhere," Blee said, her expression one of mock disgust as she turned for the door. "Servant, if you need me, I will be eating a meal fit for actual consumption."

"Good taste is wasted on the young," Matthi said to the departing aide, with the two exchanging knowing smiles before she disappeared through the closing door. Now alone with Raya, he moved without invitation to the chair situated before her desk and handed her what apparently was to be her midday meal.

"Thank you," she said as she took the proffered package. "You are a gift from the gods."

"Remember that when you add the gratuity," Matthi countered as he settled himself into the chair. "So, my young progeny, what could possibly be so important that you do not even have the time to eat?"

"Everything at once," Raya replied before biting into her leafy roll and savoring the blend of seasonings that lightly burned at her taste buds.

"Let me guess," Matthi said. "The Atmospheric and Astronomic Council again? I am surprised that they have not given you your own office, considering how often you are there harassing them. A holdover from your university days, I suspect."

Raya offered a sheepish smile and felt her face warm with some embarrassment, the same way it did every time Matthi chidingly remarked about what he referred to as her "radical youth," rather than crediting her with her schooling achievements. It was during her training as an environmental sciences teacher that Raya had joined a group of fellow students committed to the purity of the planet's air and water. Her own research into the subject turned into what she knew even then would be a lifelong passion for raising public awareness of the contaminants people ate, drank, and breathed each day.

Indeed, it was her first testimony before the Convocation—a call for the protection of wetlands threatened by a proposed reduction in emissions standards for manufacturers—and the overwhelming positive response she received from her fellow students and journalists as well as a few Servants that eventually had led her to pursue a calling to public service rather than education, with the goal of forging her passions into policy. While her role as a Servant required her consideration of matters ranging from agriculture to foreign policy and from security to transportation, issues directly affecting the environment of Larenda and all of Mestiko had always been the primary driving force behind her efforts.

"I do not harass anyone," Raya said around another bite of her meal. "I am merely persistent at making my wants known."

"Indeed you are," Matthi replied, nodding, "and the people see that. They pay attention to the proposals you make as well as those you support. They like what they see, Raya."

"I am not here to be watched on the news feeds or recognized when I am at the marketplace, Matthi," Raya said. "When I was selected to serve, I admit that I was single-minded on what I wanted to accomplish here, but I have since found that my focus has broadened in a great many ways." Eyeing her mentor as she took another bite, she added, "You have yourself to either thank or blame for that, by the way."

Ignoring the good-natured jab, Matthi smiled. "That is just the kind of thinking that will see you to a leadership position, my young Servant."

Raya actually stopped chewing at that remark. Noting the look in her friend's eyes, she frowned. "You cannot be serious."

"The Presiding Servant has started asking questions about you," Matthi replied, "wondering about your potential in an expanded role, and I am not the only one whose opinion he has solicited. That is something you should keep in mind before you go charging into any proposal reviews with your customary ire raging."

"It sometimes takes a little ire to get people to think about the things in life we take for granted," Raya said, leaning forward in her seat. "I am not about to stop pushing to protect our planet just to receive leadership of some administrative committee."

Holding up his hands in mock defense, Matthi said, "I am merely offering you some insight into how others are viewing you. You are respected, both by the Convocation and the people, and you have the chance to start building consensus. That can work very much in your favor when you need support for proposals of much greater scope than tightening emissions standards. Clear-minded thinking and the willingness to work for the middle ground is what they are hoping to see you demonstrate, and I know you have it in you." Rising from his chair, he offered a knowing smile as he nodded at the remains of the meal still in her hand. "But only if you keep up your energy, so . . . finish eating that."

He let himself out, leaving Raya alone in the confines of her cluttered office. She studied the closed door as she chewed another bite of her meal, though the greens now seemed a little less crispy and the spread just a little flatter in spice as she considered what her friend had said to her.

It was not the first time that Matthi had suggested she make some effort to expand her sphere of influence within the Convocation. Unlike many of his peers, he looked past her rebellious youth and instead saw her passion for pursuing the greater good. Still, it was not as though he was ignorant of her feelings on pursuing such a career path, one which would in all likelihood require her to rein in her outspoken manner and develop proficiency in something for which she seldom had seen use: Compromise.

Sorry to disappoint you, Matthi, she thought, *but I fear that a bit of the radical still remains within me.*

CHAPTER
5

"Approaching the pulsar now, Captain."

Looking up from the latest in what seemed to be a never-ending series of status reports handed to him by his yeoman, Kirk nodded to Lieutenant Commander Gary Mitchell, who turned to regard him from his navigator's console as he relayed his report.

"Lay in a parallel course, Mr. Mitchell," he said. Turning his attention to the officer seated to Mitchell's left at the helm station, Lieutenant Lee Kelso, Kirk added, "Mr. Kelso, match the pulsar's velocity while maintaining safe distance. Let's have a nice, smooth ride, gentlemen."

Mitchell nodded, a wan smile playing at the corners of his mouth. "We'll do our best to lull the captain to sleep," he said as he returned to his station, exchanging grins with Kelso that communicated not only their trust in each other but also the faith they knew their captain gave them. Individually, each man was an effective officer well suited to his duties. Working together, they were a formidable team upon which Kirk quickly had learned to depend.

Of course, Gary Mitchell was a longtime friend of Kirk's,

dating back to their days at Starfleet Academy, and the two already had served together on two other ships, the *Republic* and the *Constitution*. Upon assuming command of the *Enterprise*, Kirk had asked for Mitchell to serve as his first officer. That request had been overruled by Starfleet Command, however, in favor of promoting Spock to that position in addition to his current duties as *Enterprise* science officer.

The admiral responsible for making such decisions believed that Kirk and Mitchell were too much alike in their personalities to make an effective tandem as commanding and executive officer, a relationship which more often than not thrived on contrasting perspectives and approaches to problem solving. Mitchell, to Kirk's shock, actually agreed with the admiral, though Kirk himself protested the ruling. Despite that initial discord, the captain was coming to realize, based on his dealings with Spock, that the admiral's decision had indeed been a wise one.

"Strong sensor contact," Spock said from his workstation. The captain looked over to see the science officer hunched over the hooded viewer that was the dominant feature of his console and that provided him with a direct interface to the constant streams of telemetry being received by the *Enterprise*'s array of sophisticated sensors. His face bathed in cool blue light as he continued to study the scanner readings, Spock continued, "Bearing 346 mark nine, velocity 40.77 kilometers per second."

Though Spock could not see him, Kirk nodded at the report before handing the data slate and its miniature mountain of status reports to the young brunette woman standing to his right. "Thank you, Smith."

She regarded him with a startled expression. "Sorry, sir. I'm Yeoman Jones."

Kirk sighed. The ship's personnel administration department recently had assigned two enlisted women to fill the billet of his yeoman, Jones for alpha shift and a striking young blonde, Smith, for gamma. At least, he thought those were their assignments, as he had yet to address either woman by her correct name.

With a weak smile of apology, the captain shook his head in

resignation. "I'll get it right one of these days, I promise." Rising from his chair at the center of the bridge's command well, Kirk noted an abnormal tremor in the deck plates beneath his feet. "What is that?"

Spock replied without looking away from his console. "We are beginning to encounter gravimetric turbulence from the pulsar. It will have an effect on our sensors as we draw closer."

"Go to yellow alert," Kirk ordered as he stepped toward the red curved railing separating the upper deck from the command well. He could tell when the *Enterprise*'s deflector shields activated in response to the raised alert level, not only from the fleeting blink in the overhead lighting as the ship responded to the new power requirements but also by the abrupt fading of the slight yet still noticeable trembling in the deck plates.

"We're starting to receive detailed sensor telemetry from the pulsar," said Professor Cameron from where she sat to Spock's left, the station she occupied having been reconfigured for her use. She pointed to one of the eight small display screens arrayed just above her console. "Density is equivalent to 1.48 solar masses. Smaller than I expected." Looking to Kirk, she smiled. "That's a good thing."

His elbows perched atop the railing, the captain stroked his chin as he considered the professor's report. "How so?"

Turning in his seat, Spock replied, "Given its current trajectory, if the pulsar were any larger there would be a significant risk of it pulling Mestiko from its normal orbit around this system's sun."

"As it is, there's likely to be a minor disruption of its orbit, anyway," Cameron said. "I'll need to examine the sensor data more closely and conduct some computer simulations, but just from what I'm seeing here I'm willing to guess the planet's orbit will become slightly more elliptical. Long-term effects would include more extremes in seasonal weather patterns: hotter summers, colder winters, though the summers might end up being shorter and the winters longer. It's possible the orbits of the planet's moons may also be affected."

From behind Kirk, Mitchell said, "Given the circumstances, I imagine the Payav could learn to live with that."

"On the contrary, Commander," Spock countered, "according to the reports submitted by the cultural observation team assigned to Mestiko, there are several segments of Payav society with deep-seated religious tenets. They include the belief that a calamity befalling their world be considered punishment for not living up to the standards set forth by the entity they choose to worship."

His eyes widening even as he kept his attention on his console, Mitchell said, "You're saying that if we manage to deflect the pulsar's effects, we'd be seen as interfering with divine will and the fulfillment of prophecy?"

"Assuming we're discovered by any of the indigenous population," Cameron replied. "Beyond the handful of people who already know about us, of course."

As if in response to the conversation, the deck plating once again shuddered beneath Kirk's feet, and he felt the vibrations channeled through the bridge railing and into his hands. The overhead lighting flickered and he noted several of the display monitors at the perimeter stations waver as though suffering momentary disruption.

"Gravimetric interference?" Kirk asked, making his way back to his command chair as Spock and Cameron both returned to their respective stations.

Consulting his instruments once more, Spock replied, "Affirmative. The effects are increasing." He turned toward the young officer at the engineering station at the rear of the bridge. "Deflectors, full intensity."

Kirk looked to the main viewscreen, upon which was displayed an image of the blue-red pulsar. "Can we compensate?"

"Our course isn't being affected, Captain," Kelso replied from the helm. "At least, not yet. We can move away if we need to, but it'll get worse as we get closer, sir."

Satisfied with the report, Kirk turned to Cameron. "How much longer do you need?"

"Just a few more minutes, Captain," the professor replied before turning back to her workstation.

"Shields holding at full power," Mitchell reported, "but they're taking quite a beating."

Kirk could believe it, even without the added emphasis of

the renewed tremor in the arms of his chair. There was no denying that the ship was being subjected to a terrific assault on its defensive systems as it maneuvered ever closer to the rogue astral body. Despite that, he understood just how important it was that Cameron be given every opportunity to collect as much information as possible. There simply was too much at stake to err on the side of caution now.

"Have engineering route emergency power to the shields. Maintain course and speed as long as possible," Kirk said. "And Professor, sooner would be better."

Cameron nodded, both hands moving across her station's rows of multicolored controls. "Almost there, Captain. These are the most detailed scans of the pulsar we've gotten to date. Its magnetic field is stronger than we anticipated, which means we'll have to modify the way the probes are deployed."

In front of Kirk at the center of the navigation console, the red triangular alert indicator began to flash at the same time as a new, stronger jolt rocked the entire bridge. He felt himself pushed back in his seat and he saw both Kelso and Mitchell grip the edges of their consoles.

"Deflector generators are overloading!" Spock called out, shouting to be heard over the alarm klaxon that was now echoing across the confines of the bridge. Once again the overhead lighting wavered, this time dying out altogether before being as quickly replaced by emergency illumination. Despite the *Enterprise*'s inertial dampening systems Kirk still felt his stomach lurch as the starship struggled against the pulsar's gravitational effects.

"Kelso, cut speed!" he ordered over the shrill whine of the red alert siren, remembering the instructions Cameron had given him in the event the ship needed to move away from the pulsar. "Veer off!" He gripped the arms of his chair as the image on the main viewer showed the pulsar pulling away before vanishing past the screen's left edge. Almost immediately he sensed the vibrations running through the deck and even his chair beginning to abate.

"Damage reports, all stations," he heard Spock call into the ship's intercom system, and looked to see his communications officer, Lieutenant Alden, turning to oversee that task. The young African man's features clouded into a concerned scowl as he listened to the litany of status reports coming in from across the ship, channeled to his station and the Feinberg receiver he wore in his right ear.

The tremors were gone now, and Mitchell already had seen to the securing from red alert before leaving his station to assist Cameron, who had been dumped unceremoniously to the deck. "Are you all right, Professor?" the navigator asked as he assisted her to her feet.

Cameron replied, "I'm fine, Commander, thank you." As Kirk moved once more to the railing, she added, "My apologies, Captain. I should have anticipated that might happen as we drew closer." Glancing toward the floor, she grimaced as she reached up with her right hand to rub her temple. "There was so much sensor data coming so fast, I guess I just got caught up in it."

"No other significant damage or injuries, Captain," Alden said from the communications station.

Stepping toward Kirk, Spock clasped his hands behind his back. "Engineering reports that the deflector shield generators experienced severe strain, but Mr. Scott believes he can have them back to full operational status within nine hours."

Nodding at the report, Kirk said, "Have Scotty see what he can do about enhancing shield strength. We're not done here yet, and I don't want to risk further damage to the ship in the event we have to get close to that thing again."

"What about those probes?" Mitchell asked, leaning against Cameron's console, his arms folded across his chest. "They're going to have to be a lot closer to that pulsar than we got. Will their shields protect them?"

Cameron frowned. "The pulsar's gravimetric effects are more intense than we anticipated, but we tried to allow for such a variance when calculating the power requirements for each probe." Exhaling audibly, she looked to Kirk. "But I have to be honest, Captain, I'm not sure it will be enough."

Kirk could see that the admission was a difficult one for the professor to make. She—and those who had helped her, of course—had no doubt labored with a palpable level of uncertainty throughout the development of their plan and the technology to support it, insecurity only made worse when measuring the stakes. Still, that feeling could at least be mitigated with the knowledge—harsh though truthful—that the people of Mestiko were doomed if no action were taken.

Now, however, Cameron faced head-on the possibility that she might take that action and still fail. It was a prospect Kirk also had considered—a realistic assessment of the situation given the untested nature of what they would soon attempt.

That said, he simply refused to accept it.

He turned to look at the main viewer, which now showed an unfettered starfield. In his mind's eye, however, he envisioned a tranquil image of Mestiko centered on the screen, with its azure oceans and lush green and brown landmasses upon which teemed a civilization on the brink of extinction.

"It'll have to be enough, Professor," he said after a moment, feeling his jaw tighten in determination. "We don't have a choice anymore."

There could be no excuses, no rationalizations for inability to achieve what they had come here to accomplish. Too much rode on the outcome of their mission; too many lives depended on what he, his ship, and the people under his command did or did not do in the coming days.

Failure was unthinkable.

CHAPTER
6

Raya slammed the heel of her hand against the door, pushing it open as she dashed into the outer offices of Umeen or-Wenda, her longtime friend and occasional rival at the Convocation's Atmospheric and Astronomic Council. The first thing she noticed was the active oval-shaped display monitor, tuned to one of the dozens of news broadcasts currently being aired. While the audio had been muted, the stark visuals—a computer-generated star map depicting a representation of Mestiko and the sun it orbited, along with another, highlighted object emitting bright yellow lines that intersected the image of the planet—and the expression of the journalist currently reporting were more than enough to convey what was rapidly becoming the sole topic of discourse, not only here but perhaps across the entire world.

We are going to die.

The thought echoing in her ears as she tore her eyes away from the monitor, Raya noted the conspicuous absence of Umeen's assistant. That alone was an uncommon occurrence, particularly at this time of the workday when the councillor was at his busiest. With no one to stop her, she made her way across the anteroom and pushed open the door leading to the inner office.

"Umeen?" she called out.

Seated in his favored high-back chair behind an ornate wooden desk perhaps twice the size of the more utilitarian model she used and watching another monitor—a smaller, tabletop display showing the same news broadcast as was currently airing in his outer office—Umeen orWenda looked up at her approach. "Raya?" he asked, squinting to see her across the expanse of his spacious chamber. "Is that you?"

Stoop-shouldered and thin, Umeen was an elder member of the AAC, having occupied his position on the council since well before the first time Raya had encountered him. She had been a student at university and he was old, then, of course, though she had watched in recent seasons as his body seemed to succumb ever more rapidly to the onset of advanced age.

Despite his deteriorating physical condition, Umeen's mind remained as sharp as ever, something he demonstrated every time Raya saw him, either in private or as he addressed the Convocation about various matters pertaining to the mission of the AAC. She had watched him stand before her and her colleagues and argue for budget increases in order to fund new satellite technology, and it had been Umeen who first had suggested that Larenda could do worse than to assist the Gelta nation in its controversial space programs, funding Raya herself had always argued could be better spent on curing the planet's mounting environmental woes.

In the end, it seemed, Umeen always won.

Pointing to the images on the monitor situated at the corner of the councillor's desk, Raya asked, "Can this be true?"

Umeen paused, and the expression clouding his aged countenance—a combination of fatigue and perhaps regret—told Raya everything she needed to know even before he spoke the words.

"Yes, I am afraid so."

Raya felt her stomach tighten as though struck by a physical blow. "I do not understand," she said as she all but sank into the heavily padded chair positioned before Umeen's desk. "How can this be possible?"

Despite her growing apprehension, she managed to keep enough presence of mind to pay attention to the councillor's brief explanation of the compact, renegade star currently traveling across the outer boundary of Mestiko's solar system, emitting lethal radiation that eventually would wash across the surface of the planet in less than a solar cycle's time.

"*Everything* will die?" she asked once her friend finished his cold, almost dispassionate explanation.

Umeen nodded. "The atmosphere will be all but burned away, creating a seemingly never-ending series of shock waves that will cause tumultuous weather events unlike anything ever recorded. According to our calculations, our side of the planet will be shielded from the direct effects, but the radiation's impact will still be felt worldwide. There simply will be no escaping it."

Feeling the first hints of true fear beginning to grip her, Raya said, "How can you be so sure?"

"The data has been corroborated by no less than seven different scientific bodies around the world," Umeen replied, indicating the monitor atop his desk with one withered hand. "Of course, that information was not to be disclosed in this manner, and I am sorry you had to learn of it this way."

Her brow furrowing, Raya scowled at the councillor. "How long have you known about this?"

Releasing a resigned sigh, Umeen reached up to scratch his long, thin neck. "Almost two full seasons now. For reasons that should be obvious, it was hoped the information about the Pulse could be kept secret from the public. Perhaps that was wishful thinking on our part."

"Our part?" Raya repeated. "Who else knew?"

Umeen shrugged. "The councillors of the *Zamestaad*, of course, as well as a handful of my peers in the science community and the leaders of the three nations who have access to space telescopes capable of detecting the object. That is the way it was to remain until the end." Nodding toward the monitor again, he added, "Obviously, someone decided differently."

Holding up a hand in protest, Raya said, "Are you saying that the *Zamestaad* has decided that nothing can be done for us? We are to simply lie down and die without any attempt to save ourselves? There must be something we can do, some preparations we can make."

For the first time since her arrival, she saw frustration cross Umeen's features. "Child, if you do not believe that our planet's greatest scientific minds have been laboring over this dilemma in the hopes of gleaning a solution, then you are as naïve about this as you were when you took me to task during those university lectures." Then his expression softened, and he sighed once more. "There is something of a plan in place, of course. People are even now being urged to move to shelters, either storm shelters, or the more robust versions constructed long ago during the global wars. I also have heard of some groups making their way to the inland mountain ranges, to the caves and tunnels there. It will be a futile effort, though. Even if such shelters are sufficient to protect against the radiation, it is unlikely anyone will escape the Pulse's long-term effects."

Raya felt a tear sliding down her cheek as she finally began to absorb the enormity of what Umeen was telling her. "So, what are we to do?"

Shaking his head, Umeen replied, "There is precious little we can do, my dear. In the time remaining to us, I fear we shall have our hands full just keeping the public from devolving into mass hysteria and anarchy." With a tired, resigned smile, he added, "Not that I believe such efforts will be successful, mind you."

Rising from her chair, Raya made her way to the large, elliptic window dominating the rear wall of Umeen's office. Looking down into the expansive courtyard that occupied the center of the Convocation grounds, her eyes were drawn first to the courtyard's stand of revered *noggik* trees, their gnarled, fruit-bearing branches and fragrant wood a living symbol for many people of the diversity and plenty of all life. The courtyard was a regular place of respite for Raya, where she could find momentary peace away from the daily responsibilities and stresses of her duties.

As she watched now, however, the courtyard was anything but serene and calming. Dozens of armed security personnel moved about, either securing the various exits from the complex or working to bring under control what appeared to be a growing crowd of civilians. Even from where she stood, three levels above the ground, Raya still could see expressions of concern, anguish, and fear on the faces of the citizens. No doubt they had come here, to the seat of their elected government, in search of answers to what was being disseminated over the news broadcasts. The longer they went without information—some sign that their leaders were working on their behalf—the more panic-stricken they would become. Chaos would soon reign supreme.

For a short time, at least.

As she watched the growing unrest among the people she had been selected to serve and as she realized she was no longer in a position to do anything for them, Raya's thoughts turned instead to a single person.

Your words would be such a comfort now, my beloved Elee. What am I to do?

". . . sent to us by a member of the first consul's administration who has asked to remain anonymous, appear to leave no doubt that our entire planet faces an imminent threat from space. So far, all requests for clarification from the first consul have gone unanswered."

"How could you do this?"

Along with Mino orDresha, Dr. Nathan Apohatsu stood with the other two members of his cultural observation team—the three of them each sporting their Payav clothing, makeup and prosthetics that allowed them to move undetected about the local populace—at the rear of Flen etHamwora's office, watching as the elderly Payav leader rose from his chair and leveled an accusatory finger at the individual who—so far as the public was concerned, at least—remained "anonymous."

"Do you not realize what you have done?" Flen asked Celadi ilSom, who until a few moments ago had been one of the first consul's most trusted assistants. As he jabbed his long, bony finger at the younger Payav, Flen's anger seemed on the verge of racking his entire aged, emaciated frame. "Surely you comprehend the widespread panic this will cause? Why would you do such a thing?"

His hands clasped behind his back as he stood flanked by two members of the security force assigned to the capital, Celadi nodded slowly. "I felt the people deserved to know what was coming, so that they might be with their loved ones, rather than simply going about their normal lives as though nothing were amiss." Looking up, he added, "Is it wrong to want to seek peace when one's end is near?"

"Of course not," Flen snapped, "but you are not empowered to make that decision for an entire world!" He started to say something else, but the words were interrupted by a deep, gurgling cough that caused him to collapse back into his seat. Watching the first consul struggle to regain his composure, Apohatsu knew that this was yet another effect of the disease ravaging Flen's weakened body.

He had watched the progression of the first consul's ailment in the months since his initial meeting with the aged leader. In that time, he had come to respect Flen not only as an individual but also for the courage he displayed every day as he forced aside his personal struggles in order to continue his service to the people of Gelta.

As Flen reached for a carafe of water, Mino stepped forward. "Celadi," she said, reaching out to place a hand on the assistant's shoulder, "what else did you tell the journalist?"

Clearing his throat, Celadi replied, "I provided information about the Pulse's projected effects, the damage it would cause, and how soon it would begin. I supplied computer simulation data and visual records obtained from our telescopes. Additionally, I offered the names of certain scientists who could corroborate the data on the promise of anonymity."

"So, there are others who have betrayed us, as well?" Flen asked, having once again reclaimed his bearing. Not waiting for an answer to the question, he rose once more from his chair, using his cane to shuffle his way to the expansive window that formed his office's rear wall. Looking down on the vista of Yabapmat, he shook his head. "The repercussions of your actions will be staggering, if somewhat short-lived." As he said that last part, his eyes shifted so that he was looking at Apohatsu, and the doctor was sure he saw uncertainty in the elder Payav's features.

For the first time since his arrival on this planet, the doctor was acutely aware of how much he and his companions did not belong here. Apohatsu looked to the other members of his team, and saw true sorrow in the eyes of his fellow Earth-born researcher Camila Schiapp. The cultural anthropologist's somber expression seemed even more acute given her Payav disguise, which hid from view the brown hair that usually framed her face and that always refused to be tamed by the ponytail she typically wore.

Next to Schiapp, the Deltan sociologist Vlenn regarded him with hard eyes and lips pressed tightly together. While Apohatsu outranked him, Vlenn was by far the most experienced member of the team. In the doctor's opinion, no one held any greater appreciation for the duty to protect indigenous peoples and cultures from outside influences that might irreparably change the course of their natural development. Given all that had happened—over the past several months, to say nothing of the past few minutes—there was no denying the expression of helplessness and frustration now visible in the Deltan's features.

"What you did was misguided, but I know that it was without malice," Flen said as he turned away from the window, and Apohatsu now saw the strain of the past months—his disease, coupled with the need to come to this place each day in order to carry out the duties of his office, knowing all the while that he was helpless to protect the civilization he had been elected to lead—etched firmly in his pallid features.

The first consul did have a point, Apohatsu knew. That Celadi had not known of the existence of Apohatsu and the rest of the team was fortunate, in that it obviously would have led to all manner of other questions regarding their presence here, to say nothing about inquiries into their knowledge of the pulsar and whether they might be able to do anything about it.

Waving toward the guards standing on either side of Celadi, Flen ordered, "Take him down to the emergency command center." As the pair of security personnel moved to collect their charge, the first consul held up his free hand. "Wait." Walking slowly but with a renewed purpose around the corner of his desk, he moved to stand before his assistant. "Celadi," he said, his raspy voice sounding even more tired now, "your family will be brought to the shelter. You should be together when . . ." His voice faltering, he suppressed another cough. "You should be together."

As the guards left with Celadi and Flen made his way back to his chair, Mino stepped closer to the first consul's desk. "What happens now?"

"Now?" Flen repeated, lowering his withered frame into his seat. "As we speak, our police, military, and emergency first-response assets are being deployed toward quelling the mass unrest that is gripping the populace. I have already begun the steps to declare nationwide martial law in the hopes that such drastic, distasteful measures might afford us some degree of control, as fleeting a concept as that is rapidly becoming."

"First Consul," Apohatsu said, stepping toward the desk, "there is something you might wish to consider."

His eyes widening in surprise, Flen asked, "And what would that be?"

"Talk to the people," the doctor replied, his initial uncertainty at the idea fading with each word he spoke. "Tell them that the situation is not as certain as was first believed. The calculations support several conclusions. Tell them you really don't know what's going to happen."

"You can't be serious," Schiapp said as she moved toward him. "What possible good can that do now?"

"Perhaps nothing at all," Vlenn replied even before Apohatsu could open his mouth to speak. "However, there is a chance it will quell the panic, at least for a time."

"You're not suggesting I tell the people about you?" Flen asked.

Apohatsu shook his head. "Certainly not, First Consul. I merely advocate giving them some small piece of hope on which to cling. It could help for a short time, after which, either their prayers will have been answered, or . . . it simply won't matter anymore."

Reaching up to wipe his face, Flen indicated the door through which Celadi had been escorted with a nod of his head. "I can only imagine what might now be ensuing among the people if he had been privy to that information. Still, is it wise to alert the populace now? Considering that plan that your people are putting into motion is fraught with uncertainty, we risk falsely elevating our people's hopes, particularly at this late juncture."

The allegation was veiled, but Apohatsu caught it nonetheless. "As I have told you before, First Consul, the technology being employed in this endeavor took a considerable amount of time to develop, and remains untried. Further, the people currently involved in its use are doing so at great risk to their own safety."

Nodding at words he had heard before, Flen said, "We have discussed your directives against interfering in cultures that are not as advanced as yours, Doctor. For some time, I have wondered if that directive had any part in the length of time it took to arrive at a means of helping us."

"I beg your pardon," Vlenn said, the Deltan making no attempt to hide the disbelief in his voice. "Are you actually accusing our people of dragging their feet so as to somehow avoid rendering aid?"

It took a moment, but Flen eventually shook his head. "No, but trust me when I tell you that—should anyone survive the calamity about to befall our world—it will not be the last time such an accusation is raised."

"With all due respect, First Consul," Mino said, "I do not believe our friends are capable of merely standing by and watching our people die. Their actions to this point are obvious evidence of that."

Flen cleared his throat. "Their laws would indicate that they have done precisely that, at least once."

"We're here now, aren't we?" Schiapp said, her voice quivering as she fought to control her composure. "We've spent a year and a half here, immersed in your culture, watching your children grow, your world thrive." Apohatsu looked to his friend and saw the tears welling in her eyes. Reaching up to wipe her face, she drew herself straight, her jaw setting in that expression of determination the doctor had come to know so well. "And now we stand here, with you, waiting to see if your world can be saved."

Something in the woman's voice seemed to strike a chord in Flen. He studied her for several seconds before looking to Apohatsu. "Is that true, my friend? Do you stand with us and await our fate?"

Realizing what was being asked of him—and the inherent trust that hinged on his response—Nathan Apohatsu nodded.

"We stand with you, First Consul, until the end."

CHAPTER
7

Even if he had ready access to a laser scalpel, Kirk was certain he still could not cut through the tension blanketing the bridge as everyone on duty regarded the image now displayed on the main viewscreen.

"*The situation is deteriorating down here, Captain,*" said Nathan Apohatsu, looking out at Kirk and his bridge crew with tired, red-rimmed eyes. "*You've already seen the reports of mass panic in many of the larger cities. Martial law has been declared, and a number of mass-scale evacuations are still under way.*" Apohatsu sighed as he reached up to wipe away a sheen of perspiration on his forehead. "*I don't know where the hell they think they can go.*"

Sitting in his customary place at the center of the bridge, Kirk replied, "Perhaps it has more to do with them wanting to just do something." He offered a resigned shrug. "Anything to avoid sitting around and . . . waiting." According to the reports he had reviewed, the captain also knew that those Payav who had been working in the three space stations orbiting Mestiko had been evacuated and returned home. The thirty-four people residing on the planet's only lunar colony were a different story, however. Even if a vessel were available to carry them, given the insufficient warning, the colonists had no time to make the transit back to their home planet.

Kirk bristled at the current circumstances. Why had Payav leaders not taken steps to ensure those people were retrieved? While he understood the original decision to keep the approaching pulsar a secret from the general public, steps could still have been taken to ensure that the lunar colonists at least were with their families if and when the rogue object's worst effects came to pass.

Well, it's our job to make sure that doesn't happen, right?

Leaning forward in his chair, Kirk said, "Doctor, there's still time for us to return to the planet and have you beamed aboard." He left the rest of his concern unvoiced.

Apohatsu knew full well the implications of what had not been said. With a small, accepting smile, the doctor shook his head. *"If it's all the same to you, we'd rather see this thing through with the friends we've made here."* Straightening his posture, he leaned closer to the visual pickup. *"Good luck, Captain."*

"To all of us, Doctor. Kirk out." The transmission ended and the image of Apohatsu was replaced with that of a starfield, with the pulsar depicted as an indistinct red blur at the center of the screen.

Kirk noted the new silence around him, the only sounds that of indicator tones from the surrounding workstations as well as voices piped through the intercom system as other departments aboard the ship relayed normal status reports to the bridge. It was there that any similarities to just another mundane duty shift ended. He sensed anxiety in every person around him, with the notable exception of Spock, of course. The uncertainty was evidenced in the way his people went about their respective tasks—shoulders hunched as they sat at their stations, the movements of hands across consoles taut and efficient. There was no conversation, not even the normal exchange of duty-related chatter as the bridge crew saw to their various assignments.

Though Kirk's own duty at a time like this was to oversee the actions of those around him, such responsibility on occasion left him with nothing to do but sit and dwell too much on things that did not contribute to the accomplishment of the mission. When that occurred, he often felt envious of his subordinates, who at least could channel their apprehension and focus on their work.

Each of them, along with every other member of his crew, knew full well the importance of the coming moments, and that they were about to bear witness to either a tremendous act of salvation or one of immense devastation. What would the next hours bring? Would there be cause for celebration, or mourning?

With grim determination, Kirk forced away the troubling questions. Swiveling the command chair to his right, he looked to where Cameron now worked with Lieutenant Sulu at her station, coordinating the various aspects of the operation that was just now getting under way.

"Professor?" the captain prompted.

Looking up from the console, Cameron turned in her seat. "The probes are almost in range now, Captain. I'll be ready to deploy the deflector grid as soon as they've been maneuvered into their final positions." The professor's report was more a courtesy for the rest of the bridge crew than anything else, Kirk knew. Cameron had assumed authority over the mission, and the deployment of the probes as well as the positioning of the *Enterprise* all had been at her direction, and she would enable the massive deflector shield at the designated moment.

Despite his first impulse, Kirk forced himself not to ask again about the status of the shield network the probes would generate. He knew that Cameron and Chief Engineer Scott had spent a significant portion of the past several days examining the devices' shield generators, looking for ways to enhance their output and further protect them from the tenacious assault they would face as they moved closer to the pulsar.

Scott's last status report had been straightforward, if not unduly optimistic: He and his engineering staff had made all the modifications possible under the circumstances, enhancing the probes' shield output by several percentage points. Any further upgrades were simply beyond the physical limitations of the units themselves, and would require the replacement of key components not included among the *Enterprise*'s stores of supplies. As it was, Scott already had performed several unorthodox adjustments to the components he did have on hand in order to reach the level of enhancement he had achieved. In the engineer's opinion, he had done all that was possible and even a few things that flew in the face of that.

The rest, Kirk figured, would have to be left for Fate to decide.

"Position report," he called out as he rose from his chair, stepping out of the command well and making his way to the science station.

Looking over his shoulder, Gary Mitchell replied, "We're holding steady with the pulsar two million kilometers off the port bow."

"Maintaining parallel speed," Kelso added. The helmsman shook his head. "Never thought I'd fly a starship this slow except out of space dock."

Kirk nodded. While the *Enterprise*'s current velocity was but a fraction of what the starship's massive engines were capable of generating, he knew that speed was not the priority now. Professor Cameron had determined that due to the level of X-ray radiation being emitted by the pulsar, this was the maximum distance the ship could keep and still receive uncorrupted telemetry from the probes once the deflector grid was deployed and began its task of shunting the lethal radiation away from Mestiko.

Studying the sensor data being fed to him at the science station, Spock looked up from his hooded viewer. "Pulsar will reach intersection point with the planet in two minutes."

"Probes are in position now," Cameron called out a moment later. "Standing by to activate the deflector grid."

"You are doing the right thing, child. I am glad you are staying where you are needed."

The voice in her ear soothed Raya elMora as she listened to her *elor* over the wireless headset, just as it had for as long as she could remember. "How is it, Elee, that you always know just what I need to hear?" Raya hoped that the concern she felt was not making itself apparent in her own voice as she talked.

It was a difficult conversation to hold, given the current circumstances. Sitting as she was in one of several dozen small, drab offices on the lowest of the two-level subterranean shelter, Raya could barely make out Elee's words through the irregular static caused by the compromised audio signal. There also was the constant din of people moving and talking in the corridors and rooms beyond her makeshift office, the sounds generated by the hundreds of Payav who had been herded into this complex, one of four located beneath the Convocation grounds. The room was functional and afforded her some measure of privacy, but it hardly compared to her regular office, to say nothing of her home.

"*I have had many years of practice, now, have I not?*"

"You certainly have," Raya replied. She had sought Elee's words of comfort in the past for such personal hardships as adolescent heartbreaks, the difficulties of living alone while at university, and even after a few of her more strained political dealings had left her worn and frustrated. Today, though, made every personal drama she had experienced in her life seem trite by comparison, for today, Raya truly was unsure whether she might see a tomorrow.

Even though Larenda was located in the hemisphere of the planet that would be spared the initial and much more catastrophic effects of the Pulse, Raya knew from the reports Umeen had shown her that no one on Mestiko was safe. Eventually, the atmospheric and environmental damage inflicted on the planet would overcome everyone, and everything.

Or, would it?

According to the speech Raya had just watched as it was delivered by Flen etHamwora, leader not only of the Gelta nation but also the global *Zamestaad* Council, the dire predictions first given by the media regarding the Pulse's potential effects were no longer being reported with such certainty. Instead, Gelta's first consul had offered the supposed conceit that there was no way to be certain as to just what would happen during or after the passing of the rogue object. Experts were forecasting severe weather events and possible high ultraviolet radiation surges as the worst consequences.

With that in mind, the citizenry had been warned to seek every opportunity for shelter, and scores of people had gathered at the Convocation complex. Many of them had come in search of safe haven from the riots and looting that still consumed many areas throughout the province. Others had come with a mind to continue their lawless behavior, only to find themselves confronting law enforcement officers and military units deployed to protect the Convocation complex as well as other important locations. While Raya could have taken the opportunity to return to her home province and wait out the event with her family, she and other Servants instead had realized that their presence among the people would serve a grander purpose, perhaps providing a calming influence.

Then why, Raya thought, *am I letting myself be consumed with such dread?*

"I am taking up too much of your time, young one," Elee said. *"You should be using this time to call home and not worry about the likes of me."* Despite the low-quality connection that was a consequence of the inadequate audio transmissions inside the shelters, Raya still heard the ever-present strength from her father's mother, and it buoyed her despite the concerns for her family half a province away. She hoped that as the situation progressed—or worsened—she would find within herself the same composure that her beloved *elor* apparently was able to muster in the face of such uncertainty.

"Do not worry. I have already connected with everyone else. They have all moved to shelters. Will you be joining them?"

There was a pause before Elee replied, *"I am too old to be sleeping on the floor of someone's storm cellar, or on a makeshift bed alongside two hundred strangers. I will be fine here, child, in my own home."*

A beep echoed in her ear before an automated voice filled the connection. *"This connection is required for official Convocation communications. Please terminate your connection immediately so that the frequency can be reallocated."*

Feeling a sudden surge of tears well in her eyes and realizing her voice would soon betray her fear, Raya cleared her throat. "I have to go now, Elee, but I will talk to you soon. Promise me you will take care of yourself."

A burst of static that made her pull the headset from her ear was followed by the telltale tones signaling the connection's termination. It was unusual for private connects to be so interrupted, but Raya knew these were extraordinary times. Feeling a tear begin to slide down her cheek, she stared at the now inoperative handset.

"I love you, Elee."

Staring at the walls of the small office, which seemed to be closing in around her, Raya knew there was nothing to do now but wait.

Or, so she thought.

"Servant?"

Turning toward the voice, Raya looked into another pair of concerned eyes. This time, the worried gaze belonged to her trusted aide, Blee, who seemed obviously unable to mask any inner turmoil in her expression.

"What is it, Blee?" Raya asked.

"You have a connect on the Civil Security line," the assistant replied. "It is Servant orJurbes, and he pressed me to find you rather than having you connect back."

Raya followed Blee out of her office and down the shelter's narrow, dimly lit main corridor. The passageway seemed even more confined due to the press of people who mingled listlessly in small groups, and from whom Raya was sensing an escalating sense of dread and gloom, the same feelings of discomfort and worry she had detected in Blee. As they walked, Raya reached out to place a hand on the younger woman's shoulder, hoping that it might offer even the slightest consolation. Her aide did not even turn her head to acknowledge the gesture.

At the far end of the corridor was a small, drab office, not unlike the one she had just left. Inside the room was an officious-looking young man, the sash he wore indicating his affiliation with Civil Security as he sat at a portable desk that seemed too tiny to support the large, bulky transceiver situated there. As soon as Raya stepped inside, the young man rose from his chair.

"This is a hard-wired connection among the Convocation complex buildings for emergency use," the man said crisply.

"I am aware of the equipment's function and purpose," Raya said, hoping her smile might take some of the edge from the man's perfunctory yet understandably nervous tone, "but we are in an emergency shelter. Does that not imply that any connects received over this equipment are related to why we are here?"

Now looking somewhat sheepish, the man nodded. "Of course, Servant. However, I have orders to keep traffic on this channel limited to an official nature."

"I imagine that I would not be summoned by a senior Servant for anything less," she said, still smiling as she took over the man's seat at the station and leaning forward to talk into the slim microphone mounted on a pivoting arm. "Matthi? This is Raya."

"*There you are,*" replied the tired-sounding but still recognizable voice from the transceiver's speaker. "*You no doubt are very busy over there, and I just wanted to make sure you were getting something to eat.*" There was a pause before Matthi added, "*Let me guess: That poor security officer is glaring at you right now.*"

Raya turned to look over her shoulder and saw the young man displaying the very disdainful expression Matthi had predicted. She also caught the grin on Blee's face, something Raya was pleased to see given the fog of uncertainty in which each of them found themselves. "Matthi, should I interpret this connect as you using your influence to access an emergency channel for personal use?"

"*Absolutely,*" the elder Servant answered. When he continued after a pause, the humor was gone from his voice. "*Raya, the initial predictions about the atmospheric effects from the radiation may well be correct. Level 5 on the side of the planet that will see direct exposure.*"

Raya felt a wave of dread wash over her. Coded classifications for the Pulse had been determined and secretly distributed among select government officials during their preparations in order to facilitate a quick but ciphered system of passing information without spreading panic. With regard to intensity, Level 5 was the extreme end of the list, and represented a level of destruction from which few to no survivors were to be expected.

"What about everywhere else?" she asked, finally finding her voice.

"At least Level 4, but it is important to stress that there's still some uncertainty. I just thought you should know. Keep your head about you as I know you can do, and I will talk to you when this is over."

"Thank you, Matthi," Raya said, feeling the same tightness in her throat as when she had spoken to Elee. "And I want to tell you that I—"

"You can tell me later," Matthi replied, her longtime friend's voice sounding so secure and confident to her. *"We will talk soon."* Raya then heard a series of clicks from the speaker that signaled the end of the connection.

"Level 4, Servant?" asked the Civil Security officer. "What does that mean?"

"It means you should keep to your post," Raya replied, certain that her expression must be undermining the effort she was making to stifle her grave sense of the situation. "You will be needed here."

For what specifically, however, Raya could only imagine.

CHAPTER
8

"Tactical plot on main viewer," Kirk ordered, turning toward the forward screen in time to see the image displayed upon it change from that of the pulsar to a computer-generated schematic. It featured a pale yellow grid superimposed over a black background, with a bright yellow sphere—Mestiko's sun—displayed in the screen's lower left corner. Smaller circles depicted Mestiko itself as well as its six sister planets. Closer to the center of the screen, a stark blue line illustrated the course of the pulsar while a moving white arrow represented the Enterprise following its parallel course. Six smaller white dots corresponded to the positions of the unmanned probes, arrayed in a hexagonal formation between the pulsar and the general direction of Mestiko.

"Intersection point in ninety seconds," Spock said. "Deflectors are holding steady. Mr. Scott's modifications to our own shield generators are proving to be most effective."

Nodding at the report, Kirk looked to see Cameron focused on one of the sensor display monitors at her station, the index finger of her right hand poised over a control button. The finger was moving up and down rhythmically, and Kirk realized she was tapping in time to the countdown.

Spock was just announcing the forty-five-second mark when the professor's hand pressed the button. It was accompanied by a short, high-pitched tone.

"Deflector grid activating," Cameron reported, and Kirk watched on the main viewer as a web of orange materialized amid the array of probes depicted on the screen. "Starting the clock: three hundred and fifty seconds . . . mark!"

Not even six minutes. That was the window of time that stood between Mestiko and survival or all but total annihilation. It was how long the probes needed to provide their blanket of protective energy, erected between the pulsar and the endangered planet as both astral bodies made their way through the void.

"Intersection," Spock called out a moment later. "Now."

Though the interval that the pulsar's deadly X-ray emissions would sweep across Mestiko was somewhat shorter, Cameron had calculated a margin for error both before and after the event. Kirk actually felt himself flinch as his first officer provided the report, an almost instinctive reaction for which the captain had no explanation. He was unsure as to what he might have expected once the critical moment arrived, but it was heralded by nothing more than those around him offering tentative glances to one another. Otherwise, the atmosphere of the bridge remained unchanged: Tense.

"Shield status?" he asked.

His attention focused on the instruments he was monitoring with Professor Cameron, Sulu replied without looking away from his viewer, "Field generators are at maximum output, sir."

"Shield's already taking a hell of a beating," Cameron added. "The enhancements we made are helping, but I don't know if they'll be enough." She looked over to the chronometer that dominated one of the smaller display monitors at her station. "Five minutes, twelve seconds remaining."

On the main viewer, the computer illustrated the collision of X-rays with the deflector grid as a series of rapid-fire blinking lines, too fast for normal eyes to follow. To Kirk, the display reminded him of training simulations he had studied at the Academy and periodically throughout his career. He had studied vicious, merciless conflicts between spacecraft of the Federation and Klingon Empire, and before that Earth and the Romulans, all reduced to basic, sanitized, computer-generated representations created for the purpose of facilitating the learning of starship combat tactics and strategy.

While Kirk appreciated such training aids for their value in honing those skills—the possession of which was an unfortunate necessity as humans and their allies ventured ever deeper into uncharted space and encountered those who did not take kindly to such visitations—part of him always had taken issue with the cold, antiseptic portrayal of such battles and the apparent disregard for the deaths of hundreds or even thousands of people on both sides of the engagements. He knew the programs held no such imprudent intentions, but it nevertheless was a reaction he always experienced, even if only for a moment.

As he regarded the image on the main viewer, Kirk realized he was feeling the same thing now. He could not help but wonder if, in years to come, Starfleet scientists would scrutinize and dissect the sensor records of this event. Would they analyze it in the interests of furthering science and knowledge with the same tenacity that soldiers studied past battles with an eye toward improving the way they waged war? How would Mestiko's people, the fate of whom was still in question, factor into what those future students learned?

A sharp, piercing alarm signal echoed across the bridge, startling Kirk from his reverie. It took him an additional instant to realize that it was not any of the alert tones normally used aboard the *Enterprise*, but instead was something new, emanating from the station Cameron and Sulu currently occupied.

"What is that?" the captain asked as he moved toward them.

Without looking up from the console, Cameron replied, "We're picking up fluctuations in the deflector grid. One of the probes is showing strain in its field generator."

"Can we compensate?" Sulu asked, his brow furrowing in concern. "Redeploy the other probes into a new formation?"

Cameron shook her head. "The grid scheme is balanced for six probes working in tandem," she said as her fingers worked across the rows of controls, entering rapid-fire commands to the console. "Using five to cover the same area will weaken the overall strength of the shield."

"What about the *Enterprise*?" Kirk asked, feeling as he did so the eyes of the entire bridge crew turning in his direction as he voiced the question. "Can we channel more power to the malfunctioning probe? Stabilize it somehow?"

The professor turned to face him, pondering the questions for several seconds before replying, "It'd be dangerous. You'd have to position us with pinpoint precision to avoid direct exposure to the pulsar's emissions."

"And if we don't try?" the captain asked.

Sulu answered, "If the problems with the probe worsen, we could lose that portion of the shield, leaving a sizable area through which Mestiko would be exposed to the pulsar's X-rays."

That was all the information Kirk needed. So far as he was concerned, there was only one course of action open to him. "Feed the coordinates to the helm, Professor," he said as he stepped back down into the command well. "Mr. Kelso, stand by to alter course. Put all decks on the alert."

Casting a glance over his shoulder before setting to work assisting the helmsman, Mitchell said, "It's going to be a bumpy ride, Captain."

Kirk understood his friend's meaning, taking a moment to convey that concern to the rest of the crew via the ship's intercom system. Then he could only sit and observe as his officers worked to put into place a contingency plan that was being developed as they went. He listened to Sulu conversing with Scott down in engineering, crafting new protocols that would allow the transfer of power from the *Enterprise* to the troublesome probe's shield generator while at the same time preventing any compromise in the starship's own defenses.

"How much time until the pulsar passes the planet?" Kirk

asked, trying to ignore the increasing tremble in the deck plates and the arms of his chair.

Cameron replied, "Three minutes, twenty-eight seconds."

Almost there, Kirk thought. It was simultaneously a hopeful and yet frustrating thought, given how the seconds seemed to be stretching into decades from where he sat. The ship was shaking now, the toll accumulating on the *Enterprise*'s shields as they continued to combat the pulsar's gravitational effects.

"We're in position, Captain," Kelso called out from the helm.

Nodding at the report, the captain activated the intercom pickup affixed to the flexible arm on the right side of his chair. "Kirk to engineering. Scotty, start the power transfer."

There was a momentary pause before the chief engineer replied, "*Transfer under way now.*"

From the science station, Spock reported, "The connection is not stable. It's being affected by the pulsar's emissions."

"*Aye, I was afraid of that,*" came Scott's aggravated voice from the intercom. "*Too much interference, Captain. I cannot recommend taking us any closer, though.*"

Kirk looked up to see Spock stepping down into the command well, moving to stand next to him. "Doing so is the only way to stabilize the connection, sir."

The captain nodded, not seeing any choice in the matter. Things only had to hold together for a minute, two at most. Surely the *Enterprise*, which already had performed admirably to this point, could take that limited amount of additional abuse? The people of Mestiko certainly deserved everything that could be done on their behalf, did they not?

Standing before the large, ovoid window that afforded a panoramic view of the night sky above Yabapmat, one hand absently fumbling with the universal translator he carried on his belt and concealed beneath the loose jacket he wore, Nathan Apohatsu realized that at this very moment, he had never felt quite as isolated in his entire life.

He was not actually alone, of course, given the three dozen beings occupying the room with him. Along with the rest of the first consul's staff, he, Vlenn, and Camila Schiapp had listened as the Gelta leader delivered what he believed was a hopeful speech, broadcast via satellite to almost the entire planet, after which a brief prayer service was conducted by the first consul's spiritual advisor. Now, the assemblage had begun to splinter into smaller groups, some huddled in corners while others moved to other rooms, but all of them awaiting the announcement that would call for them to descend into the storm shelter situated nearly a hundred meters below the ground floor of the capitol building. The chamber, recently stocked with foodstuffs and equipment intended to keep them alive following the pulsar's anticipated sweep of radiation, held little appeal for Apohatsu.

If the worst comes to pass, that place just prolongs the inevitable.

His sense of isolation, the Starfleet cultural specialist decided, almost certainly came from what he observed outside the window. The streets of the capital city, once bustling with activity only to be all but consumed by riotous looters and panic-stricken citizens as the global menace loomed, now were desolate. Broken glass, tattered papers, and other detritus littered the pavement. Buildings that once had housed merchants and services stood mostly as empty shells, smoke-streaked and savaged. Vehicles remained where they had been abandoned in the streets, gutted, wrecked, and overturned.

And amid the chaos, not one person could be seen. Everyone had either been corralled away by security forces or else had left of their own volition, fueled by terror or madness, to places unknown.

Apohatsu turned his gaze toward the sky, clear and starry, hoping against hope it would remain unchanged in the minutes to come. For several hours, by his own reckoning, he had pondered the sight, hoping and praying that deliverance from the pulsar's effects might come in the form of intervention by the daring plan being put into motion by the *Enterprise*. News of their success would not be coming by communications signal, not under the circumstances under which the starship currently was operating.

No, Apohatsu knew, the answer would come from the sky.

"*Lloben na slu winneden, mos Naythun?*"

While not understanding the meaning of the native tongue spoken to him, Apohatsu slipped from his reverie enough to recognize the feminine tone of the voice right away. Realizing that his absentminded toying with the translator on his belt must have turned off the device, he moved to reactivate it.

"I'm sorry, Mino," he said, turning to the Payav woman who had walked up behind him. The dark circles beneath her icy blue eyes contrasted sharply with her pale skin, and her long neck seemed to bow a bit under the weight of her smooth head. "What did you say?"

"Do you see what you seek, Nathan?" Mino orDresha repeated, herself now looking past the window up toward the night sky.

"Not at all," he said, "and with any luck, I won't."

Mino nodded. "I did not know whether you would prefer the company of your own friends."

Glancing over his shoulder, Apohatsu saw the other members of his cultural observation team, who like himself had shed their usual prosthetics and other disguising garb in order to be more relaxed in front of those very few Payav aware of their existence.

He located Vlenn in the far corner of the room, the Deltan sitting motionless with eyes closed in contemplative reflection. At one of the room's two tables was Camila Schiapp, sitting with a pair of older Payav males whom he recognized as peers of Mino's. The human woman appeared solemn-faced but still attempting to engage her companions in discussion of some sort.

"Not at all," Apohatsu said, offering a small smile. "We're all friends now, I should think."

Pausing as if to consider his words for a moment, Mino asked, "May I confide in you, friend Nathan, as an observer of people?"

Apohatsu heard the hesitation in her voice. "Of course," he said. "Now more than ever."

The smile gracing Mino's petite features was the first one he could remember seeing in weeks, if not longer, and he realized in that moment how much he had missed it. He found it somehow soothing, particularly given the current circumstances.

"One of the first consul's administrators," she began after hesitating again, "before he went down to the shelter area, asked if I might accompany him to another part of the building." She regarded him for a few silent seconds before adding, "Alone."

Despite his best efforts, the look on Mino's face coupled with the sincere concern in her voice got the best of Apohatsu, and he found himself releasing an explosive laugh that echoed through the room. Mino's frantic motions for him to be quiet only made things worse, and within seconds his continued laughter had drawn the attention of everyone around him. Most understandably were startled from their conversations or quiet thoughts, with Schiapp alone offering a puzzled smile in return.

The abrupt release of tension actually felt good, he decided; it was something he'd sorely needed, given the mounting stresses of the past months. Reaching out, he placed a comforting hand on the shoulder of the woman who had become so dear a friend to him so far away from his native home.

"*Stop* that," Mino demanded in a hushed voice, her white cheeks darkened as she blushed. "It was discomforting, and a completely inappropriate request!"

"But so male," Apohatsu said, grinning, "and actually pretty human, too."

Finally seeing the humor in the situation, Mino returned the smile, though it was a small, tentative one born as much from embarrassment as amusement. After a moment, she said, "I have enjoyed your company these past seasons, but I do not believe I have ever thanked you for your friendship, Nathan. You have given me so much that I never thought I would experience in my life. This has been . . . a hopeful time."

"For both of us," Apohatsu replied.

Neither of them said anything for several minutes, both content to gaze at the stars above them. It was a calm, serene moment, one he would have been happy to share until the sun once more climbed above the horizon.

Then, he saw it.

A barely perceptible flash winking in the night, and Apohatsu felt a shiver down his spine. Was it a trick of light, perhaps an aftereffect of his blinking? He widened his eyes and stilled his breath, staring silently into the starry blackness.

"Nathan?" Mino asked.

The night sky flashed again, more brilliantly this time, like a ripple of sheet lightning across the skies of Earth. It happened again, quicker than before, and now he was sure he noted a steady glow coalescing out of the darkness, casting each star in its own aura among a wavering pattern of rich purples, eerie reds, and warm yellows.

Apohatsu sensed more people gathering at the window alongside him. He heard the gasps as some caught sight of what he was seeing, while others asked what the apparition might mean. As the colors and lights danced, not unlike a most intense show of Earthly aurora activity brought about by the harmless collisions of electrons in its upper atmosphere, Apohatsu's sinking heart filled him with dread.

"It is happening, yes?" Mino asked.

"'Not with a bang, but a whimper?'" Apohatsu recited under his breath rather than answering the question, his eyes filling with not only tears but also the cascades of electric color he so much wanted to appreciate for their beauty rather than the portent they heralded.

Reaching for Mino, Nathan Apohatsu slid his hand into hers, squeezing it slightly and pulling her close to him, saying nothing as the colors grew more brilliant and chased the darkness from the sky.

CHAPTER
9

"It's failing!" Cameron called out. "The probe's shield generator just gave out!" She uttered the report at the same time a new alert klaxon began wailing across the bridge and Kirk felt a renewed shaking in the very structure of the ship around him. His stomach lurched as the deck shifted beneath his feet. To his right, Spock fell against the railing, and Kirk saw the science officer's legs dangle in midair as he gripped the red bannister. Kelso and Mitchell somehow managed to keep from being tossed out of their chairs. Then Kirk caught sight of another body being thrown about to his right and turned to see Cameron tossed from her seat and over the railing, landing heavily on her side as she slammed into the deck of the command well.

"Professor!" Kirk yelled as he threw himself from his chair to where Cameron lay in a crumpled heap, her right arm moving listlessly as she tried to pull herself to a sitting position. "Lie still," the captain said, kneeling beside her and noting her agonized grimace. His gaze was drawn to her right leg, bent unnaturally beneath her body. "Try not to move. We'll get medics up here as soon as we can."

Nodding, Cameron lay back on the deck, her eyes squeezed

shut as she fought against the pain of her injuries. "The shield," she hissed between gritted teeth. "You have to move away from it, now!" Even as she spoke the words, Kirk felt the deck tremble beneath him once more.

"The pulsar's radiation," Spock reported, now back at his station. "Our shields will overload if we stay here."

"Helm!" Kirk shouted above the alarm, turning and pointing toward the main viewer. "Get us out of here!" As he gave the order, the captain's gaze locked on the image still displayed on the screen, the tactical diagram that had been updated by the *Enterprise*'s sensors to depict the planet Mestiko, now awash in the partially deflected yet still potent X-ray emissions of the pulsar.

Oh God.

Then there was no time to ponder the misfortune of the ill-fated world as the astrogator console situated between Kelso and Mitchell exploded.

The sound was all but deafening as it enveloped the bridge and Kirk winced as he ducked, draping himself atop the injured Professor Cameron in a desperate attempt to protect her. Glass and sparks peppered his uniform and exposed skin, and he heard the sound of several heavy objects falling to the deck. He looked up as he sensed movement nearby and saw that Kelso and Mitchell had fallen from their upended chairs. Mitchell had rolled away from the still smoldering console, blood streaming from several small wounds on the left side of his face and neck.

"Lee!" the navigator yelled, ignoring his own injuries as he tried to cross the command well to where Kelso lay unconscious near the steps leading to the upper bridge deck. Mitchell only made it a few steps before stumbling over his overturned chair, saved from falling by Kirk as he pulled himself to his feet in time catch him.

"Gary?" Kirk asked, his ears still ringing from the explosion as he pushed his wounded friend into the command chair. "Are you all right?" Though worried about Mitchell, and indeed the growing number of wounded people literally at his feet, the captain knew he could not focus on one person right now. The ship was still in immediate danger.

Intending to take the helm himself, Kirk turned around in time to find Lieutenant Sulu hunched over the console. Next to him, Alden had abandoned the communications console and taken up position at the navigator's station, a duty he often performed in relief of Mitchell while on the bridge.

"Engineering!" Sulu snapped as he pressed the intercom control on his console. "We need lateral power!"

"*We're workin' on it, bridge!*" shouted Scott's voice over the comm speaker.

Leaning over the helm console, Kirk asked, "Lieutenant, are you sure you can handle this?" He knew that the astrophysicist had been training in other departments—including starship operations—for the past several months as a way of fueling his seemingly unending desire to learn new things, but had no idea how far he had progressed in his studies.

Sulu nodded. "I've got it, sir." He spoke without looking up, his fingers moving as though of their own volition over the helm console. Kirk looked from the station's array of status indicators and lights to the image on the main viewscreen, which showed a computer-generated representation of the *Enterprise* beginning to arc away from the pulsar. Already he could feel the shaking in the deck plates ebbing as the ship put distance between itself and the rogue body.

"Nice work, Lieutenant," he said, patting the younger man on the shoulder. "Notify sickbay that we need emergency medical teams up here on the double," he ordered before turning to where Spock was now working at Cameron's station. "Spock?" he asked, a single anguished word pushing past his lips.

The Vulcan turned from the console, his eyes hard and focused as he provided the cold, merciless facts. "The pulsar has moved past the point of intersection with Mestiko, Captain. While the compromised deflector grid was able to redirect 74.893 percent of the emitted X-rays, what was able to get through was still sufficient to cause significant damage to the planet."

"Oh dear God," Cameron said from where she still lay on the deck near Kirk's chair. The captain could not help but notice that the professor's voice seemed even weaker now than just a few moments earlier.

"What the hell does that mean?" Kirk asked. "Isn't there something we can do?"

Drawing himself into a ramrod posture, his hands clasped behind his back, Spock locked eyes with Kirk. "The effects are quite unavoidable now, Captain."

"You son of a bitch," Kirk heard Mitchell say, and turned to see his friend still slumped in the command chair, holding a part of his tunic's torn left sleeve to the wounds on the side of his head. "Do you hear what you're saying? Every person on that planet could die, and we can't do a damned thing to stop it!" There was no mistaking the dulled expression on the navigator's face and the slurred speech. Mitchell was slipping into shock.

His mind still on the more immediate problems, Kirk turned to his first officer, certain he caught a hint of remorse in the Vulcan's features, but it vanished almost as quickly as it had appeared. For a moment, the captain thought Spock might even offer an apology.

"Spock," he said, forgetting all of that, "how long until the pulsar's emissions hit the lunar colony?"

"Eight minutes, thirty-seven seconds, Captain," the Vulcan replied.

There was still time! Looking over his shoulder toward the helm, Kirk ordered, "Sulu! Lay in a course for the colony. I don't care what you have to do, but get us there with enough time to transport those people to the ship. Go!"

As he spoke the words, he saw the already stressed lieutenant turn to the task of carrying out his latest orders. That accomplished, Kirk turned and knelt beside Professor Cameron. Tears welled up in her eyes and streamed down her face, though the captain knew she was not crying due to the pain she suffered.

"I'm sorry, Captain," she whispered, her voice faint and barely audible.

Shaking his head, Kirk patted her on her shoulder. "You did everything you could, Professor. No one can blame you for anything."

Even as he spoke the words, his imagination began to fill with visions of a world in flames, enveloped in chaos, death, and destruction; city streets running red with the blood of millions falling victim to the wrath of nature and its unrestrained fury. As he raced to save a small segment of Mestiko's population, he wondered about the wounds being inflicted upon the planet itself. What would they find when the *Enterprise* returned there?

The flickering of the lights was the first indication to Raya that something was wrong, a suspicion only strengthened when the overhead illumination failed altogether and plunged her small office into total darkness.

Cries of surprise and fear echoed in the corridor beyond her door even as the lighting almost immediately returned, though Raya noted its lesser intensity, telling her that the underground shelter's primary power generation systems had been disrupted or compromised in some fashion.

Rising from her chair, Raya made her way into the corridor to find Blee weaving around other evacuees as she maneuvered up the passageway toward her. "What has happened?"

"The Pulse," replied the young aide as she came closer. "It is beginning to affect power and communications systems. We just lost the news broadcasts."

Raya knew that whatever her most nightmarish imaginings of how the planet might be ravaged by the effects of the rogue object, they would not compare to the images conjured by those now cut off from the rest of their world and forced to wonder just what was happening far above them.

As they approached one of the shelter's larger common rooms, Raya caught sight of the larger, elliptical monitor suspended from the ceiling near one corner, which now displayed nothing more than colorless static. She knew that the shelter and its counterparts situated within the Convocation grounds were supported by power generators as well as communications and other equipment, which were shielded against electromagnetic interference such as that being inflicted by the Pulse—a consequence of preparations made long ago in paranoid anticipation of a global nuclear conflict which, thankfully, had never occurred. Unfortunately, the same could not be said for the vast majority of those systems utilized by the populace at large.

All around the common room, Raya observed the reactions of those gathered there. Some impulsively shouted out questions and remarks to no one in particular, while others dissolved into tears and held tightly to a friend or family member.

And then she heard the rumbling, sounding much like the rising and ebbing of an approaching thunderstorm; a slow, throaty roll echoing through the building and bringing a moment of silence to the room. Then a second clap of thunder— as loud as the first—seemed to rock the flooring beneath Raya's feet.

"Everyone, go to your emergency stations now!" she called in a firm voice as people started to shriek in alarm. As the dulled yet still raucous sounds of furious thunder echoed through the thick walls of the underground shelter, other evacuees began heeding Raya's call to action, echoing her command and passing it on to others beyond the common room.

As she moved into the corridor and made her way toward the communal dining area on this level of the shelter, Raya noticed Blee keeping pace with her rather than heading for her own emergency station. The young woman already had made her own decision to stay here rather than seek out her family, and Raya's assent to that request made her feel implicitly responsible for her aide's safety. It was a charge she intended to honor as best she could.

Another shock rocked the building and Raya stumbled into Blee. Shrieks of fear filled the air and the lighting flickered as dust filtered from the overhead fixtures. Blee grabbed on to Raya and held her for a moment, until everyone realized that the shock to their surroundings had subsided.

"It is not safe here!" yelled a voice from the congregating throng of people, followed by a series of shouts and cries echoing throughout the corridor. Raya wrested herself from Blee's clutches, dashing down the passageway and past several citizens toward the source of the commotion. Turning a corner, she found herself at a stairwell and watched in horror as a line of panic-filled Payav was trying to ascend it.

"What are you doing?" Raya called over the shouts ringing

within the bare-walled, confining space, but to no avail. Instead, the crowd flowed upward—toward the exit leading to the sur-face. Certain that whatever circumstance lay outside was more dangerous than any injuries to be sustained within the shelter, Raya struggled to be heard among the fleeing refugees.

"Stay here!" she called back to Blee before dashing into the stairwell—practically buoyed along with the surging crowd—only to be greeted by acrid-smelling air and the deafening roar of thunderclap upon thunderclap. By the time she reached the door, several dozen Payav had already made their way outside, but as she stepped to the threshold she turned to face those people still behind her in the stairwell.

"You will die out there," she pleaded, seeing the fear in the refugees' wide-eyed, ashen faces. "Go back downstairs, please!"

The crowd lurched forward—forcing her outside.

Pushed aside as her fellow citizens emerged from the shel-ter's entrance, Raya looked up to see that the light of the sun was almost scrubbed out by an orange-brown haze suspended in the sky, almost but not quite obscuring the line of storm clouds gathering on the horizon. Wind whipped at her cloth-ing, and the stark white brightness of bolt after bolt of light-ning illuminated the clouds, their surreal energy making her exposed skin tingle with their power. All around her, the Payav who had escaped the shelter's confines were all but mesmer-ized, shouting and crying in fright as they beheld the hellish scene surrounding them.

Above that din, however, Raya heard a piercing, desperate cry, and looked about her to see a young girl, one who had been swept up in the exodus, not unlike herself, standing alone and abandoned as people rushed past her. Apparently not knowing what else to do, the girl could only stand frozen and scream in abject terror.

"Over here! Come over here!" Raya shouted as loudly as she could muster over the crowd and wind, prompting the girl to regain her senses and dash toward her. Raya greeted her with outstretched arms, though the girl seemed to cry even harder as she fell into the woman's grasp. "You are safe now," Raya said, hoping her words were more convincing to the child than they were to herself. "What is your name?"

The girl sputtered several unintelligible words between sobs before finally offering something Raya could understand. "Theena. Theena elMadej. I cannot find my parents!"

Raya held the girl more tightly as she cried. "We will find them, but first we have to go back inside. Come with—"

The words caught in her throat as another cacophonous blast of lightning pulled her attention toward the center of the Convocation courtyard, where she now saw fire engulfing the revered *noggik* trees, flames licking at their trunks and reaching up to consume the entire canopy. Her eyes welled up with tears yet again as the living symbols of her people burned.

Forcing her gaze from the distressing sight as she gripped young Theena's hand and guided her back to the shelter, Raya could only think of the dying trees as nothing more than a dreadful omen of what was to come.

CHAPTER
10

Poured into a squat, octagonal-shaped glass with a thick base, the Saurian brandy sat untouched atop Kirk's desk. Though he had come to his quarters for a short reprieve from the burdens of command and the current situation with the full intention of drinking from his bottle of preferred spirits, he now found he had no taste for the liquor.

Instead he merely stared at it, as though by some miracle it might actually provide him with the answers he sought.

To his left, perched on the edge of his desk, his computer terminal continued to display the latest status reports on the catastrophe currently enveloping Mestiko. While new information was still hard to come by from the planet itself, the *Enterprise*'s sensors were performing an admirable job of conveying the simple, harsh reality.

Mestiko was dying.

It would take time, Kirk knew, as he stared at the viewer and beheld the image of the wounded planet before him. He watched with tired eyes and a heavy heart at the process that already was well under way as the once serene planet descended into what was fast becoming a stark vision of hell. A veil of sickly brown haze roiled across the sky, all but covering the entire hemisphere currently visible to him. Thick storm clouds crossed the central region of the largest continent, the dark sky broken only by frequent discharges of lightning.

"*Sensors are registering spikes in ultraviolet radiation across the planet,*" reported the voice of Spock as the image on the viewer shifted to depict the first officer at his station on the bridge. "*Average surface temperatures have increased twenty-six degrees over the past two-point-four hours. Thunderstorms and tornadoes are still active across the three largest continents as well as flash flooding in many low-lying regions. Two hurricanes have formed, each in different oceans. Average sustained wind velocities are at one hundred kilometers per hour and rising.*"

"Any word from Dr. Apohatsu or his team?" Kirk asked, running a towel through his hair to dry it after the short but much-needed shower he had taken—part of Dr. Piper's prescription of rest, recovery, and a meal after the captain had spent nearly three complete duty shifts on the bridge observing the unfolding situation on the planet.

The image on the viewer shifted again, this time to display Lieutenant Alden. "*No, sir, nothing. I'm not picking up their transponder signal or any of their individual communicators.*"

It was as Kirk had expected, of course. The nation of Gelta, where Nathan Apohatsu and his team had made their home for more than a year, had been in the hemisphere facing directly toward the pulsar. When the drones' shield grid was compromised, that portion of the planet was subjected to the full brunt of those X-ray emissions not deflected by what remained of the shield. The entire continent was among those places hardest hit, where the bulk of the casualties would be recorded.

That included Dr. Apohatsu and his team, who had upheld their pledge to remain with their Payav friends until the end.

As for the rest of the planet? The pulsar's X-ray emissions had only washed across its surface for less than two minutes, but the duration and intensity of the radiation still had been enough to cause damage on a global scale. In addition to the immediate effects on the atmosphere, the lingering, cumulative consequences would continue to plague Mestiko for generations.

And it's our fault.

The thought echoed in Kirk's mind, ate at his gut, had tortured him from the moment he had first heard the reports of the shield grid failing. Wallowing in the nearly overpowering feelings of guilt was tempting, but he could ill afford such selfish indulgences now.

"*I am picking up a few scattered broadcasts, sir,*" Alden continued. "*Probably from military-grade equipment hardened against electromagnetic pulses. The signals are fairly weak and have hardly any range, though. They're probably operating from batteries and using small antennae, but somebody is talking down there.*"

Kirk nodded at the report as he finished dressing. News from the surface would be sketchy at best for quite some time, in large part due to the damage inflicted upon any unshielded electronics by electromagnetic disruption. Adding to that issue was the loss of dozens of communications satellites that had fallen victim to the pulsar's radiation and already were beginning to drop from their orbits. While it was disheartening to observe the calamity currently gripping the planet, it also was encouraging to hear that survivors already were reaching out and looking for others.

"Stay on that, Lieutenant," Kirk said after a moment as he smoothed wrinkles from his newly donned uniform tunic. "Any information you can glean will be helpful to the rescue ships when they get here." He was about to ask for Spock again when he heard his door chime. "Come."

The door to his quarters slid aside to reveal Gary Mitchell, leaning against one side of the threshold with his arms folded across his chest. A white rectangular dressing was affixed to the left side of his neck, along with a somewhat smaller bandage placed above his eyebrow. Otherwise, he appeared as fit as ever.

"Probably a bad time to ask if you're up for a game of racquetball," the navigator said, his expression somber.

Kirk took the comment in what he knew was the intended spirit, releasing a tired chuckle. His friend's presence already was having a calming effect, and he could feel the tension in his muscles easing, if only a small bit.

Entering the room without invitation, Mitchell made his way to the chair on the other side of Kirk's desk and took a seat. "I know that look," he said, reaching for the unmolested glass of brandy and taking a swallow. "You're carrying the weight of the world on your shoulders, Jim. One world in particular, at any rate."

Kirk reached for the bottle of brandy on the shelf behind him. "If you read more poetry," he said as he poured himself a new glass of the liquor, "you'd know how truly bad that sounded just now."

"You know I never was one for that sort of thing," the navigator replied before taking another sip from his own drink, "but we're not talking about me, are we?" Setting the glass back down on the desk, Mitchell turned to regard his friend. "Tell me you're not hell-bent on blaming yourself for what's happening down there."

Though he released an exasperated sigh, Kirk said nothing in reply and instead sipped from his brandy. While he was frustrated about a great many things at this particular moment, adding to that level of his strain was his knowledge that Mitchell was right. Of course he blamed himself. Who else was there? The actions of everyone and everything under his supervision were his responsibility, regardless of the outcome. While he never would have considered taking credit for the work of Professor Cameron and those members of his crew who had assisted her had everything gone as planned, the failure of the operation could only be laid at his feet. That was the price of command, the cost of obtaining and keeping the trust of those who swore oaths to follow and obey individuals placed into positions of leadership. It also was a philosophy in which Kirk had believed his entire adult life, for which he had spent his career training and preparing to undertake.

"So," Mitchell said after a moment, making a show of tapping his now-empty glass on the desktop, "what happens now?"

Pausing long enough to refill his friend's glass from the bottle, Kirk replied, "Alden and his staff are continuing to monitor whatever broadcasts they can pick up from the surface. There are survivors, lots of them. That's good news, at least."

At this moment, Dr. Piper and his medical team were seeing to the needs of the Payav, rescued almost without time to spare from the doomed lunar colony. Guiding the *Enterprise* as though he had been doing it all his life, Sulu had maneuvered the starship into position above the moon and given transporter crews just enough time to lock on to and beam up all thirty-four colonists before moving the vessel out of danger as the pulsar's X-ray emissions once again found their deadly mark. Since then, the colonists had been sequestered in the *Enterprise*'s main shuttlebay, where makeshift sleeping, dining, and hygiene arrangements had been made based on the information about the Payav provided by the late Dr. Apohatsu and his team.

In addition to identifying and treating any medical needs, which thankfully were few, Kirk also had assigned sociology and xenobiology personnel to handle what had become a touchy first contact scenario. The early reports were what he had expected, with the Payav colonists reacting at first with fear and uncertainty to their new surroundings, followed by shock at what was happening to their home world as well as at being introduced to beings from an intelligent species that was not their own. Kirk at first thought that he should go down there, introduce himself and perhaps try to explain the situation, but common sense had quickly prevailed. He had qualified, experienced members of his crew seeing to those needs, and they would tell him when the time was right for a formal visit by the ship's captain.

Until then, all Kirk could do was sit, watch, and wait.

Not that I've ever been any good at that sort of thing.

Sighing, the captain took a pull from his glass before continuing, "Starfleet's mobilizing ships, supplies, and personnel to deliver aid. Specialists are being brought in to assess the long-term damage to the planet." On top of everything the Payav had faced, they also would have to cope with the realization that they were not alone in the universe, and that some of those other inhabitants were coming to their aid. Sociology and xenobiology experts would be required on site as well. As first contacts went, Kirk figured this one probably would end up ranking among the most heartrending such events ever recorded.

Shaking his head, he added, "These people are in a bad way, Gary. It'll take weeks just to assess the extent of the damage, and decades to complete the sort of terraforming efforts the scientists are talking about back at Starfleet Command." Reviewing the unremitting flow of reports on the scope of the tragedy only served to hammer home the magnitude of what had been inflicted upon the people of Mestiko, to say nothing of the very real possibility that those who had survived to this point might well be facing a long, slow death in the grips of the savagely and perhaps even mortally wounded planet.

Scotty was right. The bitter musing taunted him. *Those who died probably were the lucky ones.*

The door chime sounded again, and Kirk looked up, surprised. "Is the intercom broken or something?" he asked. "Come."

When the door opened this time, it was to admit Dr. Piper. "Am I disturbing you, Captain?" he asked, his expression one of concern.

"Not at all, Doctor," Mitchell said, rising from his seat. "I promised Kelso I'd look in on him before I turned in for the night. How's he doing?"

Piper nodded. "He'll have a headache for another day or so, but otherwise I think he's going to be fine." Looking to Kirk, he added, "I was planning to discharge him from sickbay tomorrow, sir."

"Probably not a bad idea," Mitchell said. "He's going to want to get back on the job pretty quick, before Sulu sneaks it out from under him." Offering his good-byes to Piper and Kirk by way of a mock salute, the navigator then disappeared through the door and out into the corridor.

"Have a seat, Mark," Kirk said, waving the physician toward the chair Mitchell had vacated. Holding up the bottle of brandy, which he noted was now missing a third of its contents, he asked, "Care for a drink?"

"Best offer I've had all day," the doctor said as he all but dropped into the seat. "Professor Cameron suffered a broken leg and hip. I've taken care of that, but she'll be off her feet for the next few days while the bones knit. Otherwise, she's fine, physically. I can't say as much for her emotional state, of course."

Kirk figured as much, just as he suspected the professor was suffering at least the same level of remorse and frustration that he currently was facing. Rising from his chair, he began hunting for a clean glass, noting for the first time as he did so that Piper was carrying a data slate, which he laid atop the desk. "What's that?" he asked as he poured the doctor a drink.

"My preliminary reports for Starfleet Command," Piper replied as he took the proffered glass from Kirk. "From a medical standpoint, all of the colonists are fine, physically speaking. Their mental state is something that may be a bit more tricky to gauge, at least right away. According to Lieutenant Lindstrom from the sociology department, the Payav aren't quite sure what to make of us just yet. They don't know whether to consider us saviors or murderers."

"Something tells me the answer to that question will be a long time coming," Kirk replied. "What about your report on what's happening down on the planet?"

Piper sighed. "It's mind-boggling, trying to put it into words." He paused, taking a long pull from his drink. "It's going to take a lot of resources to treat the various maladies they're going to suffer, Captain, in the short and long term. Melanomas and other cancers, respiratory ailments, you name it, these people are going to be dealing with it, and future generations are going to have a hard time of it, too."

"Still want to retire?" Kirk asked.

Piper did not miss a beat. "Now more than ever," he said before sipping again from his brandy. "I thought I'd seen a lot in my time, but this is a whole new level." Shaking his head, he added, "As much as I'm ashamed to admit it, Captain, I just don't have the stomach for this kind of thing anymore."

Kirk said nothing for a moment, instead regarding the doctor in silence. Piper, in his late sixties, appeared to have aged another decade in just the past few days. Deep frown and worry lines creased his forehead and his jowls, the

wrinkles and puffiness around his eyes seemed more pronounced than even was normal for him. When the doctor
said nothing else for nearly a minute, choosing instead to sit
and sip his drink, Kirk could tell that other issues were
weighing on the man.

"Something else on your mind, Mark?" he prompted.
Though he respected the physician not only as a member of
his crew but also for the long, distinguished service he had
given to Starfleet, he could not honestly think of Piper as a
close friend or confidant, or rely on his counsel to the same
degree he did Gary Mitchell's. He figured the difference in
their ages kept the doctor from considering him in similar
fashion, as well.

He should have known better.

"Actually," Piper finally said, "I'm worried about you, Jim."

Kirk could not help his surprise. Since arriving aboard the
Enterprise, Piper had never once referred to him in anything
less than a formal manner. "How so?"

"You're beating yourself up about what's happening down
on Mestiko. You figure it's your fault, and that it should be you
who falls on your sword."

Shrugging, Kirk absently spun his empty glass atop the
desk's smooth surface. "That's what captains do, Mark. It's
part of the job."

"A lot of the time, sure," Piper replied. "Ordinarily, I'd agree
with you, but not this time." Leaning forward until his left
arm rested on the desk, the doctor locked eyes with Kirk. "You
haven't been a captain that long, but you're no untried rookie,
either. Thing is, you won't last long as a captain if you don't
learn to accept that, every so often, you're going to get the
short end of the stick."

"Millions of people are dead, Doctor," Kirk snapped, feeling
his jaw tighten. "There's no telling how many more will die.
That's not the short end of the stick. It's an obscene failure."

"And that's what I call bullshit," Piper countered, his own
voice rising a notch now. "You didn't make any kind of mistake here, Captain. There was no failure to act or foresee or respond in the correct manner. The technical solution Professor
Cameron developed was the best that could be expected, con-

sidering that no one in the history of . . . hell, I don't know . . . anything . . . has ever tried to do what we attempted here. It was more than anyone could predict."

Kirk heard nothing he had not already considered, either on his own or via the reports he had reviewed as submitted by Spock and Sulu. "Your point, Doctor?"

Reaching for the brandy bottle, Piper poured himself a new glass. "My point, Captain, is that your only other option was to stand by, do nothing, and watch a planet's entire population die." He paused to take a drink, before pointing the glass in Kirk's direction. "Now, you and I haven't known each other very long, but I'm pretty sure you're not the type of captain who's going to stand around and do nothing, not while any other kind of choice is available. Am I wrong?"

"No," Kirk replied, feeling his teeth grind together. "You're not wrong."

Piper nodded. "And since we're on the subject, seems to me I recall you not having a lot of say in the matter, anyway, so I don't think you're entitled to blame yourself for decisions you didn't make in the first place."

"Starfleet sent the *Enterprise*," Kirk said, slapping the desk. "That made it my responsibility."

"And you can carry that around with you if you want," Piper snapped, "but the simple fact is that you did everything that was asked of you, everything that could be asked of you. There are people down there we can help because of that, rather than arranging funerals for an entire world."

Forcing his rising temper down a notch, Kirk cleared his throat. Once he was convinced he could speak without verbally cutting off the doctor's head, he even offered the hint of a smile as he asked, "Is this your way of telling me to look on the bright side?"

"Something like that," Piper replied. "Fate dealt these people a hell of a blow, Jim. It's up to us . . . no, it's up to *you* . . . to help them forge something better from what they've been given."

Kirk released a sigh mixed from equal parts fatigue and acceptance. While it might be easier to dwell on what had happened—or what might have been—he knew Piper was right. If there was to be any helping the people of Mestiko, that effort only could begin by looking to the future.

The desk intercom blared to life with its melodic whistle. Reaching for the desktop terminal, the captain opened the frequency. "Kirk here."

"Alden here, sir," replied the voice of the communications officer. *"We're picking up some new broadcasts from the surface, apparently from the surviving elements of their global security council. You need to hear this, Captain."*

Frowning at the report, Kirk searched his tired memory for the name used by the indigenous population for the international body to which Alden referred, but his brain would not cooperate. Nevertheless, instinct told him he was not going to like what he was about to hear. Exchanging a worried look with Piper, the captain said, "Send it down here, Lieutenant."

There was a delay as the communications officer made the proper connections, after which Kirk and Piper found themselves listening to the still in-progress broadcast being delivered by an unidentified Payav woman, and translated by the *Enterprise's* computer.

"—ful for our deliverance from this great tragedy, which has taken so many of our loved ones from us. It will be a struggle, but from this day forward we must strive to ensure that the gift of survival bestowed upon us is not wasted. To do so, we must recognize that the visitors from the stars who have been watching our planet for these many seasons acted in our best interests, who in fact took steps to save our world from total annihilation, and hope that they are as willing to assist us with our recovery."

"Uh-oh," Piper said.

Listening to the speech, Kirk heard the fatigue as well as the resolve behind the words. This was a strong woman, he decided, someone people could look to for guidance and compassion, particularly in the days ahead. Was she an established leader, or simply a person of such strength and character who had seen the need for someone, anyone, to step into the void created by the disaster and lay a firm hand on the tiller?

"Something better," Kirk said after a moment, echoing

the doctor's earlier comments. Closing his eyes, he reached up to rub the bridge of his nose, listening to the mesmerizing woman as she continued to speak, offering hope and possibilities to a world all but enveloped by darkness and despair.

Maybe there's hope for us, as well.

CHAPTER
11

"I never thought I would get to see my world from space," Raya elMora said from where she stood at the front of the *Enterprise*'s bridge, staring at the main viewer.

Standing next to her, Kirk recognized the expression on the Payav woman's face as one of almost childlike wonder. He imagined he understood at least some of what she was feeling now, as to this day he still recalled his first time looking upon Earth from the observation port of a shuttle on its way to the orbital docking facility holding his father's ship.

"As a youth I used to daydream about it," Raya continued after a moment. "My *elor* used to tell me to get my head out of the clouds and mind my studies." Kirk watched the woman's expression falter to one of resignation, even defeat. "It was always so beautiful in my dreams."

On the screen, Mestiko seemed to turn as the *Enterprise* continued its orbit, providing a sobering, bleak image of the wounded planet. Instead of the brilliant blues of its oceans and the rich, vibrant colors saturating its landmasses, everything was shrouded and dulled by the thick brown haze permeating the atmosphere.

"It can be beautiful again." Though he delivered the words with what he considered to be a confident, authoritative demeanor, which he had spent his entire career developing in anticipation of one day ascending to the position of starship command, Kirk could not help but think that the belief he was expressing seemed to ring hollow.

Turning away from the viewscreen, Raya regarded him with narrowed eyes. "Forgive me if I find that hard to believe, Captain. From what I'm being told, the environmental damage inflicted upon my world is beyond measure."

She was not far from the truth, Kirk knew, at least according to the resources currently available to her. Even with the *Enterprise*'s sensors at his disposal, it had taken nearly two days to assess the extent of the immediate impact of the pulsar's passing. Though casualty figures were still being accumulated, projections were rising well into the order of hundreds of millions already dead. As many more were predicted to die from the direct effects of ultraviolet radiation poisoning and cardiovascular ailments brought on by the unforgiving pollution now permeating the atmosphere. There also were the ravages of persistent, unforgiving severe weather to consider—thunder and electrical storms, flooding, mudslides, tornadoes, hurricanes—which already had taken a tremendous toll in the days following the pulsar's passing.

With more than half of Mestiko having suffered the worst effects of the pulsar, the surviving elements of planetary governments devastated by the disaster had been struggling to deploy emergency response assets and procedures. Primary energy production facilities across the planet were offline, and already stressed backup services were being further taxed by the demands of ongoing rescue and aid efforts. Kirk knew that such measures were temporary at best and would require bolstering in order to continue operating even in the short term.

In the long term, the measures currently being employed were woefully inadequate, and would do nothing to stave off the doom still faced by the planet. Kirk knew from the reports he had been receiving from Spock and Professor Cameron that the worst was still to come. Continuously rising nitrogen oxide levels in the atmosphere meant less sunlight making its way through to warm the planet. Further, if left unchecked, the ultraviolet radiation eventually would be responsible for killing off all plant and animal life. Along with the atmosphere's depleted oxygen content, and Mestiko would devolve into a frozen, uninhabitable rock.

Unless we do something.

After a moment, Raya's pale features softened, and Kirk even thought he caught a twinkle in her radiant blue eyes as she offered a small smile. "I apologize if I sound harsh, Captain. As you might imagine, this is more than a bit overwhelming for me." She paused, casting a glance toward the deck. "For all of us, and I do not just mean the calamity that has befallen my people." Looking around the bridge, exchanging glances with the members of Kirk's crew, she added, "Learning that you are not alone in the universe is something of a trying experience, as well."

"No apologies needed, Raya," Kirk replied, almost faltering as he remembered at the last moment that the Payav woman had stated a preference not to be addressed by any specific honorific in keeping with her position of leadership. It might have been modesty, though the captain suspected that practicality was a more likely explanation given the hasty circumstances under which Raya had assumed her current role. "I know it's a lot to take in all at once, and while I can't claim to understand what you must be feeling right now, I hope you believe me when I say I want to help you in any way I can."

Among the casualties suffered by the people of Mestiko were many members of national and provincial governments across the planet. Chief among the losses were several heads of state who, in addition to leading their own countries, had also served on the *Zamestaad*, the planetary association founded out of circumstances similar to those that facilitated the creation of both the League of Nations and the United Nations on Earth in the twentieth century. Whereas the *Zamestaad* originally had been formed with the stated goal of fostering communal peace and security, its hastily created replacement now carried the simple yet daunting task of trying to lead their people from the ashes of despair and perhaps toward whatever fleeting remnants of hope might still remain to those who had survived worldwide catastrophe.

Turning to Kirk once more, Raya did not say anything, but instead seemed to study his face as though attempting to gauge the sincerity of his words. After a moment, she said, "I do want to believe you." Nodding in the direction of the viewscreen, she added, "While many, myself included, recognize and appreciate your attempts to help us, the general consensus is to blame you for our plight."

Despite the guilt he had been harboring since the moment the deflector grid failed and sentenced Mestiko to its tortured fate, Kirk still found himself unprepared for the stark allegation. "It's an understandable sentiment."

"Perhaps for those who do not know better," Raya countered, "but not for those with access to more comprehensive information." Looking to the viewscreen and its image of her world once more, she said, "Embracing your people while we come to terms with what has happened will take much time, and it will present a formidable challenge. But as I have already told the *Zamestaad*, were it not for your efforts, we would not be here to undertake that challenge in the first place."

For the first time since the pulsar had inflicted destruction upon Mestiko, Kirk felt the initial faint glimmer of hope. "I only hope that more people come to feel as you do."

"Several members of the *Zamestaad* would not even agree to meet with you," the Payav woman replied. "Much of that is fueled by fear at the prospect of facing beings from another world, of course, but my people are very hurt, and very angry. I am here because I see the necessity of meeting with you given your pledge to render assistance." She smiled once more. "I must also admit to a bit of selfishness. The opportunity to visit a spacecraft from another world was too precious an opportunity to ignore."

"I'm only happy you agreed to transport up here to meet with me," Kirk replied. "I wanted you to see firsthand everything we're trying to do." Motioning her to accompany him around the bridge's upper deck, the captain led Raya to the communications station. "Mr. Alden, can you show our guest what you've been picking up in the way of audio broad-casts?"

The young lieutenant looked up from his console and nod-ded. "Of course, sir." To Raya, he said, "We've been monitoring various low-level frequencies since after the incident. There are numerous transmission points scattered across the planet—pockets of survivors trying to make contact with one another. We're thinking most of these broadcasts are coming from large underground structures, probably shelters similar to yours, with equipment designed to be protected against effects such as those inflicted by the pulsar." Looking to Kirk, he added, "One group in particular seems to be having a great deal of success, making contact with people at twenty-three separate locations." Alden pointed to one of the status display monitors at his station. "Their equipment is definitely more powerful than most others I'm picking up."

He reached out and tapped a sequence of colored buttons, which resulted in a burst of static from his console's intercom speaker followed by a faint but unmistakable male voice say-ing, *"Praise be to our god for your joining us in the aftermath of the cleansing. Blessed be the mar-Atyya!"*

"Interesting," Raya said, and Kirk noted the cloud that seemed to darken her ashen features, if only for a moment.

"Something wrong?" he asked.

Shaking her head, the Payav woman replied, "No, not really. What we are hearing is the broadcast from a religious sect known as the mar-Atyya. I do not pretend to understand the various tenets of their chosen faith, but I seem to recall that according to their beliefs, this event was foretold—in a manner of speaking, of course." Pausing for a moment, she added, "It seems they were right, and were prepared, if I un-derstand what you were saying about their shelters and equip-ment. I wonder how they will fare in the times to come."

"As well as anyone else on your planet," Kirk replied. "At least, that's our hope."

Raya said, "I and others have urged our peers to accept your offers of assistance in order to best serve the immediate needs of the people in our time of crisis. There has been much resistance to that idea. Several *Zamestaad* councillors are worried about how far they may have to subjugate themselves to you."

While he had expected such concerns to be voiced, Kirk nevertheless found himself swallowing a sudden lump in his throat when confronted with the issue. "Under no circumstances will that happen, Raya. Your world is yours, and always will be."

"I want to trust you, Captain," she replied after a moment. "I can sense your commitment to helping us . . . and perhaps even a bit of remorse as well. I do not wish to sound ungrateful, but such trust must be earned. Only time will allow us to see whether that can happen."

Kirk knew from the reports he had received that Raya elMora had found herself thrust into the position of leading her province simply as a consequence of being the highest-ranking individual of her people's government to live through the disaster. Only then had she been told, by surviving members of the original *Zamestaad*, about the *Enterprise* and the team from the Federation that had been working in secret with trusted Payav science and government leaders. While those original council members held seniority, of course, the captain's instincts told him that this woman was no fool, and that she soon would become a significant voice in the renewed body that would oversee the rebuilding of Mestiko.

"Captain."

Turning toward the voice, Kirk saw Spock standing behind him. The captain could not be certain, but he thought he detected the first hints of fatigue finally beginning to show through the Vulcan's stoic countenance. Kirk knew that his first officer had been working without respite since the disaster, overseeing the monitoring of its aftermath and coordinating not only the *Enterprise*'s limited ability to render aid but also status reports to Starfleet Command in order to facilitate its deployment of relief assets and personnel from throughout the Federation.

"Yes, Mr. Spock?" Kirk asked.

"We have received an update from Starfleet Command," the Vulcan replied. "They inform us that a flotilla of medical and colony support ships is en route at high warp and should be here within the week. Other ships and supplies are being dispatched as well. We can expect a steady stream of support vessels, supplies, and personnel for the foreseeable future, sir."

"Those supplies will alleviate much suffering," Raya said, "and will help build this trust we both want. Let us hope that such gestures do not become too little, too late."

The statement was not delivered in an accusatory fashion, but Kirk felt the sting of the words just the same, and he could not help but feel that such a charge was not misplaced. Could the Federation have been better prepared to deliver the much-needed assistance in a more timely fashion? Should it not have anticipated that the pulsar's effects would only be mitigated, rather than either being simply diverted altogether or allowed to wash unimpeded over the surface of the planet?

Enough.

Kirk pushed away the irritating, defeatist thoughts. Even now, the Federation was mobilizing, all of them driven by the single goal of devising a solution to the planet's staggering environmental issues. Leading terraforming experts already were hard at work studying the issue and contemplating the best course of action in the shortest possible time, knowing full well the number of lives hinging on what they did or failed to do. From her bed in sickbay and much to Dr. Piper's vexation, Professor Cameron had demanded to be included in such efforts, using a computer interface to remain in constant contact with the special team that had been formed at Starfleet Command on Earth. Should whatever efforts devised for aiding Mestiko fail, Kirk was confident that it would not be for lack of trying.

Even if there was precious little he himself could do here today, about anything.

Well, there is one thing.

"Raya," he said after a moment, "I know this won't sound like much right now, but you have my word that my people will do everything they can for Mestiko. The Federation's greatest minds will work tirelessly to heal your world. They'll do whatever it takes, for as long as it takes, to see that Mestiko is made whole again."

Looking to him once more, Raya locked eyes with his, and

Kirk could sense that she was measuring his words against whatever it was she saw in his face.

"You seem determined, Captain," she said after a moment, "and I admire your passion, but are you in a position to make such pledges, no matter how sincere they may be?" Nodding, she let her question go unanswered. "Nevertheless, I appreciate your convictions."

"My convictions are all you need," Kirk countered, feeling his confidence beginning to return, if only to the slightest degree. "Your people deserve every chance at returning to the life that was taken from them. It's the least we . . . the least that *I* . . . can do."

Despite his vow and even as he gazed once more at the viewscreen and the tarnished, aggrieved world displayed upon it, Kirk could not deny that accomplishing what he had promised would be a struggle, to say the least. The assistance Mestiko required could conceivably take decades to render, if not longer. While he was certain the Federation would provide that help without reservation, was it truly possible to repair the harm done to these people—both by nature and by the actions of those who many on the planet believed should have been friends as well as benefactors and even saviors?

Surely some revelation is at hand?

James Kirk knew that only time and effort would provide that answer.

2267

THE CENTRE CANNOT HOLD

Mike W. Barr

For Mary E. Barr
1921–2002

CHAPTER
1

Captain's Log, Stardate 3290.9:

After two years, the *Enterprise* is returning to the planet Mestiko to aid in the task of restoring the planet's ecology following the devastating effects of a rogue pulsar that has been dubbed the Pulse by the locals.

The first thing Dr. Leonard McCoy saw when he emerged from the turbolift was Spock rising from the command chair in deference to the person McCoy had ridden up with. The first officer said, "Captain, we have crossed the orbit of Mestiko's second moon."

"Thank you, Mr. Spock," said Captain James T. Kirk, replacing Spock in the center seat. "Uhura, send best wishes to Space Central and request permission to establish orbit. And summon Dr. Lon to the bridge."

"Aye, sir," came Uhura's voice from behind him.

McCoy, meanwhile, turned his gaze to the viewscreen, showing a faraway view of a planet. "So that's it, eh?"

"That's it, Bones," said Kirk. "Mr. Sulu, viewer on full magnification."

"Aye, sir," replied Sulu. A moment later, the world came into sharper focus.

"What do you think of our patient?" asked Kirk.

McCoy was silent for a long time as he took in the more detailed image on the viewscreen. Immense patches of sere, barren earth, many encompassing entire continents, were evident, unobscured by an almost complete lack of cloud cover. The oceans looked dark, their waters listless.

"My God," said McCoy, finally. "I've read Piper's notes, but had no idea. . . . It looks almost dead."

Looking up from his station, Spock said, "A more accurate diagnosis, Doctor, couched in medical terms, would be that the planet is in critical condition. The planet's atmosphere was almost entirely denuded of its ozone layer by the radiation from the pulsar. The death of most of the oceans' plankton followed, reducing oxygen levels all over the planet. Mestiko was once a Class-M planet, but the Federation Science Council has temporarily redesignated it as Class-L."

"To hear Dr. Lon tell it, the emphasis is on 'temporary,'" said Kirk.

"So the people are living in enclosed shelters?" asked McCoy. "Unless they're compensating for the lack of sunlight, vitamin D deficiency will be a chronic problem for them. And I don't want to think about the nutritional situation."

"I'm afraid you'll have to, Bones," said Kirk, "until these people can get back on their feet. Uhura, do you have Space Central yet?"

"I'm having trouble establishing contact, Captain. The Pulse ionized the interplanetary medium around the planet."

"'The Pulse,'" said Spock, with a shake of his head. "A very inaccurate term for the event."

"It's their planet that got devastated, Spock," said McCoy with a shrug. "I guess they get to decide what to call the thing that did it."

"Perhaps, Doctor, but 'disaster,' in its original meaning, would be much more precise."

Before McCoy could reply to Spock's latest bit of pedantry, Uhura said, "Captain, I have Councillor Raya elMora."

"Put her on-screen, Lieutenant," Kirk said, rising from his chair.

McCoy had seen so many pictures of wounded and dying Payav, people scarred by radiation or killed by exposure, that he had forgotten how beautiful a people they could be, until he saw the woman whose face replaced Mestiko on the viewscreen. Her features, though delicate, gave the impression of an inner strength, and the lines her face bore spoke of having faced many struggles, and losing more than she had won. But the mouth was full and mobile, curving upward with an appreciation of pleasure by a person who had lately not seen much.

Her skin was quite pale, with an almost porcelain glow, with the delicacy of a living thing that might be beaten back, but could never be entirely eradicated. She was bald and might have been taken for a Deltan, save that her face was entirely hairless and her neck, swanlike and twice as long as the human norm, was covered with tattoos that complemented the graceful lines of her naked skull.

But the most intriguing aspect of her appearance, to McCoy, were her hands. They were as graceful as the rest of her, and a casual observer might overlook the fact that, in addition to the four fingers common to Federation standard humanoid species, each of her hands bore two thumbs. McCoy noted that Raya elMora had a habit of tapping the tips of her left thumbs together for emphasis when speaking, almost like a pair of pincers with a life of their own.

In a tone Kirk used with few planetary leaders, the captain said, "Madam Councillor, greetings from the United Federation of Planets and the *U.S.S. Enterprise*."

"*Captain,*" she said. Her voice was low and musical, but gave the impression that, given the need, it could immediately sharpen and snap to enforce discipline. "*How good to see you again. On behalf of the* Zamestaad, *I welcome you and your crew to Mestiko.*"

"Thank you, Madam Councillor," replied Kirk, making a little bow. "We are looking forward to seeing the progress

Mestiko has made in healing itself over the past two years." The turbolift door hissed; McCoy and Kirk turned to see Dr. Lon enter.

"Excellent timing, Doctor," said Kirk. He motioned for Lon to join him and extended a hand at the viewscreen as if the woman whose image graced it were standing on the bridge. "Dr. Marat Lon, Madam Councillor Raya elMora."

"*A pleasure, Doctor,*" said Raya. "*I look forward to a full explanation of your satellite technology.*"

"I look forward to this chance to prove it," said Lon, "though I might have wished for less drastic circumstances." Tall and lean with ascetic features, Lon was typical of the Martian people descended from the colonists who had taken the red planet as their own centuries ago.

"*I understand, Doctor, but it is the universe that dictates circumstances to us, not the other way around.*"

"With due respect, Madam Councillor," said Lon, "the science of terraforming may enable us to do just that."

Raya chuckled a little, and McCoy saw Kirk glance at Lon with a little smile, as though a child or a trained animal had done well. "*Perhaps so, Doctor. I certainly look forward to discussing this with you. Captain, can you and your people join us for an evening meal with the rest of the* Zamestaad? *The menu may not be quite so elaborate as you're used to, but—*"

"I'm certain it will be quite sufficient, Madam Councillor," Kirk said quickly. "We'll see you tonight, then, if . . ." He paused.

"*Yes?*"

"If we may receive permission to enter planetary space."

Raya elMora laughed again, and seemed to McCoy to be grateful for the opportunity to do so. "*Of course, Captain. Permission granted.*"

"You heard the lady, Mr. Sulu. Standard orbit."

"Aye, sir," said Sulu, exchanging a slight grin with Chekov, "standard orbit."

"Thanks for introducing me," McCoy said archly after the viewscreen went blank.

"You'll have your chance to make an impression tonight, Bones," said Kirk. "I wanted to make a point of introducing

Dr. Lon, as he's going to be living on the planet for a while. What did you think, Doctor?"

"They like their tattoos, don't they?" said Lon, judiciously.

Spock, naturally, had an explanation on tap. "The Payav have a long history of skin decorations, Doctor. It is their custom to think of their skin as a blank canvas they may adorn. Many generations of the same family can be found to wear identical tattoos."

"Filthy habit, injecting chemicals under the skin," said McCoy.

"Nonetheless, it is their way, Doctor," said Spock, "though it is less common than it was generations ago. I have made a study of the Payav body art that—"

"I'll bet you have," said McCoy. "But no thanks, Spock. I've still got some medical records to go over." He glanced at Kirk. "I'm going to want a look at their medical facilities. Will that be a problem?"

"I'm certain we can arrange something, Bones," said Kirk.

"I'm certain *you* can," replied McCoy, remembering the look Kirk and Raya had exchanged.

"Such an arrangement is already in place, Doctor," said Spock. "Under the terms of the Organian Peace Treaty, inspection of humanitarian services is allowed."

"Everyone keeps citing that treaty," said Lon, a trifle aggrievedly. "I'm afraid I don't follow politics all that much, so I'm a bit unclear as to its meaning here."

"I suppose the entire landing party could do with a little review before we go planetside," said Kirk. "The briefing room in ten minutes."

CHAPTER
2

"Is everyone here, Spock?" asked Kirk as he walked into the briefing room ten minutes later.

"We seem to be missing one member of the landing party, Captain," said Spock.

Kirk looked at the large table in the center of the room. The three-sided viewscreen sat in the center of the table, and around it sat Spock, McCoy, and Lon. Spock was, as usual, next to the large computer station. Two seats remained empty. One was for Kirk himself, the other . . .

Stabbing a button on the wall intercom with irritation, he said "Kirk to—"

Before he could finish, the doors parted, revealing a young female officer with shoulder-length blond hair. Her chest rose and fell rather more rapidly than was normal, and she seemed a little wobbly on her feet, as though she had just come to a full stop from a brisk run.

"Lieutenant Sinclair," said Kirk dryly. "Glad you could join us."

"I'm sorry, sir, I was brushing up on the local customs and lost track of time." She had a straight nose, gray eyes, and a squarish jaw, which was currently thrust forward.

Sternly, Kirk said, "This is a valuable opportunity for you, Sinclair. If you're not up to the responsibility—"

"I am, sir." She brushed back an errant lock of hair that had strayed during her run.

"Well, take your place."

Sinclair nodded docilely and sat down, tucking her long legs underneath the table.

Kirk also took a seat at the head of the table next to Spock. "In fact, Lieutenant, since you've been brushing up, tell us about the Organian Peace Treaty."

"Yes, sir," said Sinclair, her high forehead furrowed a little. "The treaty forbids hostilities between the Federation and the Klingons, and provides that any planet disputed between the two sides will be awarded to the side that proves it can develop that planet most efficiently."

"And since Mestiko is already closer to the Klingon Empire's borders than Federation's, the Klingons have already claimed it's theirs," said Kirk.

"Captain," said Lon with a frown, "I don't relish the idea of my technology being taken by the Klingons."

"Your technology is secure, Doctor," said Spock. "In fact, it was your technology that convinced the *Zamestaad* to give the Federation the first opportunity to repair the ecosphere. The Klingons' plan simply proposed to mine and sell Mestiko's many stores of mineral wealth to support the population until the ecosphere restored itself by due course of nature."

"Which, left to its own devices, would take over a century," said Lon. "My technology can do it in half the time."

"And you'll have the chance to prove that, Doctor," said Kirk. "No matter which side wins, the results will be known throughout this quadrant for decades. Losing this planet to the Klingons may be more devastating to the Federation's reputation than losing a war. And I have no intention of losing this planet—let alone its population—to the Klingons."

"They've already suffered enough," said McCoy emphatically.

"Exactly, Bones. Which is where you come in, Lieutenant,"

said Kirk, swiveling to face Sinclair. "Your job as recording officer is to make sure a full record of our dealings on the planet is preserved."

"I understand, sir."

"If there are no further questions," said Kirk, rising, "then we have a dinner engagement."

CHAPTER
3

"Are you sure this is the wisest course, Captain?" asked Chief Engineer Montgomery Scott.

"You sound worried, Scotty," said Kirk, as he entered the transporter room.

"I just don't think both you and Mr. Spock should be goin' planetside when we're this close to Klingon space. Sector 418-D is practically next door to the sneakin' devils."

"There has been no evidence of any current Klingon presence on Mestiko, Mr. Scott," said Spock from his place on the platform with McCoy, Lon, and Sinclair.

"Besides, with Sulu at the conn and you in engineering, I don't think we'll be in any danger, Scotty." Kirk took his place on the platform with the others. "But just in case, make sure either you or Kyle is on duty here. I want an experienced hand in charge if this ionization shows any signs of interfering with the transporter. Energize."

"I was worried about the ship, mostly," grumbled Scotty as he manipulated the transporter panel.

"What was that?" Kirk asked even as the beams activated. The next thing he saw was the interior surface of a great half-sphere. It showed evidence of having once had windows, but these had been sealed.

Kirk looked around. Hallways led off the half-sphere at sixty-degree intervals that sank below ground level as they progressed.

"Captain," came a cool voice, "welcome from the *Zamestaad*."

Kirk smiled as he turned. Madam Councillor Raya elMora approached with a walk that managed to be somehow businesslike, efficient, and yet feminine.

"On behalf of the United Federation of Planets," replied Kirk, gallantly, "I accept." This led to a formal greeting in which Raya held out her hands with the left palm facing upward, the right palm downward. Kirk placed his own palms on hers, and the gesture was held for a moment.

Then the two of them broke into a mutual smile. "It is good to see you again, James," said Raya.

"And you, Raya, alive and well," replied Kirk. "From the reports received of your planet over the past two years, I wasn't always sure that would be the case."

"Perhaps you worry too much," said Raya, turning away from him to face the others.

"My landing party," said Kirk. "You already know Mr. Spock. This is our new chief medical officer, Dr. Leonard McCoy, Dr. Marat Lon, and Lieutenant Sinclair, our records officer."

"How good to see you again, Mr. Spock," said Raya. She approached the landing party and exchanged the same handshake with each of them. "Dr. Lon, I look forward to discussing your plans to restore our beleaguered planet. I'm afraid you have your work cut out for you."

"A scientist always enjoys a challenge, Madam Councillor," replied Lon, as Raya moved to Sinclair.

"Is something wrong, Lieutenant?" asked Raya, after a moment.

"No, ma'am—no, Madam Councillor. Forgive me if I was staring. Your hands are very beautiful."

"How kind," said Raya. She favored Sinclair with a smile that Sinclair returned with a brilliant smile of her own. Raya's eyes widened and she took an involuntary step backward.

"Madam Councillor, did I—?" began Sinclair.

"It is nothing, Lieutenant," said Raya, regaining her composure as quickly as she had lost it. "Nothing at all." She stepped away from Sinclair and gestured to a small group that had remained some distance away. "Let me present my advisors."

Kirk followed, tossing Sinclair a frigid glance as he did so.

"What did I do?" asked Sinclair, of the landing party in general.

"Your acquaintanceship with the local customs is not yet complete, Lieutenant," said Spock, before moving to join Kirk. "The Payav consider showing teeth when smiling a major cause for offense."

"Don't worry about it, Lieutenant," said McCoy, "Spock's hardly the one to give advice about smiling. I'm sure Raya didn't take it personally."

"I hope not," said Sinclair, her cheeks coloring.

"Captain," Raya was saying, "may I present my *elor*—my grandmother."

"I can easily see where Raya's beauty comes from," replied Kirk. He took the grandmother's extended hand and kissed it.

That the old woman and Raya were related was obvious from more than just the fact that several of their facial decorations were identical, though the grandmother's tattoos were somewhat faded with age, and the skin they decorated was weathered like old parchment. The grandmother's features very much resembled Raya's, but it was in a shared manner of looking at the world, of quizzically evaluating any new aspect of life presented to them more than any mere physical resemblance that most made them seem alike.

"It is good to have visitors, Captain," said the old woman. She regarded Kirk with a smile that showed an appreciation of his flattery, yet also saw through it.

"Please, this way," said Raya, motioning to one of the walkways leading off the main structure.

"Is this building aboveground?" asked McCoy, looking around. "I thought I read that your living quarters were all underground."

"Almost all of them are, Doctor," replied Raya. "But we kept this building, which used to be the main hall of our council chamber, in use, after sealing it off from the atmosphere, as a receiving point for visitors. It also—" And here she approached one of the walls, opened a small panel set into the wall, and pressed a button. "—serves to remind us of the struggle we will be fighting for years to come."

A curved section of the outer dome retracted, revealing a window of thick glass. It looked upon the landscape of Mestiko as its sun set, red rays refracted through an atmospheric slush of reddish-brown air that hung over the land, barely moving, like a lurking predator. Beyond that, remains of collapsed buildings could be seen, tumbled over vehicles and city streets that had once been filled with an industrious people.

"My God," said McCoy. The starkness of his tone drew no reproach from any present.

"Nitrogen dioxide," said Spock. "Red-brown in color. Along with nitric oxide, which is colorless. They block both light and heat from the sun, two essential elements if the planet's ecology is to recover."

"That's where Dr. Lon's satellites come in," said Kirk, heartily, trying to encourage a positive attitude. "Isn't that right, Doctor?"

"Yes, Captain," said Lon, though not as eagerly as Kirk had hoped. "Once the satellites are placed in orbit, they'll begin reconverting the nitrogen oxides—both nitric oxide and nitrogen dioxide—into regular nitrogen and oxygen."

"Because it is the nitrogen oxides that are destroying the ozone, yes?" asked Raya.

"Exactly, Madam Councillor," said Lon. Unlike Kirk's attempt at raising spirits, Raya's response seemed to engender a more encouraging tone from the doctor. "It will take some time—years, in fact—but my satellites will do the job far more quickly than waiting for Mestiko's condition to correct itself."

"I will know the world is on the path to recovery when I see it covered again in forests of *noggik* trees." For just a moment, her shoulders slumped. "I do so miss them."

"Such technology is remarkable," said Raya's grandmother.

"I do not think I shall live to see the day when we can live on the surface again, but it will help to know it is coming."

"*Elee*, don't be such a fatalist," said Raya, taking her hand. "I'm sure you'll outlive us all."

"Perhaps," said the grandmother, smiling faintly.

"This is what I would have you see," said Raya, urging the party forward. Kirk became aware that they were heading gradually downward, deeper into the earth. From the ceilings of the tunnels they walked were hung lights that, despite being strung at regular intervals, gave the impression of having been positioned quickly; bare wires and electric conduits could be seen sprouting from them.

"Were all these tunnels built after the Pulse struck?" asked McCoy. "Seems a lot of work to have to do in a short time."

"We have become experts at that over the past two years, Doctor," said Raya. "But, to be honest, most of these tunnels originally formed the access networks to the physical plants of many of the major buildings of our city. With the cities no longer in service, the access to the surface has been sealed off. Now the tunnels, some of them expanded by emergency construction, have been used to provide housing, schools, temples, and whatever other facilities may be needed. It is a rare chamber that does not serve at least three purposes."

Kirk got a look into a vast underground room as they passed, and caught the whir of turbines, powering electrical plants, and air scrubbers.

"And you live down here, too, Madam Councillor?" asked Sinclair. "In subterranean quarters?"

"Yes, our living areas are down here, too. In fact . . ." Raya paused before two wide doors decorated with bright paper stickers and scrawled drawings and tapped a button in a wall console next to it. The doors rose, revealing a large room full of families, standing, in various degrees of impatience, in line before tables full of food. Most heads turned at the sound of the doors parting. Then, when a cheer arose at the sight of Raya, all heads turned.

"Madam Councillor," said a portly uniformed attendant, running forward and bowing at the same time. "Forgive us, we did not know—"

"Actually, it is I who beg your forgiveness," said Raya, with a smile. "I did not know we would be coming."

"Raya!" exclaimed a voice at the edge of the crowd. A moment later a young girl, all arms and legs and neck, but apparently well cared for, broke through the crowd and hugged Raya, to the utter disapproval, Kirk noted with amusement, of the uniformed attendant who obviously had a great deal of a martinet in her.

"Hello, Theena," said Raya, running her left hand with affection over the child's skull. "These are the visitors I mentioned. This little *hareeja* is Theena elMadej, a friend of mine."

"I am not a demon," replied the girl, with a grin. "I am a big help here."

"I'm sure the attendants would have a different story," said Raya, with a smile.

Most of the children had gathered around Raya and her grandmother, waving and jumping up and down, but some of them regarded their visitors closely, especially Spock. Their parents stood back a little, also plainly happy to see Raya.

"Are those ears real?" asked a little girl, of Spock. Kirk couldn't help but smile.

"Indeed they are," said the Vulcan, equably.

"And you only have one thumb? How do you make do?"

"One per hand, yes," replied Spock, "but they have always seemed sufficient for their tasks."

"Loda—!" gasped an aghast parent, pulling the little girl back. "I'm sorry, sir, she meant no—"

"There is no need for apology," said Spock. "Her curiosity is natural. And quite commendable."

"These are visitors," said Raya, "from another planet."

"Oh!" gasped a little boy, enthusiastically. "Are you Klingons?"

There followed an awkward moment of silence, which Kirk broke by saying, "No. We're from the United Federation of Planets. Dr. McCoy and I are from Earth, Dr. Lon is from Mars, Lieutenant Sinclair is from Alpha Centauri, and Mr. Spock is from Vulcan." Spock gravely exchanged greetings with children who offered their hands; Dr. Lon stood back, nodding politely, but a little aloof. Many of the children

seemed in awe of these faraway names, but at the mention of
the Federation, a cloud seemed to pass over the faces of some
of the parents, and their smiles turned to concern, and, in
some instances, to outright frowns.

"That is one of our better living facilities," said Raya, as
they proceeded back up the tunnel, waving good-bye to
Theena. "I wish it were possible for each family to have a separate home, but . . ."

"They looked generally well fed and cared for," said McCoy.
"Were those sunlamps I noticed in the ceiling?"

"Yes, they're used in the mornings to simulate the effects of
sunlight. There's only so much that can be done with vitamin
supplements."

"I've been saying that for years," said McCoy, with a martyr's sigh, and Kirk chuckled.

At the central intersection of the tunnels Raya led them to
the left, down a long hall past a blank wall, then into a large
room lined with tables set with silverware and linen table-
cloths. While Kirk appreciated the effort to show grace under
pressure, the fact remained that they were in an underground
chamber, discussing the revival of a planet that was very
nearly dead. Several persons in native dress or military uniforms were already present, milling about, some with drinks;
at Raya's entrance they turned and applauded.

"Thank you, members of the *Zamestaad* and representatives
of the peoples of Mestiko," said Raya, acknowledging their applause with a graceful bow. "Join me in greeting Captain
James T. Kirk of the Federation Starship *Enterprise*." This was
followed by another round of applause, though not as long,
nor as enthusiastic. Kirk and his party made little bows, and
tried not to look self-conscious.

They were ushered to a large table at the head of the room.
As they neared it, Kirk noticed a large man wearing a military
tunic, festooned with medals and ribbons. His features were
strong and had a cast that could, in certain conditions, be considered cruel, though others might consider it merely resolute.
His eyes were the most remarkable thing about him, Kirk realized. Large and clear and carrying a sensitivity they rarely
showed; they were the eyes of a poet.

"Captain Kirk, I present Councillor Traal," said Raya. Kirk nodded and presented his hands for the standard greeting, then introduced the rest of his party.

Sinclair had prepared a thorough briefing on Traal; he was a native of a tribe called the Norrb, a tyrant and conqueror who, in the wake of the Pulse and on the backs of its victims, saw the road to political respectability and a vindication by history, and so was trading in the title of warlord for councillor. *Different world, same story,* Kirk thought with bemusement.

"So, Captain," said Traal, in a confidential man-of-the-world tone that could nonetheless be heard twelve feet away, "you have come to attempt to make amends for the damage the Federation has done to our planet, to buy our allegiance?"

Kirk had rather expected this sometime during his visit, and better now than later. "Suffice it to say, Councillor, that the Federation is extending to all the tribes of Mestiko the hand of friendship . . . as, I assume, are you to the many nations you once tried to conquer." Rather than being taken aback, Traal smiled wryly and shrugged, as if acknowledging that his first assault had been merely a test, and that Kirk had passed.

There was a round of toasts, which were followed by drinks of a native liquor, something beneath whose pungent fruitiness lurked a kick that, Kirk decided after the second toast, could easily sneak up on an unsuspecting imbiber. He had no idea what it was called, but nicknamed it "liquid dilithium" and resolved moderation in its intake.

Councillor Traal was lavish in his praise of "our new allies, the United Federation of Planets," but concealed a sting in its tail, praising also "our friends of the Klingon Empire."

Suddenly, Kirk felt all eyes on him for reasons other than that he was the next in line. He rose, hefted a glass of the liquor and delivered a stirring toast to the planet Mestiko, its brave citizens, the *Zamestaad*, and finally, "the *Jo'Zamestaad*, the first on the Planetary Council, Raya elMora." This brought the entire assemblage to its feet, and as he lifted his glass, Kirk caught a glimpse of Raya, beaming at him.

The meal was a native dish, simply prepared and quite

flavorful. Kirk gathered it to be some kind of fish, and he noted an attendant telling Spock that a vegetarian dish had been prepared for the Vulcan, which Spock received gratefully.

It was just when an after-dinner cordial was being offered that Kirk's communicator sounded. Rather than trying to hide it, he produced the device and flipped it open with a nonchalance that said such tasks were all in a day's work, knowing that any observers would be fascinated by the details of his command.

"Kirk here."

"Captain," came Sulu's voice, *"we've just picked up—"*

"Captain," said Spock, cutting off Sulu, "we are no longer the only visitors at this banquet."

Kirk lifted his gaze to the entrance of the banquet hall, where a display of silent, flickering red energy had drawn every eye in the room.

The energy coalesced, revealing itself to be four Klingons.

And at their lead, Commander Kor.

CHAPTER
4

Kirk again felt every eye in the room on him, now including those of the new arrivals. He lifted his communicator and spoke into it almost nonchalantly. "Yes, Mr. Sulu. I believe you were about to say you've picked up the *I.K.S. Klothos* in the vicinity?"

"*That's right, Captain,*" came Sulu's reply, a little confusion in his voice. "*Are you all right?*"

"We're fine. Commander Kor just made a grand entrance. Await further orders. Kirk out." As Kirk stashed his communicator, he looked down the table at his landing party. "Have a seat, Lieutenant," he told Sinclair. "The evening's not over yet."

Sinclair looked down at herself, as if surprised to find she had risen to her feet, one hand halfway to her phaser. "Yes, sir," she said, sinking slowly back to her chair.

"Commander Kor, welcome back to Mestiko," said Raya, in a hospitable tone. "How may we be of service?"

"*Jo'Zamestaad,*" said Kor with a half-bow, "we thank you for your hospitality. We trust our arrival, though unannounced, is not an intrusion." His voice carried the identical tone he had used during his short tenure as military governor of the planet

Organia, and to his grudging credit, the tone he had used with the Organians even after they were revealed to be non-corporeal life forms of nearly incalculable power: cordial, condescending, and capable of turning on the object of his attentions in a split second.

"Not at all," replied Raya, "all friends of Mestiko are welcome in the chambers of the *Zamestaad*." She gestured down the table. "Have you met Captain Kirk and his crew?"

"Commander Kor and I have . . . exchanged greetings in the past, yes," said Kirk. He rose and approached Kor, wearing a smile behind which lurked an ill-concealed reserve of defiance. Kor's landing party began to move around Kirk as he neared their commander, but Kor raised his right hand with a dismissive wave that scattered his men.

"Captain," said Kor, "how glorious to see you again."

"Thank you, Kor, it's a genuine pleasure to see you, as well."

"Is it, now?" asked Kor cautiously, smelling a rat.

"It is, yes. I always feel more comfortable when you and I are face-to-face, rather than back-to-back." Kirk gave Kor a toothy grin, hoping the Klingon was up on the local customs.

One of Kor's minions, who either was up on the customs or simply slow on the uptake, began to emit a low growl. "Silence, Kiregh," said Kor. "This is a social occasion." Nonetheless, it felt to Kirk like the air had become electrically charged, like the calm before a tremendous storm. During his walk to confront Kor, Kirk had seen the heads of every person present oscillating slowly on their long necks. A people who had suffered much these past two years, it was as if they were cautiously waiting to see which way they should jump.

"Commander, will you join us?" boomed the voice of Councillor Traal, breaking the tension like a clap of thunder.

"Thank you, Councillor Traal," said Kor, not taking his eyes from Kirk. "We will not be staying—this time. I simply wanted to wish the captain a pleasant stay on Mestiko, though I doubt it will be a long one."

"That's up to the people of Mestiko, isn't it, Commander?" asked Kirk. "Just as it was up to the Capellans, not so long ago."

"Were it up to us," trilled a familiar voice, "I know what my decision would be." Kirk turned and was surprised to see Raya's grandmother, risen to her feet and thrusting an imperious finger at Kirk. "And I think many other of the Payav would feel the same. It was the Federation that knew disaster was headed for our planet and conspired with our former leaders to hide this from us. And now we are asked to trust them?"

This statement elicited cheers and applause from many of those present; some level of Kirk's mind noted idly that applause from hands with multiple thumbs sounded no different than applause from hands with one thumb.

Kirk locked eyes with Raya, who returned his gaze, but gave him no support. And what he saw there gave him no comfort.

"Nothing more to say, Captain?" said Kor, his voice an oily smear.

"Just this," said Kirk, returning to stand behind his chair. He waited for the clamor of the crowd to die down, then waited a few more seconds, making sure he had their full attention. "If the *Zamestaad* feels the Federation has not fulfilled its promise to aid the people of Mestiko, I invite them aboard the *Enterprise* tomorrow night to witness the implementation of the first step in the Federation's plan to restore the ecosphere of Mestiko, the dispersion of Dr. Lon's satellite technology. That should convince any who doubt not only the Federation's good intentions, but the ability to act on those intentions."

There was more applause, most of it from people other than those who had applauded the Klingon. Kirk nodded his thanks.

And when he looked toward the entrance of the banquet hall, he caught just the fading flash of the Klingons' transporter.

CHAPTER
5

While Jim Kirk didn't have his chief medical officer's facility with sarcasm, he hoped that he matched McCoy's tone on the bridge earlier when he sardonically said to Raya, "Thank you for your support."

"What did you expect, James?" replied Raya.

They stood in Raya's office, a rather small cubicle, Kirk thought, for such an important post. The walls were mostly bare, which lent authority to those few pieces mounted there: a picture of a woman Kirk first thought was Raya, but was probably her mother, with a younger version of the grandmother and Raya as a gangly young girl; a picture of Raya with the girl Theena; and a photograph of the *Jo'Payav*, the warp-speed vehicle built by the Payav that had drawn them to the attention of the Federation in the first place. It was a craft so austere in its design that it almost resembled a child's toy. Then Kirk remembered Zefram Cochrane's *Phoenix*, the first Earth craft to break the light barrier, and decided the Payav craft wasn't bad-looking at all.

Occupying nearly the entire facing wall was a picture so large it could almost be taken for a window—an immense painting of the city under which they currently dwelled, in its days of greatest glory.

Hopefully, days of even greater glory lay ahead.

"Did you expect me to take the Federation's side against that of the Klingons?" Raya asked. "Though my *elor's* statement was impolitic, it was not untrue. The Federation does bear at least partial responsibility for keeping the truth about the Pulse from us."

"And the Klingons will be glad to take full responsibility for every living soul on Mestiko—for the rest of your lives."

She nodded; at least that truth had not eluded her. "But it is my responsibility to lead my people—Payav and Dinpayav alike—through this black mark in our history, and I will do so by any means available."

Nearing her, Kirk said, "You know that I have only the best intentions toward you and your people—and so does the Federation."

She replied after a moment, "My duty is to see my planet healed and its people saved, just as it is your duty to guard the safety of your ship and your crew." She paused for a moment, the thumbs of her left hand tapping together rapidly. "Would you betray your ship and crew, act against their best interests, simply on my word?"

"No," conceded Kirk, softly.

"Thank you for your honesty," she said. "Perhaps as long as we have that between us . . ."

"Perhaps so," said Kirk. Then he looked up. "The *Zamestaad* will come aboard the *Enterprise* tomorrow night, then?"

"Of course," Raya replied quickly. "This is a matter of Mestiko's future, James, and our relationship with the Federation. There is no question of trust between the two of us. At least, I hope there is not."

"Of course not," replied Kirk, perhaps too quickly. "Lieutenant Uhura will be in touch with your office about the arrangements for tomorrow night, then."

"I look forward to seeing the woman in your life," said Raya, with a teasing smile.

"I'm not so sure you haven't already seen her," said Kirk.

CHAPTER
6

"I want continuous sensor sweeps, Mr. Chekov," said Kirk. "Maximum range. Report anything you find that even seems irregular to me immediately."

"Aye, Captain," said Chekov from the science station, filling in while Spock was off the bridge, answering the same order for the third time in two minutes.

"And there have been no signs of a Klingon presence?"

"No, sir. Wherever the *Klothos* went when it left orbit last night, it's out of our sensor range. Perhaps they're hiding on the other side of the planet?"

"Possibly," said Kirk, after a moment's consideration, "but I doubt it. Too much chance of being picked up by one of the other nations and reported. But I don't want to take a chance on being ambushed by the Klingons at any time—and certainly not when we have the Mestiko Planetary Council aboard."

"Acknowledged, sir," said Chekov, for variety's sake.

The turbolift opened, and Lieutenant Sinclair emerged. Kirk turned, and Chekov, thankful for the diversion, continued the sensor sweep.

"I have that information you wanted, Captain," said Sinclair, producing a computer microtape.

Kirk nodded, but did not take the tape. "Report. Is there any record of Councillor Traal's dealings with the Klingons?"

"No hard evidence of it, sir, though it is common knowledge that he does deal with them. Traal is the most visible leader of what might be called a 'Mestiko First' movement. He denigrates the Federation, and, as we saw last night, has even implied that the Federation might be responsible for instigating the Pulse so we can secure a foothold on Mestiko, and discourage Mestiko's own attempts at space travel. He is on record as having petitioned the Payav, in an attempt to force them to share their warp technology with all the peoples of the planet, but was turned down. Traal feels he and his people can do better by helping themselves than they can by, to quote one of his speeches, 'tying themselves to the Federation's apron strings.'"

"As though those are the only options," said Kirk.

"I'm just quoting, sir."

"Of course, Lieutenant. Continue."

"Councillor Traal has a great deal of credibility among both the Norrb and even among the Payav, because he believed the alarms raised about the pulsar. His people are living in relative comfort in cities preserved under domes or in underground colonies, and he has been responsible for distributing aid and comfort to millions of Payav whose lives have been disrupted."

"Well, we can't fault his humanitarian acts, though their motivation might be somewhat suspect. Thank you, Lieutenant. Report to Mr. Spock. He and Dr. Lon are doing a final diagnostic on the satellites before tonight's ceremony."

"Aye, sir," said Sinclair. She turned smartly, headed for the turbolift, and was gone. Chekov wished he could have followed her, as he did not enjoy being under Kirk's eye when the captain was in a mood.

"Members of the *Zamestaad*," said Captain Kirk, resplendent in his dress uniform, hours later, "welcome aboard the Starship *Enterprise*." The first bunch of councillors had barely materialized on the transporter pad before Kirk was bearing down on them. "You all remember my first officer, Mr. Spock."

Some of the councillors who had probably never transported before were patting themselves surreptitiously, as if confirming that they had each arrived with all the limbs they left Mestiko with. Kirk thought of his own ship's doctor and grinned, though he did not show teeth.

"Madam Councillor," said Kirk, offering a hand to Raya as she stepped off the pad. She was wearing a gown of shimmering, multicolored fabric printed with many of the same tattoos she herself wore. This gave an observer a first impression that the gown was at least partially diaphanous, though she was clothed from head to toe. Kirk greeted Councillor Traal as though he were Kirk's best friend, then offered an arm to Raya's grandmother, which she took with a smile.

As they passed transporter control, Kirk glanced briefly at Lieutenant Kyle, observing a brief, furtive shake of the lieutenant's head. It meant that neither Traal—nor any of the other guests—was wearing any kind of recording or eavesdropping device. Kirk had debated the diplomatic repercussions of this kind of scan being performed on the guests without their knowledge, but reasoned that where the Klingons might be involved, it was better to err on the side of caution. If it were an error at all.

Leaving Spock to greet the rest of the council, Kirk ushered the first arrivals through the halls of the *Enterprise* to the officers' lounge, where there would be drinks before dinner. Kirk had deliberately chosen the transporter room farthest from the lounge for the council members' materialization, so the impromptu tour of the *Enterprise* could be extended as long as possible. The *Zamestaad* was properly appreciative of his ship, making it all the more easy for Kirk to treat them, not as representatives of a planet of which one race had achieved faster-than-light space travel, but as trusted colleagues.

"Look at the size of it!" gasped one councillor, on seeing the recreation deck. "You could land our entire ship in it!"

"You should see the size of our early space-faring craft," said Kirk, in the tones of one colleague to another, "I don't know how the crew stood it."

Traal was largely noncommittal through the tour, nodding once in a while in acknowledgment of an observation Kirk put directly to him, but volunteering little. It may have been only the calm before the storm, but it was at least better than last night's rabble-rouser.

After dinner and drinks in the lounge, they made their way to the observation deck. With this many occupants and the overlooking window closed, the deck seemed a trifle cramped. When their guests were comfortable, Kirk spoke.

"Honored members of the *Zamestaad*, and *Jo'Zamestaad*," began Kirk, "I thank you for giving the Federation the opportunity to show you the technology we offer you to help restore your planet—the satellite technology of Dr. Marat Lon."

Tapping a button on the deck's console, the shield over the window slid back, providing a view of the shuttlebay and its current cargo.

There were a number of actual gasps, which Kirk appreciated, watching their faces reflected in the revealed window, though Traal's face was not among these.

The floor of the shuttlebay had been pressed into service as the launching pad for Dr. Lon's satellites, a fleet of which hovered at various heights in the bay.

"There they are," said Kirk, through the intercom to the bay. "Dr. Lon, the author of this technology, and Mr. Spock, performing the final pre-launch check." As instructed, both men turned and waved to the observation deck. Dr. Lon seemed uncomfortable in the role of cheerleader, and Spock was . . . well, Spock. Amusingly, he was still in his dress uniform, though he of course didn't let that curtail his work in the least.

The satellites themselves were large gray globes with a pair of vents on either side and a short communications antenna. "Are there any questions?" asked Kirk.

"Why do they look like mines?" said Traal, undiplomatically. "Are explosive devices to be released into our atmosphere?" Kirk quickly started to reply, but was cut off.

"No, no," said Lon, his voice magnified and slightly harshened by the intercom. *"The function of the units is to replenish Mestiko's atmosphere by reconverting the nitrogen*

oxides into regular nitrogen and oxygen. The design is simply to make the units as aerodynamic as possible, the vents are simply for the intake of nitrogen oxides, and the emission of standard nitrogen and oxygen. We discussed this. Do you people remember noth—?"

"Yes, Doctor, thank you," said Kirk, quickly cutting off an incendiary remark. "Please join us up here when you're through down there."

There followed a few moments of uncomfortable silence that somehow seemed longer than the entire evening had so far. When Spock and Lon entered the observation deck, Kirk was tempted to hug them.

"Any remarks on this occasion, Doctor?" asked Kirk.

Lon's slender features twisted in thought for a moment. "No, Captain. Instead I feel, as I'm sure do our hosts, that I would rather begin the restoration of Mestiko's atmosphere." This was met by applause from the Zamestaad; Kirk couldn't blame them.

"If you'll begin, then," said Kirk, gesturing to the control panel. Lon nodded and took his place. Inside the sealed and pressurized observation deck could be heard the pumps that sucked the air from the shuttlebay—until, of course, there was no air and nothing to be heard.

A slight tremor swept through the observation deck; the more sensitive of the council looked around nervously. "Is the ship coming apart?" asked Councillor Jolon, representative of a tribe called the Domtos.

"Not at all, sir," said Spock. "That is simply the vibration made when the doors of the shuttlebay open, conducted through the floor, rather than through the medium of atmosphere. It is quite ordinary."

"Very well," said Jolon, returning to his seat. From the corner of his eye Kirk noticed Lon shaking his head as if in exasperation. Then he caught himself, and returned gazing at his brainchildren.

"That's Mestiko out there, in the background," said Kirk, pointing. Most of the councillors, who were not spacefarers and had never seen their planet suspended against the cosmic firmament, nodded with interest; Kirk even heard a few gasps, though they were quickly subdued. He imagined the councillors had been warned against appearing too provincial to the Federation offworlders, and that was something of a shame. Kirk appreciated the honest reactions of people experiencing space travel for the first time, not as a superior observer, but as one who had once been there himself, and remembered it well.

Lon tapped a few keys on the control panel and touched a small lever that had popped up from it. In the shuttlebay, lights at the bases of the satellites' antennae began flashing, and they stirred slightly, like children waking up after a nap.

"The navigation beacons will aid in the prevention of close-range collisions with other craft," said Spock, "and each satellite broadcasts its own unique long-range identification signal."

Looking up from the controls, as though just becoming aware Spock was doing part of his job, Lon said, "These signals will be provided to all the governments of Mestiko."

The councillors nodded. Raya tapped her grandmother on her arm and pointed at the first satellite, which was hovering at the mouth of the bay. It hesitated there for a moment, like a swimmer testing the waters, before plunging out into space.

"The restoration of Mestiko's atmosphere has begun!" said Lon, and there was a round of applause that, Kirk noticed, even Traal joined in.

"We're going to take you on a quick trip around your planet," said Kirk with a grin, "though I hope you'll forgive me if we don't have time for sightseeing." The *Zamestaad* laughed, this time with no tension at all.

"Where will the satellites be placed, Dr. Lon?" asked an elderly councillor.

"In stationary positions in Mestiko's stratosphere," replied Lon, "largely at equal distances, save over the planet's polar ice caps, where the atmosphere suffered less damage than that of the remainder of the planet. The satellites need maintenance only twice a year, which your vessels are certainly capable of performing." *Clever*, thought Kirk, *treating them not only as partners in this endeavor, but as partners performing a vital task.*

"Of course," said Spock, "no planet is perfectly spherical. It may be of interest to the *Zamestaad* to become acquainted with the calculations used to determine the satellites' positions—"

"Thank you, Mr. Spock," Kirk interjected rapidly. "I think this moment speaks for itself."

"Yes, sir," said Spock, with a raise of his brows that said such an omission was Kirk's loss.

An hour later, Kirk and the *Zamestaad* stood in the transporter room, bidding each other good night. There was not a frown in the bunch; even Traal looked somewhat less dour as he offered Kirk an Earth-style handshake.

"A great day for Mestiko, Captain, thank you," said another councillor, moving to the transporter pad.

"Would you and your *elor* care for a nightcap, Madam Councillor?" asked Kirk, approaching Raya.

"Thank you, but this has been a full day for us both," said Raya, holding hands with her grandmother. They reminded Kirk of the family picture in Raya's office. "A wonderful day," she continued, leaning forward and kissing Kirk on the cheek.

"What do you think of the woman in my life?" asked Kirk, blandly.

"I think it may take a powerful woman like the *Enterprise* to tame you," said Raya.

"Or one like her," said Kirk, with a smile, as the *Jo'Zamestaad* and her grandmother dissolved into energy.

"I think, Mr. Spock," said Kirk, as they walked the ship's corridors, "that we've done our part for interplanetary diplomacy today."

"Indeed, Captain, but I'm sure the Klingons will have something to contribute to the discussion."

"I'd like to see them top this," said Kirk, as he left the turbolift.

Hours later, Kirk was awakened from a dream in which he had four thumbs, each one ending in a miniature satellite, by the beeping of his intercom. *"Spock to captain."*

"Kirk here," he replied. "What is it, Spock?"

"Captain, Satellite 22 has struck the planet's surface."

"Struck the—?" Kirk shook his head; it was as though he were still dreaming. "Was anything hit?"

"An orphanage," said Spock. *"Thirty-six reported dead so far."*

CHAPTER
7

Two minutes later, the landing party materialized near the orphanage—or what was left of it.

Kirk surveyed the scene; if he had still been dreaming when he heard the report, that dream had become a nightmare. The air of the orphanage, buried deep beneath the capital city, was nearly opaque, like that of the planet's surface, but it was polluted with floating dust. Aid workers, pressed into emergency service, tried to lift jagged mounds of masonry. A huge hole sundered the ceiling; a makeshift emergency covering had slid into place, but it tensed and buckled ominously.

Some yards away one of Lon's satellites lay, buried to its equator. From beneath it protruded a pair of legs, still twitching.

And everywhere there was blood and the screams of children.

Kirk shook his head. It was too much like a scene from his past, the massacre at the Tarsus IV colony at the hands of Kodos the Executioner. Though the two events had little in common, the screams of children gave them a deadly similarity.

"Bones," said Kirk, "do what you can for these people."

But McCoy had already whipped open his communicator. "McCoy to sickbay! Chapel, tell M'Benga to divide the staff into emergency medical teams; tell them to be prepared for mass trauma. And beam down a box of miner's masks; they should be in the ship's stores."

"Spock, Dr. Lon," said Kirk, "find out what went wrong here. Sinclair, you're with Spock."

Spock and Sinclair each nodded and moved off, Lon trailing behind them. "But be careful, Doctor," said Kirk. "Any goodwill your invention bought us has just been exhausted." Lon's mouth opened, moved a couple of times, then closed as he walked off. He had made no sound, and his expression was like that of a father who had just learned his dearest son was responsible for a grisly murder.

Through the dust Kirk saw a willowy form approaching. Raya's beautiful features were slashed with pain, her skin paler than Kirk had ever seen it. She saw Kirk and moved toward him. "James, how—?"

Kirk motioned for patience and flipped open his own communicator. "Kirk to *Enterprise*."

"*Scott here, Captain. How is it down there?*"

"Worse than I'd feared. Trace these coordinates and put a tractor beam on the ceiling of this chamber. It looks as though it's going to blow, Scotty, and we can't have that."

"*Aye, sir.*"

"And get every available hand down here, have them bring that thermoconcrete to build emergency shelters. And send down the spare food synthesizers, calibrated for the locals, with all the emergency gear you can find."

"*Right away, sir. Anything else?*"

Kirk looked around, as though suspecting to see someone lurking. "Maintain maximum sensor surveillance. This would be the perfect time to blindside the *Enterprise*."

"*Not if I have anything t'say about it.*"

"You have your orders, Scotty, Kirk out." Looking up, Kirk started to apologize, but Raya was no longer nearby. She stood, supervising men who were trying to maneuver a board into position to lever some wreckage away. Kirk ran to them, motioned them to stay back, and used his phaser to dissolve some of the layers. The men ran in, using tools to pry the remaining wreckage out of the way and emerged seconds later, bearing seven children. They were unmoving, save for the action of their chests, which rose and fell fitfully.

"Raya!" called a thin voice. Raya's head snapped up as a small form became visible through the floating dirt, running toward her. Raya's broad mouth spread into a joyous smile and she took Theena elMadej in her arms, kissing her.

"Thank you," said Raya, fervently, to Kirk. "For everything." Her eyes brimmed with tears.

"Clean yourself up," whispered Kirk. "You have to be strong for the others."

She nodded, comprehension dawning.

"Leaders don't get the luxury of being weak," said Kirk.

Raya made some reply, but it was drowned out in the trill of transporters. Columns of energy coalesced in the courtyard, and a second later, *Enterprise* crew charged forward to aid in the rescue effort.

Kirk wandered across McCoy and Nurse Chapel, the latter performing triage in an alleyway that had been turned into a hospital. Every one of the victims being treated was wearing one of the miner's filter masks McCoy had requisitioned.

Despite the emergency, Kirk was intrigued. He approached the physician, whose face was smudged with dirt, and put a hand on McCoy's shoulder. Without looking at Kirk, McCoy pointed behind him. "Put them in the alley."

"It's me, Bones. Is it bad?"

McCoy looked up, his eyes filled with pain. "Bad enough. Anyone who wasn't stricken with shock by the impact is in danger of suffocation."

"From what?"

"These people are totally hairless, Jim, remember? No nose hair, no cilia in the ears to filter out air pollutants or dust. Without the miner's masks, half of them might have been dead from inhaled dirt clogging their lungs before we could help them."

Clapping McCoy on the shoulder, Kirk moved on.

Rounding the corner of a building, Kirk found himself confronted by a band of adult Payav, their hands cut and bleeding, their clothes in tatters. They were glaring at him in a manner he deemed distinctly hostile.

Kirk stood with his hand halfway to his phaser, facing them down. An errant breeze wafted away a cloud of dust, and behind the crowd Kirk saw the bulky figure of Councillor Traal, watching, making no move to interfere.

"You are from the Federation ship, no?" asked the leader.

"Yes. But you'll have to make the first move," said Kirk.

They did just that, though hardly in the way he expected. Like puppets controlled by a single string, the men fell to their knees. "Please!" said the one in the lead. "Take us with you!"

"We beg you!" said the second. "This planet is death! We Payav are dying! Take us with you!"

"We will do anything," intoned a third. "We will be your servants, your slaves. Just take us from this planet!"

Kirk stared at them for a moment, struck dumb with shock. To be attacked was one thing, he could fight that. But to be the object of near-worship by helpless men . . .

Bending before the leader, Kirk angrily seized his shoulders. "No. This is *your* planet! Get off your knees! If you have to kneel, do it to dig out those children!" He virtually shoved the man toward one of the numerous work parties. The others followed, slowly, looking over their shoulders at Kirk as though he might be following them.

"A stirring speech, Captain," came Traal's voice, approaching. "Would that we could practice it."

"What's stopping you?" asked Kirk, still breathing a little hard.

"The efforts of your Federation to keep us down," said Traal, with a shrug. "You pick us up with one hand and slap us down with the other." One of his hands moved to indicate the crashed satellite, his thumbs twitching.

"You think we did this deliberately, Traal? Destroyed an orphanage so we could come in and be saviors?" His head shook contemptuously. "You and the Klingons belong together."

"We shall see," said Traal, moving off into the dusty air.

Later, Kirk remembered very little of the rest of that

night. It was all a montage of crushed concrete, cries begging to stop the pain, and, underscoring it all, the wails of children.

He was stepping off an antigrav sled from a work detail securing the protective covering when he saw Spock. He had not thought of his first officer in several hours. "What do you have?" he asked, sitting roughly down on a stack of concrete slabs.

"The data will have to be processed, but I believe it will be revealing. I have transmitted it to the ship's computer banks for analysis."

Kirk felt something warm thrust into his hands, a cup of broth, no doubt laden with nutrients. He looked up to see Sinclair. "I thought you might need a break, sir."

Kirk nodded his thanks and sipped gratefully. "Where's McCoy?"

"Dr. McCoy was supervising the installation of certain medical equipment into the makeshift hospital."

"Any idea what the death count is?"

Spock said, "I have heard estimates of over two hundred dead, but that total may be in error."

Kirk nodded and took out his communicator. "Kirk to *Enterprise*. Scotty, how's the ship?"

"We're fine up here, sir," replied Scott, *"how are things down there?"*

"I'll let you know when we get back. Kirk out."

They found McCoy leaning against a support pillar in a hastily constructed thermoconcrete building. His eyes seemed dead, like marbles. As they approached, Chapel hovered briefly by his side, gave him a shot of some sort of stimulant and moved on. McCoy looked up, began to protest, then shook his head.

"Bones," said Kirk. The doctor looked first to his left, then to his right, and shook his head.

"Two hundred and fifty-seven dead, Jim," he said. "For the rest—well, take a look." He lifted a hand expansively.

Rows of field bunks stretched out, seemingly to the horizon. In the distance, Kirk saw Raya, carrying a tray of cups. She stopped by one bunk, gave a child a cup, stroked his brow, and moved on, approaching Kirk. "You look terrible," she said.

"I feel better than any of them," said Kirk, indicating the bunks. "I thought you'd be conducting an emergency council meeting or something like it."

"Of what use is another meeting? Time enough for that when we have facts to discuss."

"I understand. Bones, Spock, is there anything more we can do here?"

"The emergency ceiling is secure and the initial crisis seems to have subsided, Captain," said Spock. McCoy simply shook his head.

"Then let's get back to the ship. I want to start trying to find what went wrong." He looked around. "Has anyone seen Dr. Lon?"

"Not for some time," said Spock.

"There he is, Captain," said Sinclair, pointing across the building at a small table. Lon sat there, slender shoulders hunched as he worked on a small computer he had procured, seemingly oblivious to the chaos surrounding him.

"Dr. Lon," said Kirk, as they neared him.

"Captain," said Lon. "I was trying to analyze what little data I have on the incident."

"The ship's computers are analyzing our findings as we speak, Doctor," said Spock.

"Then let's go," he said. "I'm anxious to see what they've found. We have to prove to these people that my technology wasn't responsible for this."

"'This' is going to be a hell of a lot more difficult to explain than that, Doctor," said Kirk.

"Captain," Sinclair said, nodding toward the entrance, "there may be trouble."

Raya was standing at the portal to the emergency shelter, facing down a small but determined bunch of angry citizens who were pointing toward the *Enterprise* party.

Off to one side stood Councillor Traal, taking in the scene noncommittally, while Raya glanced back over her shoulder at Kirk. Kirk caught a snatch of their conversation, which consisted of accusations against the Federation citizens of murder and even attempted genocide, and Raya's reply: "There is no evidence at this time to recommend legal proceedings . . ."

He took out his communicator. "Kirk to *Enterprise*. Five to beam up."

A moment later they were gone, but the screams still rang in Kirk's ears.

CHAPTER
8

"Bones, this may be a long night," said Kirk, as they trudged to the conference room.

"I'd like to tag along, Jim," replied McCoy, after a moment.

Kirk shrugged. "You're the doctor. Spock, better see what the computers have come up with."

They entered the conference room. Spock nodded and accessed the interface with the bridge computer as Dr. Lon gazed at the second screen of the tri-faced viewer on the conference table. McCoy sat down with an audible sigh, and Sinclair brought a tray of beverages.

For several minutes Spock and Lon spoke in low tones as various pieces of computer circuitry were highlighted on the viewscreen. "Well, gentlemen?" said Kirk, finally.

Spock tapped the keyboard of the computer interface and lifted his gaze to Kirk. Kirk took a look at the viewer, which showed what looked like a complicated set of computer commands. "If you will examine the viewer, Captain," said Spock. "I retrieved this data from Satellite 22's computer banks just before its circuitry burned out completely."

"It looks like some sort of computer language," said Kirk, taking a cup of coffee from Sinclair.

"It is in fact a computer override code, sent to the satellite via its computer interface," said Spock. "This will prove that the satellite left its orbit, not due to a programming failure, but by interference in its programming."

"It will prove that only to those who don't have their mind set against the Federation," said Kirk. "Is Payav technology sophisticated enough to accomplish this?"

"I wouldn't have thought them capable of this," said Lon, shaking his head, "though it's certainly possible for the Klingons."

"One of the more salient features of this analysis," said Spock, "is that the override code shows no sign of having been acknowledged by the satellite's long-range onboard receiver."

Kirk leaned forward, as if this information were more stimulating than another cup of coffee. "Could the override code have been somehow . . . induced into the satellite's interface directly by some sort of short-range transmission, possibly generated by another spacefaring craft?"

"It is a distinct possibility," said Spock. "The long-range receiver would have held the override code for some time, but it was only by good fortune that the override code was detected before the satellite's more delicate circuitry expired."

"We're about due for a break," said Kirk. "Could the override code have come from the *Jo'Payav*?"

"We didn't think the Payav quite capable of that degree of sophistication," said Lon, "but it is possible."

"What about the Klingons?" asked Kirk. "Could this override code have come from them?"

"The programming is consonant with known Klingon technology," said Spock, "but it is not unique to them. It is insufficient to tell us whether the Klingons are taking a direct hand in Mestiko's affairs, or merely loaning out their technology to, for example, Councillor Traal."

"I think it's time we found out," said Kirk, getting to his feet. "Get cleaned up, and meet me on the bridge in ten minutes."

CHAPTER
9

"Mr. Scott," said Kirk, in mild surprise as he exited the turbolift. "I didn't expect to see you still on duty." It was the night shift, after all, and Scott should have been in bed. So, for that matter, should Kirk have been.

"No Scott has ever bunked down while his captain was in the field, sir, and I'm not going to be the first," replied Scott, rising from the command chair.

"Appreciated, Scotty," said Kirk, chuckling at the boast, taking the center seat. "Any visitors while we were gone?"

"Not a one, sir. Nice and quiet. Too quiet, if you get my drift."

"I think I do. Stick around if you feel like it, we may have something for you to do."

"Aye, sir," said Scotty, moving to the bridge engineering station next to the turbolift entrance.

Spock took his post at the science station and Lon at the auxiliary science station.

"Orders, Captain?" asked Spock.

"Patch into all the satellites we put in orbit around Mestiko," said Kirk. "Check for any attempts to override programming."

"Do you think they'll try the same trick again, Captain?" asked Scott.

Kirk shrugged. "If no one catches them at it, why not? Spock, anything?"

"Evaluating data, sir," said Spock, staring into his scanner. "Interesting. Satellite 158 shows attempts to override its basic programming."

"Location?"

"Satellite 158 is orbiting directly over the Norrb Refugee Center."

"Kirk," said Lon, as this bit of knowledge struck home, "you can't let them—"

"They won't catch us with the same trick twice, Doctor," Kirk said with a glance behind him, then turned back to Farrell and Riley at helm and navigation in front of him. "Mr. Riley, lay in a course to take us within ten thousand kilometers of Satellite 158."

"That's as close as you want, Captain?" asked Riley. "I can get us—"

"Have you ever seen a cat track a mouse, Lieutenant?"

"I get it, sir," said Riley, with a grin. "Course laid in."

"Mr. Farrell, ahead, maximum impulse power."

"Ten thousand kilometers from Satellite 158, sir," said Farrell, seconds later.

"Maintain this position," said Kirk. "Spock, any uninvited guests?"

"Difficult to say, Captain. The same ionization from the disaster is making sensor readings somewhat unreliable. This location is a source of maximum interference."

"And I don't need you to tell me the odds against that being a coincidence," said Kirk. "Do what you can to compensate. Lieutenant Palmer, main viewer on, maximum magnification. Can you get a visual at this range?"

"It's not the range, sir," said the relief communications officer. "It's the interference. Let me try . . ." Seconds later, a hazy, static-ridden image flickered on the viewscreen; a globular object seemed to float on a sea of ebony waves. For all they knew, it might have been a snowball dropped into a vat of dirty oil, viewed through the wrong end of a cracked telescope.

"That's the best I can do, sir," said Palmer.

"We'll have to do this the hard way," said Kirk. "Scotty, can you pick up any kind of engine readings out there?"

"It's like trying to see through that muck they call air down there, Captain. I'm picking up energy readings that indicate a matter/antimatter drive—'tis definitely a warp-capable ship. But I cannot localize the readings. It's nothing I'd care to chance a phaser lock on."

"Understood. Spock, lock on to Satellite 158. Are you too far to check if there's been any interference with the satellite's programming?"

Spock's fingers ran over the console of his station like a pianist playing a keyboard as the blue glow from his scanner washed over his face.

"I am reading some foreign programming attempting to override the original, Captain. The system is attempting to resist it."

"Part of its computer security program," said Lon, proudly.

"Attempt to track the foreign programming back to its source," said Kirk. "That may give us a—"

"Unsuccessful," said Spock.

Kirk pondered for a moment. "Mr. Riley, attempt phaser lock on that satellite, ready to fire on my command."

"Kirk, you can't!" Lon cried.

"If it shows any signs of deviating from its orbit, I can and will, Doctor."

"Captain," said Riley, "unable to attain phaser lock. Too much interference."

Kirk didn't need to see Lon's face to know it bore a smile. Kirk was silent for a few seconds, then: "Spock, do the satellites carry a self-destruct code?"

"They do, Captain."

"Enter and activate self-destruct code for Satellite 158."

Inevitably, Lon again said, "Kirk—!"

"We may not be able to pinpoint that ship, but we can make its general vicinity very inhospitable."

Dr. Lon's angular form ran across the bridge and stood before Kirk, shoulders hunched. "Kirk, I won't let you—"

"Would you rather be considered a mass murderer by an

entire planet, Doctor? Whoever's tampering with your satellite is no friend of yours, or of Mestiko's."

"Self-destruct code entered, Captain."

"Damn it, Kirk!" Lon's build was slender, but wiry; muscles worked beneath his torso like cables. "You can't—!"

"Stand down or you'll wake up in the brig, Doctor!" Kirk rose from his chair. "Spock, implement self-destruct code."

Spock continued to work his console with his left hand. The satellite's explosion was almost anticlimactic. The snowball abruptly threw itself at the screen, then vanished, leaving only a field of gently undulating static.

"Scan for radiation, Spock."

"I have something, Captain. Some kind of craft. Not precisely a lock, more an indication, gauged by the radiation from the satellite, of where the craft is not, rather than where it is."

"I'll take it. Who is it?"

"Insufficient data for identification. We know only that it is there, and it is damaged. It is likely the same energy reading Mr. Scott detected—sensor readings indicate an imbalance in a matter/antimatter reactor."

"Good enough. Mr. Farrell, take us in. Mr. Riley, ready phasers."

"Aye, sir. Phasers ready."

Spock said, "The ship is wounded, but still navigable, Captain. It is attempting evasive maneuvers."

"The masquerade's over," Kirk said, sitting back down. "It's time to unmask. Tractor beam."

"They're running, Captain."

"Or trying to. Mr. Farrell, prepare for warp drive."

"Captain," said Spock, "the craft is not entering space. Rather, it is nearing the planet."

Kirk cursed. "I was afraid they'd think of that. Get after them, Farrell."

The viewscreen was swathed in clouds, then, when those broke, the brown atmosphere of Mestiko. The ship's progress could barely be discerned by broken clouds and paths through the russet air that were already disappearing as the *Enterprise* followed.

"Hull temperature increasing, Captain," said Spock.

"Where are they?" asked Kirk, sweeping his gaze from one side of the viewscreen to the other.

Spock stared into his scanner for a moment, then shook his head. "Electromagnetic interference is blocking our instrumentation. We have lost them."

"Where could they have gone?" asked Lon.

"They may have returned to a concealed base. I read no signs of a cloaking device."

"Where are we, Spock?" Kirk asked.

"Over an area of Mestiko's easternmost continent, a region whose possession is under dispute by the Norrb and the Domtos tribes, locally referred to as 'the badlands.' A sensor sweep indicates that name is well-deserved. A more accurate verdict cannot be obtained without an investigation of the area."

"Then we know nothing about them," said Scott.

"Not necessarily, Mr. Scott," said Spock. "I would conjecture that the craft was not the *Klothos*. Such a craft would move sluggishly through a planet's atmosphere, and could not elude us that rapidly. Our quarry was, in all probability, a smaller, more mobile ship."

Kirk nodded and rose. "All right. Return to standard orbit. Continue monitoring the satellites for any signs of interference—though I think we've scared them off for tonight. And tomorrow, we're going to take the fight to them."

CHAPTER
10

"I have a mission for you," said Kirk, the next morning.

"Yes, sir," said Lieutenant Sulu, with an anticipatory nod. Sulu did not look around the conference room at Lieutenant Kyle, Ensign Chekov, and Lieutenant Sinclair, but Kirk knew they were all wondering what he had in mind for them.

Kirk played for them the bridge recording of their encounter last night with the unidentified vessel. "What do you think?"

"Not much to go on, Captain," said Chekov.

"No, Mr. Chekov, not much at all. But enough to give us an idea of where to start looking for it. You four will take a shuttlecraft and attempt to find the hidden base that berths that ship."

"Captain," asked Kyle, "isn't that something the *Enterprise* can accomplish more efficiently?"

"Not with the state their atmosphere is in," said Kirk. "Too much interference. No, a smaller, more mobile craft is the way to go. It will allow you to fly closer to the surface and scan more precisely than we can from up here."

"Yes, sir," said Sulu. "When do we leave, sir?"

"Tonight, after sunset on the eastern continent. The atmospheric interference will be playing havoc with any warning system they might have set up, too, so darkness may be your best ally. Sulu, you'll be in command."

"Yes, sir."

"You're not to play hero," said Kirk, wagging a finger at them. "If you find any signs of a hidden base, you're to document it as thoroughly as you can, then return to the ship immediately. Is that clear?"

"Yes, sir," said four voices, as one.

"Report to the shuttlebay after sunset. In the meantime, familiarize yourself with the information Spock has put together." He rose. "If I don't see you before you embark, good luck."

"Yes, sir," said Chekov.

"And thank you, sir," said Sinclair.

Kirk was halfway to the door, but turned. "Save the thanks until you return."

As the doors closed behind Kirk he smiled, remembering the anticipation seen in their faces, then he shook his head. It never got any easier to send his crew into potential danger.

"Captain," said Raya elMora, minutes later. "Please, come in."

Kirk entered her cubicle with a smile. "I hope I'm more presentable this time."

"I'm certain we both are," she said. Then her smile faded. "Thank you for all your help last night. I'm certain a number of lives were saved."

"I hope so," said Kirk, seating himself in the chair Raya offered. "Despicable act, targeting an orphanage like that."

"Of course," said Raya, with a slight tremble. She rang a small bell on her desk, and her assistant entered, bearing a tray, two glasses, and a carafe. "Will you join me?" she asked, as she poured.

"Is this the same stuff we drank last night?" asked Kirk, smiling warily.

"The unfermented version," she replied with a laugh. She handed him a glass that Kirk offered in a toast.

"To the friendship of all tribes of Mestiko and the Federation."

"I can certainly agree to that," she said. They clinked glasses, and drank.

"Delicious," said Kirk, after a cautious taste.

"I told you it was unfermented."

"Yes, but many things on this planet harbor more danger than they might seem to."

Raya drained her own glass—Kirk noted that its stem carried two small niches for dual thumbs—and put it down. "I don't know what that means," she said, finally.

Kirk smiled. "You'll have to learn to speak the language of diplomacy if you're going to head a people."

"James, what are you talking about?"

He frowned. "We discovered a spacecraft last night, trying to bring another satellite down on the Norrb Refugee Center."

Raya actually gasped. She gave an involuntary shudder that almost toppled the small tray; Kirk caught it just in time. "Thank you," she said. "But what do you want?"

"I want to examine the *Jo'Payav* and its records," said Kirk. "I have to ask you to prove that your ship wasn't the one we chased last night."

"Why . . . of course it wasn't," she said. "To even think so is absurd—"

"Not so absurd, Raya. The ship we detected had a warp drive, and there's only one warp-capable spacecraft on the planet."

"James," she said, stiffly, "I resent your implication."

"Not as much as I would resent having to pull more refugees out of more wreckage."

"How can you even think our people are involved in—?"

"I'm not saying all your people are. I'm not saying any of them are. Perhaps only some who have access to that spacecraft."

"Don't you trust us?"

Kirk shrugged fatalistically. "As much as you trust us. Your expression of support to Councillor Traal last night could have been a more ringing endorsement. 'There is no evidence at this time to recommend legal proceedings.'"

Raya waved a hand, as though to dispel Kirk's statements. "I have to use that kind of language with Traal. He has already scattered the seeds of doubt concerning me among the *Zames-taad*."

"Then you have no reason not to give us the logs," said Kirk.

Their eyes locked for what seemed a long time. On the edge of his vision, Kirk saw a steady beat in her graceful neck.

"Very well," she said. "I'll have the logs transmitted to the *Enterprise*—"

"I'd prefer a look at the actual ship—now," Kirk said. Before Raya knew what had happened, Kirk had risen, drawn her chair back, and was ushering her forward.

Her cheeks, under her tattoos, colored. "So this is a matter of trust."

"It's a matter of maintaining trust between allies," said Kirk, before he opened his communicator. "And I trust you can provide the coordinates to our transporter chief?"

"May I not at least inform the crew that we'll be coming?"

"I'd rather surprise them."

Kirk had them beamed back to the *Enterprise* and Spock summoned. When the science officer arrived, tricorder in hand, the three of them materialized in the hangar.

Raya gestured before her. "There it is, Captain, the *Jo'-Payav*." Despite her barely restrained anger at Kirk, her voice carried a measurable amount of pride.

The hangar was a Spartan affair, unadorned gray reinforced walls arcing upward to a barely perceptible hatch in the ceiling. The ship was a match for its surroundings, a sweeping silver shape that nearly blended into the walls, and looked in motion even when standing still.

A maintenance crew around the craft looked up in alarm when Kirk and Raya first appeared, confused by their presence, and became even more distraught when a squad of security forces charged the room.

"Thank you, Colonel," said Raya, nodding to the officer who led the troops. The colonel, a hard-bitten middle-aged man, looked at them with a mixture of curiosity and hostility, but he relaxed when he recognized his *Jo'Zamestaad*.

"Madam Councillor," he said, saluting. "We were not expecting you."

"That was the intent of our guests," replied Raya. "Captain Kirk, Mr. Spock, this is Colonel maTara." MaTara, impressed despite himself, gave Kirk the traditional Payav handshake. "The captain wishes to inspect the *Jo'Payav* logs."

"Will you require internal access?" asked maTara.

"I first wish to scan the craft's exterior," said Spock. He proceeded to walk slowly around the silver ship, working the instrumentation of the tricorder, his expression unchanging. "Thank you. *Now* I request access to the ship's interior."

"As Madam Councillor wishes," said Colonel maTara, his tone implying that giving offworlders access to the craft would not be his responsibility. He approached the ship, lowered a small concealed panel in its side, and tapped a security code into the revealed keyboard, dexterously using both thumbs of his right hand. Seconds later, the hatch, well disguised in the lines of the ship, arced open.

"After you," said Raya, bowing to Kirk. Kirk, in turn, nodded to Spock, who briskly climbed the stairs that had automatically lowered. Then Kirk motioned Raya aboard.

The ship was quite small; it reminded Kirk of some of the training craft he had piloted at the Academy in his first, uneasy flights. Raya followed Spock to the bridge, with Kirk bringing up the rear.

The bridge held four seats, their backs to one another at the four compass points. Spock, who had never set foot in the ship before, strode to the seat occupied by the equivalent of the science officer and scanned its console with the tricorder.

"The recording computer is at this station, Captain." The tricorder began its customary warble as Spock's long fingers worked the instrument. Seconds later, Spock, after having viewed the tricorder screen, looked at Kirk and shook his head. "The last time the *Jo'Payav* was utilized for transport was three days ago," he said.

"You're sure?" asked Kirk, then bit his tongue.

"I am, Captain," said Spock, "its log is quite specific. And while it is possible that such records can be altered, it is extremely difficult to do so without leaving some residual evidence, none of which is present here.

"Additionally, even considering an altered log as a possibility, the hull of the *Jo'Payav* contains no traces of the radiation it would have been subjected to had it been in proximity with Satellite 158, nor of the damage we detected to its matter/antimatter core. I can state conclusively that the *Jo'Payav* was not the ship that tried to send Satellite 158 out of orbit last night."

"I see," said Kirk. "Thank you, Spock." Spock nodded respectfully to Raya, and left the bridge. Kirk faced maTara, bowing gratefully. "Thank you, Colonel maTara. I hope you understand the necessity for inquiries such as this during times like these."

MaTara seemed uncertain whether he was being insulted or not, then finally chose the side of grace. "Of course, Captain. Please contact me if I can be of any future assistance." Kirk shook hands with him again, and the Payav colonel moved off.

Kirk took a deep breath and turned to Raya, who stood stiffly, as though waiting for something. "My apologies," said Kirk, with a little nod. "I trust the *Jo'Zamestaad* will understand that, with the current climate, we had to be certain."

"I understand," said Raya, after a long pause. "And *I* trust you will remember this incident the next time you deem such an investigation necessary."

"Raya," said Kirk intently, "is it possible there is another warp-capable ship on Mcstiko? That your technology has somehow been stolen by another nation?"

Raya, momentarily frustrated by this seeming change of tack, thought for a moment, then threw her hands up. "I don't know. It is possible, I suppose, but we have maintained thorough security throughout the ship's construction and maintenance."

"All right," said Kirk, bringing out his communicator. "We'll be in touch. Scotty, stand by for transport."

"Aye, sir."

"Captain," said Spock, "there is no logical reason for positing the existence of a second spacecraft. Such a conjecture is pure supposition."

Kirk nodded glumly. "Perhaps the recon party can help us out on that."

CHAPTER
11

"Scanning sector 17-B," said Chekov, peering into the scanner of the shuttlecraft *Armstrong*. "No sign of unidentified base."

"Acknowledged," said Sinclair, making a notation on her electronic clipboard.

"Scanning sector 17-C," said Chekov. "No sign of unidentified base."

"Acknowledged."

Sinclair sighed.

"Scanning sector 17-D—" said Chekov.

"Let me guess," said Kyle, from his position at the navigational control grid, "'no sign of unidentified base.'"

"Very good," said Chekov, "you must have mastered the Vulcan mind-meld."

"I'd rather have mastered the art of navigating while I'm asleep," said Kyle, stifling a yawn.

"I've seen your navigation," said Sulu, slyly. "I thought you already had."

They all laughed, the tension breaking, if only for a moment, which was Sulu's intention.

"Well," said Sinclair, "that killed a few seconds. Now what?"

"Keep scanning," said Sulu. "This is still better than stellar cartography."

"Scanning sector 17-E," began Chekov. Then he peered more intently into the scanner. "Sulu, I think I've got something."

"Send the data," said Sulu. "Let's see." After a few seconds, Sulu nodded slowly. "I think we have got something here, but it's difficult to tell."

"Those are definitely plasma traces," said Chekov, "perhaps exhaust from a spacefaring vessel."

"Or maybe a false positive," said Kyle. "These instruments are very delicate, but that makes them easier to knock off calibration."

"We're going to need more than that to take to the captain," said Sinclair.

"All right," said Sulu, "if anyone is down there, you can bet they're watching us, as well. I'm taking us to the next sector, nice and easy, just like we didn't find a thing."

"But—" began Sinclair.

"Then we'll double back on foot and see if we can't get some definite positive readings. Sinclair, find us a cozy spot to set down."

"Right," said Sinclair, bringing up the planetary maps. "Looks like there's good cover right over that next ridge."

"I'd like to get my hands on whoever designed these environmental suits," said Kyle, putting on the helmet.

"Just make sure your seals are nice and tight," said Sulu. "You don't want to get a whiff of that sewage they call an atmosphere, let alone come into contact with that acid rain."

"Yes, Mother," said Chekov.

"Everybody ready?"

"Yes, thanks," Sinclair replied. Though she had been fully trained on the use of environmental suits, she had never worn one on an actual mission. Through the visor of her suit she caught Sulu giving her a wink, and grinned in reply.

"*Intercom check.*" The other three gave the standard reply

as they heard Sulu's voice crackle over the interiors of their helmets. *"All right, let's go."* Sulu worked the controls next to the main hatch of the *Armstrong*, blowing out the atmosphere as the hatch rose.

Setting foot on Mestiko was like walking underwater, something Sinclair had actually done back home on Alpha Centauri. But the Opal Ocean back home was clear and beautiful, with visibility for several dozen meters. On Mestiko, the brown air only permitted viewing a few feet ahead. There was moonlight, but like the sun in the ocean, it was refracted through the atmosphere, its faint presence more taunting than providing any real illumination.

"Keep someone in sight at all times," said Sulu. *"We don't want anyone lost. Adjust your faceplate controls to make maximum use of what little illumination there is. And move at a steady pace. If they're using motion sensors, they won't be of much use here."*

They stalked through the plain toward Sector 17-E. It was difficult to tell what the terrain might have been like under normal conditions, Sinclair thought. Even in the suit it was incredibly cold, and the land itself was bleak and quiet. Not just still, but absolutely silent—another similarity to moving underwater. Sinclair associated the great outdoors with the sounds of birds and insects and living things making all kinds of racket. This kind of silence wasn't natural on land.

But then, what aspect of the mission to this planet was?

They tromped across the terrain for an hour, pausing twice for short breaks.

"We're coming up on it now," Sulu's voice sounded over the intercom. Ahead of them loomed a small rise of ground, seeming to waver a little as seen through the befouled air. *"We'll split into two teams, taking as many tricorder readings as we can. If you pick up any signs of interference, don't be shy about letting the others know. Chekov, you and Kyle take the southern face. Sinclair, you're with me."*

"That's right," Chekov said with mock annoyance, *"I get stuck with Kyle, and you get Sinclair."*

"Who's stuck with whom?" Kyle replied in like tones.

"Do you hear me complaining?" asked Sinclair.

"*Hasn't serving under Captain Kirk taught you anything, Chekov?*" Sulu chuckled. "*Let's go, Sinclair.*"

"Age before beauty."

Sulu and Sinclair made their way to the mound, tricorders warbling as they made readings. "*I'm definitely getting power-generation readings,*" said Sulu. "*How about you?*"

"Me, too. Some kind of technology and—whoa!"

"*What is it?*"

"I think I—" Sinclair rapidly made an adjustment to her tricorder. "Yeah, I got a warp signature for just a second there."

"*Did you get it down?*"

"Right here in my tricorder."

"*Terrific. Sulu to Kyle. We've got what we need, let's go.*"

The trip back to the *Armstrong* seemed quicker than the trip away. Once back inside, Sulu didn't even get rid of his enviro suit before activating the motor. His still-filtered voice asked, "*How are we, Kyle?*"

Kyle had at least removed his helmet. "Fine, Sulu, just take us out low and tight."

"*Exactly as planned,*" said Sulu, as the shuttlecraft rose. He removed his helmet with a pneumatic hiss, and then added, "Give me a course a couple hundred kilometers away before we take any altitude."

"Sulu," said Chekov, "I think we've got company."

"Have they picked us up?"

"I think so," said Chekov, staring into the scanner. "They may have been waiting for us to lift off to give them a better target."

"Anything to be an obliging guest," muttered Sulu. "Get ready for some turbulence."

"Sulu," said Sinclair, "I'm reading weapons powering up—"

It was as though the shuttlecraft were slapped by a giant hand. The craft swerved to port, reeled, and tried to right itself. There was a moment of nausea before the inertial dampers caught up, then they were flung to the right.

"Playing with us," said Sulu, angrily. "All right, then . . ."

"Tractor beam!" said Kyle. "They've got us!" Even without Kyle's warning, Sulu could feel their progress slow.

"Not yet, they haven't," Sulu said with amazing calm. "Sinclair, prepare to discharge the secondary fuel line."

Confused both by his calm and his orders, Sinclair said, "What? Why will that—?"

"To give them a slap on the wrist they won't forget. Prepare the discharge, and wait until I give the order."

Still confused, Sinclair said, "Yes, sir."

"We're close now," said Chekov. "I'm still having trouble making out their ship, but—"

"Now, Sulu?" Sinclair asked anxiously.

"When I give the order. Where are they, Chekov?"

"Right behind us. I'm reading machinery . . . their hatch is opening."

"Now, Sinclair, release and ignite."

Even through the forward viewports, Sinclair could see the explosion of the ignited fuel reflected off the ship behind them. There was a moment's turbulence; then they were free. Sulu feinted to port, then pitched the *Armstrong* to starboard and threw all engines into maximum.

"They're arming weapons," said Kyle.

An instant later the shuttlecraft bucked forward, sending the recon team sprawling. Pulling himself back to the main controls, Sulu took one look at them and turned to the others, shouting over the alarm klaxons that now blared throughout the small craft. "Back into the suits! We're jumping ship!"

The second volley tore the back off the craft and sent them into the planet like a greased brick.

Straining to remain conscious after the impact, Sulu extended one hand toward the control panel, pulling on his helmet with the other. He shook his head, why was he moving so slowly? He had to reach only one switch to send an emergency signal . . .

But he fell into unconsciousness with that task unaccomplished.

When he awoke, Sulu had to admit he was surprised. He had expected to find himself either dead or in the brig of a Klingon ship. But the quarters he found himself in were cramped and showed every evidence of being makeshift. The cabin's walls were unfinished and dull.

Sulu's hands were tied behind him—no surprise there. He glanced to his right, and saw Chekov, Kyle, and Sinclair, unmoving, save for their chests, which slowly rose and fell. That was something. Their environmental suits had been removed, as were their uniforms and equipment. *At least they left us in our underwear,* Sulu thought glumly.

Vibrations came through the floor; a second later footsteps rang outside the cabin. A section of the wall opened, revealing two natives—members of the Norrb if he wasn't mistaken—and, between them, a massive form that seemed to loom over Sulu like the side of a cliff.

"Sulu, Hikaru. Starfleet serial number—"

"I have no interest in such trivia," said Councillor Traal. "There is nothing I want from you."

"Then you won't mind letting us go." This was Sinclair, her voice raspy, but her tone defiant.

"Sinclair, don't—"

Traal nodded to one of his entourage who bent and slapped Sinclair smartly across her mouth.

"I said there was nothing I wanted from you," said Traal. "I did not say your capture served no purpose."

"My mistake," said Sulu mildly. "And I'll bet I can tell you what purpose we serve."

"Really?" Traal's heavy features smiled cynically, but his poet's eyes seemed interested. "And what is that?"

"Traal," growled a voice from behind the councillor.

Traal did not turn, but snapped, "What is it, Kiregh?"

From the shadows behind Traal emerged a Klingon. "My commander demands you speak to him." He held a communicator, which he thrust toward Traal. Traal eyed it for a moment, lifted his gaze to Kiregh, then took the instrument, grudgingly.

"Kor, what do you want?" He listened for a moment. Sulu tried to hear the other end of the conversation, but couldn't quite make it out. "No, the prisoners are mine. We agreed—" More chatter. "Very well, we will transfer them to your vessel. Yes, at the rendezvous. Traal out." Speech was still coming from the communicator as Traal shut it off and flung it away to clatter on the floor.

Kiregh and Traal locked eyes for a moment. "My apologies," said Traal, "I'm all fingers today." Kiregh looked at the communicator for a moment, bent slowly to recover it, then left the chamber.

Traal looked at Sulu and smiled. Sulu noted that he was showing teeth. "I wish we had the pleasure of your company for a longer time, Starfleet. I think that soon you will wish the same."

"I don't like the sound of that," said Chekov, after Traal and his men had left.

"At least we know for certain that Traal is in bed with the Klingons," said Kyle, his voice a little groggy. "Not that there's much we can do with that intelligence."

Despite the circumstances, Sulu smiled. "Everyone okay? All right, try to stay limber. You never know when we'll get a chance."

"We're in it pretty bad, aren't we?" asked the timid voice of Sinclair.

"We've been in worse," Sulu said, trying to sound reassuring. "Just stay ready for any opportunity. Get back-to-back and try to untie each other."

"You never did get to tell Traal what purpose you think we serve in this," said Sinclair.

Grimly, Sulu said, "Bait."

CHAPTER
12

"Where's Sulu?" asked Kirk, rhetorically. "He should have checked in forty-five minutes ago."

"Forty-three minutes and eighteen seconds," said Spock.

Kirk rose from the command chair restlessly. "Uhura, any luck in raising them?"

Uhura's chair swiveled as she faced Kirk. "No, sir. They're not receiving at all."

"Keep trying. Spock, any clue as to their whereabouts?"

"None, Captain. I have scanned for their engine signature as well as the transtators in their environmental suits. Neither has yielded any data."

"Captain," came a tentative voice from across the bridge.

"Yes, Dr. Lon?" asked Kirk.

Lon looked up from a console, speaking rapidly. "I've just accessed all the remaining satellites. Their sensors show no signs of having registered any spacecraft."

Kirk nodded, grateful that Lon seemed to have gotten over his snit. "Thank you, Doctor. Send your reports to Mr. Spock for calibration."

Nodding, Lon turned to do so.

Kirk turned to the helm. "Mr. Farrell, take us over the eastern continent. As low an orbit as you can get away with without alarming the authorities."

"Aye, sir."

What seemed like an hour later—though Kirk knew it was far less—he approached Spock again. "Any sign of them?"

"No, sir," said Spock, "no signs at all. That in itself is suspicious; if they had crashed or were forced to abandon the shuttlecraft, there would be wreckage left behind, but this points to the shuttlecraft having been taken into custody."

Kirk thought for a moment, then turned to Uhura. "Get me Colonel maTara."

Moments later, the Payav colonel appeared on the viewscreen. *"Yes, Captain Kirk?"* He sounded wary, as if expecting some kind of test.

"Colonel," said Kirk, with the hearty manner of one colleague to another, "have you picked up any signs of an unauthorized ship on your planet? Specifically, of any other warp-capable craft developed by any other people of Mestiko."

MaTara frowned. *"The designs of the* Jo'Payav *have been under maximum security, Captain—"*

"And as we discussed earlier today, we all know how porous such security can be. Some of my people may have been captured, and—"

"I understand. Can you please hold?" The screen went blank for a few seconds. *"Captain,"* said maTara, when the screen was activated again, *"we do have some records of an unauthorized craft in our airspace. Obviously, we have kept such reports on a need-to-know basis—"*

"Of course, Colonel. But time is of the essence here. As a ship captain yourself, I'm sure you realize how—"

"Of course," said maTara, understanding, as Kirk was hoping he would, the captain's urgency. He glanced offscreen, and Kirk heard the click of a keyboard. *"I've just transmitted the coordinates at which we've detected unauthorized activity. If such a ship is anywhere—if it even exists—that may be your best chance."*

Kirk glanced at Uhura, who nodded. "Thank you, Colonel. Would you care to join us in a little hunt?"

MaTara smiled. *"It would be an honor, Captain."*

"These are the coordinates Colonel maTara sent, Captain," said Uhura, ten minutes later.

Mestiko, looking as though caught in an eternal dust storm, hung in space a few hundred thousand kilometers away. "Spock, anything?"

"The presence of the *Jo'Payav* approaching, Captain."

"Uhura, on-screen."

"Captain," said maTara, a moment later, *"how may we aid you in your search?"*

"Captain," said Spock urgently, "I am reading the presence of another—"

His next words were drowned in the sound of an explosion. When Kirk picked himself up, he said, "What the hell was that?"

"An unidentified ship has just fired at us, Captain," said Spock. "And . . . I read a Klingon battle cruiser, type D-7, approaching at full impulse."

"Raise shields! Red alert," said Kirk. "Sound battle stations!"

CHAPTER
13

The image on the viewscreen shattered, then coalesced again, this time showing the visage of Councillor Traal, standing on a small but efficiently designed bridge. *"Kirk,"* he thundered triumphantly, *"I demand your surrender!"*

"Another signal, sir," said Uhura. "This one from Commander Kor."

"It never rains, but it pours," said Kirk grimly. He turned to his science officer. "Damage report."

"Minor hull damage along decks six and seven, Captain. No major structural damage yet. However, we are boxed in by three ships. No chance of escape sitting still as we are." Kirk nodded and turned to his left.

Kirk slammed his fist on the intercom. "Scotty, make us look more damaged than we are. Vent some plasma from the exhaust ports. Give us a fake limp. Buy me some time."

"Aye, sir," said Scotty from engineering, *"let me see what I can do."*

Uhura said, "Commander Kor is waiting impatiently, Captain."

"I'm sure he is. On-screen. See if you can make this a conference call."

"Aye, sir . . . I have them all, Captain."

The viewscreen was now segmented in thirds. The faces of maTara, Traal, and Commander Kor now glared at Kirk. Kor spoke first: *"The Organians shall not prevent our battle this time, Captain. And it will be glorious."*

"I can understand Traal being on the Klingons' leash," said Kirk, "but what about you, maTara? What do they have on you?"

"Do not answer!" Traal snapped.

MaTara shrugged. *"What does it matter, Traal?"* To Kirk, he said, *"They are going to take me and my family off this planet. To a place fit for children to grow up in."*

"More likely a Klingon relocation camp," said Kirk, tersely. "I have to hand it to you, though, Colonel—I thought I was a better judge of character. You took me in completely."

"That will make an excellent epitaph, Kirk," said Kor.

"Aren't you being a little premature, Commander?"

"I think not." The Klingon sneered, and Kirk was afraid he knew the ace Kor had under his sash. *"Traal, show Kirk your guests."*

The image flickered again, to show Sulu, Chekov, Kyle, and Sinclair, lying on a floor, stripped of their uniforms, their hands apparently tied behind them.

Knowing it to be futile, Kirk nonetheless said, "I demand you release my officers."

"I will," said Traal, *"when you and all Federation influence have left Mestiko."*

"I can't let their lives make any difference," said Kirk. "And they knew that when they signed on."

"Excellent, Captain," Kor said with a grin. *"We shall have some sport after all."*

"You have an odd idea of 'sport,' Kor—three ships against one."

"The battle shall be between the Enterprise *and the* Klothos, Kirk."

"Whenever you're ready, Kor," said Kirk, smiling coldly. "Screen off."

As the viewscreen returned to the image of the three vessels that hemmed in the *Enterprise*, Uhura said, "Sir, the ships are still communicating with one another—and their signals aren't encrypted!"

Kirk whirled around. "What?"

Uhura rarely smiled so broadly on duty, but she did so now. "My guess is that the Klingons aren't trusting Traal and maTara with their codes."

"On audio, Lieutenant."

Kor was in midsentence when Uhura put it on the speakers. "—*your orders, maTara. Proceed on your mission.*"

It was Traal who replied to that. "'*Mission'? What do you mean, Kor?*"

"*Space Central is about to receive a visitor, Traal—another satellite.*"

At the same moment, both Lon and Traal said "*What?*"

"*Your people are stiff-necked,*" said Kor. "*Their spirits need softening. Another tragedy will at once further that process, eliminate the Zamestaad, and install you as supreme ruler of the planet—as per our agreement.*"

"*Kor,*" said Traal, "*there is no need for more death. I sent the first satellite out of orbit as you demanded. Why make maTara the deliverer of a second?*"

"*So he will know obedience,*" said Kor. MaTara hissed, as if he felt the crack of a whip on his back, but made no reply.

"*Kor,*" said Traal, "*my people have suffered—*"

"*Your people have only begun to suffer,*" said Kor. "*Another Federation satellite coming to call should make them beg to become citizens of the Klingon Empire—as well as make them quite tractable subjects for you. Colonel maTara, you have the coordinates, and your orders.*"

For the first time, maTara spoke. "*I understand. The satellite positioned over Space Central has been targeted, with the satellite over the Norrb Refugee Center laid in.*"

"*Damn you, Kor!*" thundered Traal. "*You would attack my own people?*"

"Captain," said Spock, "Traal's ship has left position to pursue the *Jo'Payav.*"

"*Traal!*" Kor screamed, "*return immediately—*" The channel was cut with a blare of static.

Kirk smiled grimly. "Looks like I'm not the only bad judge of character around here. Spock, did he transfer the prisoners?"

"Both ships still have shields raised, Captain. The hostages are still aboard Traal's ship."

To Farrell, Kirk said, "Get after him, Mister."

"Aye, sir."

Spock said, "The *Klothos* is pursuing us, Captain."

The ship shuddered again.

"A disruptor blast to our aft section," said Spock. "Deflected by our shields—just barely."

"Mr. Riley, direct a pinpoint phaser beam to Traal's ship. Burrow through his shields, and find Sulu's team." He tapped the intercom. "Scotty, prepare to send a transporter beam through to get them out of there."

"*Aye, sir.*"

"Captain," Spock said, "we will need to lower shields to beam them aboard."

"I know," said Kirk. "So we'd better do it while we still have shields to lower."

Aboard the *Jo'Payav*, Colonel maTara sat uneasily in the center seat. To betray his own people and his oath by divulging the specifications of his ship to the Norrb was bad enough. But to send a satellite plunging into an occupied area, to cause destruction and death to his own people . . . this was a line he had hoped never to cross.

"Colonel," said his first officer, "we are approaching the satellite."

"Prepare computer interface," said maTara, closing his eyes. He did this for his children, so they would not be trapped on this dead planet simply because their father's orders did not permit him to be assigned offworld. *We cannot afford to lose your leadership on the* Jo'Payav, they had said. *We need you here.*

The colonel prayed his children would never learn of this. And that if they did, they would forgive him for what he did in their names.

"You don't understand," whimpered Sinclair. "You've just *got* to let us go. The Klingons will torture us, they'll—"

"Without orders to do so, Traal would have my head," replied the Norrb guard. He seemed an unimaginative sort, and did not look prone to hyperbole.

"Then let *me* go," said Sinclair. "I'll go with you, I'll be your prisoner, I'll—"

"Sinclair!" snapped Sulu, "remember you're a Starfleet officer."

"That's what got me into this," she said, maintaining eye contact with the guard. "Please! I'll do anything." Two small tears leaked from her eyes.

"Will you, now?" The guard smiled and approached Sinclair, his right thumbs scratching the corners of his mouth as he knelt to speak to her. "And how do you define any—"

This statement was never completed. Sinclair's long legs shot up like catapults. The balls of her feet, bound together, slammed against the Norrb's chin, sending his head back with an audible snap.

"I knew it was a mistake for the Payau not to allow women in their space fleet," said Kyle, as Sinclair made her way, none too gracefully, to the guard. She took the knife he wore on his belt and held it behind her, its blade tracing an uncertain path through the air.

"Who wants to be cut loose first?" she asked.

"How about if I free you?" asked Sulu, watching the wavering knife blade cautiously. "I am in charge."

"Damage to the port nacelle," said Spock, as the *Enterprise* shook.

"Mr. Riley, Mr. Farrell, evasive action," said Kirk. "And make it good. Scotty, how's that beam-out coming along?"

"*Little by little, sir,*" said Scotty. "*Their shields're strippin' away, bit by bit.*"

The ship rocked again. Kirk smelled burning circuitry. "I think you can say the same for us."

"The Earther flees, Commander," said Kor's weapons officer. "He fears us!"

"Cowards are not given commands of starships," replied Kor, sitting forward in his command chair. "Kirk has some plan, and I do not care to find out what it is." He hammered a control console and spoke into the intercom. "More speed! More power to weapons!"

"Prepare to interface with the satellite's navigational computer," said Colonel maTara. Then the ship shook.

"Captain, we are being fired upon!"

"By whom? Kirk?"

"No, sir, by—by Councillor Traal!"

"Traal?" MaTara shook his head. "No matter. Abandon the satellite interface. Target satellite and fire!"

"Firing, sir!"

Crimson energy lanced from the *Jo'Payav* and struck the nearest satellite, thousands of kilometers away. It wobbled in its orbit, then plunged toward Mestiko.

"Now," shouted maTara, "turn and—"

A moment later, the *Jo'Payav* erupted like a firecracker.

"The *Jo'Payav* is down, sir!" said Traal's helm officer.

"But the satellite?"

"On a collision course with the planet, sir," said his science officer.

"Fire upon it! Destroy it!"

The weapons officer turned. "All banks were exhausted in destroying the *Jo'Payav*, sir."

Traal shook his head. He would not have wished it to end this way, but if it must . . . "Prepare to intercept!"

"Which way's the transporter room?" asked Sulu, as they crept down a corridor.

"I don't think they have one," said Kyle. "And it's too small for escape pods."

"If the ship is that small, perhaps we can take the bridge," said Chekov. "There can't be that many of them."

"Does anyone else smell something burning?" asked Sinclair.

"Captain," Spock said, "Councillor Traal's ship has fired upon and destroyed the *Jo'Payav*, and has entered a course to intercept the satellite disrupted by Colonel maTara. Its hull temperature is two thousand degrees. I do not believe this is a maneuver they intend to return from."

"You hear that, Scotty?" said Kirk. "Send the transporter beam through, *now!*"

"*I've got only a partial lock on them, Captain! I can't be sure we'll get them!*"

"It's a better chance than they'll have if they stay on that ship," said Kirk. "Energize!"

"*Captain,*" said Scotty, seconds later, "*we've got 'em! All four of 'em!*"

"Get them to sickbay," said Kirk. The ship again lurched sickeningly. "Now let's save the ship, Mr. Spock."

"We may be beyond that point, Captain," said Spock, as if commenting on the weather. "Photon torpedoes are exhausted, phaser power is down to forty percent, shields down to thirty percent."

"Commander, Traal's ship has collided with the satellite set out of orbit by the *Jo'Payav*. It has been destroyed, with all hands, as has the *Jo'Payav*."

"Better for Traal that he died," said Kor, shaking his head. "Well, we will still wring a victory from this day. Fire full disruptors on the *Enterprise*."

"We've still got warp power, Captain," said Riley. "We can give them a run for their money."

Kirk shook his head. "Stick close to the planet. Within the envelope of interference created by the Pulse."

"Such a maneuver will interfere with the Klingons' sensors,

Captain, but probably not enough to let us escape," said Spock.

"I'm not looking to escape," replied Kirk, "I'm looking to give them some vision problems. Uhura, access the satellites we distributed over the planet."

"Let me, Captain," said Lon, approaching Kirk. He looked a little green around the gills, and sounded compliant, even desperate. Kirk guessed that this was his first taste of space combat. "I'm already familiar with their interface mode."

Kirk gestured across the bridge to an empty seat. "Uhura, patch Dr. Lon into the auxiliary communications station."

"Shields down to twenty-five percent, Captain," said Spock, as the ship shuddered again.

"What is it you want, Captain?" asked Lon.

"Contact the six nearest satellites, plot an intercept course. Bring them alongside us—and hurry."

"Commander Kor is contacting us, Captain," said Uhura. "He's asking for our surrender."

"No answer, Uhura. I can already imagine the look on his face."

"Satellites accessed, Captain."

"Reprogram the satellites, have them send the *Enterprise*'s identification signal. Spock, Uhura, give him a hand."

Spock nodded and turned to his console. "Do you think such a ruse will be sufficient, Captain?"

Kirk's reply was almost drowned out by another groan from the ship. "In a few minutes, we'll both know."

"Commander," said Kor's science officer, not taking his eyes from his console, "the Federation ship still flees."

Kor was silent for a moment. "I thought this a ruse of Kirk's. I thought I knew him better than that. How petty of him to lessen the sweetness of my victory. Still, I shall be made a captain for removing this thorn from the empire's side. Target full disruptors and—"

"Commander," said the science officer, slowly, "we now read

seven Federation ships, all carrying the *Enterprise* identification signal."

"What? One of them must be our target! Locate the true ship and—"

"Commander, electromagnetic interference from the planetary medium makes closer targeting impossible. Request—"

"Target them one at a time, then! Destroy them all! Before—!"

Suddenly the *Klothos* shook, like a branch caught in a high wind. "Commander, the *Enterprise*—all of them—have reversed course and are attacking."

"All available power to the phaser banks, Scotty," said Kirk urgently over the intercom. "It won't be long before they see through my little ruse."

"One satellite has been destroyed, Captain," said Spock.

"Send another on a collision course with their bridge."

"What was that?" demanded Kor, as a tremor passed through his ship. "That did not feel like a phaser blast."

"A collision with some foreign body, Commander. Forward shields are down to seventy percent."

"All power to forward shields. Fire again!"

"Their forward shields are weakened, Captain, they're diverting power to strengthen them."

"Target their engineering section, and fire."

"Commander, engineering reports taking—" This report was interrupted as his console exploded.

Smoke filled the bridge. Kor rose from his command seat, as if this would give his orders increased emphasis and his fist smashed his communications console. "Engineering! *Engineering,* answer or—!"

"Engineering does not respond, Command—" The *Klothos* shook again. "We are running on impulse engines only."

"Reverse course," said Kor, finally.

"The *Klothos* has broken off pursuit, Captain," said Spock. "It seems to be heading for open space. Shall we pursue?"

"No need to press our advantage," said Kirk. "I think we've taught them enough of a lesson for one day. Secure from red alert."

"Secured from red alert, sir."

"Redeploy the remaining satellites, Dr. Lon—and thanks for your help."

"You're welcome, sir," replied Lon.

Kirk hammered a button on his chair arm urgently. "Sickbay. Bones, how's the recon team?"

"No permanent damage, Jim," replied McCoy, *"unless you count the coddling Nurse Chapel is giving them."*

"Battle damage?"

The physician's voice lowered. *"Three dead, fifteen wounded."*

"Thank you, Doctor," sighed Kirk, after a moment. "Kirk out. Mr. Farrell, reverse course."

"Aye, sir."

Kirk shook his head as conversations erupted around him. Three dead. It could have been worse. But it could have been better. It could always be better.

CHAPTER
14

Captain's Log, Stardate 3297.8:

Dr. Lon's satellite fleet has been restored to full strength. With almost two hundred satellites doing the work, the loss of four is negligible to the overall effort. The satellites are continuing the work they were designed for. Dr. Lon will be remaining on Mestiko for the duration to supervise satellite maintenance and to act as liaison for the Federation.

The Federation will replace the *Jo'Payav*, agreeing with my argument that its existence serves as a vital symbol of the future of all Mestiko.

Commendations to the recon team for their meritorious service, and a special civilian commendation to Dr. Lon as well.

"And never let it be forgotten," said Kirk, pausing for emphasis as he looked out over the assembled mourners, "that

Colonel maTara and Councillor Traal gave their lives to the cause of preserving their people and their planet in the face of subjugation by the Klingon Empire." Kirk stepped back and pulled a cord, unveiling the rather severe memorial to maTara and Traal that had been erected in the center of Space Central. As he stepped back to his chair behind the dais, Spock caught his eye, and Kirk shrugged.

"Fellow members of the *Zamestaad*," said Raya, "a toast to our friends from the Federation." She raised a glass of the native liquor, and Kirk was privately delighted to see even the members of the *Zamestaad* who most hated the Federation complying, so much so that he decided not to rub it in.

"Thank you so much," said Raya, at the reception afterward.

"I was glad to speak," said Kirk.

"I mean for what you said about Traal and maTara. Their families may be comforted," she said, lifting a glass of the native liquor, "though I doubt it was the literal truth."

"Sometimes a lie can serve the bigger picture more faithfully," whispered Kirk. "Your planet needs heroes now more than ever. I decided to give them some."

Raya was silent for a moment as she surveyed the room. "I'm disappointed the Klingons did not attend," she said, "though I'm not surprised."

"The Klingons will be wiping egg off their faces for some time," said Kirk. "I don't think you'll have to worry about them."

Her brow furrowed quizzically. "I don't think you understand, James. If it is in the best interests of Mestiko to do business with the Klingons, Mestiko will do just that."

"Even after what they did?"

"After what Traal allowed them to do," she said. "And is what they did really any worse than what the Federation did? Or, rather, did not do?"

She turned to meet Kirk's gaze, and they stared at each other for several seconds. Then she turned and walked off.

Kirk stood there for a moment, then opened his communicator. "Now, Scotty. Beam the package down."

* * *

"Sometimes I almost think Spock has the right idea," said McCoy, lowering his glass. "*Almost,*" he emphasized.

"Regarding what, Doctor?" asked Spock, his curiosity piqued.

"About not having any feelings," said McCoy. "When I think of what the damned Federation Council said . . ."

"What was that, Doc?" asked Sulu.

Kirk was glad to see that he, Chekov, Kyle, and Sinclair had been working the room, enjoying themselves, seemingly none the worse for their experience, and, he hoped, better officers because of it.

"In the council's response to my report," said Kirk, "they declined to take any action against the Klingons, because Kor had been approached by a member of the *Zamestaad* to provide aid. Kor was, according to them, operating completely within the constraints of the peace treaty, and the council agreed that there was no treaty violation."

"Indeed," said Spock, significantly.

"Well, this isn't the last time we'll cross paths," said Sinclair.

"I just hope I'm there when they finally get caught," said Chekov.

"Excuse me," said Kirk. His gaze was fixed across the room as he watched an orderly deliver a message to Raya. She nodded, seeming somewhat puzzled, and exited the hall. Kirk placed his empty glass on a table and moved toward the door.

He caught up to Raya in her office, where she stared at a tall, slender package, loosely wrapped in bright paper. She turned as he cleared his throat.

"What is this? It is so beautiful."

"It's not the paper, it's what's inside it. It's a present," said Kirk, approaching her. He took her hand and lifted it to the package. "Unwrap it and see."

Kirk smiled as she gasped. "It's wonderful," she said. "Even more beautiful than the paper." She let the wrapping fall to the floor and took in the *noggik* tree seedling, running her hands over its gnarled wood, breathing its pungent fragrance.

"Mr. Sulu knows his way around our botany lab," said Kirk.

"It will be a while before Mestiko's surface can support such growth, but I didn't want you to have to wait that long."

"I'm not sure if this will make the wait easier or more difficult," replied Raya, her blue eyes brimming with tears, "but thank you, James. I only wish—"

"I think I have the same wish," said Kirk.

2271

SHADOWS OF
THE INDIGNANT

Dave Galanter

For my father and hero: Max
If I'm half the man he is, I've done well.

CHAPTER

1

"Damned violation of my rights is what this is." Leonard McCoy spat that—and a few other things that turned heads—at the blank expressions of the two Starfleet security officers as they stood next to his table. All eyes in the restaurant had been on the pair of uniforms since they'd disrupted the atmosphere by beaming directly to the hostess's station, but now the patrons were looking more at McCoy.

The older of the two security agents was on the short side, wiry, but had an air of confidence and authority. His younger, more athletic, female counterpart was inexperienced enough to look amused at McCoy's situation, a small smirk playing at her lips. "We have our orders, sir," she said.

"Where've I heard that before?" McCoy muttered. "Is there a charge, or a plan, or do I just sit here until Kingdom Come?"

This time the male officer spoke. "Our instructions are to hold you here until we receive further orders from the admiral, sir."

"I'm not a 'sir,' Lieutenant. I've resigned. I'm a civilian. Do you understand that?" McCoy tried to keep his voice in check, but people continued to stare. And why shouldn't they? How often did anyone beam into a small family restaurant in Fox Chase, Kentucky?

"Yes, sir," the man said.

"Then stop calling me 'sir,'" McCoy grumbled.

"We'll try, sir," the woman said. Her youth was showing. She was amusing herself at McCoy's expense, which was unprofessional, and it garnered a harsh look from her comrade.

McCoy noticed for the first time that while the male didn't have his phaser out, his hand *did* hover over the weapon in its holster.

"Do I threaten you, son?" McCoy asked.

The man smiled, and his brow crinkled a bit, probably at the unique thought of McCoy's thin, almost frail frame being menacing. "No, sir."

"Then take your hand away from that weapon. This is a public venue," McCoy barked, then motioned toward his half-empty dinner plate and the silverware on it. "Unless you think I'm going to fling my butter knife at your neck as I make my dramatic escape."

The hostess who'd seated McCoy less than an hour before and had wished him a good meal came sheepishly toward the table. Her gaze cast mostly downward with only passing sympathetic glances toward him, her voice was barely above a whisper. "Excuse me, Doctor?"

Poor girl couldn't look McCoy in the eye at all. When he'd signed for the credit transfer she was the one who said she'd have to check on why it wasn't going through, and she was the one who must have made the call about his flagged account. All that brought Starfleet Security barging in, and she obviously felt responsible. She was a sweet young girl—probably not more than twenty-two or twenty-three years old—and McCoy wondered at exactly what age he'd decided people in their twenties were "children" to him, but he felt as if he must allay her guilt. "Well, it's not your fault," he said to her quietly.

She smiled meekly and whispered, "I really am sorry but we really do need y'all to move to one of the banquet rooms." Her voice trailed off and as McCoy sighed and began to move she quietly added: "And . . . we still need someone to pay the bill."

"I'll take it." A familiar voice sliced into murmurs of recognition that bubbled around the man who now made his way from the entrance. The two security agents remained unmoving and yet seemed to tighten their stance as their superior neared. McCoy slumped back into his seat and waited as the murmurs hushed and the man who'd offered to pay the check lowered himself into the seat across from his doctor.

"I knew it had to be either you," McCoy said, "or Nogura."

Jim Kirk smiled pleasantly. "It's good to see you, Bones."

"Don't you 'Bones' me, 'Admiral' Kirk. What right have you got to—"

Ignoring McCoy's outburst, Kirk nodded to the two security agents. "Thank you. That'll be all."

Both nodded, stepped back to the hostess's station, and a transporter beam whisked them away in a flash of sparkle and buzz of sound as the hostess showed Kirk and McCoy to a more private room used for parties and banquets.

"Hey, listen—" McCoy tried to begin again once they were seated, but now Kirk was looking toward the doorway and into the main dining room.

"Could I get some coffee?" He called for one of the waitstaff.

The doctor did all he could to keep his eyes from rolling back into his head with disbelief. "Excuse me—I'm ranting at you. The least you could do is have the courtesy to listen."

A young man set down a coffee cup in front of Kirk and filled it, then nodded and quickly retreated to the main dining room. No one wanted to intrude but everyone was probably watching the doorway and listening as best they could.

"Go on with your rant," Kirk said, sipping his coffee. "Get it out of your system."

"Why the devil have I been arrested?" McCoy demanded.

"You're not under arrest. The guards are gone. I just wanted to be sure I didn't lose track of you."

If anything infuriated McCoy more than the situation, it was Kirk's expression. As if he'd done nothing out of the ordinary, as if he hadn't disrupted the lives of God knows how many people in the little small-town restaurant, as if it were reasonable and rational to take a friend into custody when you want to meet him for a chat.

"How about calling me and asking me to meet you for lunch?" McCoy asked.

Kirk shrugged. "Would you have said yes?"

Good question. "I'm not sure," McCoy admitted, and felt his ire calming. Kirk sometimes had that effect, when he wanted to. McCoy would be hot and bothered about this or that and just yelling at Kirk for a while could vent the steam and quiet his anger.

"See? My way was better," Kirk offered, taking another sip of his drink. "This is really excellent coffee."

"Your way," McCoy said, jabbing his finger at Kirk, "was to put a hold on my financial accounts and have guards stop me from leaving—"

"Did you try to leave?" Kirk asked.

"Of course not."

The admiral smiled, and the grin was becoming insufferable. "If you had, they'd have followed you, not phasered you."

"That's not the damned point."

Kirk said nothing for a long moment, just looked McCoy over—as much of him as he could see—and then finally said, "You lose a little weight, Bones?"

"Yeah," McCoy said, annoyed. "You gain some?"

Kirk pursed his lips a bit. "Maybe you need a drink—"

The doctor sighed, shook his head, and raised his arms in defeat. "Jim, what's this all about?"

"Would you believe I just wanted to catch up?"

"Not for a minute," McCoy said, and Kirk gave his best impersonation of a kicked puppy. "Please, spare me the wounded expression. Just tell me what you want."

Kirk took another sip of his coffee, placed the cup slowly back on the table, and looked McCoy dead in the eyes. "I need your help, Bones."

"That's a load of bull. Unless they suddenly have no other doctors in Starfleet."

"Okay, I *want* your help," Kirk admitted. "Will you at least listen?"

"Do I have a choice?" McCoy motioned toward the main dining area where the security detail had been standing as if they were still there, implying that they'd suddenly beam in again and wrestle him to the ground if he put his hands over his ears as Kirk talked.

Kirk gestured toward the entrance. "If you really want to go, without even listening, I won't stop you."

There was a tense moment when McCoy thought he might do just that—walk out and leave Kirk sitting there. Let him pay the bill to boot. *Would serve him right, too,* McCoy thought. He was ready to do it—even placed his heels squarely on the floor, prepared to stand up and walk away. But he didn't know what Kirk really wanted, and the chances were that if it weren't serious then Kirk wouldn't have gone to the trouble. Say what you liked about Jim Kirk, he wasn't prone to flights of fancy. "I'm listening," McCoy grumbled finally.

Kirk nodded and absentmindedly toyed with the spoon in his coffee. "You remember Mestiko?"

"Sure. The pulsar disaster. Some of the harshest living conditions I've seen."

The admiral nodded, and something played in his eyes that McCoy couldn't quite put a name to. Some memory that perhaps Kirk had not shared or McCoy had forgotten. It had been some time since that particular mission, and McCoy wasn't on the *Enterprise* for the original visit to Mestiko when the pulsar hit. "They've come a long way in a short time, considering the massive contamination, both literal and metaphorical, but reports I read say they're at a fragile stage."

"What's this have to do with me?" McCoy asked. "Or you, for that matter? Aren't you pinned to a desk now?"

"That desk," Kirk began, a defensive tone marbling his voice, "has given me some perspective on the big picture. I have a look at shipping-line patterns, for instance, and I've noticed something that someone without some experience 'out there' might have missed." When Kirk said "out there" he crooked a thumb toward the back of the restaurant as if the endless bounds of the final frontier were just beyond the grill of the small diner. "There's a pattern that's changed," Kirk continued. "Not in supply lines that provide Mestiko her goods, but in the carriers, lines, and merchant ships that furnish the ships that supply Mestiko."

McCoy felt his brow furrow in confusion. Somewhere in

the mess of lines and ships and carriers Kirk had lost him. "Once more, for the doctor in the first row?"

With a chuckle, Kirk seemed to realize what he was describing made sense only to someone who knew what he meant to begin with. He took in a long breath and began again. "Something has changed in the way Mestiko obtains goods from other planets. It's not very obvious, and in fact it's well hidden, but I see changes that have all the earmarks of a Klingon covert operation. We've seen similar patterns before: Sherman's Planet, Pentis II, SE-832."

As if back in the *Enterprise* briefing room again, McCoy automatically began thinking of the possible medical requirements of a conflict with the Klingons at the starship level: plasma burns, radiation exposure, broken bones— He stopped himself. That wasn't his job anymore, and it damned well better not be what Kirk wanted from him this time. Besides, what Kirk was talking about sounded like nothing more than idle suspicion. "The Klingons had their paws on Mestiko once before and it didn't work out."

Kirk leveled a cynical eye at McCoy. "How easily do the Klingons give up?"

Point made, but so what? What did it have to do with McCoy? "It's all very interesting, Jim, but I'm sure I can't help you weed out a Klingon conspiracy."

Kirk pointed right at McCoy with his left hand as he finished a sip of coffee and set down the cup with his right. "That's *exactly* what I want you to do. Help me find out what's going on. We send a starship in there, we're not likely to find out anything. Some things take a softer touch."

Before Kirk had even finished his sentence, McCoy was already shaking his head. "Then send in Starfleet Security—"

"No jurisdiction, technically," Kirk said with a dismissive wave of his hand as the waiter returned and refilled his coffee cup and McCoy's water glass. "And it would be hard to sell a covert mission on our side based on just my hunch."

McCoy scoffed. "But *you're* going to go—one of the more recognizable admirals in the Starfleet."

"I'm only recognizable to news watchers on Earth and Federation diplomats," Kirk said. "But officially we're calling it a fact-finding mission, should anyone ask. I've got Nogura's approval to go, and take you with me. Technically you'll be gathering info on Mestiko's current medical situation."

Shaking his head again, McCoy couldn't believe the cockeyed scheme laid before him. "You've lost your blasted minds. Both of you."

Kirk huffed out an amused sound. "That's just about what he said you'd say. If it's any consolation, he'd rather I not take you. He wants me to bring Lori Ciana."

"So why don't you?"

"Because . . . that comes with its own problems."

Feeling the weight of fatigue from his own recent travels, McCoy sighed and tried to let Kirk down as easily as possible. "Jim, I just got home—"

"We're talking a week," Kirk said. "Or two—at the most."

"I've been gone for too long. I want—"

"What difference will another two weeks make?" Kirk asked. "You know the planet, and I know you. I trust your guidance."

"Since when?"

Kirk smiled, probably because he sensed in McCoy's tone that he was being worn down. "Since I lost my blasted mind."

"Well," McCoy said, and allowed himself a slight smile for the first time since Kirk had arrived, "that's been a long time."

"Come on, Bones." Kirk held out his hand, offering it for McCoy to shake over the table. "What do you say?"

"Bastard." McCoy harrumphed, grasped Kirk's hand and shook it firmly. "I say I need that drink."

CHAPTER
2

It had been some time since McCoy had been to Starfleet Command, and to his mind it was too soon. There was a sterility about the place, from the neatly manicured trees that one would think were fake (but weren't), to the thin, hard carpeting that lined every corridor. And everything was painted white or beige. Even the uniforms were changing to those bland colors, it seemed. There were still many of the bright red, gold, and blue tunics he'd been used to, but they all seemed to be on visiting officers or enlisted personnel. Command staff officers themselves were all wearing plain jumpsuits now that couldn't help but remind McCoy of the footy-pajamas that toddlers wore. He wanted to ask the nearest ensign if he were ready for his nap, but willed himself to refrain. On his best behavior, he simply sat and waited for Kirk to get out of a meeting. Occasionally he nodded at a passing security officer who would look to make sure McCoy had the proper visitor's badge.

When the briefing room doors across the corridor parted, McCoy stood. A large number of officers spread out and went their separate ways, but Kirk guided one man straight for the waiting area.

"Dr. Leonard McCoy," Kirk greeted, "I'd like you to meet Captain Willard Decker."

McCoy put out his hand and the captain took it firmly. "Decker?" He looked to Kirk with a curious glance and wondered if there was a relation to the late Commodore Decker.

Kirk nodded. "Matt's boy."

Decker was a lean man—and who couldn't be in the new uniforms—with a pleasant smile and rather sunny disposition for a Starfleet captain. "I hear 'Matt's boy' so often, I'm not sure if that's my rank or my first name."

"Sorry," Kirk said, and patted the young man on the back. "It's a compliment, you know that, Will."

"Your father was quite a man," McCoy agreed.

"I have two sets of boots to fill, I suppose," Decker said. "His, and Admiral Kirk's."

McCoy looked from Decker to Kirk and back to Decker. "Oh?"

"Will's slated to become captain of the *Enterprise*," Kirk said, and McCoy wasn't sure exactly what emotion tinged his voice, but there was something there. As if "captain of the *Enterprise*" was a title akin to "philosopher-king." "He and Mr. Scott are overseeing the refit," Kirk added.

McCoy smiled affably. "Is Scotty actually letting you touch anything?"

"We have an understanding, but I'm learning quite a lot from him. It's an honor on all counts." Decker looked down at his inner left wrist and shook his head. "Speaking of which, I should be getting back to it." He offered McCoy his hand again. "Pleasure meeting you, Doctor." After they shook hands again, Decker turned to Kirk. "Admiral, I hope you'll come soon to see the progress we're making on the *Enterprise*."

"At my first opportunity, Captain," Kirk assured him, and Decker nodded a salute and walked briskly away.

McCoy wasn't sure exactly what kind of relationship the two men had, but there was a tension there, most certainly. Where it came from, McCoy wasn't sure. Jealousy, as if the *Enterprise* were a woman whom Kirk was loath to share? Guilt over feeling that he could have stopped Decker's father from dying unnecessarily? *Only one way to find out,* McCoy thought.

"Avoiding him, or the ship?" McCoy asked.

Kirk wasn't going to bite. "I'm a busy man."

McCoy grunted and decided to accept that, mainly because there was no other choice for now. Someday it would likely come up again, so he filed away the notion for later dissection. "So what am I doing here, anyway? If it's to see Nogura and have him talk me back into my commission, forget it."

Gesturing down the corridor they needed to turn, Kirk said, "You're practically paranoid, you know that, right?"

"Leave the diagnosis to me," McCoy said, "and I'll do my damnedest to not do any paper pushing or desk sitting while I'm here."

Kirk stopped abruptly and glared at McCoy with phasers on heavy stun. "You about finished?"

"Sure." McCoy wasn't certain if his skill at opening old wounds was because of his long friendship with Kirk or his medical degree.

Rather than continuing on, they were apparently at their destination. Kirk punched in a code on the door to their right and stood while a scanner glowed into his eye. A computer's voice responded. "*Access granted. Kirk, Admiral James T.*"

The door opened to a severe room, the walls of which were lined with white security lockers with only keypads and numbers on their doors, Kirk waited for the door to close behind them before going right to the locker he wanted.

"Why is everything always white here?" McCoy asked.

Kirk ignored the question as he tapped a code into the locker and pulled out what looked like a thick bracelet. "This is the new standard issue communicator." He demonstrated putting it on his wrist and showing McCoy the activation button, the controls for channel and gain, and the universal translator controls.

"It's small," McCoy said.

"And with an increased range of point two A.U. Multiband transceiver, translator, recorder."

"Thrilling."

Kirk handed it to him. "Just put it on."

As McCoy did, he nodded to the rest of the contents of the locker. "What's all this?"

Kirk pointed to each item in turn. "Med-kit, tricorder, palm phasers."

"None of this looks like Starfleet issue."

"It will be," Kirk said, pocketing one of the small phasers and handing the other to McCoy. "I've had these made without insignia or demarcation, and since they're not standard issue for another two months, no one should recognize them—or us—as being Starfleet."

"I'm *not* Starfleet," McCoy said pointedly. "But you look the part even when you're in civvies."

"Well, I don't intend to act like I'm in Starfleet."

McCoy smirked. "I'd love to see that."

"See? Something to look forward to." The rest of the contents gathered, Kirk closed the locker and gestured toward the door. "We depart at eighteen hundred hours."

"For Mestiko?"

"Eventually. First we visit the main shipping port in that sector. Indalo Station."

For someone who wanted to act decidedly non-Starfleet for this mission, Kirk had set a very military tone, other than his civilian clothes. From the time they met, to the tone he took with the dockmaster as they departed, to the commands he said more to himself than anyone else as they made their way quietly toward Indalo in the civilian vessel Kirk had procured for the trip, he was being very by-the-book.

While McCoy was no stranger to nonfleet ships, especially of late, he wondered just how often Kirk had piloted a warp-capable ship that wasn't a U.S.S. something or one of its shuttles.

"Where'd you get this thing anyway?" McCoy asked, breaking what had been at least a few hours' silence.

"This old thing?" Kirk asked, glancing up at the dorsal bulkhead and the older toggle controls to his left and right. "I own it."

"You're kidding me! This has got to be at least thirty years old."

"Forty-two." Kirk patted the console as if it were his hound dog's head. "It was Sam's. He left it to me when . . ." The thought trailed off.

"Yeah." McCoy had been there when Kirk's brother Sam was killed on Deneva. That was one wound he was willing to leave closed.

"It was junk when he got it, but spaceworthy. I had it restored when I was promoted. Took it out once or twice, but this seemed like as good a time as any to test it on a long trip."

"Test?"

"It's in good shape, Bones. Better than new, I'm sure."

McCoy looked around. The colors of the bulkheads were rich and lively. It was a pleasure craft. "I'll say this, it doesn't look like fleet issue."

"It's Andorian, actually. Single merchant ship that was redesigned into a day cruiser, and then back into a merchant-type ship when Sam had it. He would take it to research colonies to set up house before bringing the family along."

There was another long silence, but not truly an awkward one. Kirk and McCoy had known each other long enough and well enough that they could be alone with their own thoughts, sitting just feet from each other, and a long silence wouldn't be uncomfortable.

"Heard from Spock?" McCoy asked after a long while, just because his thoughts had wandered to silence and those who enjoy it far more than he.

Kirk seemed to hold back a sigh. "Not really, no."

"He's on Vulcan, I heard."

"Yes. And otherwise incommunicado." Kirk played with one of the settings on the console in front of him and McCoy believed that the controls didn't need fiddling with but that Kirk did it to have something to do. "I've talked to his father. He told me Spock could not be reached and to discuss it further would be considered an invasion of Spock's privacy. I pressed that, and learned that whatever Spock's involved in isn't for offworlders' information."

"Pleasant man, the ambassador," McCoy said flatly. "You should've talked to Amanda. She wouldn't stand on Vulcan formality."

"When Spock wants to contact me, he will." Kirk was looking blankly at the main viewer, which looked more like a windshield on a large bus but was not a window at all.

"Right." Here they were, parsecs away from much of anything, the ship didn't need constant care and feeding, and Kirk was looking out the window at nothing. *Damn. I thought about feeding. Now I'm hungry.* "You want something to eat?"

Kirk seemed to think about it for a moment and almost reply in the negative, but as if on a whim he turned and smiled. "Sure. I had my yeoman stock the galley. Why don't you see what's there?"

When McCoy returned, he had sandwiches and coffee. The coffee was instant and the sandwiches premade and wrapped individually. "Like the first astronauts used to eat," he said as he set Kirk's to one side and took his own into his lap as he sat.

"The first astronauts ate normal food, just precooked and processed."

"To coin a phrase, fascinating." McCoy leaned back and took a sip of the reasonably hot and mostly bitter coffee. "Jim?"

"Doctor?"

"Lighten the hell up."

Head pivoting quickly toward McCoy, Kirk looked as if he were about to snap something, then he smiled. "You're right," he chuckled, as if his funny bone had suddenly been switched on. "I'm sorry."

McCoy returned the smile. "I should get the medical tricorder and check your vitals. That's the second time today you've told me I was right about something."

"Do you ever think I'm wrong?" Kirk asked, setting a few buttons on the navigation console and then swiveling to pick up his coffee.

"Constantly."

"Well, maybe I was when I said you were right."

"You ruin everything," McCoy said.

The admiral took a sip, set it back down, and pushed it toward McCoy. "That's terrible coffee." Kirk reached for his sandwich but something on one of the scanner screens must have caught his eye because he spun quickly back to the ship's controls.

"What's happening?" McCoy asked, unable to avoid noticing that Kirk wasn't as graceful at the console as perhaps Sulu or some of the other *Enterprise* helmsmen were.

"We're being scanned," Kirk said.

"By whom?"

Kirk shook his head, his gaze shifting from one readout to another. "I can't tell. We're still about fifteen minutes from the Indalo system, so it could be them, but I can't place a source."

"Why the devil not?" McCoy demanded.

"This isn't a starship, remember? I had some good scanners installed, but not the best."

"Well, it might have been a good idea for this trip."

Kirk sighed. "The whole point of using this ship and not borrowing a Starfleet shuttle is to remain inconspicuous."

"Well, someone's curious."

"I think it was just Indalo. Standard procedure," Kirk said.

"Now who's paranoid? You thought it was pirates or something, didn't you?"

Kirk just frowned and time passed in relative silence, with more tension than either man would have liked. When close enough, Kirk called the dockmaster of Indalo Station and requested—and paid for—docking rights.

"How did you just pay for that?" McCoy asked out of curiosity as they passed the time it would take to be tractor-beamed into the docking ring of the station.

"Credit account of our employer," Kirk said with a slight smile. "Who just happens to be looking to branch out to this station."

"And that is?"

"Uhura Enterprises."

McCoy chuckled and propped his feet up on the lip of the console. "You're kidding. We're working for Uhura?"

"I didn't want it traced to her, actually," Kirk said. "So we're working for her mother."

Trying to remember past dinners at Uhura's home, McCoy knitted his brows. "I don't think I've met her mother."

Docking complete, Kirk rose and ushered McCoy toward the hatchway that connected them to the station. "Picture Uhura in thirty years."

"Nice woman?"

Kirk tapped at a few controls and with a hiss the door parted and showed a small walkway to the interior dock hatch. "Nice, beautiful, and if she weren't married I'd camp on her doorstep."

"Well, we see where Uhura gets her charms," McCoy said.

They stepped into a long corridor, the end of which met a large gangway that was filled with people. An employee of the station met them, checked in the ship, and had Kirk sign something, and asked if there was anything else he could do for them.

Nodding, Kirk replied. "Our employer is looking to rent cargo space and an open permanent dock. Who do we see?"

The employee, an Andorian woman with striking high cheekbones and typical pale blue pallor smiled thinly. "Your deity of choice."

"Come again?"

"You'll need a miracle. Everything is rented. But if there's going to be an opening, Nawaz Mazari is the man to talk to."

"He's the dockmaster?" McCoy asked.

"Of course not," the woman said. "You want the man who knows what actually goes on here, don't you?"

"Exactly." Kirk thanked her and he and McCoy headed into the crowd of people going about their business.

"Why don't we want the dockmaster?" McCoy asked.

"Because we didn't have to come all the way here to see if they had any openings. That information is available over the subspace infonet. What we need is—"

The doctor nodded, suddenly understanding. "The man who has his finger on the pulse of the station."

"You're catching on."

"I still don't know why you want me here," he grumbled. "You could do this yourself."

"It'll become clear." Kirk nudged McCoy in the ribs with his elbow. "Got your med-kit?"

Looking at Kirk sideways, McCoy felt a little knot of worry develop in his stomach. "Yeah. Am I going to need it?"

"One way or another."

CHAPTER
3

There were a number of small watering holes on the station, but the most active of them was called, of all things, "Duffy's Tavern," and it was where Kirk and McCoy had been told they'd find Nawaz Mazari. When they entered it wasn't what McCoy had expected. He'd thought it would be some seedy dive. It wasn't. The walls were painted a lively green, hung with spacescapes. The floor was a polished wood—not something one saw in space stations—and the waitstaff were nicely dressed.

Kirk motioned toward the man who was probably Mazari. He was seated toward the rear, his back to the bar and kitchen beyond, and his eyes toward the entrance. As they approached him, McCoy noticed Kirk was glancing also at the two large men sitting at the small table to the left.

"You're Mazari?" Kirk asked, once they were close enough.

The man looked up from behind a data slate, his dark eyes thin slices. "You are?" He was human, and his family was probably from Southern Asia originally if his look and name were any indication, but the accent sounded British.

"My name's Temple," Kirk told him. "We're from Uhura Enterprises and—"

"And he is?" Mazari asked, indicating McCoy with the end of his stylus.

McCoy smiled and nodded in Kirk's direction. "His bodyguard."

At that Mazari chuckled, but there was little humor in its tenor. He seemed like a man who often laughed, but with more malice than mirth. "Right," he said. "No doubt."

The admiral gestured to the empty chairs at Mazari's table and with a motion he invited them to sit.

They did so, and Kirk began, "My name is Jim Temple, his is Dr. Davis, and we want to buy you a drink." Kirk motioned for the nearest waiter to bring a round of drinks and then shifted his gaze back to Mazari, but "the man with his finger on the pulse of the station" was looking right at McCoy.

"Doctor, eh?"

"That's right." McCoy smiled. "And I prescribe bourbon for what ails you," he said as the waiter delivered a drink to each man.

"Okay." Mazari accepted the prescription and polished off the drink by slugging it down swiftly and then snapping the glass back to the small, round table. "Have at it. But it's going to take more than one of these to grease me slick enough to buy you two as anything but amateurs."

"That obvious?" Kirk smiled sheepishly.

Mazari nodded and waved over the waiter again. "I'll have another." He motioned to Kirk. "His tab."

"Truth?" Kirk shrugged as if assenting to everything Mazari suspected.

Another dark chuckle echoed around the edges of Mazari's thin mouth. "If you can fake that, sure."

"We really do work for a shipping concern. Uhura Enterprises. Or did, until we were let go last week."

Mock-frowning, Mazari was mostly looking at his data slate and likely only half paying attention to Kirk now. "That's a pity. Sacked before your time, to be sure."

"Worse than that, we got caught stealing. They can't prove it, but we all know it, and they're cutting their losses—and us."

"I may cry," Mazari said. "Drivel does make my eyes water so."

"He's not buying this," McCoy said, matter-of-factly.

"No, he's not." Kirk leaned over. "Okay, buy this, mister. I need to transport cargo to Mestiko. It can't go through customs or inspections, either here or at their destination. And I'm willing to pay. A lot."

"You'd have to," Mazari said. "That's a hot system."

"How hot?" McCoy asked.

"Nova hot," Mazari said. "Starfleet ships're all over the Mestiko system. And you *know* Starfleet is always crawling up everyone's arse about contraband to their pet project planets."

The way Mazari emphasized "know" made McCoy wonder if he was more on to them than even they suspected.

"What will it take?" Kirk asked, leaning forward as if a juicy deal was just about to be completed.

Mazari stared at them, seemingly at both simultaneously. "Who are you two?"

Kirk smiled that Cheshire cat smile he had. "If you make enough money, do you really care?"

Lips twisted in what could be called a snarl, Mazari shook his head slowly. "I don't like your smell," he told Kirk.

"Gee, I showered this morning. Is it my cologne?" Kirk's tone was suddenly annoyed and McCoy knew they'd dead-ended on their first foray.

"You reek of authority," Mazari said, absentmindedly fingering the rim of his empty glass with a finger. "If I had to place it I'd say you either work for the Federation or are being paid to work for them."

"I'm not Starfleet Security—"

"I don't care who you are, Mr. Temple. Our business is finished."

"You're making a mistake," Kirk said, and poked a finger toward, but not touching, Mazari's chest. "There's an opportunity here, and you're missing it."

"Just another bad day at the office, then." Mazari's eyes shifted to the two men at the nearby table that Kirk had been sure to keep an eye on. Now, they rose. "Good-bye, gentlemen."

One man grabbed McCoy and pulled him from his seat. The

other just stood, waiting for Kirk to rise. An interesting show of respect for a thug. "Get up."

Kirk rose, slowly, then pushed his chair under the small table. For a moment McCoy thought he might lift the chair up and ram it into someone's neck.

"Show them out, quietly," Mazari said, and McCoy hoped that wasn't code for "Show them out an airlock."

Mazari's muscle walked Kirk and McCoy to the door of the drinking establishment and pushed them both out. McCoy stumbled a bit but didn't fall, and Kirk made sure he held his stance like a wall.

One of the men looked back at Mazari for a moment, then pushed Kirk down a side corridor that probably led to the back of the pub for deliveries and maintenance.

"Let's take a walk," the man said to Kirk, then to his comrade: "Watch that one." He was bigger than Kirk, and a bit taller. His brown curly hair was cut close until most of the curl couldn't be seen except a bit on the top. He looked more powerful than Kirk, and if he hurt people for a living, he was perhaps more skilled.

"Jim—" McCoy began after them but was pulled back by the other guard.

As soon as Kirk and the other man were away from prying eyes, the fight began. Kirk sensed the first blow—a right cross—ducked it, and pushed into the bigger man's chest, elbowing his solar plexus.

Curly huffed out a sharp breath and then used Kirk's proximity against him to land a kidney punch. Kirk almost doubled over as pain exploded across his back and he let out a grunt, but he recovered quickly and angled away, giving himself a few meters of distance and a little time to catch his breath.

Slowly Curly drew closer, jabbing out but intentionally not connecting. Finally he lunged forward and connected his left fist with Kirk's brow, opening a cut that dribbled hot blood down his right cheek.

Kirk dodged the next blow and threw his weight into a

punch that landed squarely on Curly's jaw. As expected, he didn't collapse into a pile of jelly and instead dug his fist into Kirk's face in return. He tried to do it again, but Kirk ducked and punched Curly in the neck which got him gagging and stepping back.

Heaving in large gulps that Curly only wished he could take in, Kirk swung his leg wide and behind the larger man, bringing him to the hard steel deck with a thud.

"Had enough?" Kirk asked, dabbing at the blood over his eye with the knuckle of his right thumb.

Curly nodded and leaned against the wall but didn't pull himself up. "You a Fed?" he rasped. "You don't fight like a Fed—like you'd need a phaser to win."

"I'm not a Fed," Kirk said.

The man nodded. "Then you want to go see Fizzy."

"Who?" The adrenaline of the fight was beginning to wane and the pain from Kirk's bruised knuckles, cut brow, and tender kidney was ebbing forward. "I thought your boss wasn't going to help me." He chuckled a bit, and tasted a little blood in his mouth. "For a minute I thought he wanted you to kill me."

"Maybe he doesn't want to make any more credits," Curly said, finally catching his breath, "but I do."

"Who's Fizzy?"

"My price first, and it depends on how often your shipments will be, and how big they are." Using the wall to balance himself, Curly rose slowly. Kirk gave him his hand to help him up the rest of the way. "The more I have to work on making records change or disappear, the more it costs you, because the more I have to hide not just from the authorities, but from Mazari. And then there's Fizzy."

"You'll get ten percent of our net," Kirk said.

"Do I have to hit you again?"

"What do you want?" Kirk asked, lips pursing in mock frustration.

Without hesitation, Curly said, "Forty percent."

Kirk shook his head. "I'll give you fifteen. That's it."

After a moment of thought—probably not his strong suit—Curly partially agreed. "We'll see. It might go up later."

"Who's Fizzy?" Kirk asked again.

Curly cleaned the dust off his back and pants. "Full name is something orFizda, or something. But we call her Fizzy because it's easier. She's Mestikan."

Kirk blinked. "A Payav? Here?"

"A what? Yeah. Payav. That's what they call themselves." The man nodded to himself as if to remember that was significant. "She's the station liaison to their Customs. One of their own."

Looking at Curly skeptically, Kirk took a gentle step toward the main gangway with him, feeling tender. "And you know for a fact that she'd help us."

"For the right price, she'd give you the tattoos off her back."

"And where do we find her?"

"She's here a few times a week, but just left and won't be here again for another two days."

"She goes back and forth to Mestiko?"

"God only knows why."

"There's credits to be made there," Kirk said, staying in character. "We'll renegotiate depending on how much your friend Fizzy wants."

"We'll see."

Kirk blew on the swelling knuckles of his right hand. "Yeah, we will."

As McCoy closed the wound over Kirk's right brow, the admiral filled him in on the deal Mazari's man had made.

"You think that's legitimate?" McCoy asked.

Kirk shrugged and his brows moved up in a "who knows?" expression. "Greed is a universal concept."

"Name me a greedy Vulcan," McCoy said, then added under his breath, "And stop moving your eyebrows."

"They have a greed for knowledge and peace," Kirk offered.

McCoy rolled his eyes. "That's one way to define greed, I guess." He took Kirk's right hand and began to reduce the swelling and bruising with a device that would heal the underlying tissue at an accelerated rate. It would feel a little stiff for the next day or so, but there was no need to explain that to Kirk—he'd been the recipient of this particular treatment more than once. "So we wait for this Fizzy person to come back?" McCoy asked.

"Yes. And in the meantime we go through the motions of setting up contacts and business here."

"Now I see," McCoy said, closing up the med-kit and also indicating it with a gesture, "why you wanted me along."

Kirk raised his hands. "What were the chances someone wasn't going to hit me at some point?"

"Including me?"

The admiral smiled. "What about 'do no harm'?"

"You worried I could take you in a fight?"

Kirk chuckled. "Probably not."

"You know," McCoy said, "the longer we stick around, the more likely it is someone will make us."

"Make us? Suddenly you're from Sigma Iotia II?" Kirk flexed both hands, feeling McCoy's handiwork, and then rubbed his jaw.

"It seems to fit."

"Does, doesn't it?" Kirk tapped the tip of his chin with a finger and mouthed the words "still stiff."

McCoy replied with a tap on the man's shoulder and silently mouthed "live with it." There was actually a medical reason to not do more to his jaw, but why bother telling Kirk that?

"My point is, 'Jim Temple'?" McCoy asked as he stowed the med-kit in one of the storage bins near the galley of their small ship. "Kirk meaning church, isn't Temple just about too clever by half?"

"I based yours on your father's name."

"I noticed that," McCoy said, and did have to admit that he liked that touch. He had been very close to his father, and Kirk knew that. "Jim, we wait for this Fizzy person, and then what?"

Kirk pulled out his small hand phaser, checked its setting, then placed it back in the hip pocket of his dark brown pants. "Then we find out who we need to talk to on Mestiko who deals in illegal shipments."

"You don't want to just arrest her or something?"

The admiral shook his head. "I want the whole route. I want to know what's going on."

"Are you sure anything is going on? I mean, what shipping route doesn't have some way to transport contraband?"

Kirk seemed to think on that for a moment, perhaps weighing just what it was that were in those shipping irregularities. McCoy wondered as well. There was always something special about Mestiko for Kirk, McCoy knew. Something about some promise he made to Raya elMora for some damn fool thing that wasn't even his responsibility.

"I don't know," Kirk admitted, finally. "I need to run this to ground."

"You, personally?" McCoy shook his head and thrust himself down casually into one of the banquette seats near the small galley. "You sure this isn't about you riding in on your white horse to save Mestiko for Raya elMora?"

Kirk was now absently looking through the galley cupboards for God-knows-what. "It has nothing to do with Raya. It has to do with—"

"Guilt for something that wasn't your fault."

"Responsibility and guilt are two different emotions. A starship captain can feel one without feeling the other."

"He can also feel both," McCoy offered. "But you aren't a starship captain anymore."

"For someone who didn't want me to take that promotion, you certainly delight in reminding me of it." Finding some packets of mixed nuts, Kirk took one for himself and tossed one to McCoy. "I should think you'd be glad I'm out from behind that desk you hate so much."

McCoy opened the bag and fished around the various alien nuts for a good, old-fashioned peanut. "Not if it gets you killed, and me with you," he said.

"Just like old times."

"This," McCoy said, indicating the ship around them, "isn't a starship."

"She has some tricks up her sleeves, I promise." Kirk

poured a handful of the mixed nuts from the packet into his hand, brought the hand to his mouth and downed them all.

McCoy's lips pressed into a frown. "Well, with you picking up bruises and lacerations like they were daisies, she'll need them."

CHAPTER
4

The next thirty hours or so were relatively quiet. McCoy had kept to their small ship and Kirk was keeping himself busy chatting with the locals. He'd learned much about the activity of the station and the kinds of goods that saw port before moving on. Most of it was boring. He'd also made sure to drop some hints about what he was really after. He asked some questions that a few people seemed to feel uncomfortable about answering. He feigned apology at bothering them and moved on, but by now there were more people who were suspicious of him, and while McCoy might think that was a bad thing, Kirk knew it was not. One of the maintenance workers who fixed incoming vessels as needed, for instance, bristled at the suggestion that she might have seen wares that originated from the Klingons. A clerk in the inspections office had a similar reaction, and he was none too subtle about not wanting to speak to Kirk anymore. Part of that may have been because Kirk was a stranger to them, and was asking a lot of questions. But thinking that did him little good, so he preferred to think something else was happening.

The hard part was that having sown the seeds of suspicion

with these and a few others, there was little else to do but wait, and he hated waiting. In his job both on the *Enterprise* and now at Starfleet Command there was far too much waiting, for his tastes. At least on this mission there was a chance of some excitement, and there'd already been some. He'd not have admitted it to McCoy—and probably need not—but Kirk had enjoyed his tussle with Mazari's lieutenant. He chuckled to himself, because he still didn't know the man's name and only thought of him as Curly.

Kirk rubbed his still stiff jaw in remembrance of the event. It was by no means the first workout he'd had since giving up his captaincy, but it was the first real excitement in months. There was a big difference between hitting the bag at the gym and hitting a real person who hits back and isn't pulling punches. Just as there was a large chasm between logging desk-hours and star-hours, not that any of this mission would be logged, but—there was just a difference. Rank was important and as an admiral he could do much more than a captain . . . and yet so much less.

Having checked with Mestiko's embassy to the Federation, Kirk learned that "Fizzy" was actually Humal elFizda, and was indeed the Payav's customs officer for Indalo Station. She traveled frequently between Mestiko and the station, usually on the same transports that brought goods to Mestiko and then returned for resupply. Kirk knew one of two things was true: either elFizda knew about any shipping irregularities and was ignoring them, or someone was going to great trouble to make sure she didn't know about them. And it would take some great trouble. The Indalo Station dockmaster and people like Mazari might very well overlook this or that, or look the other way easily for a little graft. But elFizda's sole purpose was to make sure things that Kirk believed were happening wouldn't happen. And they were. He was sure they were.

When it came time for elFizda's arrival, Kirk wanted to nonchalantly be at that particular part of the station. A hairless, tattooed, quad-thumbed Payav would be hard to miss anywhere, but he was curious to size her up, maybe even find a moment to bump into her and meet her. He wasn't sure exactly, but he couldn't just sit and wait any longer in any case.

As soon as Kirk and McCoy had made their way out of their own docking area and into the main gangway that connected the other docks and also held various eateries and other shops, Kirk saw Curly standing with two other men. Curly nodded toward Kirk, said something to his cohorts, and all three walked straight for them.

"Yellow alert," Kirk said to McCoy under his breath.

McCoy looked around for a moment and then found Curly and the others when they were almost upon him. "How about we abandon ship?"

"Steady, Bones."

"Temple," Curly called when they were but a few meters apart. "Let's talk."

"Talk," Kirk said. "I'm listening."

Curly smirked the smirk that comes with superior numbers. "I thought it over," he said, "and I've decided it's time your business is finished here."

"You don't like our deal?" Kirk asked, keeping his hands in plain sight but unable to keep them from becoming tight fists he was sure to keep to his sides.

"I don't like you. You ask too many questions, and Mazari was right—you reek of authority. And around here, authority is bad."

"You an authority on that?" Kirk asked snidely, and it wouldn't have taken much to get him to hit Curly again, but the busy gangway of the station wasn't the place—station security was close by—and it also wouldn't have done much other than satisfy Kirk's personal gratification.

There began a short staring match where Kirk and Curly and his two muscular friends all sized one another up. And Kirk could tell it was making McCoy palpably nervous.

"It's a shame we couldn't do business," Kirk said, finally. "Someone will take me up on the offer, however." He moved to the left, not pushing his way past Curly, exactly, but pivoting in another direction.

Curly's arm came up and blocked Kirk's way. "Yeah? Well Fizzy's not comin' around here anymore, so you don't have business with her, either." McCoy backed up a bit, anticipating the worst, and Kirk looked down at the other man's arm that was pressed against his chest.

"You're in my way, mister," Kirk said, and realized that if anything was giving away his more military tone it would be in his anger.

Curly smiled, and it had about as much warmth as the dark side of Mercury. "See, I didn't say *our* business was finished here, Mr. Temple, I said *yours* was."

Kirk looked from Curly's arm to his face and to the other two men who flanked him. One was large enough to be directly related to Phobos, and the other was smaller, thinner, but looked just as mean. Again, Kirk had to remind himself that this was all he wanted—to have his suspicions confirmed that there was something about Mestiko's shipping concerns that people didn't want asked about.

"So you did," Kirk said, managing a weak smile. "Come on, Doc. Looks like we've overstayed our welcome."

"I noticed," McCoy replied, and it was obvious to Kirk that he was doing his best to cover the nerves in his tone.

"Gentlemen," Kirk said, as he turned on his heel and began in the direction of their ship. "It's been a pleasure."

Kirk didn't look back as they walked, but McCoy obviously had because when they were about halfway toward their docking port he whispered to Kirk that the three men were following.

"Makes sense," Kirk whispered back.

"Why?"

"Because they didn't want to kill us with a lot of witnesses and scanners recording it."

"Oh," McCoy said. "Wouldn't this be a good time to have a plan?"

"Working on it," Kirk said. "Give me a minute."

Something happened overnight to change Curly's opinion of his business relationship with Kirk. It may have been that Kirk was asking questions that made people suspicious, but that would lead Curly to want to cut the deal, not Kirk's throat, unless there was a lot more at stake.

McCoy glanced back, and now it was evident even to Kirk

that the three were following closely. Without the din of people from the main gangway, three extra footfalls traveled easily up the corridor.

"You know, they might think I'm easier to kill and take me first, right?"

"That's how I'd do it," Kirk deadpanned. "Just in case," he added with a whisper, "get your phaser ready. If we can avoid using them, I'd like to."

McCoy nodded and using a slow but steady movement reached into his pocket for his small phaser, which he palmed. "I'm assuming this means you have a plan."

"Yes," Kirk said. "Be ready."

"What do you want me to do?"

"On my mark . . . run as fast as you can to our ship, and get it warmed up and ready to depart."

"Wait," McCoy said. "Your plan is for me to run? While you do what?"

"I'm going to distract them," Kirk said and tapped McCoy on the arm as he turned to face Curly. "Now go. That's an order."

McCoy ran forward as Kirk stopped and waited for Curly to pull closer. The hallway was just big enough for his two thugs-in-arms to spread out and encircle Kirk so that he couldn't make the mad dash McCoy had made. So far, so good.

"You game for a rematch?" Kirk asked Curly. "Or do you really feel you need this help? Maybe alone you're not man enough to fight me."

Curly almost snarled, but didn't take the bait. "I don't need to prove anything to you. But I will enjoy watching *them* tear you apart." He nodded to the thinner one who was now behind Kirk and to his right. Kirk turned a bit to keep Skinny in his periphery and saw a glint of steel drop into his palm from up his sleeve. A hidden knife was impossible to detect—in use—and a phaser would be instantly detected. That was why Kirk himself was hesitant to use his own. Unless, of course, it came down to using one or losing his life.

Skinny had a knife in his hand, Curly said he was content to sit this one out—and Kirk doubted that—and big old Phobos was likely to use his mass to crush Kirk to death. Somewhere in the back of his mind he heard McCoy saying, *"This* is your asinine plan?"

Kirk quickly shrugged out of his jacket and dangled the center of it between himself and Skinny. The coat was leather and could somewhat deflect a dagger blade, but that wasn't the purpose. When Skinny lunged forward Kirk wrapped the man's entire hand, knife and all, within the bulk of the jacket. He pulled Skinny down, to his knee, kicking him hard in the face—hard enough that Skinny was down for the count.

"One down," Kirk said, thrusting Skinny's limp body away. "Two to go."

Phobos growled.

"Okay," Kirk said, backing off a pace. "Two and a half if we count you fairly."

Unwilling to let Phobos go down the way he had, and the way Skinny had, Curly took off his jacket and it dropped to the floor. He came at Kirk, fists balled into rocks, and pounded first a right, then a left, toward his head.

Kirk dodged low and to the left. He pushed Curly back into where he'd stumble into Skinny's flaccid form. Phobos bolted forward, moving deceptively quick for someone of his bulk. Kirk punched the larger man twice with his right hand, putting his weight into the thrust, but it didn't faze his opponent. Both hands shaped like cement trowels, Phobos snapped Kirk on either ear. Pain flashed hot into his eyes but he shook it off with a grunt in time to see Curly was unwrapping Skinny's hand, in search of his knife.

Kirk spun, dropped to the ground with a roll, and slipped his legs between Phobos's. He twisted and took the moon man off his balance until he fell to the deck. If he was going to do this, fight two larger men at the same time, he could only really have either one on his feet at any one time. Sweat bubbled over his lip; Kirk was beginning to tire. Phobos weighed over a hundred and thirty kilos, easily. What wasn't easy was bringing that amount of bulk down.

Knife now in hand, Curly was taking his second run at Kirk as Phobos grunted angrily and tried to scramble to his feet. There would be one chance at this and now was the time, Kirk realized.

As Curly thrust the dagger at Kirk's midsection, he pulled to one side, grabbed Curly's wrist, and braced his back on the wall. One foot stuck out, Kirk heaved Curly over and down, his outstretched arm forcing the knife into Phobos's massive torso. Curly yelled, Phobos yelled, and Kirk decided that was enough. He jumped over Skinny, reaching down for his jacket and lugging it along as he went.

By the time he was aboard the small ship, McCoy had all the systems online and had even cleared departure with the dockmaster.

"What happened out there?" McCoy asked as Kirk slid into the pilot's seat.

"We got what we came for," Kirk said. "We don't know what exactly is going on, but it's damn certain something is."

"Is that it? Can we go home now?"

Kirk shook his head and disengaged the moorings from Indalo Station. "Fizzy didn't come back here. That means that someone warned her off—so we're heading for Mestiko."

With a sigh, McCoy sank into the copilot's seat. "Oh, joy."

CHAPTER
5

Approaching Mestiko was awkward for Kirk. Upon requesting orbit he didn't want to register his ship there under his
name, but he somehow felt that was a breach of the trust he'd
tried to foster with the Payav. Still, he didn't want to announce
his presence to Space Central by broadcasting that Admiral
James Kirk had arrived. If there was anything he'd learned
from his last visit, it was that those who could be working
with the Klingons could well be anyone.

So Space Central got the fake name and registry that Indalo
Station had, and Kirk settled into first an orbit, and then a
landing approach.

"If you think you can survive without me," McCoy began as
they gathered their gear once they'd landed, "I'm going to see
if I can find Dr. Lon."

Kirk looked up with surprise. "He's stayed on this long? It's
been years . . ."

"Surprised me too when I learned of it. I've kept in contact
with him now and again. He's become quite fond of this place,
I think."

Already at the door, McCoy was ready to open the hatch

and Kirk had to wave him off. "We've landed, but the platform has to be pulled underground before we can disembark."

While Dr. Marat Lon's air-scrubbing satellites had done wonders for Mestiko's ravaged atmosphere over the last few years, much of the planet's surface was still relatively uninhabitable for long periods. It wasn't enough to have a breathable atmosphere for an hour, a day, or even a month—the air had to be clean enough to sustain life for year after year without causing long-term health problems. Mestiko was some years off that standard, and so the vast bulk of the populace was still living under pressure domes or underground. More domes had been built in the years since Kirk's last visit, but landing pads were still open to the air and needed to be pulled underground for ship storage. Should Kirk and McCoy need to make a quick escape of the planet as they had Indalo Station, that wouldn't be an option.

Once out of the ship, Kirk and McCoy walked toward the underground city that had become Mestiko's market capital simply because it was both the home of the *Zamestaad*—their main governing body—as well as their Space Central agency, which now had more than a few cargo transports provided by several shipping concerns who wanted to do business with Mestiko.

Both men were used to navigating around strange, new worlds and so they went their separate ways, McCoy off to see Lon and Kirk to the Mestiko office of elFizda. Even though Fizzy wasn't to return to Mestiko for another day, that didn't mean there wasn't something for Kirk to learn at her office.

Walking through the "city," Kirk was astonished with how the Payav had adapted to their hindered lives underground. Whereas the last time he'd visited the people were living in more makeshift accommodations, it was clear changes had taken place. Shops with doors and even windows were on either side of the main causeway and the grade was an upward angle that soon gave way to ground-level streets under the pressurized dome. The air inside the dome was clean and smelled amazingly fresh considering that just outside, the atmosphere was still thick with muck. Kirk looked up past the dome and into the sky. The reddish-brown hue was mostly gone, but that didn't mean much to one's lungs. From the reports he'd read it wasn't sound to breathe the outside air for longer than a few hours.

Mestiko was most assuredly a work in progress, which psychologically must have been something to deal with for her people. As a planet they'd just started touching the stars when the Pulse pounded them back a few hundred years. But it didn't just beat them back; it also knocked them forward quickly. It was a dichotomy: the same disaster that forced them to live primitively in relation to where they'd been was also forcing them to step too quickly into the realm of interstellar relations. There were growing pains.

As Kirk walked to the relatively nearby customs office, many Payav looked at him from the periphery only, refusing to make eye contact. That wasn't strange—many cultures crowded for space considered direct eye contact almost a violation of privacy. What did concern Kirk was that the universal translator had a more sensitive "ear" than a human, and it was picking up some under-the-breath comments from people he passed by.

"A'sloointa Dinpayav," one man spat quietly. "Step off from me." The first word wasn't in the translator's language base but Kirk knew "Dinpayav" was their word for offworlders, and the rest was pretty clear. Many other similar comments were being made, and one mother instructed her child not to look at the "offworld filth."

Upon his last visit there was a growing anti-Federation feeling among many—even Raya's grandmother. One would have thought she'd have had a bit better perspective since she was closer to the real story of all that had happened, but if anything Kirk remembered worrying whether she was going to influence Raya into turning down Federation help. Thankfully, that hadn't happened. And after the incident with Klingon interference in Payav politics it would seem the anti-Federation feeling had become an antialien feeling. That was probably why outside of the landing deck itself, Kirk had seen no other offworlders, only Mestiko natives. It crossed his mind that they might even have certain regulations about where Dinpayav could travel unrestricted, but not only would he know that from his position at Starfleet, Space Central would have informed him if something had recently changed. No, this was probably a voluntary segregation, and that perhaps made it even more uncomfortable.

The customs office was in one of the older buildings that hadn't been destroyed by the Pulse. It had obviously been braced by thermoconcrete, probably from the Federation, as the technology for such materials was as yet beyond the Payav. Well, the know-how wasn't beyond it, but their level of industry was completely geared to subsistence still, and most of that came from offworld. There was yet another dichotomy. The Payav relied on trade for their lives, yet didn't want to deal with those who supplied the very source of their survival. It was going to take decades for Mestiko to rebuild its economy to the point where it could be fully independent—if ever. Kirk mused how Earth might be if she decided not to trade with other worlds. He was sure it would be difficult. Not impossible, but difficult. It wasn't in the nature of spacefaring cultures to be economically isolated. Just as tribes gave way to city-states, which gave way to nations, and finally planetary governments, local economies gave way to national, then global, then interstellar economies. *Enterprise* was going under an almost total refit and if Starfleet were to remove all the non-Earth technology, there would be little more than an empty skin to the ship.

The trust among the founders of the Federation took years to cultivate and now those relationships were their joint strength. Mestiko had been thrust into similar relationships out of dire necessity. It wasn't easy, and the trust wasn't quickly forthcoming, especially considering how it began.

Taking a lift to the third floor of the customs building, Kirk approached Fizzy's office. It was a small, two-room affair, with an assistant in the reception room, sitting behind a simple desk, and only two chairs for the long line of waiting Payav that flowed out into the hall. Beyond the assistant's desk Kirk saw elFizda's office behind an older wooden door that was painted with gold, official-looking lettering. He didn't know what the lettering said, but he assumed it was her name and title.

Pushing past those in line, and irritating many by doing so, Kirk made his way to the man behind the reception desk. He smiled, sure not to bare his teeth, as local custom demanded. "Hello," he said, and let the universal translator relay the greeting in the Payav language.

"Greetings," replied the Payav man in Kirk's own language.

Admittedly, Kirk was taken aback. "You speak English?"

"This is a customs office," the man said in a monotone that was perhaps a universal standard for bureaucratic jobs. "I speak a variety of Terran, Vulcan, Andorian, Centaurian, and Orion languages."

Orion, too. Figured. "What about Klingonese?" Kirk asked, and searched the man's pale features for a response. There was none. Perhaps it might have been easier to see a change in skin tone if the young man's head and face had not been so covered with elaborate tattooing. The Payav were basically humanoid, and even rather Terran-looking, except for a porcelain pallor, longer-than-average necks, an extra thumb on each hand, and a complete lack of body hair. Any deficiency of decoration that a lack of hairdo might cause was often made up for with intricate tattoos.

"I speak some Klingonese as well," the man said after a long moment.

Kirk nodded, offered up his fake name, and asked to see elFizda, even though he knew she wasn't going to be there.

"She's out today," the man replied expectedly. Which meant she was neither on Indalo Station nor on Mestiko. Or at least she wasn't making herself available. All because Kirk was asking questions?

"What are all these people waiting for?" Kirk asked, gesturing to the two seated people in the reception room as well as the long line of thirty or more people that meandered out the door.

"Work," the Payav man said flatly. "We don't frequently have openings, but every day these number or more show up in hopes there will be something and they'll be first to apply for it."

Growing pains everywhere, Kirk thought, and thanked the man for his time. On his way out he asked a few people what kind of work they hoped for, but his requests went ignored. People looked away or down, avoiding him completely. One man, who stood near the back of the line but whom Kirk hadn't approached followed him to the street.

"Federation?" the man called after Kirk.

Turning back to the man, Kirk shrugged, not wanting to suggest he worked for the Federation. "I'm from Earth, if that's what you mean."

Thin, pale lips curving into a tight smile, the Payav man put out his arms in the traditional greeting that Kirk had learned some years ago. Grasping the man's hands, and having his grasped by those extra thumbs, brought back memories of his last visit.

"You have questions that people would not answer," the man said. He was an older gentleman, Kirk wasn't sure how old by Payav standards, but his tattooing was a bit faded, and his skin showed signs of having lost some elasticity.

"But you'll answer?" Kirk asked.

The man's head lolled around in what was probably similar to a nod. "I do not dislike Dinpayav. I do not believe the conspiracies that tell us the Federation did this to us."

"I appreciate that." Kirk gestured to a bench at what was probably a tram stop for the city's mass transit system. "Can we talk?"

They sat, the small man toward the middle of the otherwise empty bench, Kirk toward the end.

"What's your name?" Kirk asked.

"Izra," he replied. "Izra orCina. What is yours?"

"My friends call me Jim." Kirk smiled lightly, and then leapt into his questions. "What kind of work were you looking for with the customs service?"

"Any kind," Izra said. "I'm not so old that I can't work on a ship, or be a clerk, or whatever job you have, I can do."

Suddenly Kirk's heart sank. Izra wasn't just being kind, he was looking for work and assumed that Kirk was an offworld trader with ships that needed employees.

What now? Get more information, or risk disappointing him enough that he won't talk anymore? Kirk sighed and couldn't let the man assume something that wasn't the case.

"Mr. orCina, please understand, I don't have any jobs. I'm not looking for workers, or . . ." He let his sentence trail off as Izra's face fell into a deep, sad frown that suddenly made him look older still.

"I understand," the Payav man said, clearly crestfallen. "I appreciate your honesty. You are a journalist doing a story?"

"Why would you think I'm a journalist?"

"You are asking questions," Izra said. "Is that not what journalists do?"

"Maybe I'm just a trader new to Mestiko."

Izra laughed. "I assumed you were a trader who had come to look for help among those waiting for jobs because frequently Dinpayav do so here. But you are surely no one new to Mestiko."

Kirk looked quizzically at Izra, but couldn't help but return the man's laughter with a smile. "Why is that?"

"You knew the hand greeting perfectly," Izra explained. "So this is not your first visit to Mestiko. And you say you're not looking for workers, yet you ask questions, so you must be a journalist."

If Spock were here he'd say that logic was flawless. Kirk didn't answer the accusation, however, and instead wondered just what Dinpayav came to find workers here.

"What kind of people come here to find workers?"

Izra rubbed his chin with one hand in a motion that would look very human if it were not for the two thumbs at either side which met each other with a light tapping. "What *kind* of people? Dinpayav. Offworlders," he said as if the question truly confused him.

"Do you know from what planet? What they looked like?"

"They had fur, like you." He shrugged. "They were Dinpayav."

Kirk chuckled. To Izra, all Dinpayav looked alike. Well, that was fair. To Kirk, all Horta looked alike.

"Have you heard of anyone working for Klingons?" Kirk asked.

Izra's face crumpled into sour disdain. "No, I would remember that. I do not care for them."

Nodding, Kirk patted Izra's shoulder. "Can I tell you a secret?" He leaned in and whispered. "Neither do I."

Smiling again, Izra tapped Kirk back. "I wish I could be of more help."

"Do you know anyone who mentioned working on a ship or offloading cargo from a ship where something seemed out of the ordinary, or too secretive?"

Looking up in thought, Izra was silent for a moment. "You know, I believe so. A friend of mine recently got a job offloading cargo and clerking for one of the traders. I asked if he could get me such a job as well but he said they would not likely hire me." Izra leaned in as if confiding some great secret. "I have been told I'm too talkative, and Dedir said he could not recommend someone with weak lips."

Interesting. "Do you suppose I could meet Dedir? Do you know where he works?"

Izra hesitated. "I . . . I do not want to cause trouble for him."

"What trouble could a journalist cause?"

To that Izra laughed so heartily that he began to cough. "Forgive me," he said when he could catch a breath. "There are few people more disliked on my planet. Perhaps only Dinpayav are considered more—oh, forgive me, I meant no offense."

Kirk waved off the comment. "No offense taken. And I promise not to tell Dedir who told me where to find him."

"Very well." Izra smiled again. "His name is Dedir orTola. He works at dock seventeen of the main dock complex."

"You've been very helpful, Izra," Kirk said as he clasped hands with the Payav man again. "And if I hear of a job, I'll be sure to let you know."

"Thank you, Jim. Good luck and safe journeys to you."

CHAPTER
6

Dedir orTola was a stout figure, and that was an interesting sight for Kirk. It spoke to a rich diet, and when foodstuffs were scarce, that was what might be considered a real, live clue. If Dedir was eating well, that meant he was being paid well, and when there were people lined up for jobs, obviously trying to supplement whatever the government and help agencies could give them, a job that paid well meant someone needed very specialized skills. Hefting crates around, keeping track of them, and coordinating shipments didn't require great expertise.

When Kirk approached him on the large platform that was dock seventeen, he was standing with an older-fashioned data slate, poking in commands to its interface with a short, dirty stylus that probably used to be white but had turned grubby with time.

"Dedir orTola?"

The Payav man looked up slowly, connected with Kirk's eyes for a second, then looked back down. "What?"

Again, English, no need for a translator.

"I'd like to ask you a few questions—"

"I don't got time for no questions," Dedir snapped, and began walking toward an office cubicle at one corner of the bay.

"You speak well," Kirk said. "You've mastered the double negative, at least."

Dedir turned a half step, and Kirk could see his expression was confused. "What?"

"I've heard good things about you," Kirk said. "I wanted to offer you a job."

Chuckling, Dedir turned away again and made way for his office, and Kirk followed him. "I have job," he said. "Get missing."

"Get lost, you mean." Kirk stood in the doorway of Dedir's office as the chubby Payav folded himself into the seat behind his narrow desk. "You've not even heard how much the job pays. It might be much more than you make here."

"Get lost, I said."

"At least you learn quickly."

"Whatever, *a'sloointa Dinpayav*," he said, this time all in his own language.

Every person Kirk spoke to was different and each required his own brand of finesse. With Dedir, Kirk moved quickly across the room and pressed his hand down onto the arm of Dedir's chair, pinning his right hand down. "I'm going to assume," Kirk said, easily blocking a useless, leverageless blow from Dedir's left hand, "that *'a'sloointa'* isn't the nicest thing you could say to a person on this planet."

"Let me up." Dedir struggled, and Kirk pressed down harder on his wrist.

"I have questions, Dedir," Kirk whispered. "Starting with who pays you."

"I work for the people who own this dock—"

Kirk shook his head and spun the chair fully toward him. With his right hand he pinned down Dedir's other wrist to the arm of the chair and now a look of fear truly fell across the Payav's hairless brow. He struggled, to no avail.

"You might work for them in name, but I want to know who you work for in deed," Kirk said, and leaned close. "And don't lie to me."

"Get your furry hands off me!" Dedir insisted.

"No." Kirk pressed harder still, putting as much of his body weight on Dedir's wrists as he could. "Who is paying you to get fat?"

Finding straining useless, Dedir eventually gave up. He sank back into the chair and his face furrowed into what seemed more mentally than physically pained. "They will kill me," he said slowly, through gritted teeth, "and they will kill my family, and most pleasant of all they will kill you."

"Who?" Kirk demanded. "*Who?*"

"Alur," the Payav spat. "Now leave me to take my family away before they know I told you."

"Alur who?"

"Everyone knows Alur, now let me go!"

Kirk released him and instantly the man jumped up, knocking Kirk out of the way as he scrambled his plump form out of the office.

Moving faster than Kirk would have thought possible, Dedir was halfway across the docking bay as Kirk managed to get to the office doorway. He certainly hoped everyone knew who Alur was, because if not, his talk with Dedir was going to be just another dead end.

When Kirk went back to the ship, McCoy was waiting for him.

"I was beginning to worry," the doctor said.

Kirk raised his arm and pointed to the wrist communicator as his jacket sleeve fell away to reveal it. "I was a communicator signal away."

"Like I'm going to learn how to use this blasted thing."

Over a meal, Kirk told McCoy what he'd learned about a fat Payav named Dedir and his boss, Alur, which wasn't much, so it didn't take long to bring the doctor up to speed.

"I'm not sure which of us had the more interesting day," McCoy said.

"How *is* Dr. Lon?" Kirk asked, shunning the terrible coffee in favor of bottled water.

"Different." McCoy took a bite of his roast beef, then looked at the packet again as if to be sure it was, in fact, what it claimed to be. He shrugged and took another bite.

"Different how?"

"I'm not sure. More mellow isn't quite the word for it. A little more sympathetic, maybe? That doesn't quite fit either. I think he likes these people more . . . maybe as pets."

Kirk coughed out a chuckle as it interfered with a swallow of potato salad. "You're being too hard on him."

McCoy paused for a moment and seemed to consider the possibility. "I dunno. How do you spend all this time on a planet and talk more about its ecology than its people? Wouldn't you make some connections with the natives?" He looked at Kirk, then said, "Well, *you* would, if she were pretty enough."

Kirk ignored the dig and changed the subject back to Mestiko. "And how's the planet doing? The air looks more clear, but readings I took as we were landing tell me looks are deceiving."

"Nitrogen oxide levels are down a lot since Lon's satellites were put into operation. They've upgraded the original satellites, too, and added some to replace the ones that got blown up. Most of the acid rain is gone—or at least is more on par with what you'd expect for mid- to late-industrial societies. Oxygen levels are up enough that the ozone layer's under repair, and UV radiation is going down, too."

"That all sounds very good," Kirk said.

"Well, it's not all hearts and flowers." McCoy took his half-finished tray of food, its package, and his empty coffee cup and stowed them in the trash bin. "The planet's natural biomass was and is in steep decline. Massive flora and fauna extinctions, Jim. What the radiation didn't wipe out, the smog got. What the smog didn't kill, the falling temperatures destroyed, which is why other than what the Norrb can contribute, and some municipal greenhouses under the domed portions of the city, Mestiko is getting most of its food from off-planet."

Kirk nodded and McCoy continued.

"And while the air is clearer now, increased ice and snow cover is reflecting too much sunlight back into space. Temperatures are still way below normal. The ice caps are larger than as far back as Payav records go, because the last several hundred years Mestiko was on a warming cycle, coming off an ice age a few millennia back."

Stowing his own dinner remains, Kirk shook his head, remembering the devastation of the initial pulsar disaster, and then a few years later the ramifications of what to him always made him think of a massive planetary attack, as if the pulsar was an enemy that Kirk had failed to defeat.

It was probably a mistake to look at it in those terms—natural disasters weren't evil, they just *were*. Perhaps that was why the Payav sometimes looked for a scapegoat in the Federation. They needed someone to blame, someone to curse other than nature, and the Federation had been there since the beginning—Dinpayav who appeared when their world became an icy, poisonous rock. Who could fault them for coping in the easiest way they could?

Kirk felt McCoy's hand on his shoulder and he turned toward the doctor.

"Jim, you still listening?"

"I'm sorry," Kirk said. "I guess I wasn't toward the end."

McCoy looked at him, his brows knitted with worry. "I asked what you want to do now."

"Talk to Raya." Kirk opened a panel in the bulkhead to the right of the galley and revealed a keypad. He punched in a code, and the keypad gave way to a retinal scanner.

"Access," he told the computer.

"Identify for retinal scan."

"Kirk, James T."

"Identity confirmed."

"What're you doing?"

With a slight hiss, a safe door opened. "Just in case the ship was searched at some point, I didn't want this found." Kirk pulled out a card holder and showed it to McCoy. Out came a flashing ID card, showing his name and rank. "I don't think Jim Temple and Dr. Davis will get an audience with the *Jo'Zamestaad*. But I'm guessing this will get us past security."

It actually had not been that long ago that Kirk had first met Raya elMora. She'd appeared on the forward viewscreen of the *Enterprise*, the new leader of a ravaged planet, her position chosen by default of who survived the initial pulsar devastation. From the moment they met Kirk had the oddest feeling that he should've been protecting her, and had never quite been able to.

They kept in touch from time to time, but she was busy, he was busy, and subspace letters were never Kirk's strong suit.

"The years have been good to you." Kirk flirted when he first greeted her, clasping her arms in the traditional Payav handshake, and then giving her a good old warm human hug.

Raya smiled and greeted McCoy in the same manner. "Doctor, I trust you'll be treating the admiral's eyes at his next physical." She motioned for them to sit in front of her poorly organized, messy desk.

"If memory serves," McCoy said, lowering himself into one of the three plain chairs that adorned her austere office, "he has an allergy to the standard cure. We'll have to work out something else. But I suspect he's fine for now, because he's right: you're looking radiant."

"I see Starfleet still has training programs in flattery," Raya said. "I'd hoped it would. As *Jo'Zamestaad* I am treated more to diatribe than adulation." There was a confidence in her that Kirk had seen somewhat in their first meeting, more in their second, and now it was fully in bloom. "I am surprised to see you," she continued. "Pleasantly so, of course. But I received no subspace connect that told me you would be visiting."

"We were in the neighborhood," Kirk said, and watched her brows knit with confusion.

"James," Raya said in an admonishing tone. "I thought we were to be—I thought you of all people would know better than to be coy with me."

Kirk smiled. "Of course. We're here unofficially, however, so we need to be discreet."

She nodded. "That would explain why there was no record of your having arrived planetside, and no record of a Federation ship in orbit." When McCoy looked as if he was about to ask a question, Raya offered: "I would have been advised by Space Central had either event occurred."

A woman came into the room and handed Raya a data slate that looked much like the ones Starfleet used some years back. In fact, it might have been an old surplus item. "Thank you, Blee," Raya said, handing back the signed slate to the woman.

"You have an appointment you're late for, *Jo'Zamestaad,*" Blee said on her way to the door. "The subcommittee on housing is to deliver its report."

"I promise not to be *too* late, thank you," Raya called after her. When Blee was gone, Raya leaned forward as if sharing a secret. "I don't know what I'd do without her. She practically runs the government despite me, and the two years she was a councillor in her own right I was lost without her."

Kirk nodded and smiled politely, but something was wrong. He could feel it. Raya was different. Warm and yet distant. Despite an odd misgiving not to, he was frank with her about his reason for being on Mestiko. He explained in detail his belief that shipments from Klingons were covertly finding their way to her planet, that someone was going to some amount of trouble to keep people from knowing about it, and that by asking questions at Indalo Station about Klingons and their shipments, a lot of very non-Klingon feathers had been ruffled—which was in itself unusual if there was nothing to hide.

Finally, he told her about his conversation with chunky Dedir and the name he'd given Kirk as his boss: Alur.

She listened, hands clasped before her, the appropriate amount of shock registering in her pale expressions, until he was finished, when she steepled her fingers in a manner reminiscent of Spock, save when he did it there were not two sets of thumbs.

"This is very disturbing," Raya said, finally. "I will have the *Pesh-Manut* look into this immediately, and I appreciate you bringing this to me, finally. I only wish you might have come to me first—I may have been more help."

"I didn't know enough to bring you until now," Kirk said. "Can you help me find out who Alur is?"

Raya seemed to shrug. "I will be in contact once the *Pesh-Manut* have investigated this to the fullest, I assure you."

"Well," Kirk said, "do you think I could talk to someone named elFizda in the customs office?"

Her features becoming ashen, Raya hesitated for too long a moment. "The woman of whom you speak was killed upon leaving orbit yesterday," she said solemnly. "I am told it was an accident. An imbalance with the engine."

"I'm sorry to hear that." Kirk shared a look with McCoy.

Raya stood, came around the desk, and gave Kirk a brief hug again. "I fear I am running too late at this point and Blee will not allow me to hear the end of it. But I am always glad to see you, and perhaps if our mutual schedules allow we can all have a meal together before you depart?"

Despite being suddenly ushered out, Kirk smiled politely and gave Raya the information she was looking for. "We should be here long enough for that. Dr. McCoy needs to meet with Dr. Lon for a bit."

McCoy glanced at Kirk but said nothing about the lie until Raya was gone and they were both on their way back to the ship.

"You don't trust her," McCoy said matter-of-factly, not asking a question.

Kirk wanted to trust her. He needed to at some level. "She has a look in her eyes that I've seen before, Bones. I know a hostage when I see one."

"A hostage?"

"Of circumstance."

McCoy was silent for a moment, waiting, and finally he said, "You going to explain what you mean? I thought the reason I was here was for guidance. That's a damn hard thing to do if I don't know what the blazes you're talking about."

Nodding, Kirk took in a long breath and began. "Her assistant coming in and telling her she was already late for some meeting was a dodge. I've used it myself when someone's made an appointment with me and I didn't want the meeting to run too long."

"That could just mean she's busy—"

"It's not just that." Kirk shook his head and thrust his hands into the pockets of his jacket. "She knows there's more to elFizda's death than meets the eye. Did you see how quickly she wanted to leave after I mentioned her? And she's going to have the *Pesh-Manut* investigate."

"Yeah, what is that?"

"It's a conglomeration of intelligence organizations from several different Mestiko factions," Kirk said. "It's a mess. It was formed just after the disaster and it's too hard for all those once separate agendas to mesh well together. Raya herself has complained about them to me in letters."

"I didn't know you two kept in touch."

Kirk shot him a glance. "We do."

"So why did you lie and tell her I'd not seen Dr. Lon yet?"

Pulling a hand out from his pocket, Kirk wagged a finger at the doctor. "Ah, now I didn't say that. I said you had to meet with him for a bit."

McCoy grunted with disdain. "See, you're as much a politician as she is."

"Didn't you always tell me to be more diplomatic?"

"You're thinking of Spock."

"Must be."

"So," McCoy began as they found the entranceway to the underground part of the city where the docking platforms were protected. "Why did you tell her I needed to see Dr. Lon again?"

"Because I need more time. Dedir said everyone knew Alur. Maybe that means that Raya wouldn't, and maybe it means she would, but when I said the name there was a flicker of recognition."

"You know, you're basing a lot on the reactions of someone from a different planet and culture as you," McCoy said. "Who's to say you know her well enough to read her every twitch?"

They approached the location of their ship and Kirk said, "Who's to say I don't?"

McCoy was about to argue but Kirk used one hand to stop McCoy from moving forward and with his other hand he pulled the palm phaser out of his pocket.

"What's wrong?" McCoy whispered.

"Someone's on the ship," Kirk said, and indicated a light flashing on the keypad that gave one egress to the craft. "Internal sensors detecting motion inside." He motioned to McCoy. "Get your phaser out."

As he did so, McCoy protested. "Jim, I've not qualified with a weapon in over two years."

"Set it on wide angle stun," Kirk snapped as he cautiously approached the hatchway, "and try not to get me in front of the muzzle."

CHAPTER
7

"How do you know you don't just have mice?" McCoy asked in hushed tone.

Kirk ignored the question and punched a series of commands into the console next to his ship's hatch.

"We could lock him in and call the authorities," McCoy offered.

That wasn't what Kirk wanted, however. Every time someone approached him he learned more. While McCoy may not believe it, someone waiting on their ship, even if their goal was to try to kill them, was a good thing. Besides, Kirk wasn't sure which "authority" they should contact. "The port and customs authorities may be in on this up to their eyebrows," he said.

"They don't have eyebrows," McCoy muttered.

"Come on. Let's find out who's inside." Kirk tuned his phaser to a new setting, then hid it from view in the cup of his hand. "Bring out your weapon if you need to, but otherwise let's see what develops."

"What did you do?"

"I reset mine to the lowest nonstun setting." A stun would

knock someone unconscious. Kirk wanted whoever was inside to be talking.

With another code pressed into the key console, the hatch hissed open and Kirk took a tentative step in. "Keep yours on wide-stun and hope we're attacked by the broad side of a barn."

McCoy followed him. "That's not very damned funny."

The lights were on, and the main cabin looked clear. Kirk searched forward, looking in the head, then the galley, then finally the small bridge, which was where the two men were sitting, in the pilot's and copilot's seat.

"Gentlemen, you're on my ship."

Kirk didn't actually set foot on the bridge. He wasn't sure there wasn't a third hiding behind the lip of the doorway.

"You're Temple?" the man in the pilot's seat said. He wasn't Payav, but some non-descript thickish, human-looking off-worlder. For a moment Kirk was fooled—the man was bald and had some tattoo on his neck, but the eyebrows, eyelashes, and lack of a neck said he was not a native.

"That's him," the other of the two said. He was, in fact, a Payav, also pretty strong, but didn't have a great deal of tattooing. Kirk was able to see just how pale their skin was without the inked decorations, and it was ghostly. "He killed Dedir."

Dead? Kirk couldn't imagine Dedir killing himself, but he likely tried to run, and perhaps when the man named Alur found out, he killed Dedir. Or had it done.

"You're mistaken," Kirk said, and took a step back, which led McCoy to take a few steps back as well. Kirk wanted them out of the bridge and into the main cabin.

"You were seen on the surveillance record," the Payav said. "You assaulted Dedir."

Kirk didn't try to debate the assault. "I didn't kill him."

The oily human-looking one smirked. "You misunderstand," he said. "We saw what he told you. You pressured him into giving you our employer's name, and the result is that he was killed for his betrayal. That makes you responsible."

"Legally?" Kirk asked, allowing a bit of his anger to tinge his voice. "Maybe we should call the local constabulary and see if they agree."

Moving forward into the main cabin, the human pulled out a weapon—some type of disruptor Kirk was unfamiliar with but had a distinctly Klingon style—and aimed it at Kirk. In his periphery Kirk could see McCoy silently brace himself.

The Payav followed his human companion, and now all four of them were in the largest part of Kirk's small ship. The Payav had his own disruptor, and it looked to be specially made with a modified grip that accommodated his additional digit.

"The constabulary can't help you," the human said. "Unless you want to end up like Dedir, we suggest you leave this planet, and do not return."

Kirk nodded, more to himself than anyone else, as if weighing the offer. "You killed Dedir because he caused you trouble. Why not kill us?"

"Jim!" McCoy shifted his balance anxiously. "Let's try not to give them unnecessary suggestions."

"That is," the human said, "a very valid option . . . Jim."

"But you'd rather we just left." Kirk smiled politely.

"I would," the man admitted. "Two dead humans are harder to explain than just another dead Payav."

At this the Payav reacted, ever so slightly. Kirk saw his jawline twitch and his eyes narrow as he quickly glanced at his human comrade.

"That doesn't mean," the man continued, "that we can't choose that option should it become necessary."

"I don't suppose we could talk this over with your employer," Kirk offered.

The Payav spoke this time. "That is not an option at all."

Holding up his disruptor in a threatening manner, but not pointing it directly at Kirk, the human made the mistake Kirk was waiting for.

"Message received," Kirk said, and then without moving his hand from his side, he slipped his phaser into position and fired once—point blank—at the man's hand. In a flash an orange beam connected Kirk's weapon with the human's wrist. Skin sizzled and he dropped his disruptor with a yelp. When he saw the burning flesh wound that cut down to bone he screamed and covered it with his other hand and collapsed to his knees in shock.

"What the hell? What did you do? What did you do!" he hollered.

Pivoting quickly, Kirk now fully aimed his weapon at the Payav man who instantly tossed his disruptor to the deck.

"Best option yet," Kirk said, keeping his phaser trained on him as McCoy slipped around Kirk and pressed a hypo to the other man's arm.

With the hiss of a hypodermic, McCoy stopped the injured man from grunting in agony. He collapsed, sedated, but for all the Payav knew McCoy could have killed him where he lay.

"Now," Kirk said. "I want Alur's full name, and I want to know where I can find him."

The Payav twitched again, his expression one of emotional agony. They were an expressive people and this one in particular broadcast his fear easily. "I will be killed."

"I can try to protect you," Kirk told him. "But you have to answer my questions."

"I will not," the Payav insisted. "I will not. I will not."

Thumbing the control on his phaser back to stun, Kirk fired and the Payav collapsed back against the doorjamb to the bridge.

McCoy moved over to him for a moment, checked to make sure his head hadn't hit the bulkhead too hard, then collected the disruptor on which he'd collapsed.

He handed it to Kirk, who'd scooped up the other man's weapon as well. Kirk examined it, but found no markings, no serial numbers, no indication as to its origin. It certainly wasn't Payav technology.

"This is a Klingon design," Kirk said to McCoy, holding the weapon up. "I'd stake my braid on it, Bones."

"What do we do with them?"

"I'll contact Raya, have the *Pesh-Manut* arrest and question them." Kirk tapped the barrel of one of the disruptors on his palm a few times. "Get your tricorder and we'll send a detailed scan of these back to Starfleet. I want to know where this came from."

The next morning Kirk and McCoy had brunch with Raya and her *elor*, her grandmother. The meal was a mixture of local favorites—or what had become so since the disaster. There were foods from all over the Federation, and locally grown greens from the hydroponics fields of the Norrb. Some of it was delicious, and some Kirk found gag-inducing, but the company was more important than the fare.

"I'm glad we had the chance to see your *elor* again," Kirk told Raya, but looked and smiled at her grandmother. "You know, I don't think I even know your name, other than to call you Raya's *elor*."

A wise woman, with not just years behind her but much experience, she said, "Raya could not pronounce *elor* as a baby, and so I have been her Elee for so long within our family and to friends as well, that Elee I have been and Elee you shall call me."

"Elee it is," Kirk said, and tipped his juice glass toward her with honor.

"Oh, be careful of this one, child," Elee said to Raya, removing her spectacles and rolling them between the thumbs of her right hand. "He is a charmer."

Finishing his plate and pushing it away, McCoy covered it with his napkin. "Does that mean you've changed your mind about what the Federation has to offer?" He asked in jest but from her expression, Elee took the question very seriously.

"I imagine you ask this," she said slowly, returning her eyeglasses to her nose, "because of my comments upon my first meeting your captain."

Raya leaned toward her grandmother and whispered, "He's an admiral now, Elee."

She waved the comment away as if it were a morning gnat. "What have you. It's hardly the point." Slowly, choosing her words carefully, Elee continued. "I remember it well because I got quite a lecture on diplomacy that evening when my granddaughter and I returned to our quarters."

Kirk saw Elee flash a quick glare at Raya, then she looked back to McCoy, giving him her full attention.

"You know," she continued, "I was quite harsh, and I was perhaps speaking out of turn for such an event as that gathering was, but I believe in honesty."

"As do I," Kirk said, and looked at Raya, searching her eyes.

She looked away.

Elee drew Kirk's attention back when she took a deep breath as if to begin a long monologue.

"I understand what the Federation has done for us," Elee said. "I've seen the kindness of your hearts. But I also have seen the coldness of your bureaucracy. There were times in the aftermath of the Pulse that we wondered whether you were our saviors, or our tormenters. When a child is dying from radiation poisoning, and a shipment of medicine is overdue, for whatever reason . . . When your people's tongues swell with dehydration and clean water is on a ship that arrives too late for them, and so they've run to contaminated pools to quench their thirst . . ." She removed her glasses again and clasped her hands on her lap. "I am an old woman who should have died long before the millions of Payav I've seen pass from our world, including my own children. I simply ask that you forgive a woman, who has seen too much death and despair, her occasional sharp tongue. But you see, do you not, how it isn't a large leap for a very tired people to believe that their tormenters somehow planned the entire scenario for some malevolent purpose." She sighed and there was silence across the table. "In the darkest of times it is hard not to see the universe, even those who offer some light, as being as bleak as the moonless, overcast sky."

Next to her, a tear was welling in Raya's eye. Kirk reached out across the table, touched her hand, and she gave his a squeeze before pulling hers back to her lap.

"I fully understand," McCoy said, and Kirk thought there might have been the beginning of a lump in the old doctor's throat. "And anyone who doesn't is a fool."

McCoy and Elee went for a walk around the *Zamestaad* complex, which in the years since their first visit had grown to include many living complexes for hundreds of thousands of Payav. That left Kirk and Raya time to talk, and so they repaired to her office.

"By now," Kirk said, "you've read a report from your *Pesh-Manut* about who we found in my ship last night."

Raya nodded. "I'm afraid there wasn't much to learn. No more than you told the agents last night. Both men requested counsel when questioned, and refuse to speak until such an accommodation can be made."

"We have similar laws," Kirk said. "I suppose you don't have many active lawyers these days."

Behind Raya's desk were a number of framed pictures. Some of her and Elee, some with a young girl who looked vaguely familiar to Kirk, and one of what looked like a large family gathering under a large tree and had obviously been taken before the disaster.

"There are few lawyers, yes," she said, "and they are over-taxed. It will be some months before we can interrogate them again."

Kirk tried not to frown, but wasn't sure he managed it. "That's convenient."

"Pardon me? I don't understand."

"For them—it's convenient."

"I'm sure having to stay in custody is no convenience," Raya said, and it was the first flash of anger he'd really ever seen from her.

"So have the *Pesh-Manut* learned anything of value?"

"I don't believe so, no."

Increasingly, Kirk was both equal parts frustrated and disappointed with Raya. Before meeting with her and Elee, Kirk and McCoy had managed to do a little more legwork. They returned to the customs office that Kirk had visited the day before, and spoke to Izra orCina again. He knew well the name Alur, and confirmed it was the same man Dedir had been working for.

Even more disturbing was the fact that in their legwork Kirk and McCoy had no sign that the *Pesh-Manut* was investigating anything. They'd not talked to anyone about Dedir's death, they'd not talked to the docking crew about the men they had in custody who broke into Kirk's ship, and they certainly didn't want to step on the great Alur's toes.

"I think I can help you," Kirk said after a long moment of thought.

She looked at him across her paper-scattered desk. Maybe

McCoy was right and Kirk didn't know how to read her. Stranger things had happened. But if hunches were worth anything anymore, what he saw in her eyes was desperation.

"Can you?" she asked.

For what seemed like a minute and a half they just looked at each other, sizing each other up. When McCoy and Elee returned, Kirk stood and said his good-byes quickly and he and McCoy left the *Zamestaad* complex. He marched at such a quick pace that McCoy was beginning to fall behind.

"Jim, you're moving like a bat out of hell. Do you want to tell me where the fire is?" McCoy pleaded.

"She wants me to help her, Bones," Kirk said determinedly. "So that's what we're going to do."

CHAPTER
8

Alur orJada lived in a house, which was why once Kirk had his full name he wasn't hard to find. It was also why everyone did indeed know Alur, and why Raya's claims not to made no sense. And if it didn't make sense . . . it wasn't true.

For a Payav, Alur was rich. He had his own "estate," which consisted of an old machine shop that, like the customs office, had survived the disaster aftermath with little damage, and its two outbuildings, which had been damaged but strongly reconstructed. He had people living in the outbuildings—people who needed places for one reason or another—and such charity bought him a certain amount of goodwill with the populace.

There was no "sneaking" into Alur's compound, even at night. A tricorder reading confirmed a significant surveillance perimeter, and it was most decidedly not a technology native to Mestiko.

Given that Kirk's ship didn't have a transporter, the best way in was the direct way: through the front door.

As soon as he and McCoy approached, the door to the main house opened and four Payav swelled forward to confront them. Kirk wondered for a moment if he should have brought McCoy along for this one. It was his strong conjecture that Alur wasn't going to just kill Kirk and McCoy outright. There was little to be gained by that, and in fact had Alur thought he could get away with it, that would have been done already. Alur wasn't unintelligent—one didn't build what he obviously had by making stupid mistakes.

The lead Payav came forward as the others surrounded Kirk and McCoy on all sides, weapons similar to the Klingon-design trained on them.

"I'm here to see Alur orJada," Kirk said.

"We know why you're here," the first Payav said and motioned to the one closes to Kirk. "Check him for weapons."

Before the man could get close enough, another man stepped into the doorway of the building and ordered him to stop. "He's not here to kill me, Zizandil. Let them pass untouched." He was a somewhat older Payav man—it was always a bit hard to tell without the receding or graying hair that more easily placed a human's age—who was well dressed in a thick robe of what was likely expensive material.

He ushered his men to bring Kirk and McCoy into the building, which was obviously a very large room, not brightly lit, that had been sectioned into smaller areas. An old wooden desk was in one corner, with three chairs in front of it, and a padded wooden bench beyond. Wood meant rich on Mestiko, a now treeless planet that had adored them.

The room was far less ornate than Kirk would have thought, and he was beginning to wonder if a Spartan design sensibility had less to do with the Pulse aftermath and more to do with a certain Payav tradition.

With dramatic flourish, Alur adjusted his robes so he could sit easily in his desk chair, and he motioned for Kirk and McCoy to take seats in front of him. The chair sat lower than Alur's, Kirk noticed; that little tactic was perhaps a universal standard.

"Take your men, Zizandil," Alur told his guard. "I will speak with Admiral Kirk alone."

As the other Payav men left, McCoy grumbled under his breath. "Apparently I'm not even here."

"My apology, Dr. McCoy," Alur said, and finally Kirk noticed he was not speaking his own language but a perfectly unaccented Federation Standard. "I did not mean to slight you. I just assumed," he leveled his gaze directly at Kirk, "that it was the admiral and I who had the more pressing business. I understood you to be on Mestiko more as a favor to him, and of course to visit Dr. Lon."

"You seem to know a lot about us," McCoy said.

That he did confirmed much about Alur. "If Nawaz Mazari thought he had his finger on the pulse of Indalo Station," Kirk said admiringly, "he had nothing on you."

Alur grasped the bridge of his nose near his eyes with the two thumbs of his left hand and with the other hand rubbed his temple. "Ah, Nawaz. A bit lost, really. Good for what he does, but a bad judge of character in terms of whom he chooses to employ. I'm afraid I've had to deal with some of his bumbling associates."

What did that mean? Curly and some of the others were dead for not having killed Kirk and McCoy? Probably. That was where Alur would have wanted them killed—off Mestiko, and away from where suspicion might fall on him.

"Is that supposed to frighten me?" Kirk asked.

"No, no," Alur gestured with one hand, waving off the notion. "After last night I didn't believe you could be frightened off. And to be honest I should have realized it earlier, but it wasn't until yesterday that I learned 'Mr. Temple' was Admiral Kirk."

"And what gave that away?" McCoy asked.

Alur smiled, and for someone who didn't want to be threatening he was showing a lot of teeth.

"Bones," Kirk said to McCoy, but kept his eyes fixed on Alur, "I'd guess there's very little that happens on Mestiko, especially in the *Zamestaad*, that Mr. orJada here doesn't know about."

Bowing his head slightly, as if flattered, Alur poured himself a glass of something from a pitcher that sat on the corner of his desk and offered some to his guests, who declined. "Admiral Kirk is not incorrect. Which is why I am neither trying to threaten you, nor do I feel threatened by you, which is—forgive me if I assume too much—what you'd like."

"I'm not sure it's us you should be afraid of," McCoy said.

"If not you, then . . ."

"Not the *Pesh-Manut*," Kirk offered. "I'd guess there are as many of them in his pocket, Bones, as he has pockets."

Alur chuckled. "I am unfamiliar with the idiom but I think it clear enough." He leaned forward and in the soft lighting his features grew harsh angles. "Please do not think me arrogant when I tell you that I do not merely have the pulse of Mestiko—I am her heart."

Again Alur smiled and because Kirk realized he rarely saw a Payav's teeth, even when they spoke, it was the most jarring thing about him.

"You will not find what you're looking for here, Admiral. While it may have been suggested to you before that it was within your best interests to leave Mestiko, let me put it in terms you will understand. There is no benefit to you remaining on this planet. You have no starship in orbit, and the *Zamestaad* will bristle should one appear." Alur leaned back in his seat as if he'd created something beautiful and wanted to take it in from a distance. "In fact, if anything were going to push the people to rekindle a relationship with the Klingon Empire, a useless show of Federation force might be just the thing to do so."

Alur was right, on many levels. Not just about the Federation deploying a starship to Mestiko, but about Kirk not having one at his disposal. Not just *a* starship, but *his* starship. And all the people who went with her. Kirk wondered how different this mission might have been had he been commanding the *Enterprise* the last two weeks, or the last two years. Might he have meandered less across Indalo and Mestiko had Spock and Scotty been added to his counsel?

Kirk mentally shook off the doubt. This was neither the time nor the place for it. He could wallow in regret later, and second-guess himself on the way home. For now he had to push forward.

"You're rich on the backs of your own people," Kirk charged. "Doesn't that bother you?"

Alur shrugged. "My prices are very fair, actually. And whatever I might make is poured back into the community. A strong Mestiko is . . . well, a strong Mestiko is in everyone's best interests. You won't suggest that the Federation doesn't want us to be strong and independent, do you?"

"Strong with Klingon backing?"

"If you could prove that, we wouldn't be talking. You'd have brought it to the *Zamestaad* and—" Alur paused as if in thought, then acted as if he'd suddenly remembered an important fact. "Oh, but so many members of the *Zamestaad* might be implicated that it would be difficult for the body to recover. That would be sad. Careers would be destroyed, the people's trust betrayed. I can't imagine what would be more destructive to Mestiko, can you?" He shrugged. "But again, if you could prove what you believe . . ."

"You're a real son of a bitch, aren't you?" McCoy snapped. "You'd doom your people for your own aggrandizement."

There was quite a difference between having Spock along and having McCoy speak his mind, Kirk thought, and allowed himself the slightest smirk, not just at the doctor's righteous indignation, but his willingness to be even more blunt than Kirk.

"This isn't all for me, Dr. McCoy," Alur said, his tone still mild. "I'm more *using* the Klingons than working for them. You see, there are other causes on this planet than those the Federation is concerned with. And—"

"And," Kirk interrupted, Alur's simple allusion to "other causes" making many puzzle pieces fall into place, "the weapons parts being delivered aren't for you."

That got Alur's attention and he turned away from McCoy.

"The parts come to you, and you manufacture the weapons, but they go to a rival Payav faction of your choice. For later insurrection. It's not about the strength of Mestiko," Kirk said, eyes narrowed on Alur. "It's about the strength of . . . who?"

Alur was silent, and Kirk knew he was on to something.

"I think I see it." Kirk stood now and leaned down, his palms flat across the desk. "If it's found out that offworlders—Dinpayav—are stocking antagonistic Payav factions with weapons, the Klingons have their tracks covered with your help. The Payav will only know that various Dinpayav are to blame and . . ." Another piece fell into place and Kirk wished he'd seen the big picture sooner. "A separatist faction? Mestiko for Payav and no one else? Except for you, who can supply them with the help of the Klingons?"

"You know nothing," Alur said with a sneer.

"I know you're a fool," Kirk barked. "If the Federation and other Dinpayav are asked to leave Mestiko, we will. All it will take is a formal request from the *Zamestaad*. And then you think that with your Klingon-supplied weapons you and yours can take control of this planet. But you won't. Once the Federation is gone the Klingons will come in full force. And then what will you be? Head slave in the master's house?"

Alur was silent. He simply stared at Kirk, and McCoy was doing the same.

"You're making a mistake, Alur," Kirk said. "You think you'll survive this plan, but you'll be the first to die once it's known the weapons are from offworld." He pointed right at Alur's chest, driving his finger forward with every word. "You're the biggest link to the Klingons' involvement. You're the one they'd need to make disappear."

Kirk's muscles taut with energy, as if bracing himself for Alur to rise and strike him, ached with inaction. If Alur didn't want to hit him, he wanted to hit Alur.

McCoy sat, waiting, looking between the two other men. Silence draped the room until finally Alur found his composure and he slowly leaned forward toward Kirk as he pushed himself from his seat.

"I suppose," Alur began slowly, "it would be easier to explain one dead Starfleet officer," he nodded to McCoy apologetically, "and his doctor . . . than it would to deal with the exposure of your allegations."

Kirk was almost sure he heard McCoy take an audible gulp. Sometimes a doctor who wore his feelings on his sleeve wasn't the best thing when attempting bravado. "That's great, Jim. You convinced him to kill us. Anyone else you want dead you can talk him into taking care of?"

Alur glanced at McCoy for a moment, and when he

glanced back Kirk had his phaser out and aimed just under Alur's chin.

Kirk's free hand grasped Alur's arm through his robes. "I'm not so easy to kill," Kirk said. "Better men than you have tried."

Alur was looking at the phaser only now. It was likely he wasn't often personally threatened because Kirk could feel the Payav's body tense just through his arm.

"Indeed?" he croaked out softly.

"Open the door," Kirk ordered McCoy, and noticed the doctor now had his phaser out as well. It wasn't hard, even for a doctor, to slip into Starfleet training in times like this.

The door opened, Kirk wrenched Alur forward and in front of him, pressing the muzzle of his phaser into the small of the Payav's back. "You'll see us to safety," Kirk told him, and started him marching out the door.

McCoy brought up the rear, looking back toward the building as they all walked slowly away. When the first of Alur's guards appeared, McCoy called out to Kirk in the most military way the doctor could muster.

"Jim, his thugs are on the move at twelve o'clock."

Kirk twisted around so Alur was a shield to them. "I'm at twelve o'clock, Doctor," Kirk said. "You're at six."

"You want this blasted information or not?" McCoy bellowed. "I'm not even in Starfleet anymore."

Kirk nodded and quickened their pace but Alur was older than he looked—or could have been purposely slowing them down—and wouldn't speed up much.

"They're running for us now," McCoy said, and was far less panicked than Kirk might have thought.

"Is your phaser set the same as yesterday?" Kirk asked.

"It should be."

It better be, Kirk thought. "Stand by—on my mark." Kirk waited until Alur's men were about a meter back, just far enough and just close enough. He stopped, and shoved Alur head-on into his own guards so they almost stumbled over him.

"Fire," Kirk ordered and McCoy quickly thumbed the phaser's trigger.

A green flash washed forward, bathing the Payav in light. They buckled, falling on one another, caught in the wide-beamed stun.

Kirk nodded to himself and grabbed McCoy's arm. "Wide stuns don't last long," Kirk told him. "We have to move."

Alur and his men were left, collapsed at the gateway to the house of Mestiko's richest man.

CHAPTER
9

The capital city was more confusing at night than when light cascaded through the pressurized dome. With the help of a few good-hearted Payav—who didn't know why Kirk and McCoy were running but also didn't seem to care—they made their way back to the *Zamestaad* by daybreak.

Maybe it was paranoia, but along the way there had been several Payav they avoided. Men and women talking into small ear-worn communicators. Possibly they were *Pesh-Manut,* and possibly they were Alur's own agents—but to be honest, Kirk wasn't sure what the difference would have been. That several normal Payav could be woken from their beds in the middle of the night to show Kirk and McCoy the underground passages that led to the city center said much about these people. As much *for* them as Alur's treachery said *against* them. It really was no surprise— people everywhere could be kind or cold depending on their personal stories and manners—but it was heartening nevertheless.

Along the way McCoy couldn't help but treat a few Payav for vitamin deficiencies and they assumed he was part of the

"Doctors without Borders" organization that had visited Mestiko frequently.

When Kirk and McCoy found Raya in her personal chambers, she was already awake, already dressed, and ushered them both quickly into the central room that seemed to serve as kitchen, dining room, and sitting room, and not with much space for any of it.

"Please," she implored, "keep your voices low. My *elor* is still sleeping, as is Blee's husband in their bedroom." She motioned for them to sit.

Kirk noted the contrast between the chosen planetary leader, the *Jo'Zamestaad*, and Alur or Jada. Both could claim to be the most powerful Payav on Mestiko. One lived in relative wealth and comfort, with an entire building to himself. The other lived with her grandmother, her assistant, and her assistant's husband, in what would be considered—back on Earth—a small efficiency apartment.

Looking shaken, and not just because she was surprised to see Kirk and McCoy this early and in her home, Raya moved back and forth, pacing nervously, unwilling or unable to sit.

"We've talked with Alur," Kirk said, and Raya instantly began shaking her head back and forth in a lolling motion that could have been—well, Kirk didn't know what it meant. She looked almost dizzy.

"Raya?" McCoy rose and helped her into a chair opposite Kirk. He took out his medical tricorder, rolled a scan around in front of her and looked up to Kirk with a shrug.

"Alur is dead," she said suddenly. "I just got word."

"Dead how?" Kirk asked, and found he'd moved to the edge of his seat.

Raya lolled her head about again. "Murdered. His home destroyed." Her voice was riddled with a fear Kirk had never heard from her. It was disconcerting. Raya was a strong leader, a person of incredible will and determination. But his first inclination when he met with her two days ago was correct: she was captive to a set of circumstances and didn't know how to escape.

"Raya," Kirk said softly. "How much did you know?"

She pulled in a deep breath. Then another. Then a third.

Finally, she began, her decision to tell it all giving her a rush of vocal strength. "I—Alur, even before the Pulse, had been an entrepreneur in my district. He is—was—an important man and a generous man to the city and the people. After the disaster he helped as much as any community leader, perhaps more, to help Mestiko recover. He embraced the new ways and technology of the Dinpayav who offered Mestiko help."

So far, Kirk thought, Raya was selling him on how wonderful Alur was, which was set up for how she'd been fooled by him, and it didn't ring true. He prodded her: "How long have you known he was working for the Klingons?"

Her eyes met his, and the distrust they'd both recently demonstrated to each other melted away. "I became aware that Alur was receiving much of his inexpensive goods from Klingon-dominated areas some eighteen months ago," she said evenly, the words gathering individually on her lips, then falling sadly. "I had used Alur for my own ends, previous to his Klingon association. He supplied my constituents with goods they needed to survive, and I supplied him political cover and connections in exchange."

"But when you learned he was in bed with the Klingons?" Kirk asked, and her nose wrinkled at what in the Payav language must have been an odd metaphor.

"When I became aware . . . of that," she began again slowly, "Alur explained that we had been also," she shrugged and her hands drew up in confusion, "in bed together?"

"It's a saying," McCoy explained. "Politics makes strange bedfellows—strange agreements between people with different agendas."

Raya nodded and continued. "I believed we had the same agenda at first."

"And by the time you realized differently," Kirk said, "you were in over your head."

This metaphor she understood. "Yes. If I exposed Alur I was exposing myself and all the contacts in the *Zamestaad* that I had given him." She sighed. "I'd have not ruined only his standing but my own and those of my political—" Raya gasped, noticing that Elee had stepped into the room.

Kirk turned to see she was in the doorway between the sitting room and her bedroom, wearing a simple dressing gown and an expression of extreme disappointment. "Continue, child," she said.

With another slow intake of breath, Raya did. "I convinced myself that doing so—revealing Alur's . . . and *my* involvement—would also cut off a vital supply of much-needed goods for our people." Locked in a shared gaze that took in both Kirk and Elee behind him, Raya's voice cracked a bit now. "I deluded myself. And I also feared Alur's threats if I revealed what I knew." Looking away, she whispered more to herself than the others, "But I duped myself into believing I did it more for the greater good."

"Greater good," Elee repeated, and she sounded bitter. Two words wielded with such frequency both for good and for ill.

"I do not know what to do," Raya admitted and looked to her *elor* for guidance.

"Be your mother's daughter," Elee whispered. "You must."

Whatever that meant to Raya, it seemed to bolster her. She sat a little straighter, breathed a touch easier, and nodded to some internal decision.

"The *Pesh-Manut* are useless to protect me," she said, looking squarely at Kirk. "I am not a military leader. I have no personal security. I believe if the Klingon agents we both suspect killed Alur and elFizda are aware of my involvement, they will seek to end my life as well."

"That sounds just about right," Kirk said gravely.

"I need your protection, James," she said, and took his hand, her thumbs squeezing him more tightly than he expected. "I must reveal to the public, to the full *Zamestaad*, the extent of this ignominy. I cannot prove conclusively Alur's involvement with the Klingons, and that may actually save my career, but my career is less important than ongoing Klingon intrusion into Payav affairs."

"You can prove it," Kirk told her, and pulled his hand from her grip.

She looked at him with perplexity as he wrenched a bracelet from his left wrist and placed it in her hands.

Raya looked at it, seeing it was obviously more mechanism

than adornment, and she held it up between the thumbs of her right hand. "I do not understand."

· "It's a communicator, as well as a recorder. Transcribed for proof, on it is my conversation with Alur. He's very clear about his relationship with the Klingons, and his threats to the politicians—none mentioned by name—whom he could implicate." Kirk gestured to the communicator. "I'm assuming your people can verify his voice. It should be all the proof you need."

Studying first the device, as if it were a magical contrivance, and then Kirk's face, Raya nodded, stunned at the speed of events.

"This will mean political chaos," she said sadly. "I've brought political chaos to my people."

Kirk grabbed her shoulders and lifted her to her feet. "Any political bedlam is better than civil war," he told her.

"Or any war," McCoy said.

EPILOGUE

Kirk and McCoy stayed with Raya another week and on their voyage back to Earth Kirk went over her speech to the *Zamestaad* again and again. He was very proud of her. How often did politicians completely own up to their mistakes and take the political fallout solely on their shoulders?

The speech did exactly as expected, and the storm of political pandemonium would certainly cause her star to fall a bit. But power wasn't everything, and at least the *Zamestaad* agreed to allow an intermediary body to monitor shipments to Mestiko as well as trace previous consignments in the hopes of collecting any Klingon weaponry already distributed. Those councillors in the *Zamestaad* who protested were targeting themselves as members of groups who'd received such weapons, and would likely be the first under investigation.

"You think she'll be okay?" McCoy asked as he and Kirk played a round of cribbage and put the ship on autopilot through open space.

"Raya?" Kirk looked up from behind his cards. "She's a strong woman. She'll bounce back."

"'Some are born great, some achieve greatness, and others have greatness thrust upon them,'" McCoy said.

Kirk nodded. "In her case I think greatness collapsed in on her. But since the Payav authorities looked *seriously* for any remnants of Klingon agents, it's likely they removed themselves from the planet as soon as Raya's speech hit the newsconnects." Kirk played his cards and then counted. "Did I tell you I asked Raya to find Izra orCina a job? She said she would."

McCoy looked at Kirk sideways, studying the man as he pegged his points. "How is it you're able to gloat without saying anything? Just by sitting there."

Innocently, Kirk looked at the cribbage board and then up to McCoy. "I'm four points ahead. Who's gloating?"

"Not about the game, about your hunch. You were right— about the shipments, about the Klingons, about everything."

Kirk smiled and shuffled the cards. "Yeah, I noticed that."

"How long are you going to be this insufferable?" McCoy asked.

"How long have you got?"

Unable to keep from chuckling, McCoy refilled both their glasses with some Payav liquor he procured before they left Mestiko.

Kirk took a drink, sucked his teeth dry, and gestured for McCoy to refill his glass again. "You sorry I dragged you along for this?" Kirk asked him.

McCoy shrugged. "Someone had to save your ass. How could I leave you all alone on a hostile planet?"

This time having just short sips of a liquor Kirk could almost describe as both fruity and buttery at the same time, the admiral contemplated the confused planet and people of Mestiko. "Not that hostile, really. All things considered."

"You ever find out what '*a'sloointa Dinpayav*' meant?"

For the first time in a long while, Jim Kirk actually laughed. "I made the mistake of asking Raya," he said.

McCoy leaned forward, his brows arched with curiosity. "Well?"

"Dinpayav you know," Kirk said tauntingly.

"Yeah, non-Payav. Got that."

"It means, Raya told me with much embarrassment," Kirk chuckled and took another sip of his thick drink, "no-necked."

"Come again?" McCoy felt his neck. "I have a neck."

"Not for a Payav," Kirk said. "And it would seem it's the highest insult."

Thinking for a minute, McCoy finally nodded his head and chuckled. "You know what? I think I like it. I might use it on Nogura next time I see him."

"Don't start," Kirk admonished, and felt the drink pulling at him a bit, slowing him.

"Will you at least admit that this is where you belong?" McCoy asked. "Out here, and not behind a desk?"

"If not for the papers that pushed across my desk, I'd never have known anything was going on with the Klingons and Mestiko," Kirk said. "That must count for something." He took another slug of the drink.

"You convincing me, or yourself?" McCoy asked pointedly.

Kirk didn't reply. He dealt the cards, and motioned to McCoy that it was his crib. The truth was, he was trying to convince both himself and McCoy. There was a lot of future left for Kirk—he was yet a young man. Could he picture himself behind a desk for the next thirty or forty years, an admiral's braid on his sleeve? Maybe. Could he picture himself settling down and having a family? There was that side to him too. Did he still yearn to be in that center seat, on that starship, pushing past the frontier? Yes. Every moment of every day.

"What admiral takes a step back to captain?" Kirk said aloud.

McCoy was ready with an answer. "Since when do you wait for a precedent to act?"

Looking through the narrow doorway that led to the bridge, Kirk focused on the viewscreen above the navigation console. In the distance, stars pushed away as if spreading for his ship to pass.

This didn't feel like his ship; it still felt like Sam's. It probably always would.

Jim Kirk's ship was neither as small, nor available.

His ship was named *Enterprise*.

2274–2283

THE DARKNESS DROPS AGAIN

Christopher L. Bennett

PART ONE

**Stardate 7508.6
(January 2274)**

ON THE AIR

"Good midday, and welcome to *Mestiko This Week*. I'm Hanni orLitza. Before much longer, it will have been a dozen years—a dozen Mestiko years, I should say for the benefit of our nonnative viewers—since the Pulse ravaged our planet. For those years, we have looked outside our domes and tunnels to see a surface barren of life. Now, the *Zamestaad* and the Federation are about to institute a program that they claim will begin the gradual process of restoring the surface to habitability. Will this program be successful? Is it too slow a response to Mestiko's needs? Or is it, as many claim, merely another step in an insidious agenda to transform Mestiko into an alien colony, or worse?"

Hanni turned to face the second camera, maintaining his earnest expression but making sure his pose still afforded a good view of the elaborate tattoos on his left cheek and neck, which the director considered more photogenic than the ones on his right. "Joining me to discuss these questions today are: Blee elTorno, former councillor and current chief of staff to the *Jo'Zamestaad*." The on-air monitor cut to a close-up of Blee, a dainty, soft-featured woman who was unusually young for a person of her status. "Nal Kotyar, leader of the Payavist Inward Party." Kotyar was a tall, lean Tazokkan woman, her tattoos basic and simple, serving the traditional function of denoting caste and family rather than the modern, purely decorative use that the Tazokkans scorned. If not for that and her pinched, haughty expression, she would have been quite a beauty. "Dr. Marat Lon, the Federation's chief scientific advisor to the *Zamestaad*." Dr. Lon was a lean, ascetic-featured human, yellow-pink of skin and covered in fur over much of his body, though his neck was not quite as stubby as most humans' and his head was less fur-covered than it had been several years ago. "And Odra maVolan, spokesman for the mar-Atyya spiritual movement." Like the human, maVolan was entirely devoid of tattoos, his faith considering them impure. But with no body hair to compensate, his skin seemed austere and naked, like a blank parchment. His eyes were whitish as well; he had been blinded by ultraviolet exposure following the Pulse and had refused offworld treatment to cure it.

"Thank you, Hanni," maVolan interposed, taking his introduction as an invitation to speak. "I'd like to begin by protesting the use of the Gelta term *Mestiko* for our world, which should be more rightly called hur-Atyya."

"Uhh, thank you for pointing that out, sir. Of course, in mar-Atyya belief, our world is hur-Atyya, the Home touched by God. And of course, this network intends no slight to the linguistic or religious preferences of any of our world's diverse peoples. For clarity's sake, however—"

Kotyar interrupted. "Then why continue using a name in the language of the Gelta? Those neckless wonders are all but extinct now. And it serves them right for conspiring with the Dinpayav to keep the Pulse secret from us."

"That's absurd!" Dr. Lon exclaimed. "It was the Gelta government's own choice to keep the secret, at a time when the Federation was preparing to initiate first-contact proceedings. We simply respected their—"

"Please, Dr. Lon," Hanni said, reasserting himself. "You'll each get a chance to speak. Actually, I'm glad you brought that up, Nal, because I'd like to begin with a recap of the events of the past twelveyear. As you say, it began when Gelta scientists discovered a rogue pulsar, now popularly called the Scourer, entering our star system." The screen showed a graphical representation of the Scourer and its trajectory through the Hertex system. "Many astronomers had suspected the presence of a massive body due to the changes they had begun to detect in the orbits of the outer planets, but only the Gelta's deep-space telescopes were in the right position to detect the narrow cones of deadly radiation that sprayed out from this spinning orb.

"At the time, a Federation precontact team was clandestinely monitoring our world—"

"Spying, you mean," said Kotyar.

"—and communicating with the Gelta scientists. Opinions remain divided on what role the offworlders played in the decision to keep the discovery secret from the people."

"What?" It was Lon again. "There's no doubt what happened. The whole thing is thoroughly documented in the contact team's records, all of which have been public for years."

Kotyar scoffed. "As if that were an unbiased source."

Hanni tried to continue. "While Mestiko—or hur-Atyya, if you prefer—remained in the dark, the Federation debated what action, if any, it should take. Eventually an experimental array of force-field satellites was deployed to shield Mestiko from the pulsar's radiation, but the Federation's delay in dealing with the crisis meant that the shield was deployed with mere hours to spare."

"Now, that's not right," Lon said. "Mestiko was in no danger until the emission cones intersected it, so there was no point in acting any—"

"Dr. Lon, please. You'll be given a chance to rebut."

"Typical," Kotyar said. "You've been letting this alien monopolize the discussion already, and now you're promising him more time while the rest of us have hardly gotten a word in."

"I assure you, everyone will be given an equal chance."

"Then why are you only echoing the Dinpayav party line about the heroic Kirk of Starfleet saving us from the Pulse?

What about the large numbers of Payav who sincerely believe that the Federation set the Scourer on us in the first place in order to soften us up for conquest?"

"So it is written," maVolan intoned. "The mar-Tunyor were sent to bring about the Cleansing and test the resolve of the faithful. The Scouring Fire was their instrument."

Inevitably, Lon interrupted again. "That's insane! Federation technology is nowhere near capable of moving masses of that size."

"So you say."

"Dr. Lon, please, let's avoid name-calling here."

But Lon talked over Hanni. "That's why we had to use a shield in the first place. There was no chance of diverting the pulsar."

Kotyar, in turn, talked over most of Lon's second sentence. "A shield that didn't work."

"If it hadn't worked, none of you would be alive right now. It was an experimental technology operating in an intensely irradiated environment—it's amazing it worked as well as it did."

Blee elTorno spoke for the first time. "With respect, Doctor, that's easy to say if you didn't live through the Pulse, or its aftermath. Yes, we are fortunate to be alive and we are grateful to the Federation for its role in that. But in no way can the word *well* be used for anything we endured in the Pulse."

"Indeed," Hanni said, taking quick advantage of the opening to get back on course. "The consequences of the Pulse were truly devastating. More than a billion dead in the Pulse or the ferocious storms immediately following it. More dying ever since due to famine, lack of medicine, violence, and suicides. Our planet rendered barren, our people huddled underground. Even the heavens themselves have been rearranged. Our moons have shifted in their orbits, with Varnex growing and shrinking in the sky with each cycle and Kifau pulled out of orbit altogether to become an independent planetoid. Mestiko's own orbit is changed, bringing more extreme seasons.

"And our relationship with the worlds beyond our star system is forever changed as well. Now we have been thrust into a community of alien worlds whose power and advancement dwarf our own, dependent on them for our very survival . . . and sometimes at the mercy of their factional disputes. It was two years before the Federation brought us satellites to clear the toxic smog from our air, and almost immediately those satellites became weapons in a territorial clash between them and the Klingon Empire, hurtled from the sky to bombard refugees and orphans. Councillor Traal, leader of the Norrb nation and one of the leading forces behind Payav survival in those early years, gave his life to bring an end to this conflict."

Lon had been struggling to restrain himself, but only until Hanni took a breath. "We didn't bring the aerostats—the satellites, as you call them—earlier because our initial priority was arranging basic shelter and survival. Since then, they have successfully purged the nitrogen oxides from your atmosphere and have been reconfigured for ozone production."

"This is mar-Tunyor propaganda," maVolan said. "Our world is the holy abode of life, and its regeneration has come despite the alien elements."

"Yes, we'll be addressing that issue shortly," Hanni told him. "Certainly, our relationship with alien races has been a source of controversy. For nearly a twelveyear, we have depended on their technology and resources for our sustenance, and for the hope of our world being made habitable again. And yet many complain that the offworld powers act more for their own interests than ours. They say not enough has been done to improve living conditions, to provide medicines for the diseases that ravage our close-packed populations. Many feel the *Zamestaad* itself is an instrument of alien policy, more interested in appeasing powerful interstellar states than tending to the needs of Mestiko."

"Don't downplay it like the media always do," Kotyar spat. "Let's not forget that Raya elMora herself was implicated in the conspiracy to arm insurrectionist factions with alien weaponry."

"Excuse me," Blee interposed. "*Jo'Zamestaad* Raya had no awareness at first that Alur orJada was smuggling Klingon weapons to Mestiko—specifically, to militant Payavist factions that to this day are allied with the Inward Party and the mar-Atyya. Once she learned of this and was provided with proof by Admiral Kirk, she herself came forward—"

"*Former* Admiral Kirk," Kotyar interrupted. "He's been demoted. Even his own masters must think his performance was inadequate."

"He took that demotion willingly so he could command his ship against V'Ger," Lon said.

"Yes, and isn't that interesting?" Kotyar shot back. "The Federation had only three days' notice of this so-called V'Ger and were able to save their homeworld without a single life lost. Yet they had the better part of a year's notice of the Pulse and allowed half our population to die! That proves the lie behind their claims that they wish to help us."

"We've done nothing *but* help you! The Federation has devoted massive resources to the restoration of Mestiko. We've spent years gearing up for the major terraforming effort we're about to undertake, tasked dozens of ships to ferry personnel and materials here. That's part of the reason Earth was so underdefended when V'Ger came."

"Oh, so now it's our fault you almost lost your homeworld? Supposedly."

"The point is, we were willing to put our own world at risk to help yours. The least you could do is show some gratitude."

Kotyar thrust out a bony finger. "There it is! That Dinpayav arrogance, this insistence that we should be down on our knees thanking you for the meager scraps of food and medicine you give us."

"I'm sure he didn't mean that," Blee told her. "Let's remember all Dr. Lon himself has done to restore our atmosphere."

"And of course, the *Jo'Zamestaad*'s puppet, the puppet's puppet, does her best to underline the Dinpayav doctrine of infallibility. Every time the good people of Mestiko dare to challenge the alien party line, the government and the media remind us of how they've saved us from annihilation, and we're not allowed to question their sincerity for fear of seeming to trivialize the disaster. Well, I'll tell you, no one has profited as much from the Pulse as the Dinpayav have. Except maybe for Raya elMora and her cronies, who seized power only by virtue of being the ones who were left, and who've used the disaster to justify trampling our national sovereignty."

"Every nation in the world was devastated," Blee countered. "We have to cooperate to survive. The *Zamestaad* simply facilitates that cooperation."

"Facilitates the mar-Tunyor agenda, you mean," maVolan said. "Aids them in keeping us weak and starving as they pursue their mad experiments to contaminate our blessed abode with the unclean spawn of other spheres."

"Oh, please," the human cried, "you'd have to be mad to believe that!"

"Dr. Lon," Hanni said, "I've warned you about name-calling."

Lon stared. "What about calling aliens 'mar-Tunyor'? It means 'touched by evil'! Doesn't that count as name-calling?"

"We're not in the business of censoring religious expression here, Doctor."

"Then why," Kotyar countered, "do you insist on only reporting the Dinpayav ecological dogma in your broadcasts? The majority of Payav believe that our biosphere is regenerating on its own, that these alien plants and animals being introduced are only going to suppress its recovery."

"Pure superstition," Lon said. "Most indigenous species have been driven nearly or completely extinct. Oxygen levels are falling because there isn't enough plant life left. *Nothing* is going to recover without help. Now, the plants we're seeding were developed for terraforming my homeworld, Mars. They grow rapidly and thrive in cold conditions, their dark color absorbs heat and accelerates the melting of permafrost, and they're powerhouses of oxygen produc—"

"Their very existence is a desecration," maVolan declared. "The people of hur-Atyya will not tolerate their presence in our holy abode. Nor will they tolerate a regime that allows free rein to the mar-Tunyor desecrators."

"Our administration has done everything it could," Blee said, "to respect the wishes of the people and ensure that the restoration effort remains Mestiko-oriented. We've pushed to guarantee that Payav are involved in as many key positions as possible and to ensure that as many native life-forms as possible are preserved and incorporated into the new biosphere."

Kotyar turned up her nose. "Symbolism. Nothing but a sop to the people."

"Hardly," Lon said. "It's a politically motivated, scientifically unsound policy that has served only to delay our work."

"Your work to turn our world into another Earth!"

"It's not like that! If you'll just let me—"

"I'm sorry," Hanni said, "but we're out of time for this segment. When we return, we'll examine viewer response to our poll question: Is the alien terraforming plan the answer to restoring our world, or should Mestiko be allowed to recover on its own? You may log your response during the break, if you haven't done so already. The results should be illuminating."

"No, they won't!" Lon cried. "You can't illuminate matters of scientific fact with opinion polls! Reality isn't decided by majority rule!"

But the break had already begun, Lon's microphone was off, and no one heard him outside the studio—while the people inside mostly ignored him. Hanni sighed in relief, glad for a respite from dealing with this contentious bunch. Still, the director looked pleased. It had no doubt been a most entertaining spectacle.

U.S.S. ENTERPRISE

James Kirk leaned back in his seat as the playback of *Mestiko This Week* faded from the briefing-room monitor. He didn't have to wait long for Leonard McCoy to make his opinion heard. "That's what's passing for news on Mestiko these days? What was that, an interview or a wrestling match?"

"It may seem like a travesty," Theena elMadej told him, "but it reflects the growing mood of the populace." Kirk recalled first meeting Theena a little more than six years ago during his second visit to Mestiko. She had been a bright, cheerful girl whom Raya elMora, the leader of Mestiko's global council, had taken under her wing. Apparently, she'd been older than Kirk had thought, or perhaps Payav matured quickly, for now she had developed into a striking, elegant young woman of college age. She was officially offworld as part of her astrophysics studies yet had contacted Kirk to relay a message that Raya couldn't send through formal channels. "Many Payav are frustrated that things are taking so long to get better. They're eager for someone to blame, and the *Zamestaad* and the Federation are the obvious targets."

"So naturally," Kirk said, "it's the traditionalists and Mestiko-firsters they turn to as an alternative."

"And as you saw, the press is so afraid of being accused of pro-alien bias that it errs too far in the other direction, giving as much weight to ideological and inflammatory rhetoric as to hard physical evidence."

"Most illogical," Spock said from behind steepled fingers. Like Kirk, he wore the standard blue-gray duty uniform but was set apart by the high collar of the undershirt he wore beneath it (having not yet readjusted to the ship's cooler temperatures after nearly three years on Vulcan). "Left to its own devices, Mestiko's atmosphere would have taken centuries to recover fully, its biosphere tens or hundreds of millennia to regain significant biodiversity. The fact that most Payav alive today are expected to be able to resume surface habitation within their lifetimes is remarkable."

This brought a sidelong glare from McCoy, who, unlike the others, was clad informally in a white short-sleeved medical tunic. "And here I thought you'd finally started to understand emotion," he said. "It's hard to be logical when you're faced with deprivation and overcrowding, cut off from sunlight and fresh air day after day for years on end."

"I do now appreciate that logic alone is insufficient," Spock said, sounding oddly casual about the profound epiphany his recent mind-meld with V'Ger had brought him. "But it is still useful, especially in situations wherein the indulgence of emotion can lead only to increased frustration rather than productive change. What the Payav need is patience and discipline."

"Well, nobody outside of Vulcan ever won over the masses by appealing to their reason. And I have my doubts about Vulcan."

"I fear Dr. McCoy is right," Theena said. "Tensions are running high, and the mar-Atyya and Payavist factions are winning over the people with their appeals to faith, tradition, and purity." She shook her head. "The mar-Atyya have become much more militant since the Pulse. They always taught that Mestiko was specially blessed by God. But after the Pulse and the Klingons . . . the terrors inflicted on our world from outside . . . they came to conclude that not only was Mestiko blessed, but the rest of the universe was cursed. They condemn anything from outside as evil, and more and more of the people are willing to believe them. Or at least ready to try something different, feeling the *Zamestaad*'s policies are accomplishing too little."

"And that's why Raya sent you instead of contacting me openly," Kirk said. "She's weak enough politically already, without making it look like she's calling for alien help."

"Exactly." Theena's brow furrowed, though she had no eyebrows to move with it. "Her stature has never fully recovered since the Alur scandal. It has been a struggle to balance her support for the eco-restoration program with her efforts to avoid alienating the people further. Dr. Lon condemned her 'politically motivated' limits on his efforts, but if she had not taken those actions, she probably would have been deposed and replaced with someone openly hostile to the program."

"But what's the alternative?" McCoy asked. "Do they really think the planet can regenerate on its own? That whole extinct biomes can somehow magically regenerate themselves?"

"The mar-Atyya have advanced what they call a 'purity-based' program of restoration. It uses only those indigenous plants and animals that have survived the Pulse and encourages a traditionalist lifestyle as laid out in their holy texts. They argue that living in this way will demand little of the ecosystem and help regenerate it, and that purging it of alien elements is necessary to restore its proper balance and vitality."

McCoy scoffed. "Superstition and quackery."

"Yes," Theena said, "but with enough real science dressing it up to make it sound credible. And it appeals to the rank and file of Payav far more than the idea of importing alien plants and animals to replace extinct native forms."

Kirk leaned forward. "Tell me, Theena . . . if there's so much anti-alien sentiment on Mestiko, what does Raya believe I can accomplish there?"

Theena smiled. "You still have your supporters on Mestiko, Captain. Raya is not the only one who remembers how you have helped our world. The mar-Atyya's coalition may be gaining ground in the war over public opinion, but the other side is still fighting, and Raya believes you could strengthen them by lending your voice. You do have quite a reputation for saving worlds."

Kirk tried not to fidget. He was still embarrassed by the reputation he'd gained after muddling his way through the V'Ger encounter, but he was beginning to understand it was a tool he could wield to his advantage. "Still, that reputation could backfire. You heard the insinuations that Kotyar woman made."

"Even so, Raya feels another cool head on the scene could aid matters. An upheaval may be imminent whether you come or not, Captain, but if you are there, you may find a way to help us, as you have before."

He studied her. "Even though Raya can't publicly admit she wants my help."

Theena shrugged. "Politics."

Kirk sighed. "I know all about politics. Why do you think I went back to starship command?"

MESTIKO

"**Y**ou've been avoiding me, *Jo'Zamestaad*."

Raya elMora winced as the familiar voice called out from down the corridor behind her, accompanied by heavy footfalls as the speaker hastened to catch up. Smoothing her features, Raya turned to greet her pursuer. "Not at all, Asal. I've simply been too busy—"

"Don't try to sandstorm me, Raya," Asal Janto said. "I can tell when you're trying to dodge an undesirable encounter. Remember how you made me change clothes with you in the bushes outside our dorm so you could sneak away from Hodi orManat? I could barely fit into your things, I was so embarrassed trying to race back inside!" Asal's jowls shook as she laughed. In these times of scarcity, the councillor from Domtos was no longer as chubby as she'd been in their university days, so her skin hung a bit loose. As a member of the *Zamestaad*, however, she was still able to keep herself fairly well fed.

Raya didn't share in her jocularity, however. "I'd rather you didn't invoke our past friendship, Councillor, considering the agenda you're no doubt here to advance."

Asal's expression hardened. "You make it sound as though

I'm the one who betrayed you. I never made deals with any Klingons."

"You know that's not fair! I didn't know Alur was—"

"And once you found out, you said nothing!"

"Until I could be sure it would be safe!"

"To protect your own interests!"

"To preserve the goal of restoring our world! We can't let that fall prey to petty ambitions."

Asal shook her head. "The words are like the Raya I knew, but the commitment is not there. You used to be so strong, so determined not to compromise. When we rallied for the environment, you were right there at my side."

"That is still my commitment!" Raya exclaimed, stepping closer to loom over her former friend. "My goal is unchanged. But unlike you, I am able to see that achieving a goal requires the willingness to change one's methods. I've learned that sometimes you cannot reach the destination by the path you assumed and must find another way. You still think you can blindly barrel forward and triumph on ideological purity alone."

"Don't underrate purity, Raya. Purity is what the people want. They want our world restored to what it was, and they want our people in charge of making it so. You obstruct that will at your peril."

"I share that ideal, Asal. I have made every possible concession I can safely make to it without jeopardizing the effectiveness of the project."

"And whose judgment of that effectiveness are you going by? That human Dr. Lon? Those Kazarite brutes? Is it me, or does each new wave of aliens get more unnatural?"

Raya suppressed her own instinctive reaction to the mention of the Kazarites, knowing it was impolitic and parochial. "The Kazarites . . . take some adjusting to. But their services are useful. They and Dr. Lon have already made remarkable strides."

"At turning our world into a zoo for their castoff creatures. And meanwhile, they have done nothing to support our plans for a global radiation shield."

Raya sighed. So that was where she was going with this.

"*Your* plans, Councillor. Fortunately, the majority of the *Zamestaad* does not share your priorities."

"The people do! Listen to them, and you will hear them demanding protection in case the Pulse should happen again!"

"It never will!" Raya insisted. "The Scourer is leaving our system and will not come back. We have surveyed the skies for light-years around and found nothing approaching us. Nothing like the Pulse has happened before to any known world. It would be a criminal waste of our resources to put them into a defense against a threat that will never come again!"

"So *they* say," Asal countered. "All you have is the Din-payav's word that it hasn't happened elsewhere. And they were as surprised as we were when it happened here!" She shook her head. "You place too much faith in the aliens' wisdom, Raya. You always assume the fact that they've been in space for a grossyear or two longer than we makes them so much wiser in all things."

"Our own scientists confirm it, Asal. You know that."

"And our scientists did not see the Pulse coming, either. What I know—what the people know—is that the universe is unpredictable, and we must be ready."

"What is the point of being ready for a threat from outside when our world is still dying from within? Let us make sure we have air to breathe and food to eat first! Then we can debate what protection we need."

"What is the point of restoring our world to health if we don't know it will be here a generation from now?"

"We know."

"The people don't, Raya. They want assurances."

Raya made herself relax and speak more softly. "Of course they do. They're afraid. We all are. But sometimes it's more important to give the people what they *need* than what they want."

Asal gave her a pitying look. "You always were politically naïve."

"*I* am? You're the one who refuses to bend her ideologies regardless of popular opinion."

"I don't need to," Asal stated. "The people agree with me."

Raya heard the warning in her tone but chose to ignore it. "Is that all, Councillor? I really am most busy."

"Meeting with Kirk, no doubt."

Ah. There was her real point after all, then. "Yes, I have heard that the *Enterprise* is making the latest supply run from Starbase 49. Naturally, I will extend hospitality to its captain."

Asal wasn't buying it. "And to your old friend Theena, who just happens to be a passenger on that ship?"

Raya suppressed another wince. Her back-channel contact might have slipped by most people, but Asal was more familiar with the details of her personal life. They had still been friends until the Alur affair, so Asal had known about the young orphan girl Raya had bonded with after the Pulse and treated as a friend and protégée ever since. There was no way Asal would believe Theena's presence on Kirk's ship was a coincidence. Raya had never been any good at deceiving her.

"No need to explain," Asal said. "You hope Kirk can find one of his miracle solutions and stave off the coming upheaval, saving your career in the process." She shook her head, her face showing regret that Raya couldn't quite dismiss as insincere. "You should never have strayed from your commitment to our own people, *Jo'Zamestaad*. The future of our world—and of its government—lies with us, not with aliens. I only pray you recognize that before it is too late."

Lieutenant Commander Hikaru Sulu had flown many types of craft in his years as a helmsman and test pilot. Yet somehow he'd never expected that one of them would be a crop duster.

More precisely, he flew the *Galileo III*, one of the new multipurpose shuttlecraft assigned to the *Enterprise*. The flat, blocky shuttles, whose shape reminded Sulu of an axe head cleaving the air, could be customized for various mission profiles with attachable modules such as long-range impulse engines, compact warp nacelles, weapons pods, cargo units, and so forth. Right now, the *Galileo* was outfitted with a tank-and-nozzle assembly for aerial spraying and stout wings to improve its atmospheric performance. Since the *Enterprise*'s nominal mission here was to assist in the eco-recovery project, the ship had stopped off at Starbase 49, command base for Mestiko operations, to pick up these and other supplies for that effort. The starbase staff had been grateful for the extra help, giving the crew their first indication of how massive this undertaking was.

Still, there were signs of progress being made, as Pavel Chekov observed from the copilot's seat. "It looks better than the last time," the young lieutenant said, studying the view in the large virtual display that took the place of a window in this shuttle design. "No more brown gunk in the sky. And there's green on the ground."

"Not much," Uhura added from behind them. "No trees, no flowers . . . hardly anything more than moss."

"But it's a start," Sulu told her. "You should've seen it up close last time. I've hardly ever been anywhere so completely dead. Well, airless moons and such, of course—but those are *supposed* to be barren." He suppressed a shudder. "Compared to last time, this is downright lush." According to the briefings—which, in his new capacity as *Enterprise* second officer, he had studied more carefully than he would have as just a helmsman—the Kazarite ecologists spearheading Mestiko's restoration were starting out with simple life-forms that could thrive in cold, low-oxygen, high-UV conditions. Some were indigenous species, but most were genetically engineered, imported from alien worlds, or both, such as the Martian "frostbuster" moss that was at the foundation of the new ecosystem. What lived below them at the moment consisted mostly of plant life, but those plants relied on insects, worms, and other such forms to pollinate them and to mix, aerate, and fertilize the soil they grew in. It was a barely visible ecosystem from this altitude but already a complex one and, as Sulu was well aware from his botanical hobby, a vital one. (Charles Darwin had once proposed that no other species had "played so important a part in the history of the world" as the earthworm, for plant cultivation would be impossible without it.) The chemical mix spraying from the shuttle helped sustain the whole biosphere: fertilizing agents and growth enhancers for the plants, tri-ox compounds and radiation counteragents for the invertebrates. Yet it was a carefully designed mix of organic compounds, gentle to the environment, as one would expect of anything designed by Kazarites.

"Try telling that to the Payav," Uhura said. "From the broadcasts I've been monitoring, they're getting pretty impatient with the pace of the restoration."

Sulu shrugged. "Tell them I'm flying as fast as I can." Even as he spoke, he was turning the shuttle for another pass, making it as tight as he could to save time. He wouldn't have recommended the maneuver to a less experienced pilot, but he'd helped test this design while it was still in prototype. Still, he had to adjust for the steadily diminishing mass of the cargo tank as its contents sprayed out.

"On second thought, I don't think most of them would listen," said Uhura. She'd done her homework on Payav cultures, since her purpose on this mission was to work with the Kazarites on improving their translator algorithms to smooth over misunderstandings between them and the Payav. "The mar-Atyya and Payavist opposition have gotten them fired up about it, blaming the government and the Federation for not doing more faster. When they're not just condemning aliens in general." She couldn't help glancing back at the other passengers in the shuttle: the Tellarite biologist Bolek and the bulge-headed, gas-masked Zaranite microecologist Havzora. True, they were no more alien to Mestiko than the humans were, but the Payav would probably not see them that way.

"Don't they see the opposition is just doing that to gain political advantage?" Chekov asked.

"I'm not so sure," Uhura said. "A lot of people are genuinely angry and frustrated. They want to believe there's a quick and easy answer, and a lot of them would rather look for it in their old, comfortable traditions than in the things that aliens tell them. That's probably as true of the mar-Atyya demagogues as of the people who support them."

"Only because it suits their ambitions to believe those things," Chekov replied. "Trust me—we Russians understand these matters."

"You pessimists, you mean."

"Is there a difference?" Sulu teased.

Before long, the tank was running dry, and Sulu set course for the compound from which the Kazarites were supervising the reseeding of this part of Mestiko. "About time," Bolek griped, though he had volunteered to come by shuttle rather than waiting for his turn through the *Enterprise* transporters, which were being kept busy beaming supplies to the surface.

The Kazarite compound was in a broad valley surrounded by mountains that sheltered it from the winds. It had been chosen because the terrain provided a natural confinement for the oxygen produced by the frostbuster moss, concentrating it enough within the valley to allow humanoids free movement on the surface for longer than was possible elsewhere on the planet. Finding a natural solution like this, rather than creating it with force fields or transparent-aluminum enclosures, struck Sulu as a very Kazarite approach. Although they had only recently joined the Federation, the Kazarites were already making a name for themselves as master ecologists, thanks to their empathic rapport with animals. Mestiko, a world not too far from their own, had become their most ambitious undertaking to date.

Still, to Sulu the valley looked more like parts of Earth than Mestiko or Kazar. It was mostly filled with a forest of small, young conifers imported from Earth, chosen because they were well adapted to cold, dry conditions and heavy snows. As the shuttle soared over the forest, Sulu's eyes were drawn to a flock of Regulan pygmy eel-birds, whose shiny purple plumage, evolved to reflect the intense UV light of their hot primary star, made a vivid contrast to the deep green trees on which they perched.

Once the shuttle cleared the woods and neared the main research compound, Sulu saw a more alarming concentration of life-forms. A large crowd of Payav, wearing wide-brimmed hats, sun visors, and long-sleeved clothing to protect their pale skin, stood outside the compound's main gate, waving signs and fists in the air and chanting things that Sulu couldn't make out but that sounded pretty angry. "Mar-Atyya?" Chekov asked.

Uhura used a side screen to magnify the image. "A lot of them are. But most of them have tattoos."

"Payavists?"

"Or just ordinary citizens who've been swayed by their rhetoric. The placards are condemning alien contamination of their holy ground."

As the shuttle touched down, a Kazarite party came out to greet them, and the increasing hostility of the protesters' cries made it clear that the "contamination" they found offensive was not limited to moss, birds, and trees. To Sulu, the Kazarites' dark-hued, simian features, backswept black manes, and loose, homespun robes bespoke a quiet dignity and simplicity, but the translator caught cries of "Beasts!" and "Hideous savages!" from the protesters. He hoped Uhura could help overcome that perceptual gulf, but he doubted it would happen here and now. "Let's get inside quickly," he advised. "Make sure your phasers are on stun, but don't do anything provocative."

Sulu tried to get through the exchange of greetings with the Kazarites as quickly as possible, and they appeared to share his desire. "Maintain a calm bearing," their lead ecopath, a soft-spoken female named Hogach, suggested once hasty pleasantries had been traded. "Show no fear. But avoid eye contact with the crowd."

It was a nice theory but of little avail against someone already resolved to lash out violently. The protesters grew more agitated with each new person who exited the shuttle—*each new alien polluting their soil,* Sulu thought. But this was especially true with Bolek and Havzora. Someone actually screamed when the Zaranite disembarked, and a furor began to surge through the crowd. Sulu supposed he could understand being startled by one's first glimpse of the slit-eyed gas mask that supplied Havzora with fluorine, but this kind of panic seemed beyond the pale on a world whose people had been aware of alien life for more than eight years now.

But then Chekov sidled up to him and pointed to several tattoo-free Payav at the front of the crowd, facing the protesters and rallying them. "Mar-Atyya," he said. "They're stirring up the crowd, driving them into a frenzy!"

"Get everyone inside, now!"

But the crowd was already surging against the fence, and projectiles began to arc over it. Sulu prayed that this was an unplanned attack, that they were only rocks or bottles. But even those could be dangerous. "Cover!" he cried, leading the landing party back toward the shuttle.

But then Hogach and the other Kazarites stepped forward and spread their hands, humming in the backs of their throats. The projectiles changed course in midair as though struck by a powerful wind, falling short of their targets. Sulu realized he'd just seen the Kazarites' telekinesis in action. It wasn't as powerful as the abilities of a Platonian or a Thasian, say, but it was good enough for Sulu.

The protesters saw it differently. Already stirred up into a superstitious panic, the Payav reacted with utter horror to the Kazarites' seemingly supernatural abilities. Now one of the mar-Atyya was preaching loudly enough for Sulu's translator to pick his voice out of the crowd. "Do you see, my brethren? This is the work of demons! With their foul sorcery they will collapse our tunnels upon us, crush our hearts in our chests merely by willing it! Unless we stop them here and now! Unless we purify our world!"

"Yes! Purify!" The cry went up through the crowd, the preachers echoing and reinforcing it. Sulu began to get a bad feeling, remembering that religious purification rituals generally involved one of two elements: water or . . .

Fire! As if making his thought manifest, a crude incendiary device flew over the fence. But Chekov darted forward and hit it dead-on with a phaser beam, vaporizing it in midair. "Good shot!" Sulu cried.

But other firebombs were flying over the fence now, and even with Sulu adding his own expert marksmanship to Chekov's, they couldn't stop them all. *They did come prepared after all*, he thought as some of the firebombs made it through, shattering on the ground and splashing flaming liquid on the foliage around them. Within moments, the trees were burning, the fire spreading from several points.

No, it's even worse than that, Sulu realized. *This was a well-planned attack. We were just the diversion—the excuse. They want to burn down the forest!*

U.S.S. ENTERPRISE

"This is a disaster!" cried Marat Lon as he gazed at the image of the forest fire on the bridge's viewscreen. "Kirk, we have to do something at once!"

Instead of responding to the doctor, Kirk spoke into the com pickup. "Sulu, assessment?"

"The fire's spreading quickly, sir. Normally, that wouldn't be a problem for pine trees, but these are young and thin-barked. They might not survive."

"Neither will the animals," Lon added, his tone still urgent. "The eel-birds are nesting; their eggs will be lost, and they won't breed again for another year! Not to mention the milli-snakes, the groundhoppers—even if they could outrun the fire, where would they go?"

"All our firefighting resources in the area are being mobi-lized," Raya elMora said, her face appearing in an inset on the main viewer. *"But it will take time, and we have little still func-tional on the surface."*

"There's no time for that," Lon said. "Kirk, isn't there any-thing we can do from here?" Lon had come aboard to supervise the transfer of supplies but now sounded as though he blamed himself personally for abandoning his work down below.

Kirk pondered for a moment, pacing the bridge. "Spock, how about using the ship's phasers to cut a firebreak in its path? Sacrifice some of the trees to save the rest?"

"Feasible, Captain. Although it may not completely suffice on its own, it should delay the spread of the fire enough to allow ground crews to contain it."

"*You want to fire weapons on our planet?*" Raya asked. "*Captain, you must understand how tenuous the public's sentiments are right now. Even the appearance of aggression from Starfleet, however beneficial the result, could spark a far greater conflagration than this.*"

"We don't have time to cater to Payav paranoia!" Lon cried, then reined himself in. "With respect, Madam Councillor, the preservation of that valley is urgent. The restoration plan is on a precise timetable, countless elements all carefully balanced, and losing this facility would be a massive setback for these species. Surely the people can be made to understand that."

Kirk could see the struggle in Raya's eyes. Those eyes met his, seeking his opinion, and he sent her his wordless encouragement. *I trust your judgment and will support it.*

"*Very well,*" she said. "*Proceed with your plan, Captain Kirk. I will issue an immediate public statement explaining your action and urging calm.*"

"Thank you, Madam Councillor," Kirk said, settling back into the command chair. "Chief DiFalco, plot our new orbit. Ensign Ledoux, engage."

As the two women guided the *Enterprise* to its new orbit, Kirk listened to the feed as Raya made her announcement to the people. In the meantime, Spock calculated the optimal location for the firebreak and sent the data to Ensign Nizhoni, Chekov's second-in-command, at the tactical station. The young Navajo woman had the firing solution prepared by the time Monique Ledoux had settled the ship into a forced orbit over the burning valley. "We're ready to fire, Madam Councillor," Kirk reported.

"*You may proceed.*"

"Nizhoni—fire phasers!"

Kirk watched the viewscreen as the beams speared down through Mestiko's atmosphere and struck the valley. He ordered magnification, but between the smoke from the fire and the vapor and dust that billowed around the impact point, there was little to see. Ledoux switched the viewscreen to terahertz imaging to cut through the smoke, allowing Kirk to see the wide swath the phaser beams were scything through the evergreen forest.

In minutes, it was over. The fire was still burning, but they hoped it would remain contained within the firebreak. Kirk ordered Ledoux to keep station over the valley in case another firebreak was needed. "Spock," he said, "is there anything else we can do to fight the fire from up here? Say, use a tractor beam to suck away its air supply?"

"Doubtful, Captain. The intervening column of air is several dozen kilometers deep, and—"

"*I fear we have more immediate concerns,*" Raya interrupted. "*Apparently, my address was ineffective. I'm getting reports of riots breaking out in dozens of major cities.*"

VOSTRAAL, MESTIKO

Raya slumped behind her desk as she watched the monitors, which cycled among images of the riots raging across half of Mestiko. The government's security forces were being overwhelmed in city after city—at least, where they hadn't broken ranks and stood with the rioters. *No, Raya. This is beyond rioting now. Call it what it is—a coup.*

She glanced over to the two large guards who stood inside her office door, mirroring the two who guarded its other side and the two more inside the outer office door, and so on. She was beginning to doubt they would be enough. Kirk had offered to send down his security people to protect key government facilities, but she knew that would only make things worse. The mar-Atyya had orchestrated their coup deftly, stirring the people into a xenophobic fury. They had provoked Starfleet into action with the fire and used its response as an excuse to launch an open revolt. There was no way it could have happened so swiftly had it been spontaneous. They had been plotting insurrection for some time, just waiting for the right excuse. Perhaps even waiting for Kirk himself. Asking for help from *Enterprise* security would only add fuel to the fire.

Besides, Raya had heard from Theena about what the *Enterprise*'s crew was like now. So many aliens in one place, of more species than Raya believed she had even heard of, and many of them downright frightening in appearance. Raya liked to consider herself cosmopolitan, but her dealings had been mostly with humans, Klingons, and Vulcans, species who differed only marginally from the Payav norm. It had been something of a shock when she'd met her first Kazarite, and she'd barely avoided an embarrassing outburst of fear at the first demonstration of their psionic abilities. She knew that the rank and file of Payav would react even more badly to the alienness of Kirk's crew than she would, and would not be as circumspect in expressing it.

Now, there's an understatement for the ages, she told herself as she studied the monitors. The Kazarites and other off-worlders had already been beamed to the *Enterprise* or the other ships in orbit for their protection. But Raya had no such recourse. Kirk had implicitly offered it, but she would remain with the *Zamestaad* for as long as that institution existed.

"*Madam Councillor?*" It was Blee, calling from the outer office. "*Councillor Asal Janto is here to see you.*"

Raya's eyes widened. What could she possibly want now? Raya had grown too cynical to imagine that her estranged friend would want to—what was the human expression?—"kiss and make up" in the face of crisis. "Blee, advise the councillor to return to her chambers and wait there. Have a guard escort her."

Blee's voice was tentative. "*Uhh, Madam Councillor . . . she has several guards with her already. And I don't think they'll react well if I send her away.*"

Raya absorbed that for a moment. *Perhaps I haven't grown cynical enough.* "Send her in, then." She nodded to the guards to permit it. No point asking them to throw their lives away for a lost cause.

Asal dared to look apologetic as she entered the room. Her guards waited outside but held the door open. "So," Raya said. "You're their figurehead."

"More than that, Raya. I stand for the majority of Payav who support the mar-Atyya movement in its opposition to alien incursion and its commitment to shielding our world from all external threats, natural or otherwise."

Raya stared. So this was about her absurd radiation-shield plan? The mar-Atyya must have promised to support it in exchange for her allegiance. "They're a band of fanatics, Asal! Can you really believe the policies they'll impose will have any grounding in reality, any chance of solving the problems that face us?"

"They chose to place their support behind me, a secular leader. That should answer your question."

"You, secular?" Raya scoffed. "In title, perhaps. But you have always been driven by faith. You always assume that your own self-righteousness will let you triumph over any problem."

"Look around you, Raya. We *have* triumphed."

"No. You have merely compounded the problem. In fact—" Unable to contain herself any longer, she struck Asal across the face. "You may have just doomed our world to extinction!"

Asal rubbed her cheek but remained calm and confident. "Restoring Mestiko—pardon me, hur-Atyya—is still our top priority. But we will do it *our* way. Without alien contaminants."

"How? By wishing very hard and hoping that entire extinct taxa will resurrect themselves?"

"We're not the primitives the Federation imagines. We have genetic sciences. Samples of defunct forms can be found and cloned."

"With what resources? What animals' wombs will they incubate in? Who will perform this highly skilled work when we are starving to death in the absence of offworld food shipments? And where will you find the budget and the skilled personnel while you are wasting it all on building a shield against a nonexistent threat?"

"You accuse me of overdependence on faith, but you have none in your own people. We have endured much this past twelveyear, and in the ages before. We are a resourceful people, and I believe in us."

"I believe in us, too, Asal. But we do not have to do it alone."

"No, Raya. Now more than ever, we do. We have to prove we are as capable as any other species in the universe, or we will always consider ourselves inferior." Asal sighed. "You, on the other hand, will have to rely on aliens for assistance."

Raya studied her. "I'm to be exiled, then?"

"You and your loyalists, yes. Those who survive," she added, looking away. "It's for your own protection, Raya. I fought for it. Whatever our political differences," she went on, meeting Raya's eyes again, "I would not wish you dead."

Raya returned her gaze coldly. "Then you show more concern for my welfare than for our planet's."

U.S.S. ENTERPRISE

Kirk rose from his seat as Raya entered the officers' lounge. "Are your people settling in all right?" he asked.

"As well as can be expected," she answered as he escorted her to the seat nearest the door. "Thank you. Conditions are somewhat cramped, but we're used to that. We've managed to find room for all the surviving members of the government in exile. Fortunately, you have a very spacious recreation complex."

Kirk sat across from her, on the couch next to Spock. McCoy watched from the opposite couch, and Dr. Lon paced before the windowlike viewscreens. "And you?" Kirk asked with a solicitous smile. "How are you bearing up?"

She gazed into his eyes and let him see a sorrow and weariness he doubted she would show anyone else. "Well . . . I was betrayed by a very old friend today. I suppose that friendship ended three years ago, but it still hurts. And . . . I was unable to track down Elee," she went on, referring to her beloved grandmother. "She was not at home, and I have no idea if she escaped the violence." She strove to keep her voice controlled, but Kirk could sense her fear. After losing the rest of her family to the Pulse and its aftermath, he knew she would go to any lengths to save Elee from a similar fate.

Kirk clasped her wrist. "Your *elor* is as strong as you are. She'll survive." She placed her other hand atop his and gave wordless thanks.

After a moment, they broke apart, cognizant of the others' gazes upon them. "Then I suppose the next question," Kirk went on, "is where we'll take you."

Raya nodded. "I would assume Starbase 49. That would be a good place to establish a command post for our efforts to retake the government. Most of the infrastructure is already in place; it's just a matter of converting its purpose. Once we have a decent fleet assembled . . ." She trailed off, registering the looks on the Starfleet officers' faces. "What is it?"

"Raya . . . you know the Prime Directive won't allow us to intervene."

She stared, then laughed. "What? Isn't it rather late to be worrying about the Prime Directive *now*? Surely that was rendered moot after the Pulse. Starfleet has been intervening directly in our world's affairs ever since."

"With the invitation and consent of your world's sitting government," Spock told her. "That condition no longer applies."

"We're not conquerors, Raya," Kirk said. "We'll provide humanitarian aid when we're asked, but we're not in the business of overthrowing governments."

"Even when they have overthrown your allies?"

"It's . . . not that simple." Kirk faltered. How could he make her understand when he was having trouble with the concept himself?

McCoy leaned forward. "Raya, think about it. Say we did help you stage a countercoup and put the *Zamestaad* back. Do you think the people would just accept that? Do you think they'd be willing to work with you then? You'd be too busy putting down rebellions to do anything else."

"But what is the alternative? You all know that if the mar-Atyya's policies are enacted, all we have accomplished over the past twelveyear will be wiped out. They will destroy Dr. Lon's plants and the alien animals, and Mestiko will go back to freezing and losing oxygen again. The survival of our families, our very *world*, is at stake!"

"We won't give up trying, Raya," Kirk said. "We'll use every diplomatic means at our disposal to encourage the new government to continue the restoration work."

"And you think they will listen?" She shook her head. "What has happened to you, James? There was a time when you would not hesitate to go charging in and take on a whole society if you thought its rulers were harming its people."

Kirk cleared his throat. "Those accounts have been . . . somewhat exaggerated. And I've learned that the consequences of such actions aren't always positive in the long run. Especially if you ignore the beliefs and wishes of the people as a whole."

"The people have been lied to! Swayed and led astray by ambitious, shortsighted fools. We have to set them straight!"

"We'll do whatever we can to help the Payav make an informed decision for themselves. But our options are limited. The new regime has demanded that all offworlders leave the system, and we have to respect that."

"And what about the Klingons? With no Starfleet presence, they will sweep right in!"

"The previous Klingon regime has been overthrown," Spock told her. "The Empire seems to be concerned with internal consolidation at the moment and is not likely to pose a threat."

"Not likely. That's all you can tell me?" She stared at Kirk. "You once gave me your word that your people would do everything you could for my people."

"Yes, I did. Unfortunately, we may have done everything we can already. Aside from finding a good place for your exiles to take up residence," he added. "The Kazarites have volunteered to take you in, along with any other Payav refugees. They have a large uninhabited region on their world that they'd gladly allow you to settle."

She studied him for a long moment, then rose. "I was mistaken, it seems. I have been betrayed by two old friends today."

After she left, Kirk pounded the arm of the couch. "Damn! I

can't blame her for being angry. I wish there were more we could do!"

"Unfortunately, I can think of nothing," Spock said. "You enumerated the limits on our options most effectively."

McCoy rolled his eyes. "Spock, you still have a lot to learn about offering comfort."

"Doctor, I—"

"Send me back down."

Kirk spun. He'd almost forgotten Dr. Lon was there, since the scientist had been so uncharacteristically quiet. "What?"

"I won't abandon my work. I've put eight years of my life into this project, poured my blood into this planet. I'm not going to walk away from that. I have to do whatever I can to defend it."

"Have you seen what's going on down there?" McCoy asked. "If they see a human daring to defile their blessed ground, they'll reinvent human sacrifice right there and then!"

"Shave my head, then. Depilate my body, lighten my skin, give me tattoos and prosthetic thumbs. It's been done before. And my neck is long enough to pass."

Kirk spoke carefully. "Dr. Lon . . . don't take this the wrong way, but . . . there's more to passing as a Payav than looking like one. And you've never been particularly prone to seeing things from a Payav point of view."

"Even Starfleet's precontact team sought to minimize direct interaction with the populace," Spock added. "You propose a full-immersion undertaking, by yourself, with no ship to retreat to, no wherewithal to repair damage to your prosthetics . . ."

"I know the risks, and they're mine to take. You can't stop me from doing this."

"That is incorrect, Doctor," Spock told him. "As Starfleet officers, we are responsible for the safety of Federation citizens. So long as you remain on this vessel, we are within our rights to detain you from entering an actively hostile zone. And to refuse you the use of our medical technology to change your appearance."

"Then I'll renounce my Federation citizenship! Or I'll just let you drop me off at a starbase and make my way back here.

But who knows how much of my work may be lost in the meantime?"

"Even if you salvaged some of your work," McCoy asked, "what would you do with it? If these mar-Atyya see any alien moss growing, they'll burn it without a second thought! Along with anyone caught planting it!"

"I don't know. I don't know. But I have to do *something*. I'm not willing to let this planet die!"

Kirk looked into his eyes and made his decision. "Dr. McCoy . . . can you recommend a good tattoo artist?"

MESTIKO

Marat Lon ducked into an alley and flattened himself against its shadowed wall. He struggled to quiet his rasping breath, hoping the mob would go past without spotting or hearing him. In his life as an ecologist, he'd spent too much time in the wilds of Mars, away from the cities and their artificial gravity. And in his six years on Mestiko, he'd been too busy with his work to bother getting in shape. His doctor had warned him he needed to exercise for his health. Lon imagined even his physician would not have expected her warning to come true in such a drastic way.

What tipped them off? he asked himself for the fiftieth time. *Did McCoy bungle the operation? Was there a spy on the ship?* But he could afford little mental effort to worry about that now. Instead, he needed to find a way out of this alley before that mob of xenophobes found him and burned him at the stake or whatever they did on this planet. Wearily, he ran a hand across his bare scalp. *I miss my hair. There wasn't much left, but it was something.*

Suddenly, a hand clamped over his mouth, and he found himself being dragged backward, deeper into the alley. He struggled, but he was too exhausted to accomplish much. "Calm yourself," a female voice hissed. "Stay quiet, or you'll alert the mob!"

It began to get through his head that his attacker might be an ally. And he was just too weary to keep fighting. So he allowed her to pull him down the alley and through an open metal grate in the ground, which she closed behind them. Soon they were in a cramped, dripping drainage tunnel. He attempted to speak, but she clamped that hand over his mouth again, looking up toward the grate. Lon heard the voices and footsteps overhead and decided to take her advice and stay quiet.

As they waited, he tried to get a look at her. She was a lanky, slender Payav with an elegantly curved skull and a delicate profile. *A lot stronger than she looks, though*, he thought ruefully. But he found himself unable to look away from that profile. It was perhaps the most pleasant thing he'd seen in some time.

Her expression was not too pleasant when the noise from above finally subsided and she turned to glare at him. "You're a fool, you know that?"

"Excuse me?"

"Did you even make the slightest attempt to understand the Payav before attempting to impersonate us? Did you have a death wish, coming among us and advertising your Dinpayav ways?"

"Wait a minute, whose side are you on? I thought you wanted to save me!"

"Only because I recognized your voice, Dr. Lon. We need your knowledge if we are to salvage your work, keep your plants and animals alive while the mar-Atyya try to burn them all to ash."

"'We'?"

"We, the people of Mestiko who still have a grain of sanity left. We're not all dupes to the mar-Atyya, you know."

"No, of course not."

She glared at him. "Do not patronize me, Lon. If you want to pass as one of us, you will have to learn to cloak your ego better. Now, come."

She led him down the tunnel, and as they passed under

patches of dim light from above, he got a better look at her. Her eyes were large and dark, her lips full and mobile. Her tattoos were unusual in their patterns and color. "What's your name?" he asked.

"Daki. Daki orGalya."

He blinked. "An *or* prefix for a woman?"

"I'm Gelta. There aren't many of us left. Only those who were abroad when the Pulse hit."

"You were lucky."

She glared. "*I* was abroad. My family and my betrothed were not."

"Oh."

"You have much to learn about us, human. To start with, for your own protection, learn to think before you speak."

He bristled. "I'm not a fool! I've lived among you people for six years. I know the language, I know the customs."

"'You people'? You only know us as animals you study, an element in the biosphere you engineer. You've never lived among us, never gotten to know us. That much is obvious to anyone, as that large mob should have proven to you."

"I don't understand. What did they notice?"

"To start with, you're too careless about showing your teeth when you talk. Only a few remote tribes are so crass, and they wear scars, not tattoos. You keep scratching your head as though you're missing something that was there. You barely use your outer thumbs. Can those fakes even move?"

"They're surgical implants, state-of-the-art." He wiggled them to demonstrate.

Her face screwed up. "And you haven't learned how to move them naturally. Put those down." He lowered his hands to his sides.

"Most of all," Daki went on, "you carry yourself like someone who's never known hardship or loss. You carry yourself like someone utterly assured of his place in the universe. No Payav can do that anymore." She came up short, turned, and got in his face, her eyes captivating him. "And neither can you, from now on. Your place in the universe has just changed, Doctor, and if you want to have a hope of surviving the new regime, you will have to start by accepting that you are as lost as the rest of us."

JAROL DESERT, KAZAR

Raya stared out at the barren wasteland where the *Enterprise*'s transporter had deposited her. "This is it?" she demanded, whirling to face Kirk. "This is where the Kazarites condemn our people to live?"

Kirk looked apologetic, but that expression no longer seemed sincere to her. "Try to understand, Raya. There are only so many places on Kazar that can accommodate a large influx of refugees. The Kazarites are concerned about the ecological disruption it could cause elsewhere. As I understand it, the Jarol Desert only formed within the past century or two, after a natural shift in wind patterns deprived it of moisture from the ocean."

"So everything that was here died of thirst. And now they strand us here to suffer the same?"

"They'll share every resource they can spare for you, Raya, just as they did before." He put a hand on her shoulder, but at her glare, he retracted it sadly. "I promise you, we haven't given up. And I know you won't, either."

"That's the first true thing you've said in a long time, James. I will never stop fighting for my world. The Kazarites wish to strand my people in this . . . savage land? So be it. We will survive, and we will make it our own. We will make it the ground from which we stand and fight to reclaim our homeworld." Her thoughts turned to Elee and Theena elMadej, as they had many times during the journey here. She wished she could have her wise *elor* and her dear young friend by her side to cheer her through these trying times. But Elee's fate remained unknown, and Theena had insisted on staying on Mestiko, completing her studies as far as the new regime would allow, and perhaps beyond. That was how she believed she could best help her world. Raya admired her courage and envied the fact that, as someone with no official ties to the government, she was exempt from exile and probably safe so long as she kept quiet about her personal affiliations. She prayed that Theena would be able to find Elee and keep her safe, as Raya no longer could. Still, she would have been happier if Theena and Elee could have been safe with her, even in this forbidding waste. Or better yet, if they could all be safe together on Mestiko. But then, there had been no safety since the Pulse, had there? And if not for the Pulse, Raya and Theena would never have met.

Neither would Raya and Kirk. Right now, the thought appealed to her. "So go, James Kirk. Go off in your shining starship, and have adventures undreamed of, and shunt my people aside into this threadbare patch of this uncivilized world. That's fine. Because I was a fool to try to rely on you for help. We don't need your help. The Payav will endure, and we will triumph, and we will do it without you. Now, go! Go away!"

Kirk had a wistful look in his eyes as he raised the com device on his wrist and called his ship for beam-up. But again, Raya found it unconvincing. For behind that wistfulness, in the moment before the transporter beam took him, she could see smug satisfaction on his face, and the hint of a smile.

PART TWO

Stardate 7969.2
(November 2279)

STARFLEET ACADEMY, SAN FRANCISCO

"I have a job for you."

Kirk tried not to show his surge of excitement at Admiral Morrow's words. Morrow had found him at the Academy's track, completing his morning jog, and there were too many students around. Kirk didn't want to give any of them the impression that their commandant was unhappy with his job; that was bad for morale. True, it was no secret that Kirk would still be out there exploring if he had his way. When the refitted *Enterprise* had completed five years of service, Starfleet had insisted that the Corps of Engineers give it a thorough, months-long diagnostic to see how its prototype systems had held up. Kirk had requested transfer to another starship, but there was none available, and the Academy had needed a commandant.

Jim Kirk was a soldier, so he went where he was ordered, and he strove to execute his tasks to the fullest of his ability. And there were many rewards to the Academy posting—the opportunity to mold young minds, to get to know cadets who were the first of their species or subcultures to enter Starfleet, and, most important, to pass along the hard lessons he'd learned so that future Starfleet officers would not have to make the same mistakes.

Besides, it wasn't as if he was completely out of the saddle. That was another mistake he'd learned from. This time, he'd had enough clout to persuade Nogura to sweeten the deal: in exchange for accepting the Academy posting and the renewed admiral's rank that came with it, he'd gotten the *Enterprise* assigned as his personal flagship, with Spock promoted to its captaincy. Starfleet had come to appreciate his abilities in the field, and thus, once the *Enterprise* had completed its testing, they allowed him to take her out on special assignments from time to time, with Spock commanding the ship but Kirk in charge of the overall mission. In the past year, the two of them had undertaken a number of interesting missions, with other members of their old command crew accompanying them when feasible. In between, the *Enterprise* served as a research vessel, a test bed for prototype technologies, and sometimes a cadet training vessel—a contemplative, scholarly mission profile that suited Spock well. All in all, it was a good balance, a way for Kirk to advance in his career and assume new responsibilities without being completely cut off from the thing he did best.

So, as a rule, he tried not to advertise the crushing boredom he felt when he wasn't out there among the stars, with Spock at his side and the *Enterprise* deck under his feet. Still, he allowed Harry Morrow to see a small, private smile of thanks. Morrow, Nogura's second-in-command, had been an ally in persuading the Old Man to accept Kirk's terms, not only allowing Kirk to go out on missions but sometimes even bringing him ones, like now. "What have you got for me, Harry?" he asked as he toweled the sweat off his neck.

"You remember about ten years ago, when Minara and Beta Niobe went supernova within six months of each other?"

Kirk chuckled. "Remember? Harry, I was *there* both times. I still have the singed tail feathers to show for it."

"That's right, that was you, wasn't it? Small universe." Kirk couldn't blame Morrow for forgetting; the man had been a captain himself at the time, embroiled in his own crises and disasters. "Anyway, there are over a dozen inhabited star sys-

THE DARKNESS DROPS AGAIN 307

tems close enough to those supernovae to be at risk of lethal radiation exposure. The Federation's been scrambling to protect them all."

"I've heard about it."

"Well, the situation's trickier than we like to advertise. Luckily, the wave fronts only expand at the speed of light, so we've had years to prepare, but with so many looming disasters, we've been stretched pretty thin. Especially since some of the worlds are precontact, and we have to try to shield them clandestinely, without any local help. Like you tried to do when that pulsar hit Mestiko, what was it, about eighteen years ago?"

"Fourteen, actually."

"Right. Sorry—you know I'm terrible with dates."

"I do keep up with the news, Harry. It's hard to miss it, what with the Verzhik disaster still making headlines." Verzhik was one of the more advanced planets endangered by the supernovae—early warp era but unaligned. Its people had worked jointly with the Federation to shield their planet, but despite that, they had failed to do enough in time. Although the population had successfully retreated underground, their ecosystem had been badly damaged. The footage of Verzhik's smoggy brown skies and UV-burned animal life had been like a Mestiko flashback for Kirk. "So, what are you dancing around?"

"Your ties to Mestiko are why we need you, Jim," Morrow said. "The Verzhik are an advanced civilization, enlightened, artistic. We'd like them as a member, so we want to do right by them. And they've requested our top experts on terraforming and environmental recovery."

Kirk saw where this was going. "And the Federation's leading expert is Marat Lon."

"Right. Who went to ground on Mestiko three years ago—"

"Five."

"—five years ago, and hasn't been heard from since." Morrow's expression grew stern. "Because a certain starship commander decided to let him."

"He was a free citizen of the Federation. I didn't think I had the right to force him to go."

"But you didn't have to use your ship's medical resources to help him disguise himself."

Kirk shrugged. "Since he was determined to go, I did what I could to ensure his safety."

"All right, we won't argue this now. The point is, Verzhik needs Dr. Lon. And we aren't willing to let them down." He fidgeted. "No reflection on you, Jim, but the Federation's failure to protect Mestiko was not one of our finer moments. Of course, you did everything you could, but . . . well, the point is, we're determined not to let it happen again."

Kirk stared at a patch of ground for a while, not seeing it. "I can understand that."

"Good. Because your orders, Jim, are to go to Mestiko, find Marat Lon—if he's even still alive—and persuade him to go where he's needed."

"He's still needed on Mestiko," Kirk said, an edge in his voice. "From the reports that have trickled out, the situation is getting progressively worse there. The glaciers are advancing, the air's hardly breathable . . ."

"Exactly. I know it sounds harsh, Jim, but given the current political reality there, Lon simply can't do any good. Not as much as he can do on Verzhik, certainly." He sighed. "I can admire a man for tilting at windmills as much as you can, Jim. But there are *two* worlds at stake here, and Lon can't save either of them where he is. Take him to Verzhik, and he can at least save one."

Kirk wanted to argue further, but he knew Morrow was right. For all his personal investment in Mestiko, he was part of the admiralty now, and that meant looking at the bigger picture. That was the advantage of being an admiral—the opportunity to do more good on a larger scale than any mere starship captain . . .

Oh, who am I kidding? If there was an upside to this, it was that he would get to feel a deck rumbling beneath his feet again and not have to keep looking up at stars that stayed unnaturally still. "All right, Harry. I'll assemble a crew."

HERTEX STAR SYSTEM

"Approaching occultation point, Captain Spock."

"Very good. Take us out of warp, Mr. Haarv."

The Rhaandarite helmsman acknowledged the order and counted down to normal space reentry. The maneuver was carried out without a hitch, and the prismatic flare of warp distortion on the viewscreen collapsed into a fairly close view of Daroken, the next planet out from Mestiko in this system—albeit just barely at this point. The passage of the pulsar PSR 418-D/1015.3 fourteen years before had radically altered the structure of this planetary system. Of the original seven planets, only four were still orbiting Hertex; the outer three, which had been less strongly bound by the star's gravity, were now technically rogue planets on hyperbolic courses out of the system, although it would be decades more before they passed the magnetopause into interstellar space. The outermost remaining planet, now the system's lone gas giant, had been flung into an orbit tilted more than seventy degrees out of the ecliptic plane. Daroken itself was in a highly eccentric orbit which, at its point of closest approach, brought it within eight million kilometers of Mestiko, near enough to appear as a resolvable disk to the naked eye.

The passage of PSR 418-D/1015.3 had also disrupted Hertex's cometary belt and asteroid field, so that the system had become comparatively cluttered with debris on still-changing and unpredictable courses. As a result, even the insular mar-Atyya regime on Mestiko had recognized the need for an aggressive space monitoring and defense program, lest their world be subject to another extinction-level catastrophe as an aftereffect of the first. Although they had wasted an inordinate proportion of resources on an impractical network of radiation-shielding satellites (whose continued inability to function as the regime promised was ameliorated only by the profound unlikelihood that they would ever be needed at all), some members of the administration had evidently been sensible enough to allocate some of the project's funding toward antimeteoroid defenses—winning the support of their paranoid leaders by designing it to double as a defense against hostile spacecraft. By all accounts, it had proven very successful in that function, driving off Starfleet vessels, smugglers, and other interlopers alike. Hence the need for the *Enterprise* to conceal its warp egress behind the mass of Daroken. Stealth was essential for the success of this mission. The proximity of Daroken to Mestiko at this point in its orbit also helped, serving to minimize the length of time that Admiral Kirk's shuttlecraft would need to be in the open, at risk of detection.

If Admiral Kirk was indeed the one to go on the mission. Spock rated that probability as more than ninety-five percent, but he still felt the need to argue otherwise. "Admiral," he said, swiveling the command chair to face the man Spock still considered its rightful owner, "may I again urge you not to undertake this mission personally? According to Commander Uhura's signal intelligence, the political climate on Mestiko is still unfailingly hostile to extraplanetary life. Should you be recognized as human—"

"I know the risks, Spock," Kirk said, a faint smile conveying his appreciation for Spock's solicitousness. "But you command the *Enterprise*, I command the mission. That's the way it works. Besides, Morrow sent *me* to retrieve Dr. Lon. His well-being was my responsibility five years ago, and it still is today."

Spock rose and moved to his friend's side, his hands reflexively tugging his jacket straight. "I am more concerned for your well-being, Jim. On our recent missions together, you have shown a tendency to treat dangerous situations as . . . invigorating. Even refreshing. I believe that last time, Dr. McCoy used the term *midlife crisis*."

Kirk glared. "I'm too young to have a midlife crisis." He leaned in closer, smirking. "Actually, my plan is never to have one. Call it taking advantage of Zeno's Paradox. If I never officially reach the halfway point in my life, then it never has to end."

Spock quirked a brow at this sentiment, which was excessively whimsical even for Kirk. He could already see the excitement in the admiral's eyes, his thrill at the prospect of adventure. For a moment, he wished that McCoy's medical relief mission to Verzhik had not precluded his presence here; perhaps with the doctor's help, Spock could have persuaded Kirk to change his mind. But he decided it was just as likely that McCoy would end up accompanying Kirk into the lion's den as usual. In that case, perhaps it was just as well that the doctor was safely occupied elsewhere.

"Very well," Spock said. "But I am responsible for your safety also, Admiral. Therefore, I am ordering Lieutenant Commander Leslie to accompany you and Commander Uhura to Mestiko."

Kirk brightened as the square-jawed, curly-haired security chief stepped forward at the mention of his name. "Well, I think I can live with that. It's a pleasure to have you back in the fold, Mr. Leslie. It's been too long."

Leslie simply nodded. "Thank you, sir." He had always been a man of few words, never drawing attention to himself despite his wide proficiency in fields ranging from security to engineering to flight control to paramedics. Some might fault him for that, and for the relatively slow rate at which his career had advanced, but Spock found such a humble, dutiful approach to life quite admirable.

"And it'll be good to have another familiar face along," Kirk added, looking around the bridge. "We weren't able to corral much of the old team this time, were we, Spock?" he asked.

For the benefit of the bridge crew, he tried to keep it airy, but Spock could see the wistfulness in his eyes.

"We all have our own commitments, Admiral. Those often take us in different directions." McCoy and Scott were both separately involved in the massive supernova-relief effort, along with Dr. Chapel and many other Starfleet personnel. Commanders Chekov and Kyle were aboard the *Reliant*, patrolling the Klingon border while so many other ships were occupied in the Minara and Beta Niobe sectors. And Commander Sulu remained posted in San Francisco to oversee the raising of his daughter—a responsibility no less important than the others. Though Spock could understand the admiral's nostalgia, he felt the collective talents of the crew Kirk had trained were being put to good use where they were. "But there is always the possibility that our duties will bring us together again in years to come."

"I wonder," Kirk murmured. But he was never one to dwell on introspection for long when his duty beckoned. Shaking himself free of his mood, he said, "Well, then. I suppose we'd better get down to sickbay for our disguises."

Spock nodded. "I'll alert Dr. Duane to expect you."

"Mr. Leslie, Commander Uhura, let's go," Kirk said. But he hesitated a moment before moving to the turbolift.

"Something wrong, Admiral?"

"No, Spock," he said softly. "It's just that . . . I'm a little nervous about having my head shaved. I just hope it all grows back."

This time, Spock kept the words *midlife crisis* to himself.

MESTIKO

The landing party used a *Wraith*-class stealth shuttle to make planetfall, its black hull blending in with the night sky, its antigravs making barely a sound as it landed. Nonetheless, they came down some distance from the capital city of vosTraal, traveling the rest of the way on foot. They had to wear thermal gear and rebreather masks, for the night was frigid and the oxygen thin. The terrain was barren save for a few scraggly plants sticking up through the snow. "And it's late spring in this hemisphere," Kirk said. "Things have regressed so much in just five years," he added for Leslie's benefit.

Uhura shook her head in disbelief. "The government's broadcasts show none of this. They can't exactly claim it's a garden world, or they wouldn't be able to justify keeping people in the domes and tunnels, but it's hard to find any images of the surface in the media. Just platitudes about slow but steady progress."

Kirk sighed. "They can't admit how profoundly their policies have failed."

They came to their entry point into the underground city

just before dawn. Five years ago, this had been one of the Kazarites' bioengineering facilities, but the mar-Atyya regime had completely demolished it and sealed off the tunnel leading to it. But once Uhura's tricorder found the entrance, it didn't take long for Leslie's phaser to disintegrate the overlying rubble. There was no airlock per se, but there was a double set of doors. Once they had gotten inside the inner doors and pushed them shut, the three humans shed their protective gear, under which they wore garments that, according to Uhura's signal monitoring, would be nondescript and socially acceptable by current standards. The tunnel was warmer than the outside but still cold, so they made their way toward the city at a brisk pace.

Once they emerged into the artificial lights of the underground city, Kirk tried not to stare at Uhura and Leslie. He was still getting used to their faux-Payav appearance. Uhura looked odd with no hair and parchment-pale skin; she managed to pull it off with her typical elegance, but Kirk still preferred her usual look. As for Leslie, he and Kirk had much the same problem trying to pass themselves off as long-necked Payav, even with the uncomfortably tight straps beneath their garments that flattened out their trapezius muscles. They compensated by wearing collars and neck tattoos carefully designed to create an illusion of greater length, but still had to hope that no one would look at them too closely. Kirk wished he could be as good as Leslie at blending into the background.

It quickly became evident, though, that blending in would be harder than Kirk had expected—for the simple reason that he, Uhura, and Leslie were all adequately nourished. All the Payav Kirk could see in the city streets were gaunt and hollow-cheeked, moving slowly or seated on the ground. Kirk could imagine the profound compassion and anger that would be on Bones's face if he were there. *"My God, Jim, we have to do something for these people!"* But how much angrier would he be, knowing that Kirk's mission was to take something more away from them?

Most of the Payav on the streets seemed to be waiting in queues that stretched around multiple corners. But they just stood still, leaning against the walls or sitting in place. When the party finally came in view of the front of one of the queues, they saw that it led into a facility with a mar-Atyya religious symbol above its door. "A charity or a state bread line?" Kirk murmured.

"Probably a bit of both," Uhura said.

Higher above the door was a large video screen displaying the visage of Odra maVolan, the mar-Atyya spiritual leader who ruled Mestiko alongside Asal Janto, or rather ruled through her; although the regime was nominally a constitutional republic, the mar-Atyya held supreme authority over social policy and the religious doctrines to which the secular legislators were obligated to conform. MaVolan gazed sightlessly out of the screen with his cataract-clouded eyes and spoke in a measured, soothing tone, insofar as his gravelly voice was able. *"Conserve your energy,"* he said. *"The needs of the body are a distraction. Wasting energy wastes life. Cherish the life of the mind. Seek stillness in meditation and prayer. Commune with God, and you will be free. Give yourself to God, and God will give back unto hur-Atyya. Through prayer will our world be saved."*

"Wonderful," the McCoy in Kirk's head was saying. *"So the world falling apart around them is the people's fault for not being devout enough."*

As the humans moved through the streets, Kirk noticed many eyes watching them. They all looked away when Kirk looked at them directly, but in those fleeting moments, he detected fear and resentment. Well-fed people were out of place in this part of town—probably in every part of town except where the ruling elite lived. So much for being inconspicuous. "We'd better find the resistance and get out of sight quickly," he whispered.

"But how, sir?" Leslie asked.

Uhura gestured toward a nearby square where a crowd seemed to be gathering, looking up at another large screen. "This way. I think it's a news report."

The screen showed a state-sponsored news feed, reporting largely on events in the daily lives of the leaders and actions taken against enemies of the state. Those actions included a mass execution, using nominally humane methods but broadcast in its entirety for public consumption. *"Let us all take comfort,"* the newsreader intoned, *"in the knowledge that these criminals and heretics were redeemed by this sacrifice. For every one of them removed from our midst, two to four more children may be fed. Thus is hur-Atyya renewed, one soul at a time."*

But Kirk, following Uhura's lead, didn't watch the broadcast. He watched the Payav watching it, alert for signs of anger, disbelief in the party line . . . and, most important, *determination*. The determination to fight for a change in the way things were. He had to be circumspect, though, for the kind of people he was looking for would be wary of the kind of people he and his landing party appeared to be and would try to keep their reactions to themselves. It was a contest to see who could hide in plain sight more effectively.

But Kirk had been playing high-stakes poker for decades, both with cards and with starships. He knew the tells. And he knew determination when he saw it. Soon he spotted his quarry, a man and a woman on the edge of the crowd. He couldn't quite make out their faces in detail—his eyesight wasn't what it had once been—but he could see it in their body language, and a wordless exchange of looks told him that Uhura saw it, too. Just as subtly, Kirk pointed them out to Leslie, directing him to draw closer and keep them under surveillance. Leslie faded into the crowd, passing through it like a wraith.

Soon the man and the woman went on their way, and Leslie tracked them for the better part of an hour, staying in touch through a subcutaneous communicator next to his ear. Kirk and Uhura followed at a fair distance, hoping their subjects' path would take them to some isolated place where contact could be made. But they stayed in public places, and Kirk began to suspect that the two Payav were deliberately leading them in circles.

Sure enough, it wasn't much longer before he passed a dark alley and felt a weapon's muzzle jab into the small of his back. "Make no sound," a voice hissed. "Move into the alley."

Kirk obliged without resistance. After all, things were going according to plan.

He just hoped the Payav on the other end of the gun wasn't following a very different plan.

"I'll ask you once again—why are you here?"

Kirk faced his interrogator as forthrightly as the blindfold over his eyes would allow. "To see Dr. Marat Lon."

"Why do you want to see him?" the angry male voice continued.

"That's something I'll discuss with him." He figured it was safe to assume Lon was still alive; otherwise, the resistance would not be going to such lengths to avoid answering questions about him.

"That's not good enough!" A hand struck the side of his face, hard. Despite himself, Kirk bit the inside of his cheek. *I'll say this for the Academy job—this sort of thing doesn't happen nearly as often there.*

"Wait." It was a female voice this time, young. "They're Starfleet. This is Kirk himself. Maybe they can help us."

The man gave a bitter laugh. "Starfleet was here when the mar-Atyya took over. Where was their help then? Where has it been since? While we were fighting for our freedom, for the survival of our planet, *Admiral* Kirk here has been getting himself promoted! And obviously well fed, at that." Kirk caught himself unconsciously sucking in his gut. "So why come back now?" the man went on. "Lon's the only human who stayed to help us. If the others are back for him, I doubt it's for any reason that helps us. So we'll continue this interrogation as I see fit."

Kirk sighed. He didn't exactly have the moral high ground here, and he had to do something to establish a thread of trust. "All right," he said. "I'll tell you the truth." The man scoffed. "And you'll know it's the truth . . . because it's the last thing you'll want to hear." He proceeded to tell his interrogators about Verzhik and the Federation's need for Lon's expertise.

"I knew it!" the man exclaimed. "Not enough that you abandon us, now you want to take away our best hope of survival."

Kirk was pulled out of his chair by the front of his jacket and tossed roughly to the floor. "Maybe I should send Starfleet a warning to leave us alone . . . through you."

"You say you're fighting for freedom," Kirk called, hardening his voice. "Is this freedom? A man in a dark room, using his fists to decide people's fate? Is that what you're fighting to save?" There was no sound, no movement. The man was listening, at least. "Doesn't Dr. Lon deserve the freedom to hear me out and decide for himself?"

After another few moments, the man responded. "How do we know you wouldn't just whisk him away with your transporters?"

Well, there goes that idea. "Lon knows there are certain kinds of minerals that block transporters. Have him choose a shielded meeting place, and take us there."

After another few moments, Kirk was yanked to his feet again. "Take him to a holding cell," the man said to someone else. "What comes next . . . we'll see."

Odra maVolan stared at Asal Janto. "Admiral Kirk himself? Are you certain?"

Asal fidgeted under his gaze. In recent years, Payav medicine had regenerated to the point that a privileged few could have their sight restored. MaVolan himself had backed the effort and had been one of its first beneficiaries. But he had long used his blindness as a symbol of his purity and commitment, so in public, he always wore specially made contact lenses to simulate the cataracts he no longer had, and he took care to avoid looking directly at anything. He did not keep up the pretense with Asal and the few others who knew his secret, but even in private, he sometimes neglected to remove the contacts. It was disquieting to see those seemingly opaque pupils focusing on her so precisely. Perhaps, Asal reflected, it was not by accident that maVolan left them in. "Our operative in the resistance recognized him despite his disguise."

"And they are taking him to Lon."

"Yes," Asal said, trying to match the calculating tone in maVolan's voice, to sound more like a partner than a lackey.

"Our agent is not well enough placed in the resistance to be told Lon's whereabouts, but some kind of tracking device could be arranged."

"No."

Asal stared. "I . . . beg your pardon?"

MaVolan smiled. "Even the mar-Tunyor can do God's work on occasion. For years, Lon has been contaminating our world with his unholy mosses and worms. For every field of them we burn, another crops up within weeks. Our efforts to locate and assassinate him have always run afoul of the blasphemers who would shelter him. Yet now, one of his own fellow devils has come to take him away, so he may inflict his curse on some other world." The smile became a chuckle. "As I have preached to the people many a time, conserving energy does God's work. So let us conserve our energy. Let Kirk remove Lon and save us the effort."

"Of course." Asal laughed now, though maVolan did not join her, and she trailed off to silence. "But what if Lon refuses to go?" she asked after a moment.

"He will not. I have met the man, remember? He is a true mar-Tunyor, arrogant to the last. Our world is a puzzle for him to solve, and he stays only because he feels compelled to impose his will upon it, to remake it in his image. I often entertain myself imagining the frustration he must feel at our constant thwarting of his efforts." Asal declined to point out that maVolan had alluded to feeling such frustration himself mere moments before. "But now Kirk offers him a new puzzle, one he will not be stymied in solving. He will jump at the chance. The mar-Tunyor's own folly will bring about our triumph. Yes. I have seen it." He folded his hands serenely.

"No more Lon," Asal mused. "Imagine it. There is so much more we will be able to accomplish without the need to fight against him constantly."

"Yes. We can bring purity to hur-Atyya that much more quickly."

"Purity, yes." She paused. "Breathing the air outside would be nice, too."

"We will be able to restore our native ecology much more easily without this constant contamination."

Asal nodded. "Still . . . the moss did do a good job restoring oxygen. And it was only moss."

MaVolan's "unseeing" gaze grew sharper. "What are you saying, Asal?"

"Perhaps . . . once Lon has been gone for a time . . . we can phase some of the moss into our own plan. Once it is no longer a symbol of mar-Tunyor interference, we can control how and where it is used. The people need not even know it is not our own creation."

"I never would have thought to hear such words from you, Asal," maVolan said darkly. "They smack of . . . *compromise*. And doubt. Surely you have not let yourself be swayed by mar-Tunyor propaganda? You know there is no proof that the rise in temperature and oxygen levels was caused by the alien plants. It was simply a natural fluctuation for which they seized credit."

"That's what we've been saying all these years. It's what I wanted to believe. But it's hard to deny how cold it's getting out there. Maybe we should reconsider some of our assumptions."

MaVolan shook his head. "It is not like you to say such things. That is not the pure, constant faith of the Asal I chose to lead our people."

She did not miss the veiled threat, or the irony. Years ago, she was the one Raya elMora had criticized for believing that unwavering faith alone would always be enough. "I still believe we serve God's plan, Odra. But . . . however blasphemous they may have been, the mar-Tunyor seem to have made a difference. More of a difference than we have made since taking over. I simply suggest that we could learn something from their efforts. Let the mar-Tunyor do God's work for us, as you said."

"You have not heard my words truly, Asal, if you could use them in this way. Not a single cell of mar-Tunyor matter can be tolerated on our soil!" he shouted, slamming his fist down on the desk and making Asal jump. "Only when we are pure, in biology and in spirit, will God restore our world to what it was."

Asal gathered herself. "This is me, Odra. I don't need to

hear the party line. We need practical policies that can get things done. I believe we can do that within the confines of faith, but we can't do it with the same simplified speeches we give to the people."

"Our hold on the people is tenuous enough as it is. Too many lack faith. Too many are blinded by their own hunger. We must maintain our commitment to our principles, or we will weaken our hold and run the risk of rebellion."

"I'd like to think," Asal said after a moment, "that our policies are still motivated by something more than protecting our own jobs."

MaVolan glared. "I will choose to take that as an instance of your often-inappropriate humor. I know as well as you that hur-Atyya itself is at stake. That is why I strive so hard to eliminate threats to my authority—because only then can I ensure the salvation of our world. Do not doubt me again, Asal. Do not let your commitment to our salvation waver."

Even through the contacts, she could see very clearly what was in maVolan's eyes—perhaps more clearly than ever before. "It will not happen again," she said. But she averted her own eyes as she did so.

"No, Kirk. I'm going nowhere."

Kirk studied Dr. Lon, sizing him up. They stood facing each other in a damp, echoing cave that was lined, so the resistance had assured him, with refractory minerals that would block transporter or comm signals. Kirk was here alone, with Uhura and Leslie still being held as hostages for his cooperation. Lon was accompanied by a burly young man—evidently Kirk's interrogator from before—and a striking, slender woman with large dark eyes. Lon seemed unexpectedly at home in this ragtag company; had Kirk not known the man from before, he never would have realized he was human.

But Lon was more than a human; he was a scientist. Kirk appealed to that—and to his ego. "Dr. Lon, the people of Verzhik need your expertise. They're struggling to hold off a mass extinction. They need the best people the Federation has to offer, and they've asked for you by name."

Lon smirked. "My name these days is Cart etDeja. I doubt the Verzhik asked for him. As far as the Federation is concerned, Marat Lon is dead."

"A dead man can't help save a world."

"You talk of saving worlds? What about this world? What about its people? Do the Verzhik have a ruling clique of pathological narcissists who deny the blinding reality of their world's death throes, who would doom their whole race to extinction rather than admit they were capable of being wrong? Are the Verzhik people having more and more of their rights taken from them every season, or being forced to suffer ever-worsening deficiency diseases and epidemics because the medicines and supplements that can help them don't fit the mar-Atyya version of *kashrut*? Are their people arrested and imprisoned without trial for even suggesting that the state doesn't have all the answers? Well?" Kirk knew the answer was clear in his eyes. "There you are. They don't need me nearly as much as the Payav do."

"But you can actually accomplish something there."

"I'm accomplishing things here. We all are. Our numbers grow every day as the state gets more and more ruthless. We have a whole network, not just here but on Kazar and the other refugee communities."

Kirk's ears perked up. "Are you in contact with Raya elMora?"

"Regularly. We're building a coalition, winning the hearts and minds of the people. And soon, the state won't be able to—"

"Cart," the woman said. "Should we tell him this?"

"He won't do anything, Daki. He's forbidden to interfere."

The woman—Daki—focused those stunning eyes on Kirk. "Then you should not even be here. Cart is one of us now."

"He's a Federation citizen. A human."

"And why does that matter?" Lon asked. "Have we regressed so far as to believe that genetics defines identity again? It doesn't matter where I was born or what's in my DNA. I'm a Payav now."

Kirk studied him. "You certainly have changed, Doctor."

Lon laughed—rather startlingly, at his own expense. "I for-

get how condescending I used to be. I don't like to remember.
I thought the Payav were such primitives just because they'd
only begun to enter the warp age. I never gave a thought to
their heritage, their cultural achievements, their strength of
character.

"When I decided to stay here, I assumed I could save them
from themselves single-handedly. I almost got killed my first
day." He took the woman's hand. "Daki here saved me, and I
began to realize that if I were to survive, I needed the Payav.
More . . . I needed to *become* a Payav. And the more I saw the
faces of the people I'd come to help—the more I heard their
stories, the more I had to experience life the same way they
lived it—the more inevitable that became."

"Don't misunderstand," Daki said, smiling. "He's *still* a condescending *vikak* most of the time. But he's our *vikak*."

Kirk took in their interplay. "How long have you been married?"

Lon moved closer to Kirk. "Our son is already an avid
reader. He's starting to take an interest in ecology. He already
knows enough to doubt the state's party line. But he needs a
good teacher to help nurture that insight."

He held the admiral's eyes for a time. "Ask me again to
leave Mestiko."

U.S.S. ENTERPRISE

"I take it you did not ask," Spock said.

Kirk looked at his old friend across the briefing-room table. He was back in uniform, restored to his normal complexion, but still hairless for now. "Would you?"

"No," Spock said. "There is a distinct logic to Dr. Lon's—or perhaps I should say Dr. etDeja's—decision."

"If Bones were here, he'd say Lon followed his heart."

Spock raised a brow. "The heart has its own logic, which sometimes works in concert with that of the mind. As my longtime association with the doctor should make clear."

"I'll tell him you said that."

"I would appreciate it if you did not, Jim."

Kirk chuckled. "Well, you may see him before I do." He slid a data cartridge across the table to Spock. "Lon's notes. A copy of all his research over the past few years, developing ways to minimize the damage the mar-Atyya are doing to the environment. He believes it should be possible to adapt his processes to help the Verzhik. He also took some time to review the data I brought and offer some specific suggestions for recovery strategies there.

"That's the *Enterprise*'s next mission, Spock. Once you drop me off at Earth, I want you to head straight to Verzhik. I'm putting you in charge of implementing Dr. Lon's strategies and recommendations. Maybe they don't get Lon, but I'm seeing to it that they get the next-best thing."

"I appreciate your confidence in me, Jim, but I am not a specialist in this field."

"But you're the best generalist in Starfleet. And you'll have the help of all the specialists who are already there. You'll do fine."

"I wonder . . . will Admiral Morrow be so sanguine about this outcome?"

"You let me deal with Harry." Kirk frowned, growing contemplative. "I just wish there'd been something I could do about things on Mestiko. That's twice now I've had to leave things as bad as they were when I came, or worse."

"But you did not make them worse by removing Dr. Lon. And from what you say, there is hope that they can resolve the situation on their own."

Kirk's eyes were haunted. "But what if they can't?"

JAROL DESERT, KAZAR

Raya looked out the shuttle's window and smiled at the sight of the expansive daggerleaf forest below. The Kazarite geneticists had done their work precisely to the Payav's specifications: the trees' narrow, succulent leaves held on to water effectively, while their deep roots tapped the water table and reduced the need for irrigation. And the trees grew fast, becoming more effective as a windbreak with every season, sheltering the desert beyond from the winds that had been stripping away its moisture and its topsoil.

But Raya was finally able to realize how beautiful they were. The daggerleaf trees didn't have the deep meaning that the *noggik* tree had held for so many Payav, but Raya planned to bring some back with her to Mestiko when the time came.

Soon the shuttle passed beyond the forest, soaring over the fields of drought-resistant perennial crops that supplemented their annuals. The *kovna* grain that provided their staple food source had been successfully engineered for drought resistance, as well as for resistance to parasites and insects, for smaller crop losses meant less water wasted on plants that did not survive to be eaten. Back home, after the Pulse, even the Norrb had not been this successful at growing *kovna*. The Kazarites had been helpful with this as well, once Raya had persuaded them to spare sufficient facilities and personnel for the engineering work. But it was still helpful to have a backup food source from the perennials, for the rough years. Also, the perennials' extensive root systems helped prevent the soil from eroding and clung to whatever moisture remained in it. Season by season, the Payav refugees managed to hold on to more and more of the Jarol's water, to come closer to a day when the label *Jarol Desert* would no longer apply. But Raya was resolved that when that day came, she would be watching it remotely from Mestiko, with Elee and Theena by her side.

Not that she didn't have plenty of company here, she reminded herself as she saw the settlement's children crowding around the landing pad below. The children wore wide-brimmed hats to shield their pale skin from the sun and bandanas to protect their noses and mouths from the dust the shuttle kicked up, but she could still see their excitement in their body language. It seemed the numbers of Payav here grew every day, whether from new births or from the steady influx of refugees. Many worlds had taken in those who fled from Mestiko, but few Payav felt at home there or could easily adapt to a way of life generations more advanced than their own. As word of the exiles' accomplishments in the Jarol spread, more and more had made their way here, seeking a place that the Payav could call their own, a land they could build and grow on and make into what they needed. It filled Raya with pride that her people had achieved so much here in spite of the Kazarites who had shunted them off to their unwanted lands—in spite of the Federation that had abandoned them.

In spite of James T. Kirk.

Raya spent a suitable time greeting the children, telling them of the progress of the daggerleaf forest and how beautiful it was becoming. But she cut it short as soon as she felt appropriate, for she was eager to get to Cadi.

Cadi orMalan greeted her just as eagerly when she reached his dwelling, knocking her hat off with his kiss and his embrace. She laughed and pulled away. "Time for that later. There's news from home?"

Cadi reined himself in. "Yes. We got a new report from the resistance."

"Tell me." News from home was something to cherish—not just for its provenance but for the difficulty of getting it here. The courier ships that snuck into the system and the resistance members who beamed out radio pulses for them to intercept risked discovery and arrest by the mar-Atyya. Sometimes the couriers did not come back, or they came back with partial signals that had been violently interrupted.

Nothing untoward had happened to the signalers or couriers this time, but the news they delivered infuriated Raya. "Kirk! He did it to us again! Not enough he abandoned our world in its time of need, now he has to try to steal our best hope of its salvation?"

"Lon refused to go," Cadi reassured her. "He truly is one of us. He stood his ground and sent Kirk packing."

Raya gave a contemptuous laugh. "Kirk is getting soft. He used to be more stubborn. Or maybe Lon is just too stubborn even for him."

"He's dedicated to the cause. Like all of us."

"Yes." Raya released her tension with a sigh. "Forget Kirk. We don't need him. We never did." She stood alongside Cadi, gazing out the window. "Look what we've built here, Cadi. It's just a preview of what we'll do when we take our home back."

Cadi studied her. "Raya . . . there's no reason we can't make this a home as well. I mean . . . you're the one who keeps urging us to have more children. Why can't you . . . and I . . . set an example of our own?"

Furrowing her brow, Raya took him into her arms. "Oh, Cadi. You know your companionship has been a great boon to me. But I can't think of such responsibilities now. There's too much else I need to do."

"You need not do it all yourself. There are so many back home now, and all of us ready to support them."

"I know. But I've been working so long to coordinate it, and we have so much momentum building. I dare not risk interrupting it."

Cadi was silent for a long moment. "Raya . . . I'm not sure I'd want to leave the Jarol. I've put so much of myself into it. And it feels like home. More than Mestiko ever could again in my lifetime, probably."

Raya stopped herself from snapping at him. It was as valid a point of view as any other. Just smaller in scope than what the Payav as a whole required. "I understand, Cadi. But it can't be that way for me."

He grew somber. "I wish that upset you more. You don't see us as anything permanent, do you?"

"Oh, Cadi." She stroked his head. "I need you. I do. I need a respite from the struggle. I need someone who can take my mind off it from time to time. The fact that you don't feel it as urgently as I do is why I cherish you now. But it's also why we must part someday."

He pulled away. "And the sooner the better, to you." He walked out.

Raya hoped he would come back. He usually did. She wished she could offer him more. But her passion was devoted to a greater enterprise.

She would win Mestiko back from the mar-Atyya, no matter what it cost her.

PART THREE

Stardate 8006.5
(December 2282)

VOSTRAAL, MESTIKO

"Have you all gone mad?"

Odra maVolan's unclouded eyes glared sternly at the members of the ruling Synod, but they refused to flinch before him. Asal Janto spoke for the majority. "On the contrary. We are facing reality. The people are on the verge of revolution."

"Then we must crack down harder, not make concessions!"

"The more we crack down, the harder they resist. We must not forget that it was the people who put us in power, because we promised them a better world, better lives. And now they will take that power away from us if we do not begin serving their needs again!"

"They do not know what they need! They have been seduced by the blasphemy spread by Lon, by elMora's speeches smuggled from that alien hell she rightly inhabits. They are lost souls too deafened by their growling bellies to hear God's voice. They need us to interpret it for them."

"Because we are the only ones with enough to eat?" countered Mokar maNashol, one of the mar-Atyya cleric-administrators who had come around to Asal's side. "They hate us, Odra, and we have given them reason. If we hope to avoid being strung up by the necks like Nal Kotyar was in Tazokka, we must show the people we are listening to them!"

"By casting aside our control altogether? By abandoning everything we have fought for this past twelveyear and more?"

"Are you so certain," Asal asked him, "that we have no chance of winning a free election? If that is so, then do we even deserve to rule?"

"God decided that I was to rule. And I chose you to rule with me. So be cautious, Mokar, when you speak of being strung by the neck. That is the fate I dole out to enemies of the state."

"And that is why we keep gaining more enemies," Asal insisted. "Study your history, Odra. Killing off resistance always multiplies it rather than eliminating it."

"Then how do we retain our power if we give the rabble the license to throw us out? When they stand outside our walls right now screaming Raya elMora's name, how can we think that handing them power can save us?"

"It can save our lives, at least," maNashol said. "If we step back now, we can survive to carry on the fight."

"And be exiled, as the *Zamestaad* were? Be separated from the soil with which we share our very souls?" MaVolan shook his head. "Better to die here and stay as one with holy hur-Atyya."

"You martyr yourself if you like, Odra," said Asal. "But you're overruled. We're accepting Lon's proposal. Free elections, monitored by the Federation."

MaVolan grimaced. "Even worse—to bring those heathens back."

"At least," maNashol said, "they are the one thing we all have in common. Everyone resents them equally."

Asal was not so sure of that. Dr. Lon's resistance movement had been very effective, both at spreading its alien plants and at disseminating their results to the people. It had become increasingly impossible to deny that the alien methods were far more effective at restoring the ecosystem than the mar-Atyya strategies could ever be. A twelveyear ago, the mar-Atyya had won the people over by promising that they could have their old, familiar plants and animals back rather than settling for a mix of alien imports and engineered native species. Now, the people were eager to see anything green and growing and alive, no matter how unfamiliar it was. Indeed, the whole generation just reaching adulthood had grown up in the wake of the Pulse; to them, hur-Atyya's native life-forms would have been no more familiar than the alien forms introduced by the Kazarites. More and more, the old hostility against the Federation was fading. Many of the people now felt they had been better off with the Federation, while the long-standing resentments held by others had faded in the light of their more recent problems.

Of course, Raya elMora had long denounced the Federation in her smuggled rhetoric. She had toned down that theme in recent years, focusing more on the need for self-reliance and the power of the Payav to achieve their own salvation. But it still remained clear that she was anything but a partisan of the Federation. That made it all the easier for the people to trust the Federation as impartial election monitors. (Besides, who else was there? The Klingons? No one would risk going down that road again.)

MaVolan stood, dismissing the meeting in his own mind if no one else's. "Your lack of commitment will cost you dearly. But let elMora and the Federation come. Those of us who stand firm in our conviction still have the means and the will to deal with them."

He stormed out, and a few others on the Synod left with him—some decisively, others more timidly. Those who remained exchanged uneasy looks. The minister of security had been the first to follow maVolan out the door; naturally, the mar-Atyya leader made certain that the people in charge of the armed forces were unfailingly loyal to him. Asal had hoped that maVolan could be persuaded to accede to the elections so that matters could proceed without bloodshed. Now, that possibility seemed increasingly remote.

But she stiffened her resolve. "It doesn't change anything," she told the others. "This is still what we need to do. The cost in lives will be far worse if we do not. We have nothing to lose."

"But what does the Federation have to lose?" maNashol asked.

"They will no doubt send Starfleet to monitor the election." She sighed. "They are soldiers. They are accustomed to risking their lives."

MaNashol nodded. "Better theirs than ours."

U.S.S. ENTERPRISE

Captain Spock rose from the command chair as Raya emerged from the turbolift. He and his crew looked so formal and intimidating in the deep-red jackets and metallic insignia they wore now, as though Starfleet had finally decided to drop its friendly pretense. "Madam Councillor. Welcome to the bridge. I trust you and your colleagues find your accommodations acceptable?"

"Most acceptable, Captain," Raya replied with a hint of irony. "We are accustomed to making do with much less."

"Well, not for much longer, I'd wager," said Dr. McCoy. The surgeon was hovering behind the command chair, and Raya had to wonder what he was doing on the bridge. "You're goin' home!"

"Yes," she replied, throwing a wistful glance at the image of Kazar on the viewscreen. "Most of us are. Perhaps even to stay, if the people are willing. Though I fear we will not find it much of a home when we arrive, thanks to the treatment it has suffered from its current warders."

Spock gave what Raya supposed would qualify as a frown on a Vulcan. "Although you are naturally a welcome guest aboard the *Enterprise*, Madam Councillor, I must again suggest that a return to Mestiko might be best postponed until after the election results are in. So long as the mar-Atyya remain in power, your safety and that of your people—"

"My people, Captain, are the millions back on Mestiko crying for responsible leadership. I must be there to stand before them on the day of the election. I must step forward and face my opponents before all and be ready to take my place immediately if that is their will, or I will not be seen as an effective leader—either in their eyes or my own." She thought back to her long years among the refugees—arduous, difficult, painful years that had plowed many furrows in her face and raised thick calluses on her hands, but rewarding years during which she had worked side by side with her fellow Payav, not as a detached leader spewing proclamations but as a fellow refugee scrabbling in the soil, carrying her share of the load right alongside the others. She had come to believe that personal connection, that refusal to put herself above her people or ask them to do anything she would not do herself, was the key to effective leadership. Perhaps if she had known that a twelveyear ago, she would not have lost the Payav's trust. Now she had won it back, or so it seemed, and she was determined to be worthy of it.

"Very well," Spock said, lifting an eyebrow. "Ensign T'Lara, take us out of orbit. Ensign Domenick, plot course for Mestiko." He depressed a button on his chair arm. "Engineering. Mr. Scott, prepare for warp speed."

"*Aye, Captain.*"

Raya noticed McCoy looking at her quizzically. "Something bothering you, ma'am?"

She smirked. "It just seems odd for James Kirk not to be here. I never imagined him the type who would retire to a life of idleness."

McCoy's expressive face showed ironic agreement, and there was an unexpected coldness in Spock's voice as he said, "I would not presume to argue, Madam Councillor."

"Me, neither," McCoy said. "Don't get me wrong, Antonia Salvatori's a fine woman, a great catch. But none of us saw it coming. I—" He stopped at a look from Spock.

Raya wondered what this Antonia woman was like. Someone quiet and submissive, who would accept Kirk's overbear-
ing will without question and not stand up for herself? "Well.
It is just as well he is not here. He has no right to show his
face in these proceedings. The Payav Restoration Movement
got where it is today in spite of his efforts, not because of
them."

She was not surprised by the long silence that followed. She
could understand his former colleagues being uncomfortable
with hearing awkward truths about the man. But what puzzled her was the thoughtful, curious way that Spock looked at
her. "Captain?"

"As I said, it would be presumptuous to argue."

"If you wish to argue, please do."

"I am merely curious as to your interpretation of events. To
what specific efforts of Admiral Kirk do you refer?"

"You know full well, Spock. He refused to take any action
against the mar-Atyya coup."

"Starfleet regulations—"

"Have not stopped James Kirk when he was determined.
Yet he did nothing."

"I see. Perhaps this is one source of confusion, for you spec-
ified 'efforts' rather than a lack of effort. But did he not facilitate your resettlement on Kazar?"

"In a barren desert, yes."

Spock raised a brow. "It did not appear barren to me in our
surface scans."

"Because the Payav have made it bloom. Because we put
our sweat and our blood and our souls into it, and it gave back
to us."

"Gave back?"

"The will to keep fighting. The skill to rebuild a world. A
rallying point and haven for Payav refugees everywhere, and
an example to the people back home that we could truly save
our world."

"Excuse me, Madam Councillor. I have made an extensive
study of humanoid emotions, yet many nuances still escape
me. Your exile to the Jarol Desert accomplished all this, yet
you still feel anger at James Kirk for delivering you there?"

Raya was taken aback, floundering for words. "That . . . that was not his doing. We built that success on the results of his inaction, his refusal to help."

"His refusal to overthrow the mar-Atyya regime."

"Exactly!"

"Which the people of Mestiko itself have now learned they were in error to support."

"Yes! But only after years of suffering and terrible loss."

"Experiences that they would not have had at the time of the coup."

"Of course not."

"So they would have had no reason to agree with you that the mar-Atyya were unfit to lead. No reason to support your return to power, when they only knew your regime as one that had failed to restore their world."

"No, I . . . suppose not."

"Yet now they have tangible proof, not only that the mar-Atyya's rhetoric is hollow but that yours is backed up with concrete evidence of success. Proof that Mestiko cannot be restored without the use of alien biota, biotechnology, and resources."

Raya pressed her lips together. "I see where you are going with this, Captain. That none of this would have happened without James Kirk's choices. But Kirk does not deserve the credit. If any human does, it is Marat Lon. He did not simply retreat and leave things to work out for themselves. He went down to live among my people, to fight for them at profound risk to his life. He became one of us."

"Yes. All made possible through cosmetic surgery performed in the *Enterprise* sickbay."

McCoy smiled. "One of my finer pieces of work, if I do say so myself."

Spock turned to him. "If you can set your proclivity for subjective assessments aside for the moment, Doctor . . . is it routine for a Starfleet vessel's chief medical officer to perform extensive cosmetic surgery on a civilian at his own request?"

"No, Spock," McCoy said, glaring a bit. "Even a starship this big only has so many supplies to go around. It takes authorization from the captain to do something like that."

"What if the surgery is pursuant to a personal mission to infiltrate a hostile civilization?"

"Deliberately helping a patient put himself in harm's way? No way would I volunteer to do something like that. Again, I'd need orders from my CO."

"So I take it you received such orders in Dr. Lon's case?"

McCoy grimaced. "Cut it out, Spock. You were there in the damn room when Jim told me to do it."

"All right," Raya said. "You have established your point—though you two could stand to improve your teamwork skills." They exchanged a bemused look. "But you forget it was James Kirk who tried to take Lon away from our world three years ago."

"Who was *ordered* to take him away," McCoy corrected.

"And ultimately did not do so," Spock added. "His superiors were not pleased. But they were mollified when Lon's notes proved beneficial in restoring a degree of ecological balance to Verzhik."

"All right. You have made your position clear. But millions have died under the mar-Atyya, and countless critically endangered species have gone extinct. Kirk did not prevent that."

"No, he did not," Spock answered bluntly. "But given the circumstances prevailing at the time, can you suggest how anyone else could have?"

Only the chirping of the bridge's consoles filled the long silence that followed.

VOSTRAAL, MESTIKO

Pavel Chekov always hated beaming down into a mob. It rarely turned out well.

In this case, he thought hopefully as the transporter effect faded around him and Captain Terrell, at least the crowd of aspiring voters had not become a mob yet. And for the most part, they were probably not likely to take out their aggressions on Starfleet personnel. Over the course of this long, turbulent election day, the *Reliant*'s crew had been working tirelessly alongside the Federation election monitors, keeping watch over polling places scattered across Mestiko and ensuring that the Payav's right to free and fair elections was not infringed upon.

Since the polls opened, the reports from Lieutenant Commander Nizhoni and her security staff had felt more like a running commentary to Chekov and Terrell, who had monitored them from the *Reliant*'s bridge. Barely had one attempt at electoral fraud been exposed and neutralized than another was detected. Nizhoni's people, and the Payav police forces sympathetic to their efforts, had captured numerous Payav attempting to sneak in devices that could hack the voting computers or infect them with viruses. The science and engineering departments had been kept busy double-checking the voting computers to ensure they had not been tampered with, and in some cases purging those that had been (regrettably rendering many votes invalid but ensuring the legitimacy of those that followed). Government operatives and party loyalists had been caught attempting to vote multiple times at different polling places, using various assumed names culled from the swollen ranks of Mestiko's dead. Visual surveillance and biometric scans had helped to thwart their efforts; not every polling place on Mestiko was so equipped, but all the monitoring teams had tricorders linked into a planetwide network. In some places, poll workers had been caught giving false voting instructions or trying to pressure people into voting for the sitting regime. In others, street gangs recruited as religious enforcers had been discovered harassing voters away from the polls.

It seemed that, although the mar-Atyya government had nominally agreed to go along with the elections, many of its members saw them only as a means to quell public unrest by giving the illusion of legitimacy to their regime. Many, but not all, Chekov believed; a number of people in the government, notably High Minister Janto herself, had been unfailingly cooperative with the election monitors. They knew their regime could not survive a free election, but Chekov sensed they were as fed up with Mestiko's decaying ecological and social conditions as the masses were. Perhaps they hoped to salvage some place for themselves in the restored *Zamestaad* by supporting its return to power; maybe they were even past caring about their own careers so long as they helped their planet survive. Chekov was skeptical of the latter, but given how bad things were now, he couldn't deny the possibility that Janto and those like her had simply concluded they had nothing left to lose.

But as the day had worn on, the attempts at election tampering had grown more blatant. The street gangs had attempted to assault the polls openly, either to shut them down or to engage in booth capturing—seizing the voting computers for themselves and entering multiple votes for the sitting regime. The *Reliant*'s sickbay had been called into action treating the Starfleet and Payav security personnel injured in repelling their attacks.

And now, things were reaching the boiling point. Odra maVolan had sent in the military to shut down the elections altogether, declaring them a violation of holy law and thus invalid whatever their outcome. That was what had brought Clark Terrell down to tackle the situation firsthand.

Frankly, Chekov was surprised it had taken this long. Terrell may have been a more laid-back, soft-spoken commander than James Kirk, but he was very like Kirk in his readiness to lead the way into danger, his distaste for being left behind in a safe, familiar bridge while his crew made new discoveries or took risks on his behalf. Only his need to monitor the situation planetwide had kept him on the ship until now. As usual, Chekov had insisted on coming along to watch his back, and Terrell had cheerily welcomed the company.

Now, Terrell sighed and shook his head at the sight of the army troops blocking the entrance to the polling place, brandishing their weapons menacingly at the crowd. "People are alike all over," he said. "My great-granddaddy used to tell me about how his great-granddaddy had to go through nonsense like this to get his right to vote."

"Russian history has such stories, too," Chekov said. "Back in the—"

"Wait." Chekov followed Terrell's gaze to where a group of voters was arguing loudly with the soldiers. It looked as if violence could break out any moment. "Damnation," Terrell muttered before striding forward determinedly.

"Excuse me!" Terrell called as he came closer to the soldiers, his voice at once commanding and amiable. Many heads swung toward him, along with some video cameras operated by the local media. "Excuse me. Hello. I'm Captain Terrell of the *U.S.S. Reliant*. What seems to be the problem here?"

The leader of the troops strode forward to confront him. "Stay out of our affairs, mar-Tunyor. This gathering has been declared blasphemous and in violation of holy law. We are here to shut it down."

"Why is that, exactly?"

"Because our great and wise leader, Odra maVolan, has declared it!" The crowd booed.

"No . . ." Terrell waited for the noise to die down. "No, I meant what exactly makes this election so unholy? What specific doctrines does it violate?"

"It is impure!" the squad leader said. "It is contaminated by alien influences."

Terrell shrugged. "It was your own people who asked for it. Your own Synod who approved it and invited Federation monitors. And all the voting equipment is your own. The monitors and Starfleet personnel have only acted to ensure that everyone has fair access and the votes are counted fairly."

"Your very presence here contaminates it!"

Terrell caught his gaze. "What's your name, son?"

The squad leader paused, taken aback. "I am Squad Leader Var Nysul."

"Tell me, Var—is that what you believe? That this election is wrong?"

"I serve the will of the faithful."

"But *is that what you believe?* Look around you, son. Are you willing to start shooting these people to keep them from voting? Do you believe that would be good for your world? For your people, even the faithful?"

"Those are my orders. I serve as I am commanded."

"That still doesn't answer my question, Var."

Chekov noticed that the news cameras were fixed on Terrell now. He jogged over to the nearest one. "How wide is your coverage?" he asked the operator. "Can they see this planet-wide?"

"No," she replied. "For anyone but the state, access to the airwaves is erratic."

"I think I can do something about that." With the operator's permission, he tied his tricorder into her feed and called Kyle on the *Reliant*. "Can you send this all over the planet?"

"*If I bounce it off the right satellites, sure.*"

"Then do it."

By now, Terrell was turning to the other soldiers around Nysul. "How about you, young lady? Or you? Do you believe this election shouldn't happen?"

"They do as they are ordered!" Nysul shouted, though without much conviction.

"That's still not the question. What do you believe, people?" he asked the soldiers again. "What do you *want* for your world? What do your *families* want? What do you think is best for them?"

"You attempt to influence the election!" Nysul objected.

Terrell smirked. "You're the one saying there shouldn't be an election—why should you care?" The crowd laughed. "But all I'm asking is whether these men and women really believe that opening fire on their own people to stop a free election is good for the Payav—or the mar-Atyya, or whomever. And if so, why? All of you, please," he went on, meeting the soldiers' eyes one by one. "Can you tell me why this is the right thing to do? Can you go home to your families and tell them?"

After a moment, one soldier cursed, lowered her weapon, and broke formation, moving to stand with the crowd. A moment later, a second soldier followed. Then a third, a fourth, and more. "You are all traitors!" Nysul cried as the hemorrhaging of troops continued. "We are serving holy law!" He waved his rifle at the defectors, who readied their own weapons to defend the crowd. "Get back into formation! *Now!* I order you! I will open fire!"

"And what would that accomplish?" Terrell demanded. "You'd kill one or two of your own comrades in arms before they killed you. You'd probably start a riot that would get thousands of people killed and end all hope of avoiding a bloody revolution. And what would it get you? Would it save the mar-Atyya regime or just destroy any chance that it could avoid getting slaughtered?"

Now the rifle swung to bear right between Terrell's eyes. "You do not tell me what to do, alien!"

Terrell didn't flinch. "No. That's a decision you have to make for yourself. What you choose in the next moment could determine the whole course of this world's history from this point forward. Just make sure that you *think* about what you're doing and why before you do. Too many people use guns as an excuse to react instead of thinking. But when you're holding a gun on someone, when your finger's on the trigger, that's when you need to think the most. Because that's the most important decision you're ever going to make.

"Right now, Var Nysul, you may be the most important person on hur-Atyya. What happens next isn't up to maVolan or the Synod or even God. They may have put you here, but you're the man with his finger on the trigger. And which way that finger moves is up to you.

"So make your decision, son. Make it your own."

Terrell's gaze didn't waver. But before long, the rifle barrel did. A moment later, it clattered to the ground. But the tail end of the clatter was lost in the roar of the crowd. Terrell led Nysul aside, patting him on the back, as the rest of the troops stood down and allowed the voters to stream into the polling place once more—and then began moving to the backs of the lines themselves.

Soon, Chekov managed to catch up with Terrell, who'd just handed Nysul off to some of his fellow troops. "Captain," Chekov said, "that was amazing!"

Terrell sagged against the wall, and Chekov could see he was shaking. "Don't ever let me do a damn fool thing like that again. From now on, I'm leaving Russian roulette to you Russians."

"Nonsense, sir. You have the heart of a Russian." He clapped his captain—his friend—on the shoulder. Yes, this man was very much like James Kirk, in all the ways that mattered. "No matter what they throw at you, Clark, you will always triumph."

U.S.S. ENTERPRISE

Raya elMora stood before the bridge viewscreen, staring down the destroyer of her world. "It looks so innocuous," she said as the pulsar flickered on the screen, occasionally obscured by a burst of static. In the seventeen standard years since the irradiation of Mestiko, the spinning neutron star had traveled some one hundred thirty-two astronomical units, well beyond Hertex's planetary system though within the boundaries of its Oort Cloud. "Perhaps because I no longer fear it."

Spock would have found her sentiment commendable in other circumstances. "Nonetheless, Madam Councillor, it remains a serious navigational hazard. Ideally, we should not even be this close. The gravimetric interference—"

"Is not critical at this range, Captain Spock, as you explained before. The election is already under way. We must take the most direct route possible. I trust Engineer Scott to maintain the warp-field balance until we are clear."

Spock frowned. "I am also concerned that—"

Suddenly, the ship shuddered, and a second later, it underwent a violent deceleration. Spock caught Raya before she was flung into the forward railing, clutching the helm console to retain his own footing. "What was that?" Raya asked once she caught her breath.

"An uncannily well-timed example of the concern I was about to express," Spock replied, an eyebrow climbing toward his hairline. "We have fallen out of warp after taking weapons fire—no doubt from a ship using the pulsar's sensor interference for cover."

The ship shook again. "Three vessels, sir," Lieutenant Worene reported from tactical. "Mestikan design."

"Warp engines are offline, sir," T'Lara reported from the helm.

"Evasive maneuvers at impulse," Spock ordered.

"The mar-Atyya!" Raya exclaimed. "They will stop at nothing to cling to power."

"Fortunately, our shields were already raised against the pulsar," Spock said.

But the next hit was a strong one, making the power systems fluctuate. "Sir!" Worene cried. "Their weapons read as Klingon disruptors! Their engines show Klingon signatures, too."

Spock strode over to the tactical station to peer over the Aulacri's shoulder. From his usual place at the aft railing, McCoy asked, "Did the mar-Atyya make a deal with the Klingons again?"

"They would never deal with offworlders," Raya answered.

"But apparently," Spock added, "they are not above using leftover technology from the Norrb alliance with the Klingons—or perhaps from Alur orJada's smuggling activities. These readings match Klingon technology from that era."

"So much for purity," said McCoy.

"Lieutenant, return fire. Aim to disable only. Mr. Pilar," Spock continued, turning to the Argelian at communications, "attempt to hail the *Reliant* and request assistance."

Pilar made the attempt, but the results were as Spock anticipated. "Too much interference, sir."

"Very well. Helm, continue evasive while attempting to clear the pulsar's ionization field."

T'Lara acknowledged the order. The young Vulcan handled the helm with great skill and efficiency, though without the artistry of a Hikaru Sulu. However, the three ships were able to keep the *Enterprise* confined within a tetrahedral englobement, using the pulsar itself as the fourth point. Worene's fire failed to penetrate their shields, which must have been Klingon-made as well—and considerably overpowered, judging from the emission curves they displayed. Spock surmised that the xenophobic and paranoid mar-Atyya leaders had spent years constructing the most powerful ships possible to defend their world against alien threats. Their technology was secondhand and more than a decade behind the times, but the sheer power driving it made it formidable.

Spock lamented the absence of James Kirk's tactical brilliance in this situation. But what intuition could achieve in one leap, careful reason and hard work could arrive at as well. Needing more information, Spock relieved Lieutenant Haley and took the science station himself. Despite several years as a captain, he still felt most comfortable there, at the heart of the information flow. He scanned the pulsar as well as he could through the interference, filling in the gaps with preprogrammed simulations updated with the latest readings, displayed on one of the science station's circular screens. He modeled the enemy's englobement strategy, observing the shifting vectors on an adjacent screen. From knowledge came ideas.

"Well, Spock? Do you have a plan?" Ahh, yes—the inevitable goading from McCoy. Once it had been a distraction, but now it felt like a natural part of his decision-making process, keeping him "on his toes," as Kirk might say.

"Always, Doctor. Ensign T'Lara—take us in toward the pulsar. Use the course and timing I am sending you," he added, working the transfer controls of his console.

"You want to take us *closer?*" McCoy exclaimed over T'Lara's acknowledgment. "When did that become a good idea?"

"At impulse, the primary hazards are electromagnetic and particulate radiation, plus tidal stresses should we draw too close. However, it should not be necessary to come that near."

"Pursuers are slowing, sir," Worene reported.

Spock raised an eyebrow at McCoy, wordlessly inquiring if he saw it now.

Indeed, the doctor was beginning to smile. "Of course. After what that thing did to their world, they're afraid to get too close to it."

"Correct. I imagine it must have strained their discipline even to draw close enough to hide in its interference field. I noted that they began their attack in its outskirts."

"Captain," Raya asked, "are we not drawing too close to—" She blinked, for the pulsar had vanished from the screen before she finished speaking.

"The emission cones?" he finished for her. "Our course was carefully timed to pass between their sweeps."

She let out a nervous laugh. "I doubt they will follow us through that."

"They are no doubt already circling at a greater distance," Spock replied. "If we tried to make an end run for Mestiko, they could still intercept us at warp. We must make our stand here."

"Can't we at least get some distance from the pulsar, so they can't trap us with our back to it again?" McCoy asked.

"Negative, Doctor. This is exactly where I wish us to be."

"Because of the psychological advantage it gives us?" Raya asked.

"That is helpful. But it is not the only power the pulsar provides us with."

"Mar-Atyya ships coming around again," Worene reported. "Closing to intercept."

"Resume fire, but reduce energy level by twenty percent. Allow them to believe we sustained damage in our passage."

"Make them overconfident?" McCoy asked. "One of Jim's old bluffs."

"A proven tactic, Doctor. Helm, reverse course. Make it appear we are repeating the previous maneuver. They may well be emboldened to approach the pulsar more closely this time. Tactical, continue firing with aft phasers, but target a torpedo on the pulsar itself."

McCoy and Raya both cried *"What?"* at the same time. Spock attempted to explain quickly.

"In passing through Hertex's stellar wind, the pulsar has gathered a thin layer of hydrogen, fused to helium by the intense surface gravity. But the helium layer has not become dense enough to fuse further. The torpedo should trigger a fusion cascade, producing a burst of intense radiation in all directions." He turned back to Worene. "Tactical. Forward shields and navigational deflector to maximum." He hit the shipwide intercom. "All personnel, secure for radiation burst. Take all forward sensors offline, and deploy blast shields over all forward ports. All nonessential personnel clear forward compartments."

"You're going to blind them?" McCoy asked. "And hope we don't get fried in the process?"

"Doctor, have sickbay prepare hyronalin injections as a precaution." McCoy glared for a moment, then left the bridge to see to it personally.

"Captain," Raya asked, "is there any risk this could trigger a starquake?"

Spock contained his surprise. It should not have been unexpected that the leader of a world ravaged by a pulsar would have studied pulsars in detail. "The risk is exceedingly remote, Madam Councillor."

"But not zero."

"No."

"If a starquake were to happen, the gamma burst would be devastating for light-years around."

"Possibly. It depends on the attributes of the pulsar."

"I can't let you risk subjecting Mestiko to another Pulse!"

"At this range," Spock told her evenly but quickly, "the populace would have eighteen hours' advance notice to retreat to shelter. There is little more damage that could be done to the environment than has already been done. The ozone layer would be destroyed again, but the equipment for its restoration is already in place. And again, the odds are very remote."

"And what would happen to us?"

The ship shuddered from weapons fire again. "Madam Councillor . . . shall I proceed?"

She held his gaze for a moment, then set her jaw and said, "Yes."

"Lieutenant, status of attackers."

"Still pursuing, sir. But starting to slow."

"Fire torpedo."

The pulsar's sensor interference no doubt blinded the attacking ships to the torpedo launch. Its impact went unseen by the *Enterprise* as well, but Spock could hear the crackling that began some moments later as the intense radiation burst induced electrical discharges across the ship's outer hull. Bridge consoles sparked and flickered as some of the discharges leapt over the circuit breakers. The air temperature rose by several degrees within moments.

But soon enough, the discharges faded, and Spock ordered the sensors back online. "The pulsar?" Raya asked.

"We are still here, Madam Councillor. Therefore, there was no starquake." While Raya absorbed that, Spock ran a scan. "They are on random trajectories; at least one is drifting. Life readings are nominal, power readings fluctuating. We have gained the advantage."

After that, it was short work for Worene to knock out the ships' remaining shields, then neutralize their weapons and propulsion systems with pinpoint blasts. "We can beam the crews aboard and detain them until their disposition is decided by the proper authorities," Spock told Raya.

She smirked. "Whoever those authorities turn out to be. Which reminds me . . . I would like to get to the polls before they close, if that is still possible."

Spock nodded. "I believe that can be arranged."

Raya turned back to the viewscreen, where the reactivated sensors showed the pulsar once more, now glowing steadily with residual incandescence from the fusion burst. "This is a healing moment for Mestiko," she said.

"Madam Councillor?"

"The thing that nearly destroyed our world has now, perhaps, played a role in saving it. It is a new beginning."

"Indeed," Spock replied. "Often that which appears to be a threat can prove to be a benefit—if one's mind is open to the possibilities."

She met his eyes, and he saw that she took his meaning.

MESTIKO

"Raya! You're home!"

Raya beamed at the familiar voice and laughed as Theena elMadej rushed into her arms. The little waif had blossomed into a fine, striking woman, but she still squealed like a little girl at the reunion. "And you won!" she went on. "It's the biggest landslide in electoral history!"

"Don't get used to it," Elee said, her rough voice a tonic to Raya's ears. She had stayed safe all these years by keeping a low profile but had been one of the first to greet Raya on her return. She was more gaunt and aged than ever, trembling and brittle-boned from years of nutritional deficiencies. But she had kept on fighting while so many others had died around her, and she still had the same old fire in her eyes. "Everyone wanted the mar-Atyya out, but it won't be long before all the old agendas resurface. Enjoy this unity while it lasts, Raya."

"I think things will go better this time," Dr. McCoy said from where he leaned against the wall of the reception hall. "Raya's folks on Kazar learned a lot of useful skills for makin' dead places bloom. The people can see it's not just promises anymore. And I doubt they'll be so quick to reject outside help."

Theena threw him a glare. "What Raya and the Payav did, we did on our own. If we've learned anything, it's how to take care of ourselves instead of relying on others, whether God or aliens."

"Now, Theena," Raya told her. "True, we can and will rely on our own strengths. But one of those strengths is the willingness to trust in others. We exiles benefited greatly from the Kazarites' knowledge and resources. And the tireless efforts of Dr. Lon here did much to hold the mar-Atyya's policies at bay. Because of him, we don't have quite as far to go in restoring the biosphere, and we'll restore it far faster with his help." She turned to where the human scientist, still in his Payav guise, stood with his wife, Daki, and their son and daughter. "Or is it Dr. etDeja now?"

He shrugged. "I still think of myself that way. But everyone in the media and Starfleet is calling me Lon, so I suppose I'll have to get used to that again." He looked at his hands. "I think I'll keep the added thumbs, though."

Daki laughed. "He's learned to do some interesting things with them—I'd hate to lose them."

Captain Spock caught Raya's attention. "Madam Councillor. Have you decided yet on the disposition of our mar-Atyya prisoners?" Now that she had been officially reelected—and hastily reinaugurated—as the *Jo'Zamestaad*, and now that diplomatic relations with the Federation were officially restored, Spock had left the decision in her hands.

"They may join the rest of the deposed regime in exile on Kazar. Perhaps there they can discover the benefits of working with aliens." Privately, though, she was sure it would feel like a living hell for the fanatics. She took some pleasure in that. Except that maVolan himself had committed suicide just before the new security troops came for him. Apparently, he would rather die on his homeworld than spend a moment away from it. Or perhaps he just could not live with failure. "However, those members of the regime who supported the free elections—and did not attempt to subvert them—may remain and be allowed to do their part in rebuilding Mestiko, albeit without the power and wealth they were accustomed to under the mar-Atyya regime. They will have to earn their keep with the rest of us."

It had been hard for Raya to make that choice about Asal Janto. True, her onetime friend had been instrumental in helping the mar-Atyya achieve their coup and implement their policies. But had it not been Asal, it would have been another figurehead. And Asal had been one of the leading voices for reform. Upon Raya's return, one of her first actions had been to have a long talk with Asal, wherein she'd realized that her old classmate felt true remorse and genuinely seemed to understand that unwavering faith was not enough. She wanted to make amends, to go on fighting for her world as she had always striven to do even when her methods had been in error. Raya had reluctantly granted her request. It would be hard to deal with the emotions of sharing the same planet with the woman who had betrayed her, and hard to appease the many others who felt the same way. But as she had said on the *Enterprise*, it was time for the healing to begin. And this was a good place to start. Perhaps someday, even the mar-Atyya could learn from their exile and be welcomed back into the fold.

Spock met her gaze approvingly, and though his face did not change, she imagined she saw a smile in his eyes. "Thank you, Madam Councillor. I believe the future of Mestiko is in good hands."

EPILOGUE

Stardate 8061.3
(September 2283)

SIERRA NEVADA, CALIFORNIA

Jim Kirk was out in the yard chopping wood, stripped to blue jeans and enjoying the cool mountain air on his skin, when the Starfleet security people beamed in. He let the axe dangle unthreateningly in his hand but still rewarded them with a glare. "If Morrow sent you, remind him I'm a civilian now."

The lieutenant, a young Asian woman, stepped toward him. "That won't be necessary, sir. A foreign dignitary is here to visit you, and we had to check the area."

Kirk chuckled. "For what? Grizzly bears?"

"Procedure, sir."

"Thanks for reminding me why I retired," Kirk muttered as he retrieved his flannel shirt. He was glad Antonia had gone into Lone Pine for the afternoon. She'd never had any patience with Starfleet discipline and militarism. After more than a year, he was still trying to figure out how she put up with him.

The male guard finished his tricorder sweep and gave the all-clear. The lieutenant signaled San Francisco, and a moment later, the transporter chimes began again. Kirk sighed and turned to greet whoever it was.

And gaped when Raya elMora materialized before him. "Raya! My God!" He reflexively ran forward to hug her, then slowed, remembering that she might not be receptive to such a greeting. But she laughed and met him halfway. "What are you doing here?" he asked when she released him.

"Affairs of state. Negotiating for the next round of relief supplies. And recruiting scientists."

"Don't you have plenty there already?"

"Ecologists, yes. But we're making plans to open a general research center at our old lunar base. It's Theena's idea—start a facility that can draw the brightest minds from across the galaxy, a place where they can pursue any research they wish."

"Can Mestiko spare the resources to support that?"

"Theena's convinced me that we can't afford not to have it. We need to start giving something back to the galaxy, proving we can be equals instead of a charity case." She smiled. "And of course, the more geniuses we have on hand, the better our chances of finding quick solutions to whatever future problems might arise as we rebuild Mestiko. Perhaps we could even find a way to restore our orbit someday."

"Makes sense."

"Anyway, I just had to come and see you. I wanted to surprise you, but these officers insisted—"

"It's all right. I'm more than adequately surprised. Come in, come in!" he said, ushering her toward the cabin he shared with Antonia. "Frankly, I never thought you'd want to—"

Raya suddenly yelped and pulled up short as Butler appeared in the doorway and began barking. Kirk strode forward. "Butler! Easy, boy." The dog subsided, and Kirk knelt by him, stroking his head. "That's right. Raya's a friend."

"What . . . is that?"

"A Great Dane. A dog!"

"Are you sure? From the descriptions I've read of Earth animals, it seems more like a horse."

Kirk laughed. "It's all right. Just let him sniff your hand, you'll be fine." She gingerly followed his advice and skirted around Butler as he led her into the cabin. "Wait until I introduce you to a real horse. You could come riding with Antonia and me."

"Yes, where is this Antonia I have heard your colleagues speak of?"

"She'll be back in a little while. Say, can you stay for dinner? I'm sure she'd love to meet you."

"I'm sorry, I have a meeting this evening. Several, in fact. Give her my regrets." She looked around, taking in the cabin's rustic features—the stone walls, the wood beams and panels, the potbelly stove, the antiques and books on the shelves. "I never would have expected to see anyplace so . . . primitive on Earth."

Kirk chuckled. "We take pride in our heritage. Some of us, anyway."

"No offense intended. It reminds me of the homes we built on Kazar. I spent many a day chopping wood myself. And planting fields, and building houses, and making tools, and—"

"All right, all right, you win." He chuckled. "This must seem . . . dilettantish to you. But . . ." He sighed. "After so many years out there . . . I just wanted to get away from it all."

"You are never what I expect, James. I thought you loved your ship more than anything."

"I thought so, too. Then I met Antonia, and I realized . . . maybe it was time I started loving something else for a change."

"She must be a remarkable woman."

"She is that. Would you like some coffee?"

Raya hesitated. "I never developed a taste for it. Do you have hot chocolate?"

He grinned. "A discerning woman. I think I can scare some up."

As he rummaged in the cabinets, Raya's attention was drawn to his trophy wall, the one concession to modernity in his home, where his collection of antique weapons shared space with a portrait of the *Enterprise*, its original dedication plaque, and a photo of its command crew taken at the end of their last five-year tour together. "I see you haven't completely stopped loving your ship."

"There were certainly some special times there. For all those years, I fought hard to get her back, to keep her. But eventually, one by one, the crew started to drift away, to pursue their own careers. And I realized I wasn't enjoying it as much without them. I realized that maybe it wasn't the ship that mattered to me so much as the people. The family."

"Yes. I understand that feeling."

"So once Antonia and I became involved, I began to think that maybe it was time for me to try a different kind of family."

"Family?" Raya asked. "Is there a child yet?"

The spoon clinked loudly against the mug. Kirk cleared his throat. "Well . . . we're taking this one step at a time."

"So much for the bold Admiral Kirk."

"He had his day." He finished adding the marshmallows and brought their mugs over to her. As she sipped the chocolate gingerly, he studied the crew picture. "I realized something else, too. I was holding Spock back. He may not like to admit it, but he makes a great captain."

"He has taken to it rather well," she agreed.

"So how are things on Mestiko?" he asked, leading her to a seat in the living room.

"Rapidly improving. The frostbuster moss is back with a vengeance, and the Kazarites are already planting the first pine and daggerleaf forests. They're adapting some of our desert animals from Jarol for cold climates—there should be enough oxygen to introduce them within a year or two. Within a twelveyear—sorry, nine years for you—people should be living on the surface again. And they'll be living free, and, I hope, not so quick to throw it away this time."

"I'm delighted to hear it."

She lowered her eyes. "And I suppose I need to thank you for it. And to apologize."

He shook his head. "You don't owe me either."

"I do. I thought you were abandoning us. But you planned this from the start. You helped us by refusing to help us. By putting us in a position where we would have to learn to help ourselves—and to learn for ourselves that we could not do it alone."

Kirk stared into his mug. "I only regret that so many people had to die in the interim. Once . . . I would've fought to keep that from happening. Would've barged in and made people play by my rules and patted myself on the back for saving them. But over the years, I learned it doesn't work that way. People don't trust solutions you impose on them from outside. They have to find answers within themselves. And that means sometimes you have to stand back, let them make their own mistakes, and hope they learn from them before it's too late."

She came over and placed a hand on his shoulder. "You did more than that, James. You sent my people to Kazar, where we could learn to rebuild a world and be free to build a coalition. You let Dr. Lon go underground where he could do the most good. Even as you left us to make our mistakes, you gave us the tools we needed to fix them when we were ready." She shook her head. "You saw all that, years in advance. You saw it long before I did, before any of us did."

"I guess my time as chief of operations taught me how to play the long game. And playing chess against Spock for a couple of decades helps, too." He repressed a sigh. Antonia had never taken to chess, certainly not the three-dimensional kind. He missed it sometimes. "Still . . . on occasion, that means making impossible choices, like at Mestiko. I'm glad to be free of that responsibility."

She looked around. "So what *do* you do instead, James? What use do you make of the wisdom you've gained?"

"Who says everything has to have a use? I *live* my life. I share it with a woman and a dog who love me. I commune with nature. I read. There's so much literature I missed out on all those years hopping stars. So many other things I always wanted to do but never had time. I'm writing a book, did you know that? Well, trying to. I haven't gotten very far. But there's no rush."

Raya looked him over. "So, basically . . . you just exist."

"That's a little harsh."

"I take it back, James. This place is not like our homes on Kazar." She laid down the empty mug and stood. "Everything we did there, we did for a purpose. We had no room for indulgence. We dedicated our own lives to making a difference in the lives of others. And that has enabled us to make our homeworld better once again—to help the millions still in need.

"That is something that, although I did not admit it at the

time, I got from you, James. That determination, that commitment to making a difference. You put us on the path."

He looked away. "Then I've done my part. I'm entitled to make things better in my own life for a change."

"Is this better, James? No challenges to face, no problems to solve? Can you really sit here contentedly, chopping wood and reading books, when you know there is a galaxy of worlds out there needing someone to make a difference for them?"

"There are others who can do that."

"And there is still you."

"I have what I always wanted."

She sighed. "Maybe so. But you know something? That rarely lasts. You never know what will come swooping out of the heavens to take it away. And you can sit around and wait for it, or you can go out there and dare it to try."

After an awkward moment, she moved closer and took his hands. "Complacency doesn't suit you, James Kirk. This is a pleasant sabbatical, and you've earned it. But you'll be back in Starfleet before long. I guarantee it."

"Antonia couldn't live with that."

"Then that will be her problem to solve. For her sake, I hope she does. It would be a shame if she let you get away." She kissed him on the cheek. "I need to go. Thank you for the chocolate."

He showed her to the door. "Will we ever see each other again?"

Raya grinned at him. "I'm sure we will, James—in *my* home. On Mestiko."

2291

THE
BLOOD-DIMMED
TIDE

Howard Weinstein

HISTORIAN'S NOTE

The Blood-Dimmed Tide takes place in 2291, Stardate 9121.4—approximately eighteen months prior to *Star Trek VI: The Undiscovered Country.*

He who lives by the sword dies by the sword.
—human proverb

Live by the sword. Die by the sword.
Capture eternal honor.
—Klingon Laws of Honor
from the Scrolls of Kahless

Wield the sharpest blade
with the greatest care.
—Vulcan scripture

PROLOGUE

Seen from space, certain worlds—with wide blue oceans, emerald lands, and swirling veils of white clouds—whisper, *Welcome*.

This particular planet—with wind-scoured, cratered plains, rusty mountains, and one ragged, inadequate sea filling a basin left behind by some ancient cataclysm—*this* planet snarled, *Go away*. Only its location, in treacherous unclaimed space near the Klingon and Romulan Empires, made it worth the skirmish taking place there.

The lone, cloaked Klingon bird-of-prey in orbit was no match for two Romulan warships shedding their own cloaking fields as they opened fire. Several torpedoes found their target, confirming that no stealth technology was completely undetectable. A few explosive seconds later, all that remained of the Klingon ship was a bloom of shards glinting in the starlight as they hurtled away into space. Then the Romulan vessels turned their weapons on their primary target: a military outpost on the planet.

Hunkered in an equatorial valley, the Klingon base consisted of two structures linked by a tunnel—one a bunker housing a half-dozen soldiers and a bank of deep-space scanners, the other a turret capped by a pair of disruptor cannons. With only one big gun operational, and deflector shields failing fast, the Klingon troops were all too aware that they were overmatched by the warbirds pounding them from space. They expected to be marching into their honored afterlives in *Sto-Vo-Kor* shortly.

What the Romulan commanders didn't expect, and did not detect in time, was the Klingon battle cruiser *K'tanco* sweeping in with its own weapons blazing. The element of surprise tipped the brief battle in favor of the Klingon cruiser. With precise fury, the Klingon ship routed the Romulans—one vessel destroyed, the other making a hasty retreat.

Lusty victory cheers filled the Klingon bridge. The weapons officer called for song, but their commander glowered, dark and angry. "No," Captain Kang said, "not when we must prepare for war with the Romulans . . . and perhaps the Federation as well."

Kang's bridge officers roared their approval once again, since the prospect of battle in the name of honor was always welcome. But Kang didn't share their enthusiasm. He knew what they did not—that the Klingon Empire was rotting from within, teetering on the edge of a forbidding abyss promising none of the eternal glory of *Sto-Vo-Kor*. Kang had shared these fears only with Mara, his wife and first officer, and his two oldest comrades, Kor and Koloth.

Since before he had the strength to pick up a *bat'leth*, Kang had dreamed of living and dying as a warrior. His ancestors created a culture that prized uncompromising power so the Klingon people would never be subjugated. He'd served his empire with all his heart and soul, always marched into battle willingly, ready to shed his last drop of blood if his sacrifice would preserve the Klingon way. Now Kang faced the unthinkable. *I know no other life. If the empire ceases to exist, what will I be?*

CHAPTER
1

Dressed in the comfort of her coziest robe and slippers, Raya elMora stood at the window of her bedchamber and looked longingly out toward the placid S'rii Tuuliie meandering past the grounds of her official residence. The river's ripples reflected the full light of Varnex, the larger of Mestiko's paired moons, and the only one still orbiting the planet, presiding over the midnight sky. Back when she was a girl, this was just another provincial Larendan town, called Hur-tuuliie. She and her friends spent many a lazy summer day sailing with the river's gentle currents, pretending to be explorers, collecting the sweet fruit which fell from the *noggik* groves along the marshy banks.

That hometown was long gone, ravaged like most of the world by the same disaster that had sent the planet's second moon, Kifau, careening out of Mestiko's orbit. A new cosmopolis stood in its place. Renamed vosTraal, it was Mestiko's global capital city. Raya's childhood home was home again, but it wasn't the same. *Then again,* she thought, *nothing is the same, and it never will be.*

She padded across the carpet and sat at her simple desk

made of *noggik* planks, which never lost their fragrance. Bathed in the soft glow of a lamp and her computer screen, she scrolled through a revised proposal for celebrations marking the upcoming twelveyear anniversary of her return to leadership of the planet's ruling *Zamestaad* council. How could it be that long since the end of her exile on Kazar and her smashing election victory over the remnants of the corrupt, mar-Atyya regime? Raya sighed. She'd rejected the first ceremonial plans from her staff as too elaborate and self-congratulatory, and her chagrined aides had retreated to craft something more in keeping with their leader's modesty.

Frankly, she'd have preferred that the occasion pass with no more notice than the turning of a calendar page. But there was no escaping the tendency of civilized beings to pay considerable attention—*too much, maybe*—to milestones marking time's progress.

Bureaucracies possessed that same tendency, if only to justify their own existence. With the approach of the somber thirty-sixth anniversary of the devastation of their planet, government agencies worldwide spared no effort in preparing voluminous reports measuring Mestiko's progress. When her staff offered summaries, Raya insisted on reading the full documents. So she knew as well as anyone that her people had indeed come a long way since the days after the radiation-ignited firestorms, whipped by violent winds and fueled by vast forests, had incinerated wilderness and cities alike. The boundless flooding storms that followed had quenched the holocaust but left behind a toxic, seared surface, nearly stripped of life.

Call it the Pulse, the Scourer, or simply the disaster . . . no one knew back then if Mestiko could survive, much less flourish. Yet, even in those literally dark days of crushing despair, with a billion dead and wretched survivors forced underground, development and trade of natural resources had rebounded steadily and stabilized the planet's economy. Once freed from Klingon meddling, the miraculous satellite system created by the Federation's Dr. Marat Lon had restored the atmosphere, settled the climate, and permitted accelerated terraforming. That enabled the Kazarites to work their brand of

ecological magic and achieve enough environmental regeneration to make the planet increasingly habitable and arable.

Though it would take generations more for the population
to even approach predisaster levels, people did what people do
and the birth rate had begun to blossom. Many *Zamestaad*
council members insisted on heralding those triumphs, and
Raya could hardly dispute that her world had made an amazing recovery, considering the near-fatal blow dealt by the
rogue pulsar.

It was the curse of politics that Raya's public statements focused on success while her private thoughts dwelled on fail-
ures and frustrations. Food production and land reclamation
still lagged behind predictions, which had been conservative
to begin with. Ugly swaths of the planet remained barren, like
wounds reluctant to heal. *Will we ever truly recover? Or is this
as good as it gets?*

Raya sighed again, slouched back in her chair, and picked
up her mug of herbal tea. Never mind the debatable measures
of material progress—it was the social-services reports that
most troubled her. Rates of suicide, depression, and crime
were rising. The planet's once-thriving arts communities had
failed to reinvigorate themselves. It might have seemed trivial
that few important new dramatic works, novels, or musical
compositions had been created since the Pulse. But Raya
knew that culture sustained the soul, and the Payav soul
seemed as charred and barren as the *noggik* groves after the
disaster.

Mestiko faced a looming spiritual crisis, one resistant to the
calculus of charts and graphs, and nothing worried her more.
Various studies attempted to quantify a rift in attitudes between generations born before and after the disaster. Those
old enough to remember the good old days often found themselves drifting into nostalgic lethargy. Those just coming of
age seethed with frustration, knowing they might never taste
the halcyon existence whose loss their parents lamented. Lost
souls flocked to the latest lunatic-fringe fundamentalist faction, this one preaching yet another new twist on the corrosive
mar-Atyya belief that the Pulse was punishment for having
abandoned the old religious ways, and warning of an even

greater and final apocalypse to come. *Just what this wounded world needs.*

Things could certainly have been worse at this point. But they could also have been better. Even Raya's closest aides were unaware she'd been considering stepping down from *Zamestaad* leadership before her term was up. Not that she wasn't proud of her stewardship, but maybe it was time for fresh hearts and minds. . . .

A frantic pounding on her apartment door disrupted her ruminations, and she immediately felt queasy. In all her life, Raya had never known a late-night knock to be a harbinger of good news. She swung the door open to find Jaarg etDalka, her young chief of staff, standing there, looking even more harried and pale than usual. "What's wrong?"

"The Discovery Center." Jaarg swallowed and tried to quell the shiver in his voice. "It's been attacked."

"What? Who—?"

"We don't know yet."

Raya's head sank. She rubbed her long, still-elegant neck with both hands. She forced herself to breathe slowly, fighting off that spark of panic she always felt at the onset of a crisis. It was a reflex she'd learned to live with, and she knew the antidote: *action.* "Does Blee know?"

Jaarg nodded. "I called her first."

"Good boy." Raya smiled despite the situation, knowing her old friend and chief adviser Blee elTorno was already organizing a response.

"She's gathering all the information she can, and I've already summoned the security minister and the military chiefs. They'll be at your office in ten minutes."

"Good. Oh—one other thing. Contact Ambassador Settoon and tell him I'll need to see him within the hour. Now, *go.*"

As Raya ducked into her closet and quickly threw on some casual clothes, she couldn't even begin to guess why anyone would target the science institute on Varnex. It was no secret that some regional leaders still chafed at the surrender of sovereignty necessary for the *Zamestaad* to manage a generation-spanning global recovery. But even the naysayers generally saw the Discovery Center as a crowning achievement, built up from the ruins of Mestiko's first lunar outpost, which had been severely damaged by the Pulse. To this day, almost a twelveyear after the center opened, it still infuriated Raya that anyone could object to an institution established not only to improve life on Mestiko but also to enhance the planet's stature in the quadrant.

Yet, the sentient capacity for discord apparently knew no bounds. Some contrarian politicians and civic leaders considered it their veritable vocation to pick at the center's annual budget, though never with a vehemence that suggested they would sanction a violent attack on the place. And while she knew for a fact that certain religious zealots hated the progressive symbolism of the lunar science colony, she doubted they had the ability or reach to do something like this—not on their own, anyway.

No, rooting out those responsible for this crime would entail poking under some altogether new rocks, and Raya dreaded what might come slithering out. As much as she did *not* want to drag the Federation into this, that might prove unavoidable.

Just when things seem to be going along smoothly, somebody has to blow something up. . . .

CHAPTER
2

"So . . . what's wrong, Bones?"

"What's *wrong?*" Leonard McCoy sputtered over his coffee mug. "I'll *tell* you what's wrong."

Seated alone at a private corner table in the *Enterprise*-A mess hall, McCoy looked up at Captain Kirk looming over him. Noting the anxious twitch of McCoy's eyebrows, Kirk mulled the option of hasty withdrawal. But, after all these years, he knew McCoy was willing to blurt what others bottled up, protocol be damned, and that made his cantankerous chief medical officer a useful barometer of the crew's general mood.

"Assuming that wasn't a rhetorical question," McCoy said, biting off each syllable, "the Klingons and Romulans are at each other's throats, Spock's gone, and there's mayhem on Mestiko."

Well, Kirk thought with some consternation, *that sums things up pretty accurately.*

Alliances between predators were notoriously prickly, so Kirk had long believed the Klingon-Romulan connection would eventually fray. That inevitable final act had apparently begun, with reports of sporadic scuffles along the Klingon-Romulan border setting the entire quadrant on edge. Saber-rattling drowned out depleted attempts at diplomatic conciliation. The difficulty of getting reliable intelligence out of either insular empire made it impossible to know with certainty their relative strength or even the reasons behind the hostilities—which only made the situation more tense. Kirk had no love and little respect for either of the Federation's brutal enemies, and in his rosiest personal scenario, a war between them might lead to the demise of one and the weakening of the other. But wars rarely worked out according to anyone's optimistic prophecies, and Kirk preferred to avoid dwelling on the nightmarish alternatives. When the time was right, he intended to make his opinions clear to Starfleet Command.

He couldn't help wondering if Spock's sudden departure was related to the Klingon-Romulan nastiness. Not three days ago, with the *Enterprise* in Earth orbit, Spock had been summoned unexpectedly to a private meeting with Federation President Ra-ghoratreii at his office at the Palais de la Concorde in Paris. Then, without returning to the ship or providing any explanation to Kirk, Spock was dispatched on a mission so classified that Kirk could not extract a shred of information from any source on his whereabouts or when he'd be back from whatever the hell he was doing.

Without Spock aboard, Commander Chekov had added the role of first officer to his duties and Lieutenant Saavik had taken over as senior science officer. But even though it had been five years since Spock's stunning death and resurrection during the Genesis incident, Kirk and McCoy retained a shared raw memory of the void they'd felt without him then. Both felt uneasy about his absence now.

As Kirk sat across the table from him, McCoy leaned over and muttered, "Don't you ever tell Spock I said so, but he's as close to indispensable as anybody on this ship."

Once again, Kirk knew McCoy was right. "Maybe that's why the president picked him for this assignment."

"So meanwhile, we've got a mess on Mestiko, and we don't even know what we're dealing with."

"Whatever it is, it'll have to be handled minus one Vulcan."

Kirk hadn't been to Mestiko in more than a decade, when he had clandestinely tried—and failed—to extract Dr. Marat Lon. He'd been enjoying retirement on Earth when the *Enterprise* delivered Raya elMora home from exile three years later. Their relationship had certainly had its ups and downs since the rogue pulsar dispassionately designated PSR 418-D/1015.3 had devastated Raya's world. But once Raya had realized Kirk's role in subtly engineering events to assist her return to power, their friendship had mellowed to a level of supportive warmth that had remained unwavering over time.

Kirk always found Raya's personal letters more satisfying to read than official reports. And although she often voiced her frustrations, Kirk believed the Payav were doing more than creating their own miracle—Mestiko was, in essence, an ongoing real-life restoration experiment, providing invaluable lessons that would likely save millions of lives on other planets facing future global disasters.

In fact, Kirk had been so upbeat about Mestiko's rebirth that he'd allowed himself to believe Raya and her people would face only smooth sailing ahead. That was why this attack on their lunar science center was so troubling. He also knew how stubbornly independent his friend preferred to be. She was always conscious of the need to prove her recovering world didn't need constant aid. Though he didn't know all the details yet, the situation had to be pretty bad for Raya to call for help.

As the *Enterprise* approached Mestiko, Kirk contacted the Federation embassy in vosTraal, and Ambassador Settoon appeared on the viewscreen. Settoon was a burly being from Ana'siuol, a planet inhabited by humanoids whose general affability made them natural diplomats. The Ana'siuolo's otherwise unexceptional facial features were defined by a single, startlingly large, multifaceted eye set just above the fleshy nose. Though Kirk had never met Settoon in person, they'd spoken often since the ambassador's posting to Mestiko eight years earlier. Kirk recalled being mesmerized by that large central eye at first, but Settoon was even more jovial than most of his people; before long, the smile dominated the eye.

Today, however, that smile was a bit sad. *"Captain, good to see you again."*

"Same here, Ambassador."

"This is a most unfortunate incident. I was surprised that Raya came to me so quickly; that indicates the gravity. And I wanted you to know she specifically insisted that Starfleet send you and the Enterprise. *She has a deep and abiding trust in you, Captain."*

"I appreciate that, sir. What's your general impression of things on Mestiko these days?"

Settoon's expression brightened, just a little. *"Ahh! Quite good, actually. It's all too easy for diplomats to get caught up in official events that keep us from truly knowing the planet and people we're visiting. So I always like to put on comfy shoes and walk, walk, walk everywhere. I also love to cook, and I do not consider my job done until I've learned to cook local dishes like a native. When I first got to Mestiko, the atmosphere was still unfit for long exposure. And native ecosystems were so damaged there was almost nothing indigenous to cook. Now I am able to walk, walk, walk wherever I choose. And I've mastered enough native dishes to write my own* Meals of Mestiko *cookbook. So that's all good. But now this . . ."* His voice trailed off, but then his smile returned. *"You will set things to right, Captain. I am at your service. And before you leave, allow me to cook a meal for you."*

Unable to help smiling at the ambassador's enthusiasm, Kirk said, "I'd like that. Kirk out."

As soon as the *Enterprise* entered Mestiko's orbit, Raya beamed aboard. As she stepped off the transporter platform, Kirk greeted her with a boyish grin and the traditional Payav handshake, his arms outstretched with his left hand up and right hand down, Raya placing her palms on his. But Raya looked as grim as he'd ever seen her. "It's bad, James, and the more we learn, the worse it gets."

"The briefing room is this way," Kirk said as he escorted her down the corridor. "You look good."

The compliment caught her by surprise. "Oh! Thank you." Her eyelids fluttered in embarrassment and a pearly blush darkened her pale gray cheeks. "You too."

She really did look great, Kirk thought. The passage of time was fairly discernible in the deep furrows that had been etched in her face. How much of that was the stress of running the planet and how much was the result of her difficult years of exile on Kazar, Kirk couldn't say for sure. However, her long, graceful neck showed none of the sagging skin so common to humans and Payav alike as they aged. And the delicate tattoo filigree running the full length of her neck seemed more vibrant than he remembered.

"Your tattoos," he ventured, "they look . . . different."

"Yes," she said with a touch of satisfaction. "I had the colors brightened a bit. Payav men don't usually notice such things, which is quite annoying. Are human men more observant?"

"Not according to human women."

In the privacy of the turbolift, Raya's fingers gently brushed the silver flecks feathering Kirk's hair above his pointed sideburns. "You look . . . distinguished," she said with a twinkle in her dark eyes.

Kirk chuckled. "One of the Payav advantages? Not having hair to turn white and betray the fact you're not as young as you used to be."

"Believe me, James, I don't need hair to tell me that. Don't some humans change their hair color?"

"Are you kidding? Those gray hairs?" Kirk said, pointing to his head. "I've earned every one of them."

They arrived at the briefing room, where McCoy, Scott, Chekov, and Saavik were already seated around the table. Though Kirk gestured for her to sit, Raya remained standing and presented the facts in a soft, careworn voice, bolstered by charts, graphics, and images on the viewscreen.

"We started this science institute eight standard years ago. It was the idea of one of our most accomplished young scientists, my friend Dr. Theena elMadej. Like many of our young ones, she was tired of Mestiko's being thought of around the galaxy as a *tu-prait*—a beggar—holding our hands out for charity."

"We never thought of Mestiko that way," McCoy said.

"But we thought of ourselves that way, Doctor. Theena wanted to create something brand-new to restore our self-respect. She wanted to recruit the best scientists from many fields and many worlds, and give them funding and a free hand to pursue pure research, with no pressure to produce commercial products. We hoped they would make discoveries and advances that would help Mestiko's recovery, and help the rest of the galaxy, too. That's why Theena named the colony something simple and obvious—the Discovery Center."

Scott smiled. "Havin' read your reports, I'd say you've achieved everything you set out to do."

"Thank you, Captain Scott. Not everyone on Mestiko shares that sentiment. Funding has always been a battle. There's been . . . disagreement . . . on priorities. On a world with as many problems as ours, it wasn't easy to justify the expenditures."

"Well," McCoy said, "some people don't see the value in setting out on a journey unless they know exactly where they're going to end up."

Raya shrugged. "And I can't say they're wrong. But I thought we were reaching the point where the center was finally recognized as a symbol of unity, and a beacon from Mestiko to the rest of the galaxy. And now this." She keyed the computer to display a series of images of the facility, showing the damage, the injured and the dead. Kirk's officers watched in silence as Raya narrated. "They attacked with grenades, toxic gas, and small-arms fire. Of the eighty-nine staff present at the time, we had twenty-three casualties, nineteen of whom were fatalities. Fortunately, most had the good sense to stay in their quarters when they heard the explosions."

"What kind of security did you have?" Chekov asked.

"Not much, I'm afraid. The center was as open as we could make it without interfering with the work. We even had public tours. Theena wanted our schoolchildren to see that there was a place for their dreams to become reality. It was on the moon, for stars' sakes. It's not like anyone could sneak up on it."

"Not anyone from Mestiko, at least," Kirk said.

"Yes," Raya said with a solemn nod. "We never thought any Dinpayav would attack. But we now believe the attackers were alien terrorists."

"Terrorists?" Kirk's eye narrowed. "Why terrorists?"

"Because, as bad as the damage looks, it's actually minor. Once they were inside, they put on a big diversionary show. Lots of smoke and explosions, gas that smelled more toxic than it really was—all designed to keep the residents hiding and out of the way. Very little of the colony was badly damaged. If they were trying to destroy the place, they didn't do a very good job."

"Madam Councillor," Scotty said, "do you have any idea why it was attacked?"

"They apparently had a specific target."

"And I'm betting," McCoy said, "that it wasn't a cure for the common cold."

"No. It turned out to be a weapon. A subspace weapon. They took all the files, and the prototype. And they took Theena."

CHAPTER
3

When the autopilot announced final approach to its programmed destination, Spock opened his eyes, instantly shook
off the residual effects of his meditation period, and resumed
manual control of the sleek courier craft with the cramped
cabin and oversized warp nacelles. Though marginally
Class-M, the arctic planet on the viewscreen looked deservedly
uninhabited, so forlorn that it bore no name, just an astronomical designation. Spock banked the ship toward the
surface and, with a rueful twitch of one eyebrow, glanced
at the parka on the copilot seat. The more he aged, the more
he found himself feeling an almost irrational desire for
the accustomed warmth of Vulcan—and the more he found
amusement in such occasional twinges of illogical emotion.

Nothing like a little dying to change the way you live. How
typical of McCoy to say something so illogically homespun,
yet imbued with a nugget of irritating wisdom. Spock's experience twenty years ago with the vast though ultimately barren
machine intelligence of V'Ger had confirmed for him one of
his innermost nagging concerns—that the pursuit of *Kolinahr*,
the Vulcan spiritual state of perfect logic, was, paradoxically,

not logical. Diverted permanently from that goal, he'd spent much of the past two decades searching for his highest and best purpose, without much apparent direction—until his premature death at the Genesis planet. In ways he did not fully understand, his fortuitous rebirth had set him on a course toward that purpose. With *this* mission, it was possible he had finally found it.

Spock landed his craft softly on a glacial plateau, and saw that a battle-scarred Klingon bird-of-prey was already there. Sensors confirmed that the climate and atmospheric conditions were adverse, but survivable. He zipped the parka over his civilian clothing, pulled the hood over his head, slipped his thermal respiration mask over nose and mouth, opened the hatch, and stepped outside. Under the bleak beauty of a twilight-violet sky, the air was oddly still, but so frigid it would have been painful to breathe without the mask's protection. Spock trudged carefully across fresh snow toward a large humanoid wearing a hooded, fur-trimmed cloak, standing under the furled wing of the Klingon vessel. As Spock approached, the figure gestured up the gangway, and Spock followed him into the belly of the ship. The ramp closed behind them and they both lowered their hoods. Spock looked into the leathery face of a grizzled Klingon warrior.

"Welcome to my ship," said the Klingon in an unexpectedly soft voice.

Spock spread the fingers of his right hand in salute. "Live long and prosper, General Navok."

A second figure came out of the interior shadows. Spock recognized the dark-skinned human immediately and nodded in greeting. "Admiral Morrow. It is agreeable to see you again."

"You too, Captain Spock. Let's get something hot to drink and get down to business."

Over tankards—bloodwine for Navok, coffee for Harry Morrow, and pungent herbal tea for Spock—they sat around the wardroom table. Now, in better light, Spock noticed a deep, slicing scar across Navok's throat, the probable explanation for a voice which barely rose above a hoarse whisper, quite unlike the usual Klingon growl.

"When Curzon Dax arranged this meeting, he told me I could trust you two," Navok said. "The Great Curzon is like a brother to me, but trust must be earned."

"That's a two-way street," Morrow said.

"Ahh, but your government approves of your journey. If the High Council knew I was here drinking with two Starfleet officers, I would be executed for treason."

"True enough," said Spock. "But our immediate safety is entirely in your hands."

Navok clapped Spock on the shoulder. "Haah! So we all risk much. But the greater risk is inaction. Martial forces in our quadrant are driving toward a collision which could destroy us all. Vulcan, do you speak for the Federation and Starfleet?"

"Unlike Admiral Morrow, I am on active duty. While my visit is tacitly sanctioned by the Federation president, my presence is covert. Therefore, I have no official authority to make decisions."

Navok huffed in disgust. "Then this is a waste of my time! I need—"

"Shut up, Navok," Morrow said, surprising Spock with his less than diplomatic choice of words—though toughness might actually be the preferred approach with a Klingon. "Captain Spock *is* what you need. I'm *retired* Starfleet, so I speak only for the influential private citizens who are so worried about the future that they sent me to talk to Klingons. Spock is one of Starfleet's most respected senior officers, and Vulcans are renowned for their objectivity. That's why the president sent him. He's your link. Convince Spock you have the same goal as we do—to avoid a pointless, calamitous war—and he can convince the Federation Council and Starfleet. So make your best case, General. Why are we here, what do you want, and what's in it for us?"

Navok chuckled. "I never knew humans could be so direct. I like it! We usually think of you as mincing creatures unwilling to bare your steel. Very well, then. There is an ascendant faction of madmen within the High Council that is boiling up plans for preemptive war—not only against the Romulans, but the Federation as well. They ignore the fact that we are no longer capable of defeating one enemy, let alone two at once."

Spock's eyebrow arched in muted surprise. "Indeed? While the Klingon character is typically bellicose, it is not known for self-destructive recklessness."

"Times change," Navok said sardonically. "Chancellor Kesh pursues the fantasy of military superiority, while the empire chokes on its own pride. No outsider has ever *conquered* us, but the cost of arming against two dangerous adversaries is *bankrupting* us. We are becoming a paper fortress, a hollow husk to be crushed by the Romulans if we engage them in war."

"The Federation might welcome such an outcome," Spock said. "With one less antagonist—"

"*You* would be the only obstacle to Romulan dominion. Without a strong Klingon Empire on their other flank, the Romulan *HaDIbaHpu'* will be unleashed and it will devour you, too."

"Who's to say," Morrow parried, "that the Federation wouldn't win?"

"Oh, you might. But you might not. And even if you do, at what price? The Romulans are cunning savages who will fight to their last blood and bone. The destruction will be—" Navok shook his head. "—unimaginable."

Morrow narrowed his eyes at the Klingon. "And you have a way for us to avoid all that?"

"Yes. By preserving a three-way balance of power. As Kahless said, a warrior with two enemies cannot afford to turn his back on either."

Spock nodded. "Logical. Multilateral equilibrium makes all-out war a less attractive option." He leaned his elbows on the table and peered past his steepled fingers. "For whom do *you* speak, General?"

Navok sipped his wine. "A fair question. I speak for a growing, secret network of officers who believe that a military coup is the only way to save our empire from this mad course toward bloody oblivion. To succeed, we need Federation help."

Morrow almost choked on a mouthful of coffee. "*Whoa!* Never mind the dubious tactical wisdom of a coup. We don't have the moral right to assist in the overthrow of *any* government, even one we oppose."

Navok smiled. "Whether by coup or by battle, defeat is defeat. You claim to value life more than we Klingons. Ask yourselves: If your goal is victory over a ruthless foe who plans to attack you, which path costs more dear lives?"

"A reasonable query," Spock said. "But the question is moot until we gather definitive information about the condition of the Klingon Empire. Are you prepared to provide that?"

"It is risky business shuttling Federation spies around Klingon space. But our cause is just, and our deaths would be honorable." Navok hoisted his drink. "So—to death with honor!"

As their tankards clanked together, Morrow muttered, "What is it with you Klingons and death? How about to *life* with honor?"

Navok downed the last of his bloodwine, slammed his tankard on the table, and wiped the dregs from his mustache. He gave Morrow a quizzical half-smile. "You humans. To *life*, then—however brief it may be."

CHAPTER
4

With Raya's permission, Kirk quickly transported teams led by Scott, Chekov, Saavik, and McCoy over to the Discovery Center to conduct speedy forensic investigations. To have any reasonable chance of pursuit, they needed to know as much about the attackers as possible. And if there was a trail to follow, they needed to sniff it out before it grew cold.

While awaiting their reports, Raya gave Kirk a tour of the less damaged portions of the facility. Though he knew his friend to be modest, she made no effort to hide her pride in what had risen from the wreckage on Varnex. The equipment was all top-of-the-line, and from what Kirk could tell, the Discovery Center had certainly lived up to its name. Brilliant minds from a dozen worlds had created advances in disciplines from, quite literally, agriculture to zoology and virtually every theoretical and practical science in between. Kirk wryly noted that they'd even built a better mousetrap (an attempt at humor which got lost in translation once he had to explain its Earth origins).

For a world still recovering from a nightmare, this science

colony had been a pristine dream come true. Kirk kept wondering: *Who would attack a dream?*

As they strolled through an atrium lobby lush with plant life from many planets, Raya said, "The day of the Pulse—do you remember it?"

"Like it was yesterday. If we'd gotten here a few minutes later . . ."

"Your ship saved everyone living in this colony. Otherwise, this would have been a tomb . . . and I don't know if we could've ever come back here to rebuild. It was abandoned for years. But thanks to Theena, it became a symbol of hope . . . until now."

"We'll get to the bottom of this."

"Maybe. But I'm a little afraid of what we'll find. And Theena . . . if the people who did this hurt her . . ."

"At this point, we have no reason to think she's anything but fine. If they are terrorists, she's more valuable to them alive than dead."

Raya gave him a quirky look. "I know I'm supposed to find that comforting."

Comforting turned out to be the last word Kirk could apply to the reports delivered by his officers in the center's conference lounge, with a view of Mestiko and space visible through the clear dome above it. Chekov confirmed Raya's initial impression that the pattern of damage appeared to be more distractive than destructive, intended to draw attention away from the terrorists' apparent target—Theena's lab and the weapon they came to steal.

Scotty concluded that the attackers had pulled their punches, using munitions that packed more sound and fury than actual destructive force. McCoy determined that they used a gas formulation intended less to be lethal than to frighten residents into hiding. Chekov's review of security-surveillance imagery revealed no visuals of the terrorists' ship.

"How could that happen?" Kirk said.

"Their vessel could have been cloaked," Chekov said, "or somehow screened from external scanners."

"Or," said Saavik, "they knew where the scanners were located and positioned their ship to avoid detection."

"Or," Scotty said, "the simplest possibility of all—someone inside either shut down those scanners at the right time or tampered with the records."

Raya reacted defensively. "I can't believe any of our people were part of this."

"You do have offworlders working here," Kirk said. "What about them?"

"Their backgrounds are thoroughly checked, James."

"Background information can be faked."

"Well, yes, but—"

"We have to look at every possible scenario," Kirk insisted. "This attack was carefully planned. I'm betting it's no accident that we have no visuals of that ship."

There were no clues to the marauders' origins or physical identity, either. All the interior security cameras showed were a pack of humanoids in generic protective gear which obscured their faces. And they were prepared to be ruthlessly efficient, killing anyone who attempted to interfere. Kirk's jaw tightened and Raya gasped when they saw one attacker shoot down six scientists with a phaser-type sidearm, without any perceptible second thoughts.

But it was Saavik, accompanied by an elderly Payav woman, who brought in the most chilling information—on the stolen weapon itself. "Captain," Saavik said, "this is Dr. Hovda elZana."

The elfin Dr. elZana shuffled forward and gently shook Kirk's hands. "Captain, I am the director emeritus of the center," she said in a strong voice that belied her frail appearance.

"She refuses to retire," Raya said in a stage whisper, "no matter how many honors we give her." Despite the situation, Raya managed a warm smile as she placed an affectionate arm around the older woman's stooped shoulders.

"Well, I'm smart, Raya. I figured out if I keep coming back to work after each retirement ceremony, someone will throw me another party the next time I announce it's time to go. At my age, every party is a good party."

"Hovda was Theena's mentor and the center's first director," Raya said, "until Theena was ready to take over."

"Theena was ready when she was a child," Hovda said with

a deep sigh. "But everyone thought she was too young, so I warmed the chair until she achieved a proper age for leadership. Theena and I are the only survivors of the team working on the stolen weapon. The other three were killed."

"Hovda," Raya started to say, "Theena may also be—"

"She's *alive*," Hovda insisted fiercely. "The other three were hunted down. The only reason I'm alive is because I wasn't where I was supposed to be. These people wanted the weapon, they wanted Theena, and they wanted to eliminate everyone else who knew about it."

"Was this a secret weapon?" Kirk asked.

"No," Hovda said.

Kirk turned to Raya. "Then you knew about it?"

"No," Raya said.

McCoy squinted. "Then I'm confused."

"The faculty here operated on their own," Raya explained. "It wasn't the government's job to tell them what they could or couldn't do."

"And that's only the tip of the *noggik*. The root of this evil grows deep," said a harsh new voice, belonging to a portly woman marching in from the lounge entrance. Though Kirk hadn't seen her in almost ten years, he immediately recognized Asal Janto. Once Raya's close friend, Asal had spent many years as her political nemesis, and had led the opposition that had exiled Raya.

"Captain," Raya said, "I'm sure you remember Councillor Janto—"

"Captain Kirk," Asal interrupted, "you have stumbled into the meat of the matter—the *total* lack of supervision by any responsible agency over this so-called Discovery Center. And they trusted Dinpayav. There's no telling how many alien spies could have been working here. *This is a scandal!* I have repeatedly warned the *Zamestaad* that precisely this sort of disaster might happen."

"I'm sorry, Madam Councillor," Kirk said, with exaggerated deference, "we're only here to help the *Zamestaad* investigate this incident. As you know, it's not the Federation's intent to interfere with your government's policies. Lieutenant, please continue your briefing."

"Yes, sir," Saavik said. "The weapon was developed for defensive use. But in the wrong offensive hands, it could have the potential to change the quadrant's balance of power."

McCoy bit his lip. "Oh, I sure don't like the sound of that."

"*If* it actually functions as designed," Saavik added.

Kirk's glance flicked from his science officer to Hovda and back again. "Are you telling me it doesn't work?"

"The prototype had yet to be tested," Hovda said. "But our computer models and simulations have removed all doubts. Our team was certain it would work as designed. It was ready for test-deployment."

"All right, assuming it works," Kirk said, "*how* does it work? What makes it such a threat?"

Saavik moved to a computer console adjacent to a large wall-mounted viewscreen and inserted a data card. As she spoke, everyone watched a sim-sequence showing exactly what the weapon could do. "It is a subspace disruption-distortion field. When deployed via a generated pulse beam, it creates a predetermined and specific pattern of torsions in the fabric of subspace itself. Power systems within that field, including but not limited to warp reactors, would be rendered immediately inoperative. Depending on the dispersion of the field, the weapon could neutralize a single ship or an entire fleet, without using traditional destructive force."

Scotty's eyes lit up. "That's brilliant."

Chekov found himself nodding in agreement. "It would be the perfect defense against all enemies, no matter what kinds of weapons they used."

"If it's so damned brilliant," McCoy said, "how come *we* never invented it?"

Kirk allowed himself a grim half-smile. "Cutting right to the 'meat' of the matter, eh, Bones?"

"There are practical problems," Saavik continued. "It requires prodigious energy output in order to maintain field integrity. If the energy supply drops below a certain level, the field matrix collapses, allowing inoperative power systems to reenergize after some interval."

Scotty shook his head. "Not much good if you can't maintain matrix stability for any length of time."

Hovda looked insulted. "Problems have solutions. And we would have found them."

"But what about the ship generating the distortion matrix?" Kirk asked. "Why doesn't its warp drive shut down, too?"

"The source platform can be protected by specially tuned deflector frequencies," Hovda said, "which, admittedly, also uses a great deal of power to stand up against incursion by the distortion matrix. This, too, is a surmountable obstacle."

"It may have to be," Kirk said tightly. "If we go after these terrorists, and they use it on us, we'll need a defense."

"We'll work it out, sir," Scott said with a confident nod. "No ship of mine goes into battle with her britches around her knees."

"Saavik," McCoy said, "why do I have a feeling it gets worse?"

Her upswept eyebrow elevated slightly. "Because, according to Captain Spock, you are an inveterate pessimist, Doctor. But, in fact, it does get worse."

McCoy rolled his eyes. "I have to be so damned smart."

"*How* much worse?" Kirk prompted.

"As long as field integrity is maintained, the torsions remain within secure specifications. If power generation fluctuates beyond certain parameters, the oscillations within the matrix may become unstable, inducing tears in subspace, which are self-repairing once the matrix collapses. But while they exist, they may exert an attractive force on ships caught in the disruption field."

"And if a ship gets sucked into one of those tears?" Kirk asked.

"It would be destroyed, sir."

"Hnnh," McCoy grunted. "So much for no destructive force."

Saavik continued. "If the torsion oscillations accelerate at an uncontrolled rate and surpass what the development team referred to as a 'breakaway threshold,' then the subspace tears will enlarge into irreparable rifts, with greatly augmented gravimetric forces, which could theoretically pull in objects of considerable mass."

McCoy's eyes widened. "Like . . . *planets?*"

"Yes, Doctor."

Asal Janto stared goggle-eyed at Raya. "*Jo'Zamestaad,* is *this* what your great Discovery Center was doing with funds that could have been used to reclaim land and grow food? *Creating doomsday weapons?* When the councillors find out about this scandal—"

"Councillor Janto! This is not the *Zamestaad* hall. You are more than welcome to bring this up for debate in the proper time and place—"

"You can count on that, Raya."

"—but now we need to get that weapon back. And that's what Captain Kirk is here to help us do."

"For all the good that's done us before. You're going to need more than Captain Kirk to save you from the investigation I'll be launching immediately." With that threat, Asal turned and stalked away from the briefing.

"Saavik," Kirk said with a sigh, "anything else to add?"

"No, sir."

Kirk blew out a breath. "Until we know otherwise, we have to assume the weapon will work as advertised. We also have to expect a worst-case scenario—that it's destined for the afore-mentioned wrong hands."

"Captain," Chekov said, "there is some good news. The development team's data-encryption protocols were extremely effective. Whoever tries to use the weapon will have a very hard time accessing information on how it works. At the very least, that should buy us some time."

McCoy spread his hands. "Time for *what?*"

"To hunt down the terrorists," Kirk said, "and get that weapon back before anybody figures out how to use the damned thing."

"And how the hell do we do that?" McCoy growled.

"Commander Chekov," Kirk said, "get everyone back to the *Enterprise,* coordinate everything we've got, and find us a trail."

Raya huddled with Kirk. "James, if Commander Chekov is right about the data-encryption, and they have Theena, they're going to interrogate her to get what they need."

Kirk and Raya had been through too much together to even

think of lying to her. There was only one truthful promise he could make. "We'll do everything we can. I'll keep a channel open at all times, so you'll get real-time updates."

"I won't need them. I'm going with you." Her tone made her determination clear. "But there's one thing I need to do first, and I could use your help."

CHAPTER
5

As elder-nurses went, there were none better than Sarli Preel. That sterling reputation was why Raya had hired Sarli to care for her ailing grandmother. Even after a broken hip, Elee had stubbornly rejected Raya's appeals for her to move into a care-home. And since Raya knew all too well the frustration of feeling vulnerable and dependent, she'd decided to respect that choice and do what she could to preserve her *elor*'s dignity in the face of the myriad indignities of old age. Sarli Preel did not come cheaply, and she did come with her own set of demands. But she was worth the cost, and Raya loved how she bustled about, determined to stay one step ahead of her patient's needs. Raya felt confident that Elee was always in good hands with this elder-nurse who seemed girded for any eventuality.

Any, that is, other than the unannounced materialization of Raya herself (courtesy of the *Enterprise* transporter) in the center of her grandmother's apartment, two strides short of a head-on collision with the ever-industrious Sarli.

"*Hoy'an-Atyya!*" Sarli shrieked in heart-stopping surprise, literally jumping out of her sandals.

Just as flustered, Raya threw her hands up to protect herself from an impact that didn't quite happen. Even in that split second, Raya thanked the stars that Sarli somehow managed to neither drop the teapot she was carrying nor splash its steaming contents on either of them. Raya reached out to steady the startled nurse by the shoulders. "Sarli, I am *so sorry!* There was no one in that spot when they started to transport me."

"Sarli moves quickly," Elee's sturdy voice sang out through the double doors leading to her bedroom. "That was the funniest thing I've seen in quite some time."

"Well," Sarli said, quickly resuming her unruffled demeanor, "no tea spilled, no harm done. Can I get you a cup?"

"Thank you, but I can't stay long." Raya's voice dropped to a whisper. "How is she doing?"

"My hearing is excellent, dear," Elee called.

Sarli shrugged and smiled, replying in a normal tone as they went into the bedroom. "As you can see, your *elor*'s spirits are annoyingly fine. If her legs worked as well as her sense of humor, she'd be taking care of me."

Elee sat up straight and adjusted her pillows behind her back. "Legs, lungs, eyes . . . shall we make a list?" she asked her granddaughter with a twinkle. Then she pursed her lips and her eyes narrowed. "Something is bothering you . . ." A statement, not a question.

Raya squinted back, annoyed at her transparency. "How can you tell?"

"Because I've known that face since the minute you were born. I was right there, you know."

"I know. It's . . . I have to go away for a while. I don't know when I'll be back, so . . . I wanted to stop by and see you."

Sarli backed out of the room. "I'll be in the kitchen, if anyone needs me."

Grateful for the privacy, Raya sat on the edge of the bed and held the old woman's hand. Elee's face was deeply lined and dappled with age spots, but the skin on her hands was still soft, and her grip remained strong. "I guess I should have called ahead."

"I don't mind surprises, but you almost gave poor Sarli a heart attack." Her laugh was musical and youthful. "Ahh, I would love to get beamed again. That was so much fun, all those years ago, visiting your friend's starship."

Raya shook her head. "It makes me queasy. Always did, always will. Getting my atoms all mixed up like that. Reminds me of the gravity-coasters at Chooloo Park. You *always* wanted to ride those."

"And you *never* did." Elee smiled at the memories.

"You always did like defying gravity. I had the only *elor* with a pilot's license. I'm sorry I would never go on your annual balloon rides across Tuuliie Bay."

"You've defied gravity in more important ways, Raya. I'm the only *elor* whose grandchild saved her world from doom."

"I didn't do it alone."

"That's not what I tell my friends," Elee said, laughing. "When you come back, I want to go on one more balloon ride across the bay. Will you go with me?"

"You may have to blindfold me and get me drunk . . . but yes, I'll do it."

"So where are you going now?"

"You heard about the attack on the Discovery Center?"

"Yes. Terrible . . . unbelievable."

"I'm going with the *Enterprise.* We're going to track down the terrorists responsible and get back the weapon they stole . . . and rescue Theena."

"You do what you have to, Raya."

"I'll come see you as soon as I get back. And we'll go on that balloon adventure." Raya enveloped her grandmother in a gentle hug. Then she started toward the door.

"Wait. Let me watch you beam out."

Raya laughed. "Why, so you can see me suffer?" With a shake of her head, she flipped open the communicator Kirk had loaned to her. "*Enterprise*, this is Raya elMora. One to transport."

Three seconds after Uhura's acknowledgment, Raya felt that alarming tingle which indicated the transporter device had her caught in its mysterious aura. "Good-bye, Elee!" she said quickly, never sure of when she was no longer where she started, or where she thought she was . . . or something like that. *I will never get used to this. . . .*

As the bedroom faded from view, Raya was isolated with the loneliest of thoughts. With each visit and departure, she had to fight the fear that it would be the last time she'd see Elee. One day, soon, it would happen; she had no way of knowing when, and there was nothing she could do to prevent it. For the most powerful person on Mestiko, such fundamental impotence was unnerving. Inevitably, Raya would soon be the last surviving member of her entire family, once teeming with uncles, aunts, and cousins. Just the premonition of that certainty emptied the light from her soul and left behind an aching, hollow darkness.

When it came to issuing orders, the center seat on the bridge of the *Enterprise* was the starship's symbolic and literal locus of authority. At times, however, it was merely the place where Captain Kirk had to sit and wait (not always patiently) for his crew to do whatever it took to fulfill those orders. As was often the case, McCoy hovered at the railing behind him. This time, with Chekov and Saavik working on the bridge, and Scotty and Dr. elZana making preparations down in engineering, he expected the wait would not be long. The whistle of the intercom confirmed that expectation.

"*Scott to bridge.*"

Kirk keyed the switch on the arm of his chair. "Kirk here."

"*Captain, we're all set down here. We've got the new deflector-modulation protocols programmed, and we've added an extra blanket of magnetic-containment insulation. But . . .*"

"But what?"

"*It'll take almost all warp-engine output to maintain the deflector intensity needed to protect us against that beastie. As long as we've got warp power, then the shields'll stay up. But if the shields fail, the warp core shuts down. And without warp power, we've got nothin' for the shields. So we've got ourselves a wee bit of a chicken-and-egg situation, sir.*"

Kirk frowned. "I see. If this works, you'll have earned your pay for the week, Scotty."

"*More like the year—plus a bonus,*" said Scott. "*Dr. elZana's installed a shielded 'black box' for the sensors. If we are attacked, it'll keep recordin' no matter what, so at least we'll have data on how the weapon works—assumin' we survive.*"

"Let's be optimists. Thank you both. Kirk out."

Chekov looked up from his old seat at the navigation console. "Captain, we have isolated the intruder's warp trail. If they stay on course, their projected heading appears to be taking them toward the Neutral Zone . . . and into Klingon territory."

Kirk's jaw clenched. "You're sure?"

"Captain," Saavik said from Spock's usual post at the science console, "we cannot confirm whether or not the ion trail is from a Klingon vessel, but direction is confirmed."

Kirk opened the intraship comm channel. His voiced echoed throughout the *Enterprise*. "All hands, this is the captain. Our heading will take us toward the Klingon Neutral Zone. With a little luck, we'll complete this mission without firing a shot. Maintain yellow alert. Kirk out." Kirk stood and stepped up to the bridge's outer ring. "Commander Chekov, lay in that course. Break us out of orbit and go to warp seven. I'm going to brief Councillor elMora."

McCoy followed the captain into the privacy of the turbolift. Kirk shook his head. "I knew the Klingons had something to do with this."

"Now, we don't know that for sure," McCoy said. "You and the Klingons—"

"This isn't about David," Kirk snapped.

McCoy regarded Kirk with probing blue eyes. "*You* said it, Jim, not me."

"Bones, I know you well enough."

"And I know *you*. Can you *honestly* say it's not about David?"

"The Klingons murdered my son. That's with me as long as I live. But it's irrelevant to this mission."

"Is it?"

"Whoever took this weapon," Kirk said, dodging the question, "whatever they plan to do with it, we have to find them, and stop them . . . and soon."

"So we keep going."

"We do."

"And if we violate the Neutral Zone, we could trigger a war."

"And if we don't go where we have to . . . *do* what we have to . . . we could *lose* a war."

CHAPTER
6

Down on the floor of a small, dim cabin in the ship that took her from the Discovery Center, Theena elMadej contorted her body into the most difficult stretching pose known to practitioners of the ancient Payav discipline of *tor'kaat*. Roughly translated, *tor'kaat* meant "defying pain."

When she'd first tried it during her second university year, it was mostly because she felt fat and ugly, and needed a structured physical regimen to challenge and tone her body, much as her advanced science classes challenged what Raya had playfully dubbed her "big brain." By the day after her first lesson, with agonizing aches in muscles she wasn't even aware she had, she knew that "defying pain" didn't mean *avoiding* pain.

She could still picture her idiot boyfriend Straik shaking his head reproachfully when she'd insisted on going back for more (and that superior attitude of his definitely contributed to the hasty cessation of their romance). The trick, she eventually learned, was persisting past the pain, using the energy of the pain to fuel the work. She recalled with a smile how her *next* boyfriend appreciated the benefits of her enhanced flexibility, strength, and stamina. *Oh, well . . . Straik's loss.*

Persisting through pain was something all the people of Mestiko had been forced to do after the Pulse. But Theena believed the time had come to transcend that, and that was why she was on this ship. As she lowered her body to rest from a position most people presumed impossible to attain, she opened her eyes. The view of the stars through the window confirmed that they had slowed down from warp speed. Despite the *tor'kaat* workout, she still felt a knot in her stomach over the uncertainty of the path she'd chosen.

The door to her cabin slid open, and Terli, a young Payav woman dressed in a crew jumpsuit, stood outside. "Vykul wants to see you."

Theena nodded, slipped her bare feet into her shoes, and followed Terli down a short cramped corridor, up a ladder to the next deck, through a hatch onto the bridge. Two Payav men and two women sat at the chevron-shaped control console in front of a large viewscreen.

Vykul Marto swiveled the command chair to face Theena. He was compact and muscular, with flashing eyes and a bold, handsome face framed by unusually vivid tattoos—particularly for the Tazokkans, who generally favored very traditional, austere tattoos. Vykul's, though, covered so much of his neck and bald head that many would have dismissed it as a garish affront to good taste. They drew stares, which, Theena figured, was exactly what Vykul wanted. Even sitting still, he radiated the presence of a person accustomed to being in charge. But when he opened his mouth to speak, Theena angrily cut him off.

"The Torye are supposed to be liberators, not killers! Vykul, you swore to me none of my colleagues would die when you attacked the center." When Vykul tried to stand up so he could be eye to eye with her, Theena shoved him back into his chair. "I counted at least ten bodies. Those were our people!"

Vykul waited for her to take a breath, then spoke with a stoic serenity in sharp contrast to her roaring temper. "Were some our people? Sure. Were some Dinpayav? Yes. Did you agree it was acceptable to sacrifice some lives to advance our cause? You did."

"I meant *our* lives—the lives of people who *volunteered* to be Torye. We pledged our defiance to free our world from its cycle of dependence, even if that meant dying in the process. But those scientists? They were minding their own business, doing work to help Mestiko. They didn't deserve to die. They were innocents!"

"When a world is subjugated, there are no innocents," he murmured.

Theena rolled her eyes and shook her head. "Okay, the next person who spouts a political slogan gets a kick in the neck." For effect, she glared around at the rest of the bridge crew, all of whom tried rather intently to focus on something— *anything*—other than the verbal jousting between their two leaders. Theena couldn't blame them. Somehow, every disagreement with Vykul ended up this way, with her (the ostensible voice of nonviolent scientific reason) snarling, while he (the trained warrior from the Tazokka, the nation with the longest, most militaristic history on the planet) purred in response. Even in mid-argument, she found this behavioral irony maddening, which further fueled her fury at the barrelchested man now lounging casually in his seat.

"Are you losing sight of the goal, Theena? Maybe. We'll be sharing your weapon with allies who are also fed up with a government too feeble to seize control over its own destiny. In alliance, we create power. I'm sorry, I hope that's not another political slogan," he said with a charming grin.

Although Theena often found herself loathing the magnetism Vykul could wield like a pheromone, she knew that the first and most loyal Torye members he'd recruited were firmly under his spell. Mostly, they came from among the many Tazokkans sick of their world's dependence on the mercy of outsiders. It was odd, she thought, how such self-styled rebels could be so passively content to follow the man who'd cooked up the Torye out of their *dis*content. But Vykul was the bolt of energy that ignited this defiance movement—not so different from her own role as the catalyst behind the Discovery Center. Even though he'd created the Torye, and she'd had to join secretly so her career would not be jeopardized, she regarded herself as an equal in leading this mission. If she had to spar with him every step of the way, so be it.

The Torye themselves were anything but secret on Mestiko, where their disapproval of *Zamestaad* policies was well known—personified by Vykul in his frequent appearances on news and debate programs. He'd often reiterate how strongly he had been influenced by the life of Traal, the Norbb warlord turned *Zamestaad* councillor who had been among the most outspoken leaders of the Mestiko-First movement in the years just after the disaster. Vykul portrayed the Torye as the natural and sophisticated evolution of those early dissenters. Where the Payavist and religious fundamentalist parties advocated turning inward and shunning outsiders, the Torye aggressively advocated pushing ever outward in search of more and better alliances and markets—with the specific goal of breaking what they saw as Mestiko's sickly reliance on the Federation. For years now, Vykul had been a gleeful critic of Raya's government, ridiculing the *Zamestaad* for its failure to enhance Mestiko's stature and independence.

Though Theena knew all of that when Vykul had invited her to a clandestine meeting a year ago, his proposal of a partnership with a purpose came as a surprise. But Theena could no longer deny her reluctant conclusion that her beloved friend and mentor Raya elMora was growing too cautious with age, and too beholden to her subservient association with James Kirk. Raya had served Mestiko admirably, and she would be forever revered by her people. But her time had passed. Mestiko needed bold new leadership, and Theena had to step out of her mentor's shadow. When Vykul reminded her of the religious opposition's visceral distrust of science, and warned that the fundamentalists would shut down the Discovery Center if they came to power, she had to listen.

Theena had grown up believing that science and religion were simply different paths toward the same purpose—enlightened understanding. While they might not embrace, they could coexist. But in recent years, it seemed that zealots were bent on hijacking all of Mestiko's many religions. One by one, they twisted each faith until it was drained of spirituality. Even without Vykul's prompting, Theena was genuinely afraid of what might happen if the religious fundamentalists once again gained influence.

So, here she was, allied with Vykul, heading for a rendezvous at which they would voluntarily share an overwhelming weapon with a new, unfamiliar partner. If she harbored any lingering doubts about the wisdom of their choices, the time had come to set them aside. There could be no turning back.

"Vykul," said Fiota, the older of the two women at the central console, "incoming message."

"Anything on sensors?"

Fiota shook her head. "Nothing, other than a shimmer of interference."

"All right, then," Vykul said as he stood and turned toward the viewscreen. "It must be them. Put it through."

The starfield on the big screen winked out, to be replaced by the image of a warship's dark, smoky bridge. The swarthy commander sat on his throne, biceps bulging as his arms folded across the chest of his sleeveless body armor. He nodded in greeting. *"Vykul, it is good that we meet."*

"Captain Klaa, it is our pleasure to meet a representative of the new Klingon Empire."

"Together," Klaa said, looking quite pleased with himself, *"we are the future!"*

CHAPTER
7

As Navok's bird-of-prey crossed carefully back into Klingon territory, keeping a deliberately low profile, Spock and Morrow reviewed what they'd known before, what they knew now, and what they still needed to find out. Morrow had been sent on what his influential private Federation patrons had hoped would be the beginning of a process reducing tensions, bolstering galactic stability, and promoting peace. If there were indeed Klingons who grasped the limits of conquest as a foreign policy, Spock's presence was intended to signal them that the Federation Council and Starfleet were amenable to such a process—and that it would be in the empire's best interest to accept the offer.

But neither man had expected that they were being invited to dance at a Klingon coup d'état.

According to Starfleet's unfortunately sketchy intelligence, revealed to both Spock and Morrow at the outset of their mission, the new Klingon mining colony on Tiranax was purportedly a state-of-the-art mechanized operation. Liberated from the archaic and inefficient need for slave labor,

Tiranax would soon be producing vast amounts of strategic resources needed to meet the surging appetites of an expanding empire.

The woeful inaccuracy of those reports became instantly clear when General Navok took them to see the facility for themselves. Shortly after his ship landed, they hiked over a hill to a towering industrial building which turned out to be little more than a hollow shell. Navok guided them through a gaping entrance. Shafts of daylight pierced through jagged holes in the walls and roof, illuminating a jumble of abandoned processing equipment—conveyors, giant vats, pipes, catwalks, ore tumbrels, tracks to nowhere, cobwebs everywhere. Spock scanned it all with his tricorder for the official mission log.

Navok spread his arms wide. "Behold! The mighty forge of the empire!" A flock of batlike creatures reacted to the unaccustomed sound of voices in their domain, stirred from their perches in the rafters, and flittered in a mild panic above the heads of their unwelcome visitors.

"Looks like this place hasn't been used in years," Morrow said.

"Used? It was never even completed. This is the true condition of the Klingon Empire . . . decay. Do you need to see more?"

"Not if those records you showed us are accurate," Morrow said.

"I wish they weren't."

"And the High Council is aware that Tiranax and other colonies are not productive?" Spock asked as Navok led them back toward his ship.

"They are."

"Most irrational. Planning expansive military ventures without the industrial capacity to support them is tantamount to suicide."

Navok nodded vigorously. "Yes! That is why we must take action, before it's too late." He looked at his companions. Morrow chewed on his lower lip, while Spock's face revealed nothing of his thoughts. "This facility may be a piece of *trigak* droppings, but Tiranax itself is a treasury of resources. If the Romulans take hold of such planets . . ."

"That," Spock said, "would be undesirable. How prevalent among the Klingon officer corps is knowledge of the empire's infirmity?"

"It is spreading, quietly and deliberately. The idea is to create a unified force, not panic. There are command-rank officers of high repute in all sectors who are carefully recruiting dissidents among their troops. When there are enough of us, and we remove our support, the imperial fleet will collapse like a tent with the poles chopped down."

"Then what do you need us for?" said Morrow. "Sounds like you'll be able to incapacitate the Klingon fleet all on your own. And without it, the High Council falls."

"Unless we have the force to establish a viable new military hierarchy immediately, the Romulans will gut us like a bloated *targ*. And they will not stop with us. Only a reborn Klingon Empire stands between *you* and war with the Romulans. Only with Federation backing can we stop the High Council's march toward a war we will lose. We are trying to rescue our empire, not kill it—and a stable Klingon Empire is good for the Federation. Either you help us, or you throw us to the Romulan jackals. And once they've tasted blood, they will tear out your throats, or die trying."

"Colorful commentary aside, General," Spock said, "your scenario is not without strategic logic."

"Spock," Morrow said, "this is insane. Blowing up the Klingon Empire to save it, and us?"

"Admiral, the current iteration of Klingon leadership is apparently proceeding on a path to self-immolation, with or without us. If Federation involvement enhances the likelihood that a stable alternative will succeed it, then that is beneficial, is it not?"

"So you're in favor of this?"

"I merely state that General Navok's case is worth presenting to the Federation and Starfleet Command."

"Well, that's your prerogative, Captain. But I came out here to craft a peace, not fire up a war. Navok, you've got to understand, the Klingons aren't going to find a lot of sympathy in the halls of Federation power."

"I am not counting on their sympathy," Navok said. "But their enlightened self-interest? Now, *that* is another bowl of *gagh*."

Morrow's eyes narrowed. "What are you talking about?"

"I'm talking about how a Klingon defeat will make the Romulans an even deadlier foe to the Federation. I will show you."

Once they were back aboard the bird-of-prey and under way, Navok summoned Spock and Morrow to the bridge science station and called up a classified file. On the screen above the console, he showed them a three-sixty fly-around of an object unlike anything they'd ever seen before. It was an enormous, free-flying delta shape, bristling with oddly juxtaposed angular and geometric surfaces. With no identifiable engines, command or personnel modules, or weapons, it bore no resemblance to any known ship or space station design. Even Spock was stumped.

"What the hell is that?" Morrow said.

"Our newest weapon system, a self-supporting mobile battle base . . . as big as ten battle cruisers, with the power of fifty. Armored to withstand an attack by a fleet of opponents. One has already been deployed, at the edge of this sector. It was to be the first of a dozen. It would allow us to project Klingon power into new territories without need of outposts on planets or moons."

Morrow nodded. "Like nautical aircraft carriers on Earth back in the twentieth and twenty-first centuries."

"Exactly," Navok said. "I believe the development of this weapon is what tipped the balance in favor of preemptive war. The majority of the High Council thinks that more of these battle bases will be ready soon. I know differently."

"How?" Morrow asked.

"Because I worked on the development and testing of the first one. Oh, it is *potentially* as formidable as we hoped. It represents an advance in the technology of warfare you would do well to fear. But we do not have the resources to complete the others."

Morrow took a deep breath. "But if the Romulans capture this one, and finish the rest . . ."

"Ahh," Navok nodded. "That would not be good for the Federation, would it, Morrow?"

"No."

CHAPTER
8

As the Torye and Klingon vessels hung motionless in space, Vykul and Klaa faced each other on their respective bridge viewscreens, each seated comfortably in his ship's command chair. Theena, however, was anything but comfortable as she listened to them haggle. While the Klingon ship wasn't a battle cruiser, it was larger and considerably better armed and armored than the comparatively primitive Torye vessel. The only advantage her ship had was its stolen subspace disruption weapon, and even Theena couldn't be completely sure it would work. But that untested weapon was why the Klingons were here.

The understanding which led to this fateful meeting had been predicated on mutual self-interest. Klaa's Klingon faction would be gaining access to a weapon system that would enable them to take over an as-yet-unrevealed but coveted target—which, in turn, would give them the might they needed to set their misguided empire back on a course to glory and conquest. Vykul and his Torye band approached this partnership believing that they would retain control over their unique weapon, which would establish them as a force to be reckoned with throughout the quadrant. But Theena recalled a human axiom mentioned by Raya, who had learned it from Kirk: *The devil is in the details.* And the details of this deal were proving troublesome.

Klaa wanted the weapon transferred to his ship. Vykul explained that it was already integrated into *his* ship's systems. Even if it could be removed, they had no guarantee that Klingon systems would be compatible; it could take days to work through the engineering problems—with no assurance of success. But Theena knew Vykul had no intention of giving up control of their weapon, to anyone.

Vykul pressed the Klingons for a full description and the location of the planned target. Klaa huffily refused to give up that information without getting the weapon in exchange. They were at a classic impasse, and neither seemed willing to bend. But Theena, who prided herself on her observational skills, noted with amusement that the more tense and argumentative Klaa got, the more relaxed Vykul became. As their verbal sparring continued, body language told the tale. Vykul remained slouched in his seat, his relaxed elbows resting on the chair arms, hands folded across his stomach—while Klaa hunched his shoulders, then popped up and strutted in front of his command throne, flexing his muscles like a frustrated gamecock belatedly realizing that his potential mates were flying to other nests.

"Captain Klaa," Vykul finally said, "why don't we take a short break from our talks? Can we come at this from a fresh angle? I think so. Will we be able to get on with the mission in a way that satisfies both our needs? I have no doubts." He reached for the switch to end the transmission.

"*Wait!*" Klaa blurted. "*What if some of my crew boarded your ship so they could participate in deployment?*"

"I'll think on that, Captain," Vykul said—and then cut the signal. He turned toward his crew, looking rather pleased, murmuring almost to himself, "I handled that quite well."

"You did, actually," Theena agreed. "But it's obvious we can't trust these Klingons any more than the ones we've encountered before. This partnership was a mistake."

"You may be right."

"Then let's end this and go back home. When we tell our people that Klingons were forced to treat us with respect, they'll understand why we did what we did, and they'll join us. The Torye will become a mainstream movement and we'll have the influence to change our government's foreign policy and bring a new day to all of Mestiko. That's what we've wanted, and we don't need the Klingons for that."

"No, we don't, really. In fact, we don't need anyone."

"Then we agree."

"Mmm . . . not exactly. Can we intimidate Klingons? So it appears. Do we have to settle for merely becoming yet another mainstream movement? Not when we can rule."

"Vykul, what are you talking about?"

"I'm talking about using our assets." Brimming with enthusiasm, Vykul stood and prowled the bridge as he spoke. "Why share this weapon of ours with anyone? Why not keep it for the Torye? Use it to take over the *Zamestaad* and replace their weakness with our strength! Our world takes its place as a feared and respected power instead of a charity case. We've risen from the ashes, but now it's time for us to tower over the quadrant."

Theena stared at him. "You're talking about overthrowing our government?!"

"Overthrow . . . such a harsh word. Isn't it time for a new generation with new ideas and new power? It's *our* time. Will the old guard simply stand aside? Nobody gives up power willingly. It's time for our revolution."

"I can't allow it," Theena said with a stern shake of her head.

"I was afraid you would say that." Vykul slipped his sidearm from its holster and pointed it directly at her.

"What the hell are you doing?"

"Confining you to quarters." Vykul turned to the young woman who had brought Theena to the bridge. "Terli, take her and lock her in her cabin."

Without question, Terli drew her own weapon and gestured toward the hatch. Theena took three steps, then hesitated. "Vykul, what are you going to do about the Klingons?"

"I'm going to use our leverage. Would you like to watch, and maybe learn?"

"No, I don't think so." Theena turned and left the bridge, with Terli behind her.

Come on, Theena . . . use that big brain of yours! Confined to her cabin, Theena ricocheted between pondering how she got into this mess and trying to think of a way out. She paced, she swore, she argued out loud with herself, and she lost track of time. Then the lights flickered, the ship shook momentarily, and she assumed that Vykul had engaged the subspace weapon and turned it on the Klingons. On one hand, she was furious with Vykul and his disciples. But on the other hand, she desperately wanted to know how her weapon was working—and she got her chance a few minutes later, when the lights dimmed and stayed that way, and the shuddering resumed, with increased intensity. As the deck-plates quivered under her feet, the cabin door opened and she saw Terli standing there, looking scared. "Vykul needs you—*now!*"

They rushed up to the bridge to find Vykul and two technicians huddled around the separate console dedicated to the subspace weapon. Theena allowed herself a fast, curiosity-satisfying look at the viewscreen—though the disruption field itself consisted of an energy stream invisible to the eye, ionized atoms caught in its path created a glowing, translucent torrent washing over the Klingon ship. Vykul and the flummoxed technicians stepped aside, and Theena slid behind the controls. It took her only a moment to determine that the weapon had indeed rendered the Klingon ship helpless, but matrix instability was accelerating at an alarming rate.

"We have to shut it down—*now,*" she said, expecting an argument from Vykul.

Instead, he simply replied, "Okay. Shut it down."

Caught off-guard by his lack of resistance, Theena gave him a quizzical glance, wondering just what had gone on while she'd been locked in her quarters. Then she initiated the programmed disengagement sequence, monitoring closely, ready for manual override at the first hint of anomaly or malfunction. Happily, there was none. Once the field generator was off, the ship stopped shaking, and only then did Theena notice the cold sweat under her arms. She called up a summary report of the deployment period.

"Well?" said Vykul, looking over her shoulder.

She was so pleased at this first operational test that, for the moment, she forgot how angry she was at Vykul. "It worked. And even that destabilization was within predicted parameters. I need to take a closer look at the specific data, and then I can make some adjustments."

Vykul patted her on the shoulder. "I had faith in you, Theena. Since it worked, how long will it take their power systems to recover?"

"At least an hour for minimal power restoration. Warp core recovery could take hours longer. Or, their circuits could be so fried they'll never get warp drive restarted."

"Good, good. That buys us plenty of time to put some distance between here and there."

"Between here and *where*?"

"Fiota, you've got the coordinates. Set our course, and go to warp speed."

With a nod, Fiota followed orders. A moment later, they were in motion, wheeling away from the disabled Klingon ship, and then jumping to light speed.

Theena's eyes narrowed at Vykul. "*What* coordinates?" She swiveled her seat around as Vykul settled back into the command chair.

"The location of what was supposed to be our shared target."

"Klaa just *gave* you the coordinates?"

"Well, not right away. Did we dance for a while? Sure. I had to make him believe we were willing to take our weapon and go home. Showing him all the data from your simulations again, that helped a great deal. Reminding him what this thing could do . . . it was almost cruel, the way he drooled over it."

"How did you get the coordinates without giving him what he wanted?"

"Did I make a concession? In a manner of speaking. I promised to allow three of his crew aboard our ship as part of the weapon deployment."

"Which you never intended to do."

"He had his crewmembers all ready to transport over. That's when I asked for the target coordinates, as a show of good faith."

Theena shook her head at Vykul's apparent audacity. "What made you think they'd fall for that?"

"Because they needed us more than we needed them. Just as he was about to engage his transporter, we engaged the weapon. Now we'll go and take their target."

"Do we even know what it is?"

Vykul chuckled. "I have no idea. But was it important enough for them to let their guard down? Yes. Will it be worth our while? I think so."

Theena turned away from him, toward the viewscreen where the stars streaked by. In case her expression betrayed even the slightest hint of admiration for his ability to swindle the Klingons, she didn't want him to see it. She was still smarting over his imperious treatment of her, and had serious disagreements with him about the wisdom of his intended path. But, for the moment, that conflict was tempered by her satisfaction with the weapon's performance—and by her curiosity about their impending target.

What had Klaa been so eager to seize that he'd allowed Vykul to make a total fool out of him? There would be time to debate strategy later—and she intended to, since overthrowing Raya's government was never in *her* plans. For now, though, while she vowed not to let Vykul get the best of her again, maybe he was right about one thing.

Maybe it *was* time to think big.

CHAPTER
9

The automated distress signal was a complication General Navok could easily have done without. The transmission was so weak, it was barely readable when his bird-of-prey picked it up less than an hour from their destination—the battle base he planned to show to Spock and Morrow.

The signal originated from a Klingon vessel without authorization to be where it was. And its location put it directly between Navok's ship and the battle base, so he could hardly ignore it. Was it commanded by a fellow dissident? If so, had they been attacked by a ship loyal to the mad *targ*s running the High Council? That would be unfortunate, since it might mean the mutinous conspiracy had been exposed. But if the damaged ship carried a crew still loyal to the High Council, then Navok could not allow himself to be caught with Federation representatives aboard his ship. Either way, the ramifications could be unpleasant. He would have to play the encounter with deliberate caution.

As they approached the damaged ship, Navok hid Morrow and Spock in his cabin. Scans of the other ship showed minimal power output, with life support barely operational. When its commander appeared on Navok's viewscreen, the signal quality was oddly degraded by local interference despite their close proximity.

"*General Navok, I am Captain Klaa.*"

"What happened to your ship, Captain?"

"*We were attacked.*"

"By what? I see no battle damage."

"*It was an unknown weapon, capable of neutralizing a warp reactor without warning. And there are no known countermeasures.*"

"Who wielded this super-weapon?"

Klaa hesitated for a heartbeat, and Navok knew he was being lied to. "*An unknown invader, General. But they pose a grave threat to the empire.*"

"So it would seem. How many casualties do you have?"

"*None, sir.*"

Navok's eyebrows arched in surprise. "*None?* They overwhelmed a shipful of warriors with a weapon that made you helpless, yet they didn't destroy your ship and harmed not a whisker on your pretty head? Can you explain this?" As Klaa squirmed under questioning, Navok couldn't help but enjoy it, just a little bit.

"*No, sir, I cannot. But consider this—had they left nothing but debris, there'd be no one to report what happened to us. If it's their goal to strike fear in Klingon hearts, our destruction would not suit their needs.*"

"And did they strike fear in *your* Klingon heart, Klaa?"

"*No!*" Klaa snarled with a jolt of rage. "*They will pay with their blood!*"

"Yes, blood . . . always blood," said Navok distractedly. "Your ship's status."

Klaa shook his head. "*Our warp drive is inoperable. My engineer says it cannot be repaired in space.*"

"Well, I don't have time to tow you to a maintenance facility. Prepare to abandon ship."

"*General—no! We want to hunt these invaders and punish their arrogance!*"

"Not without a warp core, you won't. I'll drop you and your

crew off at the nearest fleet base and you can take it up with the commandant."

It was obvious Klaa wanted to argue, but thought better of it and followed orders—which only fortified Navok's suspicions that Klaa was hiding some major secrets. When Klaa and his crew of fourteen materialized on the cargo-transporter platform, they found themselves facing the general, his security squad, and an intimidating array of disruptor rifles. Klaa took a bold step ahead of his officers, then reconsidered when three disruptors aimed at his chest.

"General, what is the meaning of this?"

"The meaning?" Navok glared. "What were you doing here in the first place, Captain? Your ship had no authorization to be in this sector."

"We . . . we were on a classified mission." Despite the defiant jut of his chin, Klaa's eyes betrayed a flash of panic.

"I am a senior general, Klaa. I have access to all classified orders, and you are on no covert mission."

"We are on a classified assignment, General," Klaa insisted, without much assurance. "If you allow me to return to my ship, I can prove it."

Navok turned to the massive officer at his side. "There are too many for the brig. Strip them of all weapons and communicators, and confine them here in the cargo bay. If they cause any trouble at all, kill them." Then he marched out.

Spock and Morrow heard the whirring of the lock keeping them in Navok's cabin, and the door opened. Navok entered and quickly updated them on the situation. "I'm afraid you'll have to accept my word on the existence and capabilities of our battle base. The longer our little tour of Klingon space, the more likely you will be discovered. And that suits neither my needs nor yours."

Morrow agreed. "It does seem to be getting a little too crowded for comfort in these parts. Spock?"

"Since we cannot know if Klaa's distress call was picked up by other Klingon vessels, we cannot calculate the odds of encountering further interference. Therefore, expedited with-drawal does seem logical."

Spock, Morrow, and Navok returned to the bridge—where they were greeted with the next piece of bad news. In apparent response to Klaa's signal, a Klingon battle cruiser had already detected their presence and was closing fast, leaving no time for cloaking or escape.

Navok cursed, and pounded his fist into the bulkhead, leaving a noticeable dent. Then he strode to his female weapons officer. "Vijak, target Klaa's ship with disruptors. Destroy both engines."

Vijak's long fingers danced across her console. "Targets locked."

"Fire."

Spock and Morrow watched on the viewscreen as Navok's disruptors blew a gaping hole in one nacelle of Klaa's vessel and sheered off the other entirely. Then Navok turned toward the male officer at the communications station. "Mox, open a channel to the approaching battle cruiser—*audio only*."

"Channel open, sir."

Navok stepped up to the command throne and eased back into his seat. "This is General Navok. You have no authorization to be in this sector. Identify yourself and your mission."

There was a moment of silence, and then Spock heard a familiar rumbling voice from the speakers. *"This is Kang. We are responding to a distress signal from your coordinates. Report your status, General."*

"We also responded to the same distress call," Navok said. "We found the damaged bird-of-prey under attack by an unidentified intruder. Our intervention forced the intruder to retreat. As you can see, the ship commanded by Captain Klaa was severely damaged. We sustained only minor damage to our communications system."

"And the status of Klaa's crew," Kang said.

"Multiple casualties, several dead or dying."

"Yet you did not pursue the intruder."

"They fled at high speed. We will analyze all sensor logs of the encounter and make a full report to the High Council. Your assistance is not needed, Kang. Return to your assigned patrol."

At that moment, it appeared to Spock that Navok had successfully bluffed his way out of their current entanglement. Then, after a deliberate pause, they heard Kang's voice again. *"Our sensors detect little evidence of weapon use consistent with a firefight between three ships."*

"The enemy used a weapon we've never encountered before. That's why it is so urgent that we report to the High Council at the earliest possible time. Your interrogation is delaying that, Kang."

"We will escort you—" Kang started to say, but Navok cut him off.

"Your assistance is not needed, Captain. I gave you a direct order to return to your assignment. Or do you not consider the Romulan threat to be worthy of your attention?"

"I merely wished to be sure this incident did not involve Romulans, General."

"It did not. The security of the empire—"

But before Navok could finish his thought, they heard sounds of a clash *within* his ship—disruptor blasts, shouts, the crash of bodies against walls and deck, the brutal bedlam of large warriors fighting to the death in the corridor leading to the bridge. There could be no doubt that Klaa's troops had somehow overpowered their captors and escaped from the makeshift brig. Navok's surviving security officers were quite literally fighting for their lives in those close quarters, trying to keep the insurgents at bay.

Navok's bridge crew tensed, unsure if they should stay at their posts or join the battle. Seconds later, the fight came to them, as a brawling jumble of flailing fists and flashing blades burst through the bridge hatch. Two of Navok's crew whirled and started to draw their sidearms—but both were killed by disruptor fire before their weapons cleared their holsters. Two others charged into the fray and had their throats slashed. Two of the intruders grabbed Spock and Morrow at knifepoint, and Klaa's voice bellowed over all else: *"Mev!"*

His single word froze combatants on both sides, leaving no doubt that Klaa's crew had commandeered Navok's bridge. Klaa stepped over the dead and swaggered up to Navok at the command throne, clenched his fist as if readying a sweeping backhand—and then simply grinned and gave the defeated general a hard poke in the chest. "Your ship is mine." He gestured to two of his crew and they grabbed Navok, pinioned his arms behind his back, and dragged him down the steps. "The human and the Vulcan, with him."

Klaa's men shoved Spock and Morrow over toward Navok, while their commander stood with hands on hips, looking quite pleased with his conquest. "Two spies and a traitor. The High Council will be happy with the catch of the day."

"They're not spies," Navok said, "they're diplomats. And since we are not at war with the Federation, their safety is now your responsibility. If you kill them in the absence of any evidence of espionage, you will be committing an act of war against the Federation."

"War with the Federation . . . would be glorious," Klaa said, "unless you are a *bIHnuch* as well as a traitor."

"*General,*" Kang's voice boomed from the speaker, "*what is going on over there?*"

Klaa looked toward the viewscreen image of Kang's battle cruiser. "Put us on visual."

A moment later, Kang's face appeared on the viewer. He frowned as he took in the scene on Navok's bridge, then centered his gaze on Klaa. "*And who are you,* petaQ?"

Klaa squared his broad shoulders. "Before you call me *petaQ,* know that I have captured the traitor Navok and his two Federation spies. And I know of a weapon which will help the empire conquer *all* its enemies."

"*Ahh, the invincible weapon wielded by the mysterious enemy.*"

"It is real," Klaa insisted. "I know all about it. I can prove it."

"*And how do you happen to know so much about an enemy weapon?*"

"I . . . I can't tell you that now."

Kang's temper began to simmer. "*General,*" he barked, "*do you have an explanation for all this?*"

Not one that he may share, Spock thought.

"What I do," said Navok, "I have done for the good of the empire."

"Ghuy'cha'!" Kang thundered. *"You both speak like guilty* taHqeq *with something to hide. Prepare to be boarded. If there is any resistance, I will destroy that ship and everyone on it. Both crews will be transported to my brig, and that is where you shall remain until I can discover who is the greater liar. Your fates are now bound up as one. If anyone from either crew attempts escape, all of you will be executed on the spot."* Kang turned to his wife at her exec station. *"Mara, see to it."*

"With pleasure."

CHAPTER
10

Just as Kang poured himself some bloodwine, the door to his cabin opened. Mara entered, accompanied by two burly guards and Klaa, his hands and feet securely bound by sturdy manacles. Kang, whose hair had started to turn gray, studied the younger officer for several moments. "You asked to see me."

Klaa nodded eagerly. "Yes, Kang. I was not lying about this alien weapon. I was engaged in negotiations to gain possession of it, for the glory of the empire."

"Negotiations? With whom?"

"A group of renegades from Mestiko called the Torye. They stole the weapon from their own people, and made it look like a terrorist attack. They were supposed to share it with us."

"And what happened?"

"They are without honor. They used it on us, and then they fled."

Mara eyed Klaa suspiciously. "Fled where?"

"I do not know. But I can help you track them down."

"You don't seem smart enough to think of this plan on your own," Mara said with a smirk.

Klaa's eyes flashed at the insult and he jerked his shackled hands toward Mara, trying to hit her. She deftly sidestepped the attempt, landed a crushing kick behind his knee, and clubbed him on the back of the head as he crumpled to the deck, grunting at the searing pain from his buckled leg.

Kang used his foot to roll Klaa onto his back, then looked down at him. "If your foolish defiance was intended to impress us with your courage, it served only to reinforce my wife's appraisal of your intelligence. And even without those shackles, Mara would have little trouble beating the *baktag* out of you."

"I did not work alone," Klaa offered. "I am part of an alliance of brother officers, most of us young."

"And impatient," Kang intoned.

"Yes! We are impatient with the old women of the High Council who cower at the thought of crossing swords with the Federation. Their inaction forced us to create this conspiracy. The Torye weapon would give us all the advantage we need to crush the Federation *and* the Romulans. Our empire would once again be invincible."

Kang pressed his boot on Klaa's ribs. "I have seen no weapon."

Now Mara leaned over him as well. "And if you are telling the truth," she said softly, "the Torye seem to have changed their minds about sharing it with you. When you're ready to tell us the *whole* truth, we'll listen. Take him back."

The guards hauled Klaa up and out.

Alone with Mara, Kang retrieved his wine and took a pensive sip. "So . . . what do we make of our prisoners?"

"The general is guarding a secret he's willing to take to his grave. No one of his stature would risk being caught with Federation spies unless he was playing for very high stakes. We need to know his secret before he is executed."

"Agreed. And Klaa?"

Mara shook her head in contempt. "He is a pitiful liar. And he doesn't have the brains to make up what he's already told us."

"So you think this weapon exists?"

"I do. And whatever it is, it apparently made short work of

Klaa's defenses. Whatever his mental deficiencies, he doesn't seem the sort to go down without a fight. *QI'yaH!* How in the name of Kahless do idiots like him get to be commanders?"

Kang frowned. "The decline of the empire. Perhaps it is the natural order."

Mara stepped close to him, took the heavy metal wine tankard from his hand, and set it down on the desk. Then she scraped her talonlike nails along his neck and nuzzled him so he could feel her hot breath in his ear as she whispered, "I have told you to banish these dark moods. Warriors like you will save the empire from itself. And if you keep the faith of your fathers long enough, worthy young warriors will stand by your side."

Kang bowed his head. "How do you know this?"

"What have you always wanted?"

A moment of doubt flickered across Kang's eyes. *Was this a trick question?* "A *kyamo*-looking personal aerobatic flyer . . . ?"

Mara rolled her eyes. "How about someone you can teach to fly it with you?" Then she took her husband's hand and moved it down to her stomach. "Say hello to your firstborn son."

After a stunned, blank-faced moment, Kang reacted with a blink of disbelief. Then his eyes met her unwavering gaze. "Our *son?* How long have you known?"

"I suspected. The test confirmed it this morning." She took a step back. With a smile of wonderment, Kang placed both his hands on her belly. "You know how swiftly time passes. Before you know it, he'll be a great warrior like his father."

"And his mother." Kang chuckled, recalling the way she'd leveled Klaa.

She smiled back at him. "He will fight by our sides for many years. He will help us redeem the empire's honor, and together we'll drink the steaming blood of our enemies. We should start thinking of a name worthy of the son of Kang and Mara."

They were interrupted by the shrill blast of the ship's alarm klaxon. A gravelly voice from the bridge shouted, *"Battle alert!"*

Kang punched the intercom switch and the tense face of his

tactical officer Darog appeared on the screen. "This is Kang. Report, Darog."

"Long-range sensors have detected a Federation starship. It has crossed the Neutral Zone into our space."

"Continue tracking. I'll be right there."

By the time Kang and Mara rushed up to the bridge, Darog met them with an update: "The intruder has been identified, sir. It is the *Enterprise,* heading this way."

Kang exchanged a knowing look with his wife. "Kirk's ship. Our son will witness his first victory today, and over a worthy opponent." Then the captain took his seat and Mara returned to her science station. "Weapons, stand ready. Tactical, prepare for cloaking."

Kang's ship banked into a majestic turn, leaving the two derelict birds-of-prey in its wake, then faded from view under cover of its cloaking device.

On the *Enterprise* bridge, Saavik peered into the science viewer. "Confirmed, Captain," she said. "Two Klingon birds-of-prey, one with severe damage and no power output . . . the other with no apparent damage. No life-forms on either ship."

Trying to ignore McCoy pacing along the rail behind him, Kirk leaned forward in the command seat, focusing on the viewscreen image of the drifting ships in the distance.

"Abandoned? Now, that's damned strange."

"Maybe not so strange, sir," Scott said from the engineering station. "Sensors have confirmed residual spatial distortion consistent with deployment of the subspace weapon. The ship with the conventional battle damage has a dead warp core, so it's lookin' like the weapon worked the way it was designed."

Raya spoke up from the auxiliary console near Uhura, where she'd parked herself in order to stay out of everyone's way. "At least we know we're on the right trail."

"Right," McCoy muttered to no one in particular. "If we get our damned fool heads blown off by Klingons, it'll be a great comfort knowing we weren't on a wild-goose chase."

Kirk flashed him a look of annoyance. "So, we can guess what happened to one Klingon ship. But that doesn't explain why there's a second one out here, deserted but intact. And it doesn't explain what happened to two Klingon crews."

"Captain, there are only two logical possibilities," Saavik said. "Either the terrorists took the Klingons captive, or there was another ship involved."

"Do sensors detect evidence of a third ship?"

"Nothing definitive, sir," Saavik said. "But residual interference from the subspace weapon is making it difficult to differentiate warp signatures."

"Scotty, are we still picking up the trail from the terrorist ship?"

"Aye, sir."

Kirk swiveled toward Saavik. "Lieutenant, do a full sensor sweep on both those ships, as well as the surrounding area. Make it fast. The less time we spend loitering in Klingon space, the better."

"Amen to that," McCoy said.

"As soon as that's done," Kirk said, "we get back on the hunt."

"Captain," Saavik called out with uncharacteristic urgency, "there is a neutron radiation surge off our starboard side."

McCoy reflexively grabbed onto the railing. "This can't be good."

"It is a Klingon vessel," Saavik said. "It's the *K'tanco*, Captain—it's decloaking, with weapons charged."

At Kirk's order, the *Enterprise* heaved hard to port in a desperate evasive maneuver, but it was too late. As the enemy cruiser swept past, its disruptors scored point-blank hits and sent the starship reeling. Knowing what was coming, McCoy had barely kept his footing, but Raya went flying. She came up with a bloody gash on her head, and McCoy ducked over to help her.

Meanwhile, the *Enterprise* shook off the first salvo and righted herself. "Phasers," Kirk barked. "Return fire."

The Klingon vessel was momentarily vulnerable as it came about, and four rapid-fire phaser blasts found their mark along its flank. With each ship twisting through its own evasive dance, both became harder to hit with energy-beam weaponry—and both captains ordered torpedoes away. A pair hit the *Enterprise* engineering hull in quick succession and the ship shook down to its beams. Smoke and sparks filled the bridge.

Scott called through the smoke, "Captain, warp drive's offline. Forward shields're down to forty-three percent!"

"Captain," Uhura said, "we're being hailed."

"On speakers."

A moment later, a deep voice came through, all too loud and clear. "*Kirk, I am holding two Federation spies of your acquaintance.*"

Kirk's jaw clenched. He knew the voice. "Kang," he whispered.

"*They will be tried and condemned to death.*"

McCoy grunted to Raya. "You've gotta love Klingon due process."

"Seeing is believing, Kang," Kirk said.

"*Very well, then.*"

"Visual signal coming through, sir," Uhura said. "On main viewscreen."

Reactions from everyone on the bridge crew were immediate and simultaneous—gut-punched shock at the sight of Captain Spock and retired Admiral Harry Morrow held under the gun on Kang's bridge. While Kirk made a superhuman effort to maintain a poker face, his mind raced. *How the hell did Morrow and Spock end up in Klingon hands?* When he spoke, his tone was commanding but quiet. "Release them, immediately . . . and guarantee our safe passage back to the Neutral Zone."

Now it was Kang's turn to be thunderstruck at Kirk's audacity. Not knowing what else to do, Kang actually laughed. "*Bold talk for an invader with no warp drive. You will pay for this act of war with your lives.*"

"Klingons or Klingon agents attacked a science colony orbiting Mestiko," Kirk parried. "*That* was an act of war that justifies our presence in Klingon space."

"*Kirk, I have it on good authority that the weapon you seek was stolen by terrorists from Mestiko.*"

Barely able to find her voice, Raya rose from the seat where McCoy was tending her head injury. "What?"

On the viewscreen, Mara stepped forward, alongside her husband. *"Yes, dissidents who call themselves the Torye formed an alliance with renegade Klingons, and they were to share the stolen weapon. But the Torye had a change of heart. They are still somewhere in Klingon territory. After we're done with the* Enterprise, *we will hunt them down and destroy them."*

Raya looked queasy, and Kirk couldn't blame her. McCoy helped her back to the seat.

"How do you know about the Torye weapon?" Kirk said.

"Because," Kang replied, *"we have those Klingon renegades in custody—and they will face harsh justice. As for you, Kirk, stand and fight . . . or run for the Neutral Zone."*

"We're not leaving without Spock and Morrow."

"Then battle it is. I grant you an honorable death."

"Thanks just the same," Kirk said, cutting the comm signal.

Raya glanced at McCoy. "What's he going to do?"

McCoy shrugged. "Damned if I know."

"Captain," Saavik said, "another ship has just entered sensor range."

"Klingon?"

"No, sir. Unidentified."

"Scotty," Kirk said, "will your modified shields block the subspace weapon at less than full power?"

"I don't know, sir. We're sailin' uncharted waters."

"Divert all power to deflectors."

"You mean other than weapons?"

"All power."

"Then how do we fire back at the Klingons?"

"I'm betting we won't have to."

"Captain," Saavik said, "you may win that bet. The unidentified vessel is closing, and its warp signature matches that of the terrorist vessel . . . and they just deployed the subspace weapon."

"Scotty . . ."

"All power diverted to shields, Captain. But I don't know if it'll be enough."

"We're about to find out."

On the main viewscreen, the terrorist ship appeared barely bigger than a speck out beyond Kang's warship, but the weapon's sparkling matrix rippled across the distance in a heartbeat, cascading over both the Klingon cruiser and the *Enterprise*. Bridge lights flickered out, replaced by the red glow of emergency illumination, and computer consoles went dark.

Kirk took a deliberate breath. "Scotty, status report . . ."

"We're gettin' some frequency fluctuation, so we're only at eighty-eight percent efficiency. But, so far, warp power and shields're holdin' up."

But for how long? Kirk glanced anxiously around the bridge. Only the science and engineering stations remained functional, and he surmised from Saavik's intent focus on her sensor viewer that they were receiving data from the special scanners installed by Dr. elZana. Battery reserves kept life support and communications minimally operational.

"Captain," Uhura said, "we're being hailed."

At Kirk's nod, Uhura patched the signal to the main viewscreen, where they could see the tight quarters of the Torye bridge, and a Payav with unusually elaborate tattoos sitting comfortably in his seat. Raya was the only one who recognized him, and she gasped so loudly that Kirk whirled in her direction, thinking she'd been hurt. As she stood up unsteadily, her face betrayed her mix of emotions: shock, confusion, and anger. "Vykul?" she whispered.

"Raya. Commanders, I am Vykul, of the Torye. We will be the new rulers of Mestiko."

"Vykul," Raya repeated. *"You're* behind this?"

"Just me? Hardly. Thousands have joined the Torye. Have we had our fill of your government's complacency? Oh, yes. The weapon is now ours, and we plan to use it to make sure our world gets the respect it deserves from those who would conquer us like the Klingons, or subjugate us with 'kindness' like the Federation."

Raya closed her eyes, as if trying to blink away this nightmare. "Theena elMadej . . . you kidnapped her. If you're forcing her to help you . . ."

Then Raya got her next big shock, when Theena stepped into view alongside Vykul.

"Nobody's forced me, Raya."

For an instant, Raya brightened at the sight of her friend . . . until the reality of Theena's words registered. "What . . . what do you mean?"

"I'm not a captive. I've belonged to the Torye for some time. I'm sorry you had to find out this way."

"You—you *helped* them? They killed nineteen people at the Discovery Center! *You* killed . . ." Raya shook her head, stunned by a truth more staggering than anything she could have imagined. Kirk wanted to go to her and put a supportive hand on her slumped shoulders, but instead he circled around to the engineering console.

"Scotty, report," he whispered.

"Assumin' the shielded scanners are operatin' without distortion, the Klingon ship's warp core is disabled. And the Torye ship shows no signs of energizing standard weapons."

"Maybe they don't need to . . . or maybe they can't do both at once." Kirk turned his attention back to the wrenching conversation between Raya and Theena.

"Raya, no one was supposed to die. That's Vykul's fault."

"But they did die . . . and if you helped these monsters, it's *your* fault."

"So many of our people have died for nothing. At least the people at the center died so our world can become proud and free," Theena said, with a catch in her voice. *"Someday . . . someday, I hope you'll understand why we had to do this."*

Raya shook her head. "I'll *never* understand."

"Both your ships have been disabled by a weapon which makes us more than your equals," said Vykul in an easy tone, as if discussing a rain shower and not a sea change in galactic power. *"Could we destroy you? Yes, but that's not our goal. This was a demonstration. Will we meet again? Yes, and the next time, we'll have the force to dictate the terms by which Mestiko will take its rightful place as a dominant power in this quadrant."*

The comm signal winked out. The Torye ship disengaged its super-weapon, moved off at a stately pace, then jumped to warp speed, leaving the drifting *Enterprise* and *K'tanco* behind.

Kirk stood with Raya, who looked more shattered than he'd

ever seen her before. "James, I can't believe Theena would do this. I've known her since she was a child. It's not who she is." She kept shaking her head.

"What about this Torye group? Did you see this coming?"

"No. And that's my fault. Maybe I should have."

"We don't know that. And sometimes, even if you see something coming, there's not much you can do," he said, referring as much to the past as to the present. But here and now, they needed to make a rapid assessment of their situation, before the Klingons could attack again, and before the Torye could do . . . *what?*

CHAPTER

11

While McCoy took Raya to sickbay to patch up her head wound, Kirk huddled down in engineering with Scott, Saavik, and Hovda for an analysis of the Torye attack. To Scotty's great relief, the modified deflectors succeeded in protecting warp-drive systems against all but minor degradation from the subspace weapon, beyond the battle damage inflicted by the Klingons.

And Hovda was quite happy with how well the shielded scanners worked, yielding a wealth of useful information on the weapon and its inaugural performance. That data indicated that the Torye were having trouble mastering the weapon's full potential. Even running at only half-capacity for a relatively brief period of time, the subspace weapon consumed all of the small ship's available engine output, with nothing left for conventional weapons. As Hovda phrased it, it was lucky that the Torye vessel was underpowered compared with a starship like the *Enterprise*. Scotty was convinced the Torye cut their attack short because they were close to overloading their engines. Saavik noted that the subspace distortion field never achieved optimum matrix stability or power utilization—problems, Hovda confirmed, that were predicted by computer models and tests conducted by the development team. Still, the "demonstration" left little doubt they faced a formidable threat.

"How does Theena's involvement change the equation?" Kirk asked. "She knows this weapon system as well as anyone. Will she be able to get the bugs worked out?"

"Not easily," Hovda said. "We didn't want any lone wolves working on this. We worked in teams of at least two. Crucial data was segregated into self-contained, encrypted memory units. Each scientist on the project was assigned a secret passcode, and it takes a minimum of two simultaneous passcode entries to gain access to those encrypted data units."

"Can Theena solve those problems even without access to blocked information?" Kirk asked.

"She is brilliant," Hovda said, with mixed pride and regret. "With enough fiddling time, she'll fix some of it by sheer determination. But that won't happen soon. Given the power limitations of their ship, they may not be able to surpass what we've already seen."

"Aye," Scott said, "but what if they get their hands on a better power source?"

Kirk's brow furrowed. "Vykul said they'd have the force to dictate terms. Idle boast, or real threat?"

Scott looked grim. "If they capture a ship like this one, or a Klingon battle cruiser, and hook that thing up to bigger engines . . ." His voice trailed off. No one needed that peril spelled out.

"Then we have to keep that from happening," Kirk said, his jaw tightening at the thought. "But we've got a more immediate concern."

Scott allowed himself a half-smile of satisfaction. "The Klingons? They're in a wee bit of a mess, sir. Their warp drive's completely offline, so they'll not be so eager for battle."

"Is their warp core disabled permanently?"

Dr. elZana shrugged her shoulders. "We don't have enough real-world data to know for sure. In theory, it could recover. But it's likely to take at least a few hours for them to regenerate enough capacity for warp speed and weapons capability."

"So, for the moment, we've got an advantage," Kirk said. "Let's use it to fix our battle damage, and then we'll deal with the Klingons."

Aboard the *K'tanco*, Mara coordinated damage reports from her barely operating bridge station, and repair teams scrambled throughout the ship. Batteries sustained minimal life support, but their warp reactor was stone-cold dead. Though damage inflicted by the *Enterprise* was mostly superficial, the knowledge that his vessel could neither fight Kirk nor pursue their attackers left Kang seething.

Under interrogation, Spock, Morrow, and Navok maintained that they knew nothing more about the Torye weapon beyond what they'd all observed. "But I suspect Captain Kirk knows more," Spock said calmly. "If you destroy the *Enterprise*, you will lose that knowledge. It is in your own self-interest to deal with Captain Kirk, and expeditiously, I should think. The Torye may strike again at any time, or they may use their weapon against other Klingon ships and installations."

That, of course, was the last thing Kang wanted to hear. But Mara took him aside and emphasized that the Vulcan's logic was inescapable: Kirk might in fact hold the key.

"They invaded our space," Kang said. "Kirk must pay for that."

"Whatever he may be, Kirk is not foolish enough to undertake a one-man invasion. He told us why they violated the Neutral Zone, and we've seen this weapon for ourselves. Which is the bigger threat—one Starfleet ship, or an unknown weapon that left us paralyzed?"

"Trust Kirk, to defeat a common enemy?"

"You did it once before," Mara reminded him.

"That was a long time ago. We have learned the hard way that humans cannot be trusted. And Kirk will not trust a sworn enemy he holds responsible for the death of his son."

Measuring her husband's stony resistance, Mara modulated her approach. She knew better than anyone how Kang hated forced inaction. When it came to revenge, he had a hard time waiting until that particular dish was sufficiently cold. It was his main flaw as a commander and warrior (and husband, too, for that matter), this inability to accept that stillness was sometimes required in order to make the best decision. Someday, when it mattered most, Mara believed he would master this art. In the meantime, after all their years together, she had evolved various means of diverting Kang's impulse to act at moments when patience was the better choice. She leaned close to him. "Information is power, is it not?"

"It can be."

"Then it's time Klaa told us whatever he's withholding."

"He is a Klingon. He will not yield under interrogation, or torture."

"We have another option."

The unexpected invitation from Mara kicked Admiral Morrow's guard up a couple of notches. Would he and Spock join her for Klingon tea in the private quarters she shared with Kang? *Do we really have a choice?* Since gentle persuasion wasn't a customary Klingon tactic, he was pretty sure something was up—he just didn't know what. But despite his heightened level of suspicion, he was unprepared for the proposal Mara made to Spock.

"A mind-meld?" Morrow blurted, almost choking on the sip of bitter brew he had in his mouth. "With Klaa?"

"We believe Klaa has information of value to us as well as Kirk."

Spock's eyebrow arched. "An intriguing request."

"Spock," Morrow said, bug-eyed at the very notion and stunned that the Vulcan hadn't already rejected it, "you can't do it."

"There is no physiological obstacle, Admiral."

"Why would we want to help the Klingons get information from one of their own?"

"Admiral," Mara said, "we are being asked to trust Captain Kirk solely on the basis of his pleasant smile. Are you unwilling to grant reciprocal trust?"

Morrow chuckled without humor. "You don't trust us, and we don't trust you."

"I beg to differ. You and General Navok seemed to be getting along quite well."

"That was a work in progress."

"This is not merely a matter of trust," Spock said to both of them. "It could be a matter of survival. Based on Klaa's admission of partnership with the Torye, it is logical to conclude that he intended to use their weapon against a specific, strategically valuable target, which remains unknown. If the Torye have decided to proceed against that same target without Klaa's participation, any collaborative efforts at contravention would benefit from information on its description and location."

Morrow spoke to Spock but glared at Mara. "How do we know it'll be collaborative?"

Mara smiled. "Admiral, at the moment, this vessel's systems are almost totally nonoperational. But I have enough data to suggest that the *Enterprise* was somehow able to withstand the Torye attack better than we were. If Kang has intelligence Captain Kirk will find useful, Kirk may be more likely to share his defensive countermeasures with us in trade. On the other hand, if the *Enterprise* doesn't know where to find the Torye ship, all the countermeasures in the universe will be of little use. And without adequate defenses, we won't be able to defeat the Torye even if we know where to find them. However, our two ships on a cooperative mission have a much better chance of success."

Spock took a pensive sip of his tea. "Inescapably logical."

Mara nodded graciously, but Morrow was no less unhappy with the direction in which this conversation seemed headed. "All right, say Spock does a mind-meld and finds out where Klaa planned to use this weapon. How do we know you'll share that with Captain Kirk?"

"How do we know Kirk will give us the technical information on his countermeasures? I suppose that will be the moment of truth—are both sides intelligent enough to override our natural hostility toward each other in order to achieve a mutually beneficial goal?"

"You are correct, Mara," Spock said. "Without knowing the Torye's likely target, any effort directed at stopping them will be moot. I will accede to your request."

"Spock," Morrow objected, "are you crazy?"

"It is a logical choice, Admiral. Indeed, it may be our only choice at this juncture."

Morrow shook his head. "I don't like it. But I can't stop you." Then he turned to Mara. "Have you already plied Klaa with tea and blood-crumpets to get him to go along with this?"

"Klaa will require another means of persuasion."

That "persuasion" took the form of four strong officers hauling Spock's violently unobliging partner to a brig interrogation chair, strapping down his legs and arms, and clamping a cage around his jaw to keep him from biting. Then two guards held Klaa's head still as Spock approached. As Morrow listened to Klaa's brutish snorts and bellowed threats of vengeance, he wondered how the hell anyone could pierce that shell of furious resistance. But seconds after Spock's fingertips pressed against the Klingon's face and skull, the fire in Klaa's eyes gave way to a trance of fear and his breath came in short, shallow huffs.

"I . . . am . . . Spock," said one.

"I . . . am . . . Klaa," the other answered.

"Our minds are moving closer . . . closer . . ."

"Nooo," Klaa grunted.

"Closer . . ." Spock took a deep breath. "Our minds . . . are one."

Morrow glanced away for a moment to find that Mara and Kang and the rest of the Klingons were watching with what could only be called a mixture of fascination and revulsion at the thought of a Vulcan mind invading their own. Spock's eyes were slits of pure concentration. Klaa's eyes were pools of terror, his mouth gaping but unable to speak.

The Vulcan spoke for him in a guttural snarl that sent a chill down Morrow's spine. "I . . . am . . . Klaa. The empire . . . dying . . . paralyzed. *bIHnuch'yej* . . . a council of cowards. We will act . . . *I* will act . . . *Ha'DIbaHpu'! Bljeghbe'chugh vaj blHegh! Bljeghbe'chugh vaj blHegh! Bljeghbe'chugh vaj blHegh!*"

"What does he keep repeating?" Morrow said to no one in particular.

"A challenge to our enemies," Kang said. "Surrender, or die."

Spock's fingers dug into Klaa's face and his voice took on a rising intensity that made Morrow very uneasy. "I . . . am . . . Klaa. We will conquer. I am . . . Klaa!" Then the few words became drawn out and it took greater and greater effort for Spock to form them. Beads of sweat coursed down his face. "I . . . I . . . I . . . aaaamm . . . K-k-k-klaaaa. I . . . aaaamm . . . I . . . *aaaamm* . . ."

Klaa's face contorted in silent agony as he attempted to fight off Spock's mind reaching into his own. Morrow had no idea what was going on but he wanted this to end, *now*. He lurched forward and grabbed Spock by the shoulders just as he grunted his own name: "Spock!" The Vulcan yanked his hands away from Klaa with such repellent force that he stumbled back against Morrow, who barely kept them both from tumbling to the deck. Klaa lapsed into an unconscious stupor.

It took several long moments for Spock's breathing to slow to normal and the glaze to clear from his eyes. Then he squared his shoulders, stepped back from Morrow, and looked around the room, as if reorienting himself. "A fascinating experience," he murmured. "A mind of cunning determination, and simplistic aggressive certainty as to the rectitude of his own decisions. Klaa's universe is black and white."

"Did you find out what we needed to know?" Morrow asked.

Spock nodded. "His intended target was to be the mobile Klingon battle base. Presumably, that is where the Torye are now headed."

Kang frowned. "Battle base?"

The reactions from Kang and Mara made it clear they'd had no prior clue about this addition to the empire's arsenal. "Like it or not," Morrow said, "you're going to want to release General Navok. He can tell you all about it. And I can tell you this—if the Torye capture that battle base and use it as a platform for this new subspace weapon, they're going to pose a grave threat to the Klingon Empire, the Federation, and anybody else who gets in their way."

CHAPTER
12

"You wanted to see me, Bones?" Two strides into sickbay, Kirk stopped short when he saw McCoy was not waiting for him alone. Scott and Saavik were there as well. "Am I being ganged up on?"

"Saavik was willing to do this by herself," McCoy said, "but Scotty and I thought senior officers should be present . . . when she questions your sanity."

Saavik's eyebrow rose with a muted Vulcan variant of alarm. "Doctor," she said sharply, "please."

McCoy made a two-handed gesture of surrender, and allowed Saavik to take the lead.

"Captain," she said, "cooperating with the Klingons is the logical option."

Kirk glanced at all three of them. "And you all agree?"

"So do Uhura and Chekov," Scott said.

"Opinions noted. But this isn't a democracy. Have the Klingons sent any olive branches I haven't seen?" Again, he looked at each of them. "I didn't think so. The Klingons view peaceful overtures as a sign of weakness. I need this crew focused on coming up with ways to fight the Torye alone."

"The Torye?" McCoy blurted. "Jim, we're not even ready to fight the Klingons."

"Mr. Scott," Kirk said, "how are repairs going?"

"We should have warp drive and phasers back online in an hour, sir. But . . . we're in Klingon space, Captain. And we've no idea where the Torye went. We cannot just cruise around, hopin' we'll run into them."

"The needs of the many," McCoy said tartly, "outweigh the paranoia of the one."

Kirk managed a weary chuckle. "Logic, Bones? How quaint."

"Then to hell with logic! I find the fear of getting blown to bits in Klingon space *emotionally* taxing."

Kirk stiffened, trying (and failing) to avoid looking defensive. "Even if I agree, Kang never will. He loves humans as much as I love Klingons. Now, if you'll excuse me—"

The whistle of the intercom interrupted him, followed by Uhura's voice. *"Bridge to Captain Kirk."*

Kirk keyed the intercom on McCoy's desk. "Kirk here."

"The first officer of the Klingon vessel is asking to speak to you, sir."

Kirk didn't even try to cover his surprise. "Oh? I'll take it down here." Mara's face appeared on the comm viewer. "Mara. If you're calling to rescind Kang's honorable-death offer—"

"No, I am proposing cooperation between us, Captain. Will you consider it?"

"Will Kang?"

"He has no choice. Neither do you." Mara paused. *"We know you blame Klingons for the death of your son at the Genesis planet."*

"The *murder* of my son," Kirk corrected through clenched teeth.

"As I understand it, your son died an honorable death."

"Talk to me after *your* son dies an 'honorable' death," Kirk whispered.

"Captain." It was Spock's voice, and the view from the Klingon ship widened to reveal Spock and Morrow standing alongside Mara. *"The Klingons have obtained intelligence regarding the Torye's likely target. They are willing to share this information."*

"In exchange for what?"

"*Assistance enabling them to defend against the Torye weapon.*"

"How do I know they don't have disruptors aimed at your heads right now?"

"*We are under no coercion, Captain. Kang has accepted the logic of the situation. You each have information vital to the other, and you share a common goal—stopping the Torye. The odds of success are considerably improved if the* Enterprise *and* K'tanco *work together.*"

"*Jim,*" said Morrow, "*I don't like this any more than you do. But Spock is right.*"

Kirk felt the muscles in his jaw twitch. *Has everybody but me gone insane? Klingons can't be trusted.* But it was a high tide he was swimming against. Was McCoy right? Was his obstinate opposition *really* about David? Never mind trusting the Klingons—a lot of people he did trust were telling him he was wrong. "Mara," he finally said, "I need a sign of good faith. Return Spock and Morrow first."

"*Don't insult our intelligence, Captain. You need us as much as we need you. And our prisoners ensure that you won't double-cross us. As a sign of good faith, I pledge that they will not be harmed, and they will be released when our mission is complete. Now it's your turn.*"

"All right. Assuming we're successful, I'll see to it that the stolen weapon and plans are destroyed."

"*If that is acceptable to the Klingons,*" Spock said, "*I propose an immediate truce between our two vessels, and a simultaneous mutual exchange of the information on the defensive countermeasures and the Torye target, to be carried out in thirty minutes.*"

Mara nodded. "*Agreed. Captain?*"

Kirk forced out the words. "Agreed. A truce. Thirty minutes. We go after the Torye . . . together."

With negotiations concluded, Mara and three guards accompanied Spock and Morrow back to the brig. "Spock," Morrow said quietly, "I'm not saying you should've, but you could've simply told Captain Kirk what you got from Klaa."

"Had I done so," Spock replied, "the captain would not have been motivated to cooperate with the Klingons."

"And," Mara said, "I would have had no choice but to kill you both on the spot."

"It is imperative that the two ships undertake this mission together," Spock continued. "Additionally, actions we take now may yield collateral beneficial consequences in the future."

Morrow reacted with a small, knowing smile. "Spoken like a diplomat, Spock."

Kang paced the perimeter of *K'tanco's* bridge like a penned *klongat*. He was not pleased about the agreement he'd authorized Mara to make with Kirk. He hated logic, and hated to be ruled by it, when passion was so much more satisfying. But an astute commander should know enough to recognize and use the expertise of his officers, without diluting his own authority. It did not wound his pride to acknowledge that Mara was not only smarter than him, but also more attuned to psychological nuance. And he had learned to trust her judgment in matters other than battle, so he was secure enough to defer to her today. The deal was struck, and he would honor it as long as Kirk did. At the first sign of treachery, however, he would slit the throats of Spock and Morrow with his own *d'k tahg* and transport a cup of their blood to Kirk.

"Captain," the tactical officer shouted, "weapons fire in the brig!"

"Mara is down there." Kang reached for his *d'k tahg* with one hand and drew his disruptor pistol with the other. "Summon all available security teams to meet me there."

As Kang raced through his ship, the roar of his blood rushing in his ears, he attained the controlled frenzy of the warrior who would give no quarter and take no prisoners. The lift door opened and he charged toward the sounds of combat echoing down the narrow corridor to the brig. In a matter of seconds, through the smoke and noise, all of Kang's senses measured the chaos of carnage. At least five dead bodies in and around the hatchway into the brig, all Klingons . . . pools and rivers of Klingon blood . . . hand-to-hand fighting . . . *but who were the aggressors and who the defenders?*

In a corner, he spotted Mara, one of Klaa's men, and Morrow. The human held a *d'k tahg* . . . and was trying to kill Kang's wife. But, wait, no . . . Mara was down, wounded, and it was Klaa's warrior attacking her. Morrow flew forward, and his vicious slash nearly severed the Klingon soldier's arm. The attacker screamed, and his long-bladed knife clattered to the deck. In one desperate motion, Mara lunged for it, grabbed it, and ran it through her assailant's gut.

Now Kang knew Klaa was the instigator, taunting fate with his second mutiny attempt of the day. Kang's eyes searched the bedlam: *Where is that* Qu'vatlh *Klaa? I will cut his throat and slice out his heart!*

Then, he saw Klaa on the fringe of the melee, trying to reach the exit. "To the bridge," Klaa shouted, "to restore the honor of our fathers!"

But before Kang could wade in, a cudgel struck him in the center of his chest. He fell to his knees, momentarily breathless. Kang saw the cudgel rushing down toward him for a death blow when, suddenly, it froze in midair. A new pair of hands had seized the arms of the Klingon about to crush his skull . . . *Spock's hands*. Kang had no idea Vulcans were that strong, but Spock gripped the cudgel, gave it a thrash violent enough to dislocate his opponent's shoulders, and bashed the man into unconsciousness with a single uppercut stroke. Without a word, Spock reached down, grasped Kang's wrist, and hauled him to his feet. Face-to-face with Spock, Kang looked into those slitted eyes and saw, for a fleeting instant, all the savagery that Vulcans tried so hard to bury under their stifling blanket of dispassionate logic.

Another one of Klaa's men hit Morrow from behind with a flying tackle. Morrow crumpled, with the Klingon on top of him. The Klingon's immense hands wrapped around Morrow's head as if to snap his neck. Spock interceded with a precisely aimed kick to the back of the Klingon's head, accompanied by the fatal crack of splintering bone.

A moment later, a dozen of Kang's security reinforcements flooded into the fight, and it was over in a matter of minutes.

"Are you all right, Admiral?" Spock asked as he helped Morrow to his feet.

"More or less, thanks to you."

They stood aside as two of Kang's men carried a corpse past them. Morrow's breath caught in his throat as he realized it was General Navok.

Morrow sat on a bench in the *K'tanco*'s medical bay as a nurse tended to his and Spock's injuries. Morrow had assorted cuts and contusions on his hands and face, and what he guessed to be a cracked rib, based on the sharp ache in his side. Spock had a gash over one eyebrow and a swollen right hand. Morrow winced as the nurse roughly applied a slimy salve to a one-inch cut on his cheekbone, then pressed a skin-sealant device against the wound. The burning sensation caused by the device hurt more than the cut.

"I guess the Klingons don't believe in painkillers," Morrow muttered to Spock after the nurse left to work on other patients.

Spock flexed his hand gingerly. "Indeed. Submission to Dr. McCoy's ministrations would be preferable."

"Did Klaa get killed?"

"Negative. I saw him being reincarcerated with his surviving mutineers."

"I guess he won't be getting invited to tea anytime soon."

"Unlikely."

Making small talk with a Vulcan was not the easiest thing, and Morrow was acutely aware that he was babbling. He wondered if Spock was thinking what he was thinking . . . and whether he should just confess or forget the whole subject, the elephant in the room with them. *I condemned this man to death on Genesis a half-dozen years ago when I ordered Jim not to go back there. I didn't mean to. How the hell was anybody supposed to know he'd end up being . . . reconstituted? Even Jim didn't know. He just had this feeling, like he had to go there, even if there wasn't a snowball's chance in hell. I've never had that kind of connection with anybody . . . can't even imagine it. If I'd understood what Spock meant to him, I'd have let him go.*

Hell, I'd have ordered him to go. But I didn't. And now Spock saves me. I have to say something. . . .

"Spock," Morrow said in a hoarse whisper, "you know you saved my life back there."

"You would have done the same, had the situation been reversed. You saved Mara's life."

"I owe you my life, but I very nearly cost you yours."

Spock arched one eyebrow. "When?"

Morrow stared. "Are you kidding me?"

"Explain."

"At Genesis. The only reason you were here to save me today is because Jim Kirk ignored my direct order six years ago."

"He has been known to do that from time to time."

"Are you saying you've never blamed me?"

"For what?"

Morrow almost laughed, wondering if Spock was being deliberately obtuse just to annoy him. But Vulcans didn't do that . . . did they? "Nobody knew you were alive. If Jim hadn't stolen the *Enterprise* and gone back there, you'd have died there . . . again . . . when the planet came apart at the seams."

"That is correct. But your judgment at that time could not have reflected facts unknown to you. Assigning blame under such circumstances would be illogical." Spock paused and frowned ever so slightly. "Though I may never fully understand the thought processes which led them to undertake my rescue, logic does not prevent me from being grateful for what the crew of the *Enterprise* did for me."

"Don't you think it's a little ironic that I gave the order that would have left you for dead? Jim Kirk disobeys and saves you, and that's the only reason you were here to save me."

"Then it is fortunate that we are both here to appreciate that irony. Though it defies logic and cannot be supported by rational evidence, things, as you humans like to say, sometimes do work out for the best."

Morrow smiled and shook his head. "You're an interesting creature, Spock."

"I shall take that as a compliment."

Mara limped over to them, making a stoic effort to ignore

her own pain. "I trust our medics have given you satisfactory treatment for your injuries."

"We'll survive," said Morrow lightly.

"Mara," Spock said, "I should like to invoke a Klingon tradition."

She smiled. "I know what you are about to say, Spock." Then she turned solemn. "You have shed blood in a Klingon cause. As fellow warriors, you have earned the right to be treated as honored guests, no longer prisoners."

Morrow looked surprised. "Well! Thank you. We appreciate that."

"Don't abuse the honor," Mara warned. "If you're ready, we're needed on the bridge. It's time for the information exchange with the *Enterprise.*"

CHAPTER

13

We're helping the goddamned Klingons.

It was a perversion of all Kirk believed, the last thing he expected to be doing. But their immediate situation left him little choice, no matter how justified his animosity toward the Klingons might be. So it was that an *Enterprise* team worked side by side with Kang's engineers to repair the *K'tanco*'s warp drive, and Scott and Dr. elZana guided Mara and her specialists through the precise deflector modifications needed to defend against the Torye weapon.

Meanwhile, using sensor data collected during their initial exposure to the subspace weapon, Chekov reconfigured the *Enterprise*'s photon torpedoes to make them less vulnerable to the subspace disruption matrix. The trade-off worked out to a fifty percent reduction in explosive power in exchange for fifty percent more shield protection for the internal components of each torpedo. Kirk wasn't thrilled with that—but maximum destructive potential wouldn't mean much if torpedo guidance systems failed and they missed their targets. Once Chekov was satisfied with the alterations, he shared the details with the Klingons.

Then there was that damned mobile battle base. As Kirk reviewed the meager information Kang had retrieved from Klaa's ship and was willing to share per their truce, he couldn't believe what he was seeing. His starship, the pride of Starfleet, was three hundred and five meters long and displaced a million metric tons. The Klingons' dreadnought creation was ten times longer, with thirty times the mass. *Enterprise* armaments included nine double-barreled phaser banks; the battle base had fifty. *Enterprise* could accommodate a handful of shuttles on its hangar deck—*this* thing could carry thirty birds-of-prey. Resembling neither a vessel nor a spacedock, it could move at warp five. It was ungainly, functional—and lethal, on a scale far surpassing anything in the Starfleet arsenal. *Hell, we don't even have anything like it on the drawing board.*

As a student of military history, Kirk recognized that such gargantuan bases could be the modern equivalent of old-time naval aircraft carriers, playing a key strategic role and changing the face of galactic warfare. But massive aircraft carriers eventually outlived their usefulness (as battleships had before them), becoming little more than oversized, unwieldy targets for ever-more-deadly and precise long-range offensive weapons.

Whatever its ultimate function and fate, this battle base was a grave current threat to the balance of power in the quadrant. Steamed over Kang's refusal to share little more than the battle base's location and minimal specifications, Kirk was determined to gather as much intelligence as possible once they got close to it.

Yet, for all its military transcendence, Kirk's lasting impression of the battle base remained one of surprise: How the hell did the Klingons muster the resources to build something like that, given the economic stresses chipping away at the empire? That they'd been crazy enough to plan on constructing a whole fleet of the things confirmed Kirk's unsettling suspicion that lunatics were calling the shots in the High Council, lunatics who appeared more concerned with bellicose chest-thumping than survival. Surely, the cost of a dozen copies would break the empire's strained treasury.

Finally, after two hours of unstinting work, both the *Enter-prise* and *K'tanco* were sufficiently repaired and fortified, and they headed for the battle base.

What neither captain knew was that the battle base was heading for *them*.

Not exactly what we expected, Theena thought as she walked through the dimly lit bowels of this Klingon monstrosity. The Torye had been pleasantly surprised to find it occupied only by a skeleton maintenance and construction crew, so the actual capture turned out to be bloodless. With the subspace weapon working better the second time, they'd been able to catch the Klingons completely defenseless. Once their immense set of warp reactors were suddenly offline, the Klingons found themselves without power for weapons or shields, and they had no reason to disbelieve what Vykul told them—that they'd been conquered and had no option other than unconditional surrender. Since they were engineers and workers rather than dedicated military warriors, they complied with only token resistance.

By sheer mass alone, the battle base was initially quite impressive. But its deficiencies started becoming apparent the moment the Torye crew stepped off their ship in the cavernous hangar bay, and found not a flotilla of battle-ready birds-of-prey but a mere pair of work-worn shuttlecraft. Once aboard, Vykul split his people up for a more detailed inspection of their new acquisition.

Three-quarters of the base's interior turned out to be unfinished, mostly skeletal superstructure still awaiting installation of decks and bulkheads. Less than half the disruptor banks were operational, and the armory inventory was mostly vast empty racks where thousands of torpedoes should have been. And even in the sections which were more or less completed, Theena noted substandard materials and shoddy construction—a general observation rendered frighteningly specific when she stepped out of a balky turbolift and twenty feet of decking partially collapsed under her, leaving her dangling from a set of rickety crossbeams. It was almost as if the base had been built by apathetic slave labor—which, knowing the Klingons, could have very well been the case.

Had Klaa been able to realize his dream and seized the battle base, he would have been extremely angry and disappointed by the reality. Considering all its shortcomings, Theena would have had substantial misgivings about taking the base into actual combat. Fortunately, the Torye had other plans. All they really needed was a more powerful source of reliable energy for the subspace weapon, and the base's warp drive was among the few systems actually functioning up to nominal levels.

As she made her way back to the command center, Theena wondered how she'd ended up here. She thought of all the moments when she might have been able to stop Vykul, all the internal doubts she'd squelched, all the questions she chose not to ask . . . all the opportunities she'd had to break the chain of events that led to this looming confrontation. *Where was that big brain of yours when you really needed it?*

Disclosing her implacable opposition to Vykul's delusional plans had been a stupid, stupid mistake. She was now an object of suspicion, limiting any chance she might've had to sabotage the weapon. Despite the fact that Theena knew more about it than anyone else, Vykul made it clear he was blithely determined to use it with or without her cooperation—no matter the risks. That left her with two awful alternatives: apply her knowledge and expertise to make sure the weapon was used as safely as possible to advance a cause in which she no longer believed . . . or walk away, knowing that no one else would be able to fend off disaster if the temperamental weapon became unstable.

If she believed her absence would assure Vykul's defeat, even if she and her erstwhile comrades would die in the aftermath, she'd have chosen that course without hesitation. But in reality, leaving the operation of the weapon in less skilled hands simply increased the likelihood of triggering a cosmic catastrophe of almost unimaginable proportions. Even she was uncertain of the theoretical extent of potential damage to the fabric of subspace. It was her responsibility to make sure that didn't happen, no matter how much she'd have preferred curling up in a ball of ignorance.

"James," Raya said, looking Kirk in the eye, "what are we going to do when we find them?"

Kirk gazed down into the depths of his coffee mug for a long moment. He and Raya sat at a small table next to a window in the recreation lounge. Out in the star-strewn darkness, the Klingon battle cruiser kept pace. "We'll do what we have to do."

"Does that mean destroying the Torye ship?"

Kirk finally looked up at his friend. She looked tired and worried. "Raya, that's never my first choice. But we've seen what that weapon can do. Do you want them coming home to Mestiko and using it to overthrow your government? Getting your world into wars of conquest?"

"I keep hoping Theena can find a way to talk some sense into Vykul . . . or beat it into him."

Kirk managed a smile. "Either way would be fine with me." He glanced out the window at the Klingon ship in the distance. "We've both got friends in trouble."

"I've got a whole planet in trouble. There's a political firestorm brewing. Opposition parties are going to see this as their big chance to knock us down. It's not even about governing to them, it's all about winning. But there are also going to be honest questions about how we could let research like this go on without controls and oversight . . . about funding priorities . . . about the very existence of the Discovery Center."

"And you'll have honest answers. You always do."

Raya shook her head sadly. "What if I don't? This happened on my watch. I'm responsible. And if we get out of this mess, I need to know how something like this happened . . . and I need to make sure it never happens again."

"Then that's what you'll say. Good leaders are secure enough to admit when they don't have all the answers, and then they get on with searching for them."

The intercom whistled, followed by Uhura's voice: *"Bridge to Captain Kirk."*

Kirk slid out of his seat and walked to a nearby comm panel. "Kirk here."

"Captain, we're receiving a message . . . from the Torye."

"On my way. Kirk out."

Kirk and Raya strode out of the turbolift onto the bridge, and Uhura played back the message on the viewer abover her console. It was Vykul, seated in an unfamiliar control chamber. He rambled on for a stretch, answering his own questions about how the Torye were leading Mestiko into a future of limitless possibilities. He heaped magnanimous praise on Raya and her government for all the progress made in recent years, with special acclaim for the concept of a center devoted to unimpeded research and learning. *"Without it, this great leap forward would not have been possible. We share the credit for our achievement with you, Raya."*

Raya rolled her eyes and muttered a curse. "Just what I need."

"We've used the new weapon to annex a Klingon battle base. Why? To lead Mestiko to its rightful position as an independent power in firm control of its own destiny. We stand on the shoulders of giants, and reach toward a new golden age for all our people."

And that's where the message ended, leaving Raya with her head bowed as she tried to rub the tension from her long neck. "He almost makes it sound reasonable," she said.

"Almost," Kirk reminded her. "Saavik, do we have a fix on the origin point of that message?"

"Affirmative, sir. They made no effort to hide their location."

"Yes," said Kirk, 'Walk into my parlor,' said the spider to the fly."

Raya gave him a quizzical look.

"One of my favorite old children's poems," he said. "They want us to know exactly where they are. Vykul figures the sooner we find them, the sooner he defeats us and starts his 'golden age.' Let's accommodate him. Saavik, confirm coordinates with the Klingons and change our course."

"Yes, sir."

Theena arrived at the command center and took a deep breath before entering. Vykul looked up. "Is everything ready?" he asked.

"Not quite everything," she said as she assumed her post at the weapons-control console. "But we have about seventy-five percent engine power available to us, which is at least three hundred percent more than we had with our ship alone."

"Will that be enough to overwhelm any augmented deflectors on the starships?"

"Impossible to say for certain, since we don't know what countermeasures they may have initiated. But I'd rather be us than them when the subspace distortion matrix hits."

Vykul nodded. "Well, we find out soon enough."

From the tactical console, Fiota said, "Vykul, two ships just appeared on long-range scanners."

"Good. Then everything we've worked for is within our grasp." Vykul smiled as he activated the internal comm system and addressed his crew. "Red alert. All hands to battle stations!"

Those words made Theena's blood run cold. Vykul's scheme, unfolding with her right smack in the middle, would not have been possible without her complicity. *This is all my fault. How will you ever be able to make up for it, Theena? Wrap your big brain around* that.

CHAPTER
14

On the outer ring of the *Enterprise* bridge, Kirk perched on the rail and studied the star chart on the screen above Saavik's science station. Two decades ago, Sector 418-D had been an Alpha Quadrant backwater. Then one rogue pulsar changed everything. *Look at it now,* he mused. One little sector encompassed the troubled planet Mestiko, a swatch of the Federation-Klingon Neutral Zone, the key Klingon colony of Tiranax, and a ribbon of Klingon-Romulan border sufficiently contentious for the Klingons to have deployed their new battle base there. It was as if all sides had heedlessly tossed discordant ingredients into the same pot, disregarding the noxious stew boiling up inside. And now the lid was about to blow.

If he and Kang were going to prevent that, they'd need a unified strategy—easier said than done. Kang's impulse was to sweep in like the avenging Sword of Kahless and obliterate the battle base and its conquerors in one stroke. With McCoy and the rest of the bridge crew watching, Kirk reminded his stern Klingon counterpart that destruction of the battle base wasn't an option, since excessive destabilization or uncontrolled shutdown of the weapon had to be avoided at all costs. Hovda elZana stressed that they simply had no way of knowing how much damage that might do to the very fabric of subspace.

When Mara reminded Kang the base was still a valued Klingon military asset which might yet prove useful in defense of the empire, he dismissed it as an abomination created by the fevered minds of a High Council gone mad. *I actually agree with him there,* Kirk thought. *How about that?*

Kirk contended that their initial attack should probe for weakness and avoid exposing their own strengths and vulnerabilities. Kang was impressed (and more than a little surprised) when Kirk quoted an ancient human warrior-philosopher named Sun Tzu: "If you know the enemy and know yourself, you need not fear the result of a hundred battles."

"Kahless said the same thing," Kang replied. *"I did not know that any human possessed such wisdom when it came to the art of war. What else has this Sun Tzu taught you?"*

After a moment of thought, Kirk recalled a relevant passage: "'You can be sure of succeeding in your attacks if you attack only places which are undefended.' We already know what the subspace weapon can do. But the Torye haven't had a lot of time to integrate it with the battle base. We need to find their undefended places."

Kang agreed. *"Kahless said, 'The prepared warrior waits to take the enemy unprepared.' Our first attack will measure our enemy. Our second will vanquish him."*

"From Kang's mouth to God's ears," McCoy whispered to Uhura, "and that's a phrase I never thought I'd utter."

The *Enterprise* appeared to be alone as it approached the battle base and fired its first salvo of photon torpedoes. The Torye immediately unleashed the subspace weapon, and its cascade of scintillating energy rippled rapidly out in concentric spheres, flooding over the *Enterprise*. Just as Vykul wondered about the absence of the Klingon ship, *K'tanco* decloaked on the opposite side of the base. A spread of Klingon torpedoes sliced through the distortion matrix and exploded sequentially along the base's armored flank. The armor plating seemed almost sentient, shimmering, flexing, and settling once the blast energy had dissipated.

As the distortion matrix smothered the *Enterprise*, power generation took a precipitous plunge (much to Mr. Scott's alarm). As his starship twitched, Scotty held his breath. But the shields held, power surged, and the *Enterprise* escaped the subspace weapon's domain.

The *K'tanco* weathered the same rough ride and also slithered away, and the two ships met up again at a safe distance. Both crews immediately set about analyzing the wealth of sensor data gleaned from their sortie. Neither commander had to wait long for the results. The subspace weapon registered at *twice* the intensity of their first encounter, and the additional energy enhanced the distortion matrix's stability. Saavik felt compelled to make an inconvenient point: They had no way of knowing if the Torye were utilizing maximum power, or holding something in reserve.

However, it appeared that the power demands of the subspace weapon precluded simultaneous use of the base's disruptors. As Scotty put it, "There's only so much energy to go around." And not only were the battle base's warp engines fueling deflectors and the subspace weapon, they were also providing power to its unique adaptive armor. As Saavik and Chekov reported, unlike typical passive plate armor or energized force-shields, this defensive shell was constructed of an energy-infused alloy able to shuffle its molecular structure in response to attack, giving it an unusual capability for refraction and absorption of offensive energy.

Kang insisted he knew nothing of the development of this revolutionary armor. General Navok might have known about it, but he was dead. Kirk was privately certain only that they'd witnessed the application of a new and worrisome technology that could give Klingon ships a huge advantage in future battles.

The modified torpedoes had worked well enough, unaffected by the subspace distortion—but with the diversion of destructive capacity into shielding, they'd barely made a dent in the combined protection afforded by the base's deflectors and reactive cladding. Faced with one level of protection or the other, the torpedoes might inflict more damage, but against the combination they were unlikely to prove decisive.

Mara was the first to locate a ray of hope, which Saavik quickly confirmed: There were a few gaps in the base's deflector coverage—an indication that some of its shield emitters were either inoperative or improperly aligned. Though admittedly small, those gaps might be the fatal flaw Kirk and Kang had hoped to find—if they could figure out a way to exploit it.

They could try firing torpedoes through them—but that courted the risk of catastrophic destruction while the subspace weapon was deployed. One gap appeared large enough for a shuttle carrying commando teams to dock, but would they be able to breach the armor and get inside? Even if they could, that would take time, during which the shuttle would be vulnerable.

"Could we beam people through one of those gaps?" Kirk asked.

Everyone looked at Scott, who appeared dubious. "Captain, we've no idea how that subspace distortion could affect the transporter. If it disrupts the annular confinement beam, our people could arrive as puddles of protoplasm—if they got there at all."

"What if we minimized the distance?"

"Aye, that'd help—but it'd have to be point-blank. And droppin' our shields at close range? If they have torpedoes, we'd be sittin' ducks, sir."

"Not if one ship does the beaming while the other provides cover."

"Jim," McCoy said, "it could be a suicide mission. We have no idea what they'll run into over there."

"I'm aware of that, Doctor. But this could be our best—and only—chance to retake the base and shut down that weapon."

Kirk knew it was an option fraught with peril. But they had to do something, and time was one luxury they didn't have, considering the destructive power now concentrated in unpredictable Torye hands. Advised by their senior officers, Kirk and Kang finalized a plan: A six-person tactical team combining Starfleet and Klingon personnel would be transported from the *Enterprise* while the *K'tanco* provided heavy covering fire. Then both ships would harass the battle base and distract the Torye crew while the boarding party attempted to shut down the subspace weapon and secure the base.

Mara and Scott were assigned to lead the group of three officers from each ship. Their task: to take down the subspace weapon without blasting a disastrous hole in the universe. As they completed final preparations in the transporter room, Raya chipped in with her appraisal of Vykul and his crew.

"He fancies himself a military leader," she said, "but he and the rest of the Torye have no real experience at this. You people obviously do."

"Well, that's something," Kirk said. Then he turned to the boarding team. "But don't forget: Fanatics can make formidable opponents. Good luck over there. Remember, you'll have two starships doing our level best to give you the time you need to accomplish your mission."

From her console at the heart of the command center, Theena tracked the two ships as they wheeled around and began what looked like a side-by-side run at the battle base.

"Status?" said Vykul, still exuding supreme confidence. He leaned back in the commander's seat on its raised platform, his hands clasped comfortably behind his neck.

Theena checked her panels. "All internal systems normal. Deflectors and armor battle-ready. Weapon system on standby."

"Phase two power?"

"Ready."

One console to Theena's right, Fiota peered intently at her tactical screen. "The Klingon ship remains uncloaked."

"They could engage their cloaking device anytime," Theena said.

"Or, maybe they've just decided on a refreshing frontal attack," Vykul said. "They may have realized we have an overwhelming advantage and it doesn't much matter what they do. This could be a suicide run."

Theena gave him a quick, queasy stare, not even bothering to conceal her apprehension. Did he really believe what he was saying? Was he actually unaware of all that could go wrong? Had he forgotten that the opposing warships had been able to escape from the distortion matrix this last time around? They'd obviously determined how to adapt their shields to put up greater resistance. *So we've modified our tactics in response—but we can't be sure it'll work. What if it doesn't? We don't have any more tricks up our sleeves.* Yet Vykul radiated blissful assurance, without a hint of doubt. *Is he right—or insane?*

As *Enterprise* and *K'tanco* approached, Theena kept waiting for them to split up. But they stayed alongside each other, as if tethered together. Her hand hovered over the weapon trigger. *Enterprise* and *K'tanco* each fired a volley of torpedoes, but remained in tandem.

"Deploy weapon—phase one," Vykul ordered.

Theena followed the command. "Distortion matrix engaged." She paused while the fusillade of torpedoes exploded against the base's armor like distant, rolling thunder. But the command center barely shivered. "Targets acquired."

Vykul leaned forward slightly. "Effects?"

"Same as before. Fluctuations in their power output, but their warp drives are still online."

Suddenly, the two starships broke formation. *Enterprise* dove down, passing beneath the battle base, while the Klingon ship veered and came about sharply, unleashing a rapid-fire barrage of a dozen torpedoes in a matter of seconds.

"Phase two," Vykul said, "full power—now!"

Theena engaged the rest of the warp reactors. For just a heartbeat, lights dimmed and the background ventilation hum muted; then it returned to normal. On the main viewscreen, the shimmering distortion field billowed out and flared brightly.

"All warp engines . . . now at maximum," Theena said in a hushed voice. Her eyes widened as she waited for circuits to overload and systems to blow. But, to her astonishment, nothing failed. The augmented subspace distortion matrix flowed over both starships from behind as they accelerated away—and both appeared to falter as the distortion field interfered with their propulsion output. Despite the fact that she hated what Vykul was doing, she felt a thrill seeing how her handiwork performed.

Theena felt her stomach churn as she observed what the sensors told her: The *Enterprise* and *K'tanco* shunted almost all their respective primary warp-drive energy to their deflectors, providing a precious few seconds of .extra protection while the ships limped away on impulse power. Both ships had escaped the trap she'd set for them.

Then she felt Vykul's hand squeezing her shoulder. "Don't look so depressed. We have what we came for. We continue on course for home."

Theena shook her head. "Kirk and Kang aren't going to allow that."

"They don't have a choice. With your weapon and this battle base, we are unstoppable."

Fiota suddenly looked up from her internal-status monitors. "Vykul, we have intruders aboard. We're detecting residual transporter signatures in the lower levels."

"How could they beam people over through our deflectors?" Vykul strode over and grasped the edge of the console.

"I don't know," Fiota said with a nervous shrug.

Theena sensed that Vykul's largely untested crew was starting to panic, and for the first time, Vykul's frown betrayed his own concern.

"We have to protect this command center," he said, making a conscious effort to sound confident. "Full security alert! Seal it up! If they can't get in here, they can't stop us."

"They *can* stop us," Theena countered, "if they get to engineering ops and disrupt power flow from warp drive to weapons systems."

"Can you prevent that?"

"Not from up here. I have to do it down in ops."

"Do you need any help?"

"It's faster if I do it alone. And you need all available personnel for security."

"All right . . . but take these." He handed her a Klingon tricorder and a disruptor. "Scan for the intruders. Avoid them if possible—I don't want you captured. If you have to, shoot to kill. Go—but be careful."

Theena bolted from the command center. Running through one corridor to another, she heard muffled explosions and felt the deck shake under her feet. The two starships were attacking again, with a steady bombardment of torpedoes fired from a safe distance. *How long can this thing take the pounding?*

. She ducked into a turbolift, which dropped fifteen decks so abruptly it felt like free fall. The pod jolted to a halt, the door opened, and she jumped out onto the engineering level. Then she paused to scan for life forms—and there they were: humans and Klingons, aft of her position and three decks below. Whoever got to the operations section first would be able to lock out intruders. She couldn't allow the boarding party to beat her there.

The deck shook again, the explosions outside the hull louder than before. *They're targeting engineering! If they're trying to force us to stand down, they don't know Vykul.*

Theena kept running until she felt like her lungs were burning. And then she ran some more, until she arrived at the hatch leading to engineering operations. She leaned against the wall for a rest, her chest heaving as she tried to catch her breath. She checked the tricorder again—the boarding party was almost here. But instead of entering ops and locking the hatch behind her, she bypassed it. She moved toward the intruders as they came toward her. As an afterthought, she pulled the disruptor pistol from her belt and held it in her hand.

Twenty meters from a corridor intersection, Theena stopped to check the tricorder one more time, and then she waited. A few moments later, the boarding party rounded the corner and saw her. A Klingon female was an instant away from shooting when a burly human with gray hair and mustache stopped her. Theena recognized the human. "Mr. Scott!"

Scott squinted at her. "Theena?"

CHAPTER
15

Mara still wanted to shoot Theena. "You know her?" she said to Scott.

"Aye. Uhh, lassie, unless you're plannin' to use that weapon, you might want to lower it."

Theena looked at her disruptor, as if she'd forgotten she was even holding it. Realizing the likely ramification of pointing a weapon at a Klingon, she clipped it back onto her belt hastily. The boarding party approached her. "I'm here to help you."

Scott stared at her. "You're here to *what?*"

"Help you. We have to shut down the subspace weapon."

Mara hadn't yet holstered her weapon, and looked like she didn't intend to. "Are you going to trust her?"

"Well," Scott said, keeping a wary eye on Theena, "that all depends. Why would you be helpin' us?"

"Because Vykul's lost his mind. All this . . ." She waved her hand around them, and her voice grew increasingly frantic. "This was never my intention. I don't know how long this base will hold together, and I sure as hell don't know how long the subspace distortion matrix will remain stable. Now, you can shoot me and try this yourself, without having the slightest idea what you're doing. Or you can let me help you. Whatever choice you make, do it fast, because this much I do know—we don't have a lot of time."

On the *Enterprise* bridge, Commander Uhura swiveled to face the command chair. "Captain, message from Mr. Scott."

Kirk nodded and Uhura put Scott on speaker. "Kirk here. Status, Scotty?"

"We've reached main engineering—and we've got Theena helpin' us shut this beastie down."

Kirk's eyebrows rose in surprise. "Theena?"

"It's a long story, Captain. But I don't know if we could do this without her. How's the Enterprise, *sir?"*

Kirk couldn't help smiling at Scott's concern for his pride and joy. "Minor degradation to the warp engines, but they're regenerating. The torpedoes aren't having much of an effect on the base . . . and our inventory is starting to run low. So . . . our fate is pretty much in your hands, Scotty."

"Aye, sir. We'll do our best. Scott out."

Kirk's jaw tightened. He was all too aware that they'd be unable to retrieve the boarding party unless they could get back to the beam-in point at the battle base's shield gap, or unless Scotty's team succeeded in cutting power to the base's deflectors altogether. The Klingons might've regarded this as a good day to die, but Kirk refused to accept that his people over there were expendable until he had absolutely no alternative.

"Captain," Saavik said urgently, "the subspace distortion matrix is becoming unstable. They cannot sustain this level of output."

Kirk leaned forward in his seat, his attention on the viewscreen where the distortion field had begun to waver. "But do the Torye know that?"

"Maybe we should tell them," Raya said from her perch next to McCoy near the communications station.

"You're right," Kirk said, rising to his feet. "Uhura, open a channel."

"Channel open, sir."

"Vykul, this is Captain Kirk. Shut down the weapon, before it's too late."

The Torye leader appeared on the screen above Uhura's console. *"Why would I do that, Captain? We have the most powerful weapon in the quadrant and we're safe inside an invincible flying fortress."*

"I don't think so. Our boarding party's already breached that fortress of yours. And if you check your diagnostics, you'll find that your super-weapon is on overload. You know the consequences."

"I've been told."

"Then shut it down and surrender. Or are you planning to be a martyr?"

"I'm not a religious man, Captain; I'm sure Raya has told you that. But I'll blow this base up and take you and the Klingons with me before I surrender. So if you don't withdraw . . . you know the consequences."

Though he was outwardly calm, Kirk's mind raced. *Is Vykul all bluster? How far is he really willing to go? You don't have to be religious to be a fanatic. What if we call his bluff and we're wrong?* "You've made your point. You've got Raya's attention."

"That was never the point, Captain. But do I expect you to understand? No. You take orders, I give them. You're just a cog in a machine, but I'm the power that makes the machine go. And do I mind going out in a blaze of glory? Not at all."

"Glory?" Raya blurted, stepping forward alongside Kirk. "Is that what you call this? If you and your Torye want to vaporize yourselves, I don't really care. But this weapon . . . it could cause even more devastation than the Pulse! Did our people fight back from the brink of oblivion just so you can wreak destruction on a cosmic scale?"

"You have the power to stop it, Raya." With that, Vykul cut his comm signal.

Kirk moved toward Saavik. "Lieutenant, what's their status?"

"Distortion pattern integrity is degrading at an accelerating rate. Matrix oscillations will soon exceed acceptable limits. Subspace tearing is increasing in magnitude, with a concurrent increase in tetryon, gamma, and hyperonic radiation."

"Dammit. Uhura, contact Mr. Scott."

Uhura nodded. A moment later, they heard Scott's voice again. *"Scott here."*

"Progress report," Kirk said tersely.

Scott began with a prefatory deep breath. In Kirk's experience, that was never a positive sign. *"It's no good, sir. Theena's doin' all she can, but . . . it's too late for a controlled shutdown."*

"What if you just cut power to the weapon? Won't that collapse the distortion matrix?"

"She's past the breakaway threshold. Cuttin' power won't do a blessed thing to stop her."

"Then we're getting you out. Can you shut down the base's deflector system from there?"

"Captain, there's no time! Leave us and save the ship! If subspace is comin' apart at the seams, you're already seein' enough radiation to interfere with the transporter."

"I'll be the judge of that, Mr. Scott. Shut down those deflectors and stand by. That's an order."

"Aye, sir."

McCoy frowned at the main viewer, where he noticed a new development—ethereal tendrils of ionized particles swirling away from the main distortion field. "Ohh, that can't be good," he said, and all eyes turned toward the viewscreen image.

"Captain," Saavik interjected, "the subspace tears are starting to exert gravitational attraction on proximate matter and energy."

"Which, at some point," McCoy hissed, "is going to include this ship."

Kirk ignored the comment and activated the comm panel on his chair. "Uhura, contact Kang."

Vykul paced behind the noticeably jittery Fiota. "What's going on?"

"The weapon's on overload." She chewed on her lip as she checked her status monitors. "Warp reactor output is fluctuating all over the place. Maybe if we shut it down, the subspace damage will stop."

"Shut it down?" Vykul echoed. "I don't want to shut it down."

That pushed Fiota beyond her limit. She spun around in her seat, and was about to scream at her leader when she heard a shrill alarm beeping at her console. She whirled back and stared at the screen.

"What is it?" Vykul prompted.

Fiota swallowed hard. "Deflector emitters . . . they just shut down."

"Ours? Or theirs?"

"Ours."

A second later, a clockwork flurry of five torpedoes blasted the starboard hull just outside the command center, with enough violence to throw Vykul off his feet and knock his crewmates out of their chairs. Lights flickered, and the starboard consoles sparked and caught fire.

Out in space, Kang's battle cruiser swerved hard about for another torpedo run, while the *Enterprise* edged in so close to the belly of the battle base the two were almost touching. The ship was shaking and straining to escape from the cosmic turmoil unfolding around them.

Saavik and Chekov delivered status updates: The moaning warp engines were operating at not quite eighty percent capacity; shields were down below seventy percent. The weapon's distortion matrix had collapsed into chaos, shredding subspace, with new tears opening all around the battle base and rapidly expanding into gaping rifts. Increasingly intense gravimetric turbulence buffeted both ships like kites in a gale, holding them back as if by a string that stretched but refused to break. And the *K'tanco* was in even more trouble, some distance behind the *Enterprise,* as a vortex of matter and energy formed with the battered Klingon base at its raging heart. The more matter and energy it dragged into its maw, the faster the vortex bloomed.

Finally, the report came from the transporter room. *"Tuchinsky to bridge. We've got the entire landing party, plus one, sir."*

"Mr. Chekov, shields to maximum," Kirk said, relieved. "Get us out of here." Then to Tuchinsky, he said, "Chief, have

Mr. Scott, Theena, and Mara report to the bridge, and have security escort the other two Klingons to the recreation lounge as our guests."

"Yes, sir."

When Scott arrived at the bridge, he went straight to the engineering console, while Theena and Mara stood near the turbolift doors next to McCoy and Raya. "Scotty . . . ?" Kirk began.

Scott shook his head. "You've already got all she has to give, sir."

As the two starships labored to pull away, the battle base skidded back, then began to break apart as it was swallowed up by the spatial whirlpool. As it disappeared inside the roiling cloud of energized particles and vapors, everyone on the bridge waited, breathless. . . . The vortex coughed out three hot flares—and then a great fireball with the fury of a small sun going nova. The massive ejection of gas and gravitons slammed into the two ships and flung them away, tumbling into the distance.

On both ships, bodies and equipment went flying. Somehow, Scotty and Chekov clawed their way to the controls and coaxed the *Enterprise* out of her wild spin. Those who weren't hurt helped those who were. Kirk wiped away the blood dripping from a gash over his eyebrow and made his unsteady way back to the center seat. The viewscreen revived in time for them to see the final frenzied moments of the gravimetric maelstrom consuming all matter and energy within its savage grasp. It collapsed and twisted itself into an unimaginably dense, searingly bright pinpoint. Finally, all that compressed mass exploded into a fountain of rainbow plasma which swiftly began coalescing into the beginnings of a shimmering new nebula.

Raya and Theena stood transfixed by the awful beauty of what they'd witnessed—and survived. Brilliant colors from the viewscreen image danced across their faces. "It's . . . so beautiful," Raya whispered.

"But lethal," Theena added softly. "Radiation levels in this region will be deadly for centuries. There could have been planets . . . civilizations . . . destroyed. And it's my fault."

Raya looked into her young friend's haunted eyes. "Some of it, yes."

"I was responsible for creating a terrible, dangerous weapon."

"But it didn't have to be used. You helped Vykul use it."

"I know . . . I do know. And I'm sorry," Theena said as two security guards approached to take her away. "Here I am with this big brain. But it took all this for me to understand . . . the most dangerous thing in the universe is a creature convinced beyond doubt of his own virtue."

Kirk overheard Theena's humbling, hard-won wisdom . . . and he knew, beyond doubt, it applied to all of them.

EPILOGUE

Mara and her crewmates returned to their ship, and Spock and Morrow beamed over to the *Enterprise*. As both crews assessed damage and made repairs, Kang's vessel escorted the *Enterprise* through Klingon space and back toward the Neutral Zone. Kirk informed Kang he planned to urge the Federation to ban any further development of subspace-disruption weapons, by the Payav or anyone else—and he warned that the Federation would not tolerate deployment of the provocative battle stations.

When they reached the Neutral Zone, *Enterprise* and *K'tanco* went their separate ways. With his ship on course for Mestiko, Kirk left Chekov in command and stepped into the turbolift, with Spock and McCoy following. Noticing that Kirk looked especially grim, McCoy tried to lighten the mood. "Those Klingons might be writing one of their caterwauling songs right now, commemorating for the ages the day when the great Captains Kang and Kirk worked together to save the galaxy."

"Indeed," said Spock, "future generations may look back on recent events and recognize them as a key step toward peaceful coexistence between the Federation and the Klingons."

Despite the fact that he'd cheated death yet one more time, and escaped with his ship and crew intact, Kirk did not warm to the spirit of the occasion. "The Klingons . . . can go to hell. And I don't mind showing them the way."

So much for lightening the mood. They rode down in silence, until Kirk grabbed the control grip and brought them to an unscheduled halt. He fixed his first officer with a hard, accusatory glare. "Spock, what the hell were you and Morrow doing in Klingon space in the first place?"

"We were asked to undertake a sensitive mission by President Ra-ghoratreii himself, which remains classified. I regret that I cannot discuss it further."

"So do I." Kirk looked away and restarted the turbolift.

When they reached their destination deck, and the door opened, the captain took a deep breath and his expression softened, permitting his friends a fleeting glimpse of the heartache he'd carried with him since the day his son was killed. "We . . . can't negotiate with them, Spock. You know what they are . . . what they've done."

"Jim," Spock said, "there are some Klingons who recognize the imperative of change."

"They'll never change." Then Kirk turned and walked down the corridor.

McCoy sighed as they watched him go. "Well . . . you can't blame him."

"Doctor, after all these years, I do understand that emotions can be a heavy burden for humans," Spock said, not unkindly. "His feelings toward Klingons are substantive and understandable. But a starship captain cannot allow judgment to be impaired by emotion."

"Maybe he keeps us around to remind him of that. But as a doctor, I can tell you . . . some wounds never heal."

Kirk found Raya in her cabin, looking exhausted by the ordeal they'd all endured over the past few days—and troubled by the consequences waiting for her back on Mestiko. She managed a melancholy shadow of a smile. "Maybe I won't go home. Maybe I'll just join your crew and explore the cosmos . . . and you'll be in charge and I won't have to worry about a thing."

"Have you talked to Theena?"

"I know she has to be in the brig, but it's just . . . depressing. She says she doesn't want an advocate. Just wants to plead guilty, no matter what the charges."

"That would be simpler."

"Part of me agrees. But part of me wants to put her through a trial." She clenched her fists and shook them. "Part of me wants to *strangle* her! She *betrayed* me, James . . . betrayed a lifetime of friendship and respect. Is that . . . petty . . . of me?"

"Not after what she did. But she didn't intend to do it to you personally."

"I know that—but it feels that way. Not now—it's too fresh—but I'm going to have to sit down with her and talk, really talk. I need to know why she did this. How could such a brilliant girl go down such a dark and foolish path—and without my noticing? How many more of our young people feel so much despair and frustration? After all we've been through, all the strides forward . . . are we doomed by our demons? Do some wounds never heal?"

"Those are the questions your people have to ask, out loud. And I can't think of anyone better equipped than you to listen—really listen—to the answers." Kirk gave her what he hoped was a reassuring smile. "Well, I'll let you get some rest."

"No, wait. Stay. I . . . don't want to be alone." Raya blinked to hold back a wave of grief. "I called home to check in. Blee told me . . . my grandmother died."

Kirk sighed and reached out for her hand. "I'm . . . so sorry. I liked your *elor*."

"She liked you too, James." Then Raya laughed despite the tears sliding down her cheeks. "But she really liked this ship of yours. You know, when I left her this last visit, I . . . I had a feeling." Raya squeezed her eyes shut. "She told me to go do what I had to do."

"So on top of everything else, you have to make funeral arrangements."

Raya nodded as she wiped her eyes. "Something I can't delegate to my staff. I have no idea . . . ."

"If there's anything I can do to help."

"Just listening helps." She let out a weary sigh as recollections of Elee filled her head. "You know, she loved to fly—in anything. Gliders, props, jets, balloons . . . your starship. She's positive she'll be reincarnated as a bird. Then she'd get to spend the rest of her *next* life flying over . . ." Raya's voice trailed off and she frowned, then brightened slowly. "Wait . . . I do know what she would want . . . where to scatter her ashes. And, *yes,* you can help me."

"Whatever you need."

"James, would you please join me and Elee for a balloon ride across Tuuliie Bay?"

Kirk's careworn face broke into a boyish grin. "I'd be honored."

2293

ITS HOUR COME ROUND

Margaret Wander Bonanno

Dedicated to Thira Grace Corona,
just for being herself

CHAPTER

1

Raya elMora hooked her four thumbs into the buckle of the shoulder harness and snapped it into place.

"Computer? How much time before the Federation delegation arrives in vosTraal?"

"*Starship* Excelsior *scheduled to make orbit in approximately two hours, Jo'Zamestaad,*" the onboard computer replied crisply. "*Estimate time for necessary formalities before beamdown, additional six to twelve minutes.*"

"Thank you," Raya said, considering.

A Mestikan hour was one hundred and forty-four minutes. A low-altitude orbit of her world, Raya knew, could be accomplished in approximately ninety-six minutes. Side trips to investigate particular phenomena would add to that time. And she *did* have to land the orbital flyer and get back to her quarters to change from the borrowed flight suit into her diplomatic best before the delegation arrived.

Raya sighed. One orbit it was, then. Waiting while the computer checked wind speed and direction, she adjusted the wing cameras that would gather the information she was seeking, feed it back into the central computers in vos-

Traal, and digest it into the brief document she would present at the opening ceremonies of the Plenary Council tomorrow. Manually setting course and speed, she allowed the little craft to rise straight up to the desired altitude, then hovered for a moment to look around at her city in the rising sun before the thrusters kicked in and she headed out on her mission.

What she was doing today was an indulgence, she knew. Better-trained pilots scanned the surface of her world daily to report on the progress of its recovery from the passage of a rogue pulsar two twelveyears ago—a phenomenon so devastating that only the intervention of a Federation starship had kept the pulsar—or as Mestiko's citizens, the Payav, referred to it, "the Pulse"— from destroying the planet entirely.

Despite the *Enterprise*'s intervention, the destruction had been considerable, the immediate casualties staggeringly high; and the ensuing nuclear winter, with its toxic atmosphere and frigid temperatures, had claimed still more lives over the ensuing years. The total death toll might never be known.

And yet, the Payav were still here, a proud and stubborn people, aided by that same Federation in recovering their world and their autonomy.

And that, Raya mused, her thoughts grim despite the sheer beauty of the landscape below her, was where the current troubles began—and, she hoped, ended.

In any event, an indulgence. There was enough data from the regular pilots' runs to include in her opening remarks, but she'd wanted to come up here and see for herself. Paperwork had kept her at her desk until the last possible moment, and so these two hours of a pristine morning were all the time she had.

She'd tried not to notice the knowing smiles when she'd shown up in a flight suit just before dawn, the exchanged glances among the veteran pilots that said, *Yes, of course. Let the Jo'Zamestaad take the new prototype craft out on a morning survey run. The onboard computer will do most of the work, and if she gets into trouble we can send another craft out to help her. Let her see what we've been doing these past months to catalog every hectare of land on Mestiko and compare what is now with what was and has been since the Pulse nearly destroyed us two twelveyears ago.*

Raya knew her piloting skills were only average and a recent acquisition. Her *elor* had loved to fly, and in homage to Elee after her death, Raya had gradually overcome her own fear of heights and mastered the rudimentary skills. After all, she reasoned, she had been on starships, visited other worlds, even been exiled on one of them. Could learning to fly a craft on her own be that much more frightening?

Besides, the course was laid in automatically, and if she instructed it to, the computer would do everything for her, even sparing her the effort of steering around the occasional flock of birds.

Her first thought was: *At least now there are birds. This wasn't always so. Having been introduced from other worlds, they may not look like the birds we of the generation before the Pulse remember, but they are better than skies filled with toxic dust, and no birds at all.*

Her second thought—as she said "Computer, manual," and allowed herself to test the controls, dipping the nose and coming back up again just for practice—was: *The prototype responds far better than anything the Federation's given us.*

Was the thought disloyal to that nation that had saved so many Payav lives in the wake of the greatest natural disaster ever to befall the planet?

It is, Raya thought, *and it isn't. And there, as the Dinpayav would say, is the rub. For everything the Federation has done for us, there is, some would argue, more they could have done. And, still others would argue, less they should have done, so that we could claim our recovery for our own.*

Raya's *elor* used to say, "Put two Payav in a room and you end up with three arguments." It was as true in the recovery following the Pulse as it had been before any Payav knew such things lurked in the far reaches of space, deciding in a very short time who would live and who would die.

During the early recovery years, the Payav hadn't had the luxury of argument. Tribal and regional differences were forgotten in the daily struggle for survival. However, that hadn't stopped religious fanatics in the form of the mar-Atyya, represented by her old school chum Asal Janto, from fomenting revolution, sending Raya and those loyal to her into exile for years until they could take their planet back.

Since then, the more their world recovered and returned to normal, it seemed, the more Payav found to squabble about.

And now, Raya thought, banking the little craft to starboard as she cleared the last of the structures in the suburbs and headed out over open land before returning the controls to the computer, *we will bring their internecine squabbles under the scrutiny of our neighbors, as for the next month—or longer, if necessary—representatives of both the Federation and the Klingon Empire sit with us in an attempt to determine our future.*

Were they ready? As ready as they'd ever be. Left to their own devices, Payav would argue into the next grossyear. Besides, there was a matter of some urgency in the Federation's request for a Plenary Council. It seemed the Klingons had recently suffered a similar disaster, the explosion of one of their moons called Praxis, which had compromised the atmosphere of their homeworld Qo'noS, meaning it would have to be evacuated within the next fifty years.

At least, Raya thought, noting with satisfaction that the forward screen adapted to the light as the small craft turned into the sun, *the Klingons have the luxury not only of taking their time leaving their homeworld, but of choosing among other planets within their empire upon which to relocate. We on Mestiko were not so fortunate.*

This raised another thought. If the Pulse had never passed their world, might the Payav already have chosen membership in the Federation? Their fate then might have been a very different one. Was this sufficient argument for joining the Federation now?

Because that was the crux of this Plenary Council: for the Payav to decide whether or not they wished to join the Federation.

The Klingons would be there, officially to learn from the Payav how to cope with a disaster of the magnitude of the Pulse or the explosion of Praxis. But there was no mistaking that, if the Payav and the Federation parted company at the end of the Council, the Klingons would be waiting in the wings.

As for whether their intentions were peaceful . . . Raya had studied the Klingons. If their intentions were peaceful, that would be a first in their long and bloody history.

The whir and beep of the onboard computer "talking" to the wing cameras shook her out of her reverie. The cameras had been programmed to begin gathering data when her little craft reached the first of the areas most devastated by the Pulse.

Below her the Kemong River meandered through its littoral. Once a flourishing agricultural region, later reduced to frigid desert in the wake of the Pulse, the area had at last been restored to grazelands and grain fields. Like most of the planet, it had been reclaimed from devastation, but it would never be the same.

Everything—the number of Dinpayav (humans, Vulcans, Klingons, Kazarites, and a dozen other species Raya didn't even recognize) in the cities and even the remote areas; the introduction of new species, from Dr. Lon's Martian ice-mosses to far more complex forms; the attempts to reintroduce native species—had resulted in a patchwork of failed and successful and partly successful experiments. Good or bad, everything was *different*.

Was that necessarily good or bad? Raya wondered. Once again, the only answer she could come up with was "yes." And "no."

Monitoring the data-feeds from the wing cameras, she wondered: Did she want her people to decide to join the Federation or not? She honestly didn't know.

Well, if nothing else came of the Plenary Council, she thought, at least it would be good to see James again.

She stayed out longer than she'd planned, and barely had time to make it back to vosTraal to change into her formal clothes before the arrival of the Federation delegation. After fastening the several small buttons on the cuffs of the first new robe she'd allowed herself this year—with so many of her people still emerging from hardship, after having done without so much for so long, it didn't seem appropriate to acquire more—

she checked in with her office staff to make sure everything was still on schedule.

"We've received a communication from Captain Sulu of the *U.S.S. Excelsior, Jo'Zamestaad*," an aide informed her. "The starship is in synchronous orbit above vosTraal, and the delegation has requested permission to beam down."

"Permission granted, of course." Raya beamed, genuinely excited. "Just give me a minute to get to the reception area without running. . . ."

The Martian scientist Dr. Lon—or Cart etDeja, as he had been known since becoming a citizen of Mestiko—was there ahead of her, as was the Federation's ambassador, the ever-jovial Ana'siuolo named Settoon, and Raya exchanged the traditional two-handed greeting with each in turn. On her way here she had passed through the public corridor, where about a third of the various regional representatives—governors and Servants and tribal leaders of various persuasions—who had been invited to observe the Summit in conjunction between the *Zamestaad* and representatives of the Federation and the Klingon Empire had begun to gather. The rest would arrive within the next day or two.

Greeting each of them personally, making certain not to slight anyone—tempers were touchy enough, given that many from the more remote regions could not get there for the opening ceremonies and had to be persuaded that their opinions would be taken just as seriously over video feed as they would have been in person—Raya had barely had time to reach the reception area before she heard the familiar-after-so-many-years sound of a Federation transporter.

Three figures materialized before her. She had been expecting four.

CHAPTER
2

Consciously or not, Spock, McCoy, and Uhura had beamed down in the Missing Man formation.

Begun among Earth's air forces during the early era of flight, the tradition of leaving an empty space in a delta formation where a fallen comrade's plane should have been had been carried forward into the era of spaceflight. Not being from Earth, Raya elMora could be forgiven for not recognizing the tradition or its significance and, if asked, Spock himself would have been surprised to find that he and his companions had unconsciously left a space for one more person when they had stepped onto *Excelsior*'s transporter platform.

Raya had last seen Spock in a Starfleet uniform, not civilian clothes. A distinguished diplomatic career, as well as his past involvement with the fate of Mestiko, had made it inevitable that he would be the Federation's chief negotiator at the Summit. On either side and slightly behind him were Dr. McCoy and Commander Uhura. But immediately to his left there was a blank space, as if someone else had once stood there, but no more. Consciously or unconsciously, Kirk's friends and longtime crewmates had left a place for him when they'd beamed down.

Wordlessly, Raya looked to Spock, whose expression was unreadable. It wasn't until she saw the expression in McCoy's eyes that she knew.

James T. Kirk was dead.

The news had spread throughout the fleet, both via official sources and by word of mouth, from Scotty and Chekov, who were there when it happened, to Sulu aboard *Excelsior,* to Uhura and McCoy and Spock.

Scotty had been all but inconsolable.

"It should've been me, lass!" Tears coursed unashamedly down his weathered face on Uhura's commscreen. He knew she'd heard it through official channels, but he seemed to need to talk to someone, to explain himself. *"But there's him giving orders and me obeying without thinking until it's too late. I thought I'd seen everything in my years, but the sight of open space where he'd been standing only moments before . . . it sent a shock right through me I can still feel."* The veteran engineer mopped at his face and sighed. *"Ah, lass, I should've gone myself."*

"Sometimes it takes just as much courage to stay as to go" was all Uhura could offer him.

Scotty had muttered something about finding a bottle of Scotch big enough to drown himself in and never setting foot on a starship again, then terminated the transmission.

On the way to Mestiko, in an eerie repetition of a scene that had taken place in Kirk's apartment on Earth almost a decade ago, the rest of his shipmates had gathered in the officers' lounge aboard *Excelsior.* This time it was Sulu who led the toast to "absent friends." No one seemed to know what to say after that, until Chekov broke the silence.

"Captain Kirk was a hero," he announced solemnly. "Heroes are not supposed to die."

The voyage to Mestiko was meant to have been a festive occasion, a celebration. Captain Kirk, as the Starfleet liaison to the Payav through all their troubles, was to have accompanied Ambassador Spock to the Summit. Dr. McCoy had been assigned to follow up on his original study of the physical and mental health of Mestiko's inhabitants, and Commander Uhura would be overseeing the final synchronization of the planet's global communications grid with Starfleet configurations. *Excelsior* was to have brought them to Mestiko, with time for a rare reunion en route.

The reunion had now become a memorial service.

"I disagree," Sulu said somberly. "It's the heroes who step into the path of danger in place of us ordinary mortals."

It wasn't the first time he and Chekov had disagreed about something, and it wouldn't be the last. Not for the first time, Sulu found himself questioning the ambition that had driven him to pursue the captaincy of his own ship even as it separated him from his friends.

"I still can't believe he's really gone" was all Uhura said. "It's as if we expected him to live forever."

The thought had crossed all their minds. How many times had Kirk diced with death and won?

Not this time, apparently.

It was McCoy who took Raya aside and told her about the accident aboard the *Enterprise*-B and Kirk's heroic actions, sacrificing himself to save the ship. It was McCoy who took her elbow and steadied her when she paled and it looked as if her knees might buckle.

"The *Zamestaad* will not be happy," Raya finally said once she'd recovered herself. It was an understatement, to say the least. Kirk's absence could only complicate an already precarious situation. But Kirk's death could not delay the Summit, which was why his companions, grieving though they might be, were here.

It had been difficult enough settling regional squabbles in order to determine which nations could send how many delegates and which among those hundreds of delegates would be invited to the table and which would have to content themselves with participation by video link. Once Payav were gathered around the conference with Dinpayav, an uneasy spirit of cooperation could be hoped for, but not guaranteed.

We are, Raya thought, *back where we were before the Pulse came, haranguing each other over petty things, our decades of suffering all but forgotten. Have we learned nothing from the experience?*

In the past she had almost always welcomed Kirk's presence. The sheer brute force of his persuasiveness had kept her people and his from each other's throats, had even prompted them to clasp hands on more than one occasion. Without him . . . Raya sighed, dashing tears out of the corners of her eyes with both sets of thumbs.

Alone as she had felt once leadership of Mestiko fell on her narrow shoulders, she could always depend on the wisdom of her *elor* and the support of James T. Kirk. Now that they were both gone, she truly was alone.

She remembered the day she had returned home after Elee's funeral—the formal state funeral, not the lighthearted balloon trip she had shared with Kirk in memory of a woman who loved any form of flight—and found that the last of the sacred *noggik* trees was dying. A gift from Sulu, cloned in *Enterprise's* botany lab, it was the only true specimen known to have survived the Pulse. Once power had been restored to her part of vosTraal, she had kept it in a special environmentally controlled case, watered and fed it and made sure it got enough artificial light.

Even this had been something her people had squabbled over. People were dying, they argued, yet the *Jo'Zamestaad* wasted resources on a tree, however sacred. Still others had argued that it wasn't just an indulgence, that the tree symbolized the Payav people and its existence gave them hope.

Once communications were restored, Raya had fostered this second opinion by providing weekly newsfeeds about the young sapling as it grew and flourished. When she had been driven into exile on Kazar, she had entrusted the tree to Theena's care, and her young protégée had kept it hidden through those desolate years so that the mar-Atyya wouldn't find it and destroy it, for it was a symbol of Raya's regime, which the mar-Atyya had taken great pains to subvert.

Restored to its proper place in Raya's office on her return and apparently none the worse for wear, it had just begun to show evidence of new buds which, it was hoped, could be self-pollinated to produce seed that would breed true. But Raya had returned to work immediately following Elee's formal state funeral, where, knowing that the eyes of the planet were upon her, she had kept her composure. After all, there was not a family on Mestiko who had not lost loved ones, and few had had the luxury of dying peacefully as Elee had. So Raya had not lost control at the funeral, but remained dignified and contained.

She had not felt her control slipping until she had locked herself in her office to go over some paperwork, and saw that the tree was dying.

In the time she had been away—overcoming her fear of heights to scatter Elee's ashes from a balloon over S'rii Tuuliie with James Kirk at her side; turning the event into a celebration, not a funeral; then bidding Kirk good-bye and countenancing the state funeral a week later—the tree's blossoms had shriveled and dropped off, the leaves had turned yellow and the branches had begun to droop the way they ordinarily did only on very ancient *noggik* trees. The attempt to clone the tree had failed. It was dying, and there was nothing Raya could do.

It was too much. She'd broken down then, curled up in a little ball, her arms wrapped around her delicate-looking skull as if to ward off blows, shaking with sobs as she hadn't since she was a child. After all those deaths, culminating in her *elor*'s, and after not being able to cry in public because of who she was, she could at least cry in private at the sight of the last living thing on the planet that could be said to be unchanged by everything that had happened.

She had been ready to give up, to step aside and let someone else decide her planet's future and savor the victory, such as it was. She could not go on.

Only a subspace message from Kirk that very afternoon, sent from wherever he was about his duties in the quadrant, telling her how much he'd enjoyed the balloon ride, had brought her out of her misery. He was always thoughtful enough to keep track of what time it was in her part of the universe before he called, even if it meant communicating at some ungodly hour where he was, and she'd always appreciated that.

So it had continued over the years, despite the times they had not seen eye to eye on the future of her world; and not only officially, not only due to Kirk's sense of responsibility to Mestiko, but because he valued Raya's presence in his life. That was why this last time he had contacted her ahead of the official communiqué, to let her know that Mestiko's time had come.

"You'll receive official communiqués from both the Federation Council and the Klingons," he'd told her, his smile strangely shy on such a powerful man. *"But I wanted to be the one to surprise you. Ambassador Spock will forgive me a little . . . self-indulgence."*

"Ambassador Spock now?" Raya had responded, her own smile warm. "How wonderful! I look forward to seeing you . . . all of you . . . once more."

She had considered what the outcome of the Summit could mean. The future was heady, full of promise, the much-deserved reward for their struggle. She would savor announcing it to her people, regardless of the inevitable disgruntlement from a few corners. She would also calculatedly *not* announce the demise of the *noggik* tree, and if anyone asked she would change the subject, saving the bad news for a time when it could be slipped in as inconsequential in light of all the good news she had to share about the future.

She had immediately thrown herself into a frenzy of preparations for the event. When she stopped to think about it, she did not honestly know which choice she would make, if the choice were hers alone. For ultimately, of course, it would be her people who would decide.

CHAPTER
3

Assuming her people ever stopped squabbling over who would sit where at the conference table. At least Kirk's conspicuous absence distracted them from that momentarily. But count on the representative from the Tralva Nation to raise a ruckus from the start.

"Where is Captain Kirk?" Deman elKramo demanded in a voice that carried from the back of the crowd of representatives as he elbowed his way to the front. "We were told he would lead the delegation. Is he delayed? Too busy to attend? Ashamed at last for his part in Mestiko's suffering?"

His was not the only dissenting voice.

"Truly, *Jo'Zamestaad*, Kirk called this Summit, and he doesn't have the grace to appear?"

There were further murmurs, both of agreement and dissent.

". . . Kirk is a busy man. . . ."

". . . not the only world under his aegis . . ."

"If he hasn't the time to attend, neither do we. . . ."

"Doubtless there's a reasonable explanation. . . ."

". . . not going to tolerate this nonsense . . . important matters to tend to in our home provinces . . ."

"We will be on the next transport home!"

Raya counted to twelve before she trusted herself to speak. "Captain Kirk is dead!" she shouted, her voice breaking at the end. In the stunned silence that followed, she added, "You disgrace yourselves with this behavior! Go home, then! I will find other representatives from your districts who at least have some manners!"

Where she found the words or the voice to carry them through the crowd she would never know. Just as she ran out of words and voice, and before any of her fractious people could demand to know how long she had known and why *they* hadn't been informed, the sight of a transporter beam—different from the familiar Federation one, and totally noiseless—stunned everyone into silence.

When it ended, a phalanx of seven Klingons stood in their midst. At their head was the most formidable woman Raya had ever seen.

Chancellor Azetbur herself had come to Mestiko.

Flanked by two of her ministers and four bodyguards, each one larger than the next, Azetbur was nevertheless the focus of power within the group. Without saying a word, she commanded. The several dozen Payav ministers, so vociferous moments before, seemed scarcely able to breathe. Even Raya took a moment to remember herself.

"Madam Chancellor," she managed, hoping her voice didn't sound as strained as it felt as she held out her hands in the traditional Payav greeting. "Welcome to Mestiko."

Azetbur, resplendent in a gown that was equal parts leather, metal, and some sort of stiff glossy fabric that might have been satin and that rustled when she moved, stepped forward, taking Raya's hands in her own. The gesture was accomplished—she had studied her hostess's world and its traditions—and the chancellor neither started at the feel of the two-thumbed Payav hands in her own, nor showed her teeth when she smiled.

"*Jo'Zamestaad*," she replied flawlessly and with a slight bow. Almost a head taller than Raya, she made it elegant. "I hope we can learn much from each other."

Azetbur then drew back slightly, letting Raya's hands slip out of hers as she acknowledged the other Dinpayav.

"Ambassador Spock, we meet again."

"Madam Chancellor," he replied.

"My condolences," she said. "Kirk was a great warrior, and a man of honor."

How she knew, no one asked. But if the gathered Payav still had doubts, Azetbur's words quelled them.

Spock inclined his head in gratitude. It was the only public acknowledgment he would make of his private pain.

"Inflicting my thoughts on others will not bring the captain back" was how he explained it to McCoy when the doctor brought it up, as Spock knew he inevitably would.

"No, but it might help them get a little catharsis," McCoy suggested.

"As you have?" Spock asked dryly.

He had a point, and both men knew it. Ever since they'd shared the same brain, McCoy hadn't been able to bluff him.

"I'll grieve when I'm ready to, Spock. I'll thank you to mind your own business in the meantime."

"As I would expect the same from you."

Impasse, then, only one of many. Then McCoy brought up what he'd come here to say in the first place.

"You don't need me on this mission. Uhura caught me in a moment of weakness and dragged me along. There's still time for me to beg off."

Spock arched an eyebrow. "And do what?"

"It isn't really necessary to bring McCoy along," Uhura did not ask Spock so much as tell him. "Dr. Lon—er, Dr. etDeja—has enough staff by now, supplemented by Starfleet Medical personnel, to do a final assessment of Payav health to be submitted to the steering committee."

She waited for Spock to respond, and he waited for her to finish her thought. "For that matter, the Payav have done a pretty thorough job of restoring the communications grid. Anyone with comm training can help them synch with Starfleet systems. There was no real reason to bring me along to double-check them, except that I might have wanted to see the place again."

"Indeed," Spock said.

Uhura came straight to the point. "You want me to keep an eye on him."

"I am concerned for his emotional state," Spock said. "It has been my observation that he will express his grief either through immersing himself in his work or in less . . . salutary activities."

"So if we can keep him busy . . ."

"Precisely."

"Which would also keep me busy."

"Indeed."

"And what about you, Spock?" Uhura remembered how she'd sat very quietly when she got the news, tears flowing down her cheeks, the room growing dark around her without her realizing it. They'd all been close to Kirk, closer than any ordinary crew. But none of them had been as close to him as Spock.

The Vulcan's face was as somber as ever. Not unreadable to those who knew him well, but whatever grieving he would do, he would do alone. Getting no answer to her question, Uhura had the wisdom to let it go.

"I'll do my best to keep Leonard out of trouble," she promised.

How often over the next few weeks would she regret promising that?

She'd had to literally get him out of bed so they'd be on time for the rendezvous with *Excelsior*, overriding the lock on the door to his quarters, then running the shower and banging cabinet doors to make enough noise to rouse him from his stupor. It was the sound of breaking glass from one of several bottles of exotic liquors he'd lined up by the replicator to finish off one at a time that finally got him out from under the covers, a baleful look in his eye.

"Goddammit, why can't you let a man die in peace?" he muttered.

"You don't have time to die, Doctor. You've got an assign-ment and a deadline," Uhura said crisply, returning his glare with one of her own, but handing him a mug of hot coffee at the same time. "Let's get it in gear."

He managed to stagger from *Excelsior*'s transporter plat-form to his assigned quarters without more than a nod to any-one, only to find that someone had programmed the replicator in his suite so that it wouldn't deliver anything alcoholic. By the time they'd gathered in the officers' lounge to memorialize Kirk, he was sufficiently dried out to function, but he still wasn't talking.

Except to try to weasel out of the assignment.

"I am afraid your presence is nonnegotiable, Doctor" was all Spock had to say on the subject.

"Man doesn't even get a chance to grieve. . . ." McCoy mut-tered under his breath, then caught himself, remembering Vulcan hearing. By the time they'd made orbit around Mestiko, he was grumbling, for which Uhura was grateful. The quiet McCoy worried her; the grumbling one she could deal with.

CHAPTER
4

The Summit began the following morning with *Jo'Zamestaad* elMora's opening remarks.

"Honored Guests, Members of the *Zamestaad*, People of Mestiko," she began from the dais in the *Zamestaad*'s Grand Hall as video feeds captured her from all angles and broadcast her words to every place on the planet that had comm. "Permit me to welcome you all to these proceedings, and to show you what has transpired on our world in recent years."

There was pride in her voice and her demeanor, but also something else not easy to read—hesitancy, perhaps, or even regret, though it was difficult to see, at first glance, what the leader of this battered but emerging world might have to regret.

As she spoke, a series of holos appeared around the room.

"Gentles, you can see here the rebuilding everywhere in our cities and our agricultural regions as our people once more remember what it is like to go out under a sky that is welcoming and a sun that is warm, to breathe fresh air, to smell the scent of growing things, and to feel the rain on our faces. For those who have come of age underground, it is almost as if they have been transported to a new world.

"In fact," she said, her face and voice going solemn, "it can be said that, to almost all Payav, this is a new and not always welcoming world where we find ourselves living.

"In the nearly three decades since the Pulse ripped away our world's ozone layer, plunging it into a new ice age and destroying virtually every living thing, the tireless efforts of many, both Payav and Dinpayav alike, have reclaimed our atmosphere, replenished our food supplies, and restored most of Mestiko to habitability. We cannot begin to express our gratitude to Dr. etDeja and the many who have done this mighty work. However . . ."

She paused, the years of diplomacy thrust upon her by the passing of the Pulse having taught her perforce how to play to a crowd for maximum effect.

"This is not, nor will it ever be, the Mestiko that we who grew to adulthood before the Pulse remember. We can rebuild the cities leveled in the disaster. We can dredge our waterways and restore our shorelines and reforest and plant crops on purified soil, and we have done so. We can find new and creative ways to utilize the vast regions of topography altered in the original disaster, and we have done so. Ours is now a flourishing world. But while the flora and fauna have been almost completely repopulated, they are . . . different.

"Wherever possible, Dr. etDeja and his team have been able to preserve and/or replicate genetic samples of the known species on the planet, down to insects, wildflowers, even blue-green algae. But the cloned species tend to have shorter life spans than their donors and, in the more complex species, they often don't even resemble the donors at all."

Again Raya paused. Before the Pulse, she had been a gifted teacher, and the years that followed had only augmented her ability to hold an audience's attention.

"Before the disaster, nearly every Payav child had a beloved pet *laanur*. . . ." The screens around the room showed a series of images of something with a feline body, lustrous fur in a distinctive blue-and-silver striped pattern, webbed back feet and prehensile forefeet, with the luminescent dark eyes of a lemur, some of the pets gamboling about in a garden, others being cuddled affectionately by children or adults. "But most succumbed to cold and lack of sunlight in the shelters in the early years. Recent attempts have been made to replicate them from stored DNA, but the fuzzy newborn pups have grown into vicious, untamable creatures who live only a few months and more often than not have to be destroyed."

The screens showed several wild-eyed feral creatures with matted fur and bared fangs being held at bay by trained handlers attempting to capture them before they hurt anyone.

"Our revered *noggik* tree, once native to all of the temperate regions, a religious and cultural symbol sung of in story and legend and featured on many nations' flags, has been replaced by something which, at the genetic level, may be identified as a *noggik* tree. But what grows on the reforested hills and plains of modern-day Mestiko does not look anything like the trees we remember.

"Dr. etDeja will tell you that native species have been supplemented and interbred with carefully screened imports from other worlds, mostly successfully," Raya concluded. "Except for a few places, all abandoned now, where the scars will take centuries to heal, Mestiko has by and large been restored to a comfortably habitable planet. But as my people emerge at last from their underground shelters, many feel like exiles on a world they barely recognize.

"One wouldn't think that after all we as a people have been through, the simple loss of a pet or the fact that we will never smell the scent of *noggik* wood again would sadden us so much, and yet it does."

She hesitated, as if she had lost her train of thought. She hadn't meant to end on such a negative note. Kirk's death was affecting her more than she realized.

"I do not mean to sound ungrateful, Gentles," she managed. "But it is necessary for you to understand that the decision whether or not to join the Federation will not be an easy one. Some are concerned that it could mean a continuation of our dependency on your charity. . . ."

There were nods and murmurs from some members of the *Zamestaad*.

"Others need time to understand exactly what such an alliance would entail, how much more of ourselves and our identity we would need to sacrifice in order to fit in."

Still more consensus from those gathered.

"Ultimately," Raya concluded, "we will hear all arguments and discuss all details, and should the vote end in a tie, I will cast the deciding vote. But in all honesty, as of this moment, I cannot tell you what my vote would be. . . ."

"Well," McCoy said, watching the proceedings on a feed that Uhura had just patched in to the datacenter where he'd be working for the next few weeks. "At least she's being honest."

"Raya's always been honest," Uhura replied from a comm center across town. "Often to her detriment."

On their respective screens, Raya had stepped down from the podium, and several members of the *Zamestaad* were already trying to be heard, even though protocol required that both Spock and Azetbur add their remarks to Raya's.

"Let the games begin!" McCoy remarked, then muted the broadcast. He pretty much knew what Spock would say, and anyway he could get a replay later. For now, he had work to do.

He'd been paired with a Klingon healer from Azetbur's party. Their assignment was to review all the medical data on outcomes from the Pulse that had been gathered since the last time McCoy had been here. Where it wasn't heartbreaking—people were still dying of melanomas and respiratory ailments, birth rates were down, there were incidences of blindness and questionable genetic mutations, and the Payav life span overall was still nearly a decade lower than it had been before the Pulse—the work promised to be tedious beyond measure.

The Klingon healer's name was Rajhemda'la, and she eyed McCoy skeptically underneath her brows and shrugged.

"You're almost as thin as a Payav. We'll have to fatten you up. How do you like your *gagh*?"

"Not at all, thank you," McCoy replied, trying to be civil.

His Klingon counterpart was anything but thin, and as he observed her eating habits over the next two days, he could understand why. She seemed to spend as much time at the replicator as she did at her console. Still, despite his initial grousing, he found he was able to work with her. They divided the sector grids exactly in half, collected the data, and then flagged it for the other to cross-check and verify. There was no small talk, just a lot of demographics flowing by on a screen, and by the end of the second day, McCoy couldn't tell if he was awake or asleep. It was somewhere in that in-between state that he stumbled on something that intrigued him.

"Hello," he murmured, suddenly very much awake. "What's this?"

Once the initial shock value of having the Klingon chancellor herself on their world had worn off, the Payav lost no time in peppering her with questions, both during the official sessions of the Summit and during press conferences and even casual encounters in the corridors.

"You would have us believe that you are here solely because your homeworld has suffered a similar fate?" Deman elKramo was the principal gadfly, but he had plenty of allies. He made certain always to ask his questions when there were news cameras about. Even the growl and reflexive reach for his weapon on the part of Kra'aken, Azetbur's bodyguard, did not faze the man.

Inwardly, Spock sighed. He had expected that the negotiations would entail a long and arduous process. He hadn't expected open hostilities to erupt quite so soon.

Excelsior and its Klingon counterpart had left orbit as soon as both diplomatic parties had beamed down. Both would return within the month to retrieve their respective parties, regardless of what decision was reached. The month would be spent in negotiating, first with one faction, then another, to try to reach some consensus on what was best for Mestiko.

The first order of business, Spock realized, was to convince the Payav, despite past history, to trust the Klingons.

After three days surrounded by these hairless, fragile-looking, contentious creatures, Azetbur had stopped trying to tell them apart, addressing each simply as "Minister." It seemed to serve.

"Is that not sufficient reason?" she asked tightly. "Or is the fact that I am Klingon reason enough to suspect my motives?"

"Your people and ours have a past!" an elderly female Payav piped up from the back of the crowd. "A past that cost me several family members. Don't blame us if we are bitter!"

"Bitter about the past?" Azetbur inquired. "So you should be. But neither my father's regime nor mine has ever done you any harm."

"So you don't care if Mestiko joins the Federation in defiance of your empire?" someone else demanded in a non sequitur which made sense, Azetbur supposed, only if one were Payav.

"Frankly it's my belief that you and the Federation deserve each other!" she said with an edge to her voice just as Raya reached for the ancient *noggik*wood gavel which would, hypothetically at least, restore order to the proceedings.

"Alternatively, you could always ally yourselves with the Klingon Empire," Azetbur said, just loud enough to be heard. "What better way to learn how we deal with contentious citizens?"

This caused further uproar, which Raya did quell with a rap of her gavel before adjourning for the first day.

"I honestly don't know what made me do that," Azetbur told Spock wryly at the small reception in their honor that evening. "But they squabble worse than Romulans. The urge to knock their fragile little egg-heads together . . ."

"You are playing devil's advocate," Spock suggested, then was compelled to explain the term and its origins.

"Am I?" Azetbur asked, and so it went.

The Federation, in the person of Spock, became the target of the next day's session.

"Can you restore our world to exactly what it was before this accursed Pulse destroyed it?" one delegate demanded. "Of course you can't. So what are you offering us? It's your fault all of this happened in the first place. We will overlook the loss of our many dead, but unless you can give us back the world we once knew . . ."

"You are aware, Councillor Jolon," Spock said, and the party in question seemed surprised that he remembered his name, "that restoring Mestiko to its original state is not possible. Nevertheless, every effort has been made to—"

"Then we're not interested!" Jolon shouted. The man did not seem to be able to speak in a moderate tone of voice.

As much as she hated it, Raya let them rant. But by the end of the third day, even she had reached her limit. She pounded the gavel for a full six-minute, long after the last Servant had shouted himself hoarse.

When the room had been brought to silence, Raya waited a judicious moment before announcing, "We will adjourn until tomorrow. Any further grievances, accusations, or simple complaints about the weather will hereafter be delivered in writing, and all such documentation must be read by all of the delegates before any can comment on them. That includes—" She raised her voice slightly over the expected groundswell of muttering. "—comments on my decision that all complaints must hereafter be submitted in writing. We are adjourned until tomorrow." She kept her eye on Deman elKramo and Servant Jolon in particular. "I hope by then you can all remember your equanimity."

That evening there was no reception. All of the delegates retired to their respective quarters for dinner and reflection.

Spock found both interrupted by McCoy.

"I need to talk to you!" McCoy burst in on Spock with a rudeness tolerable only in someone who had once shared the same brain, and got right to the point. "Assign someone else to the data gathering. There's somewhere else I can be more useful."

It was the most animated Spock had seen McCoy in a very long time. "Indeed?"

"There's an ethnic enclave in the Ayanava province—a tribe,

really," McCoy said. "They call themselves and their valley the Nehdi. They refused to relocate when the pulsar passed, even though they were practically in its path. The folks in that region have lived through some of the greatest hardships of anyone on the planet." McCoy paused for breath. "Still, they're a resourceful lot, and they'd adapted, begun to reclaim their land so that they no longer needed to be dependent on government handouts, and now this . . ."

"'This,'" Spock repeated.

"Some sort of wasting disease that targets the young people," McCoy explained, "those who were children or young teens when the Pulse struck. As soon as they reach early adulthood, they begin to age rapidly for some reason, at a ratio of about a decade to a month. Organs break down, and they die. Local medical authorities are stumped."

Spock considered. "Only the young people?"

"So far," McCoy said gloomily. "I'm hoping it's just a local phenomenon, but I've got to know for sure. I want to go in there and have a look around."

Spock pretended not to notice the spark of interest in McCoy's eye, the slight straightening of his posture, which had seemed stooped with defeat and the burdens of the universe since the news of Jim's death. He was rubbing his hands together in that *Let's get down to business* gesture of his.

"Have the Nehdi asked for your help?" Spock wanted to know.

"Well, not exactly, but—"

"I am concerned about the completion of the global medical survey," Spock mused. The best way to make McCoy dig his heels in was to tell him he couldn't do something.

"C'mon, Spock. Anyone with a premed degree can stare at those grids and make a determination. You don't need a senior medical officer."

"Perhaps not. But there is also the diplomatic delicacy. There should be a Federation presence of equal rank to Rajhemda'la so that the Klingons will not be offended."

"Nonsense!" McCoy snorted. "As long as no one gets between her and the replicator. Tell you what, that young pup from *Excelsior* that you brought down as an observer can fill in for me. What's his name, Tuvok? Just on a hunch, Rajhem-da'la would be a lot happier sharing the office with a handsome young Vulcan than with an old wreck like me."

Spock seemed to be thinking it over, timing it precisely so that McCoy would not guess he was being manipulated. He waited for the inevitable explosion. It was not long in coming.

"Dammit, Spock! I've been watching the newsfeeds. You and Azetbur and the rest are going to be stuck haranguing with the *Zamestaad* for weeks. The sooner I can get my hands around this thing, the better. Maybe I can save some lives. What's the usual mode of transportation in that part of the world?"

CHAPTER
5

"I had to ask!" McCoy grumbled as the ancient bus paused for breath at the top of a switchback and some of the stronger Payav got out and began to push.

As the normal change of seasons had given way to two decades of winter temperatures and poisonous atmosphere, transportation on most of Mestiko had been a challenge, but in these far-flung wilder areas it had often been close to impossible. With most roads at first inaccessible under several feet of toxic snow and eventually upheaved and torn apart by permafrost, the locals had learned to improvise.

Every surface vehicle became a multitasker. McCoy and Uhura had traveled most of the way from vosTraal in a wallowing skimmer-van that lumbered a few meters above the surface, picking up and delivering essential goods to certain hub cities along the general route they were headed. It took them three days to reach Ayanava province, but much of what they were onloading were medical supplies and a redi-lab for the new hospital that was under construction in the Ayanava Valley, and McCoy was kept occupied with inventorying and rearranging everything down to the last tongue depressor.

Uhura, for her part, took advantage of the skimmer's leisurely path to make onsite inspections of every communications relay in every town she visited. It was as much a sightseeing tour as an assignment. When McCoy got off in Ayanav, the regional capital at the southern tip of the valley, to continue his journey via local transportation, she would stay on the van as it looped around the entire valley and eventually returned.

She was well on her way, mercifully, before McCoy had a chance to grouse about riding the local bus. That "honor" fell to Sorodel, the Nehdi Elder who had met the van when it touched down in the town square.

"The bus," Sorodel told McCoy, "predates the Pulse. You should be grateful you weren't here during the depths of the nuclear winter. The mountain passes were impenetrable. And it wasn't always possible for the flyers to navigate the poisonous murk. When the airdrops couldn't make it, people starved."

That shut McCoy up for the moment. Whatever discomfort he was feeling, it was nothing, compared with what these people had been through.

A particularly stubborn and resilient group, the Nehdi had steadfastly refused to be resettled in the more temperate, better-restored regions of the planet, despite the loss of over half their population in the immediate aftermath and the dreadful hardships of survival in the years following.

"Our ancient myths told that the gods brought us to this valley when the planet was just formed," Sorodel explained as the bus started again with a roar and those who had been pushing scrambled to get back aboard. McCoy, wondering if this leg of the journey was better or worse than the skimmer-van, noticed that the other passengers were pointedly not staring at him, though he imagined they didn't get many Dinpayav in these parts. "And while most Nehdi no longer believe that we will lose our souls if we venture away from our ancestral land, most of us refused to leave.

"The Nehdi have belonged to the Land for as long as it has been the Land, at least as it is written in the ancient lore. Even the Pulse could not drive us away. Partly this is stubbornness, but the rest is about who we are."

Sorodel, McCoy guessed, was about his age, and he found her voice particularly melodious. It soothed his impatience.

"Tell me more," he said as the bus swerved around a hairpin turn and he grabbed the first thing he could reach to keep from tumbling out of his seat. He'd learned enough about the Nehdi Elders to be aware that Sorodel carried the history of her people in her mind. He wanted to keep hearing that voice to take his mind off the jolting of his bones.

"In ancient times," Sorodel obliged him, "it was forbidden for the Nehdi to leave the Land. This is not to say that some did not try. Throughout our history many had gone away to the wider world of Mestiko and not come back."

The bus coughed, stalled, made some sort of horrible gear-shifting noise, started again, and began to move slowly down an improbable downgrade, loose scree scattering under its rear wheels.

"In ancient times, those who left and did not return were spoken of as if they were dead, mourned briefly, then not spoken of again," Sorodel explained. "Those who went away for a time and came back were studied closely by the kin they had left behind, to see if they had lost their souls.

"In ancient times, those who it was decided had left their souls behind in the wider world would be prayed over. Some would recover their souls, some not. The latter were shunned, forming little groups of their own on the outer borders of the Land.

"There was the occasional muttering that the Alangabi, who live on the other side of the ring of mountains which form the borders of the Land, are descended from those soulless ones, though modern, more urbane Nehdi dismiss that as ancient prejudice.

"In short," Sorodel concluded with a wry and closemouthed smile, "my people have not always been without prejudice. But the Pulse and its aftermath showed us how petty those ancient feuds truly were."

"So I take it you and the Alan . . . Alangabi?" McCoy asked, and Sorodel nodded. "Your two peoples are no longer feuding?"

The bus had begun what he hoped was the final descent of

the final mountain. He didn't think his innards could take much more of this. He thought he saw buildings in the distance on the hardpanned valley floor, and hoped they weren't a mirage.

Beside him, Sorodel sighed. "The hardships following the Pulse created an uneasy truce between us as we struggled to survive in its aftermath. But now that the world is returning to something resembling normalcy after all these years, the old rumblings have begun again.

"In any event," Sorodel concluded her narrative as the bus did indeed level out and begin to pick up speed across the hardpan, though it seemed to be cutting directly across the desert, and there was no road McCoy could see. "The role of the Elder, even before the Pulse, is to somehow reconcile opposing forces. Not only to make our ancient beliefs compatible with modern life, but also to try to keep the peace between Nehdi and Alangabi without losing her mind. My sphere of influence is smaller than *Jo'Zamestaad* elMora's, but I know something of what she's going through." She held out her hands to McCoy in the characteristic Payav gesture of welcome, and he returned it—though he noticed that the Nehdi custom called for the arms to be angled inward and for each side to grip the other's wrist tightly. He suspected that this was an older form that the isolated Nehdi had never changed. "And I cannot tell you how relieved I am that you are here."

The bus ground to a halt at last in a kind of central plaza surrounded by the odd mushroom shapes that indicated the entrances to underground shelters, some of them as much as a mile away through tunnels into the nearby mountains. Interspersed among them were older structures, many of them rickety-looking stilt-houses, incongruous in a land now so obviously devoid of water.

As McCoy stepped down from the bus and stretched out the crick in his back, he noticed a group of teens loitering in the central plaza around an assortment of patched-together vehicles that appeared to be part motorcycle, part skateboard, part skimmer. Staring boldly at the Dinpayav doctor for a moment or two, they scrambled onto their vehicles and left the plaza in a roar of badly tuned machinery and a cloud of dust.

Beside McCoy, Sorodel looked rueful.

"Our wild ones," she explained. "Some of our children are still afraid to play out under the sky. Others roam the land as if wondering why it betrayed them. There was a time when we were one with the rhythm of climate and weather. I wonder if we will ever recapture that? As for the wild ones, they are just on the cusp of the age where our young people begin to die of this withering disease. One can hardly blame them for mistrusting us."

"Do you suppose some of them would trust us enough to give me tissue samples?" McCoy wondered. "I'd need them to compare with the sick, with mature adults, children. . . ."

"We will try," Sorodel said. "But first we must make you comfortable. You'll stay with us as our guest. We have plenty of room. My husband Ejo is Leader. He and my grandson Chimeji and I are all that are left of the family. My daughter and her husband were among the first to die of the disease. . . ."

When the Pulse came, Ejo had been standing at the mouth of one of the underground shelters, making sure his people got to safety before he sealed the entrance behind him. He had not been quite quick enough, and a brilliant flash of lightning had both scarred and blinded him. The livid scars across his face and running down his long neck only accentuated the stark whiteness of the cataracts obscuring his almond-shaped eyes, and McCoy's surgeon's fingers itched to do an intervention on either the scarring or the cataracts or both. But when Ejo had been offered the choice of ocular implants, he had refused.

"I see more this way," he explained with a chuckle in the back of his throat. "Yes, call me a crazy old man, but I can form a mental image of you, Doctor, from your voice, from the sound of your boots on my parlor floor, from the way you look around the room, assessing the many excellent pieces of tribal pottery you see displayed here."

Found out, McCoy stopped fidgeting.

"I see also," Ejo said with a benevolent smile, "that you

have come to learn what killed my daughter and my son-in-law and so many more of our young people before it kills them all."

"I certainly intend to try," McCoy said.

The first thing he did was visit the temporary hospital units set up in tents outside the little town's main building when the wards had overflowed. New construction was everywhere in this part of the world, mostly replacing housing that had been destroyed either by the ferocious winds accompanying the Pulse or by the crushing weight of the snows that followed, but a new hospital complex was also being built just across the plaza from the old one.

"We are not quite sure what to do," Ejo explained. "This is our warm season, and the tents are adequate for now. But given the usual course of the illness, these citizens will not live to see the cold season. If all of our young people die, are we mad to keep building?"

McCoy, having just come from seeing the rows upon rows of cots set up in the bright airy tents, and the silent, wizened forms and vacant stares of the victims, tried to sound more optimistic than he felt.

"We'll find the answer to this thing, I promise you. For now, I've instructed your medical staff to keep doing what they're doing, making the ill as comfortable as they can while I get to work."

While he waited for a lab to be set up according to his specifications, McCoy got in touch with Rajhemda'la.

"Are there reports of anything similar in other regions?" he asked.

"*Negative, McCoy. I have completed the global survey, and run your specific algorithm beneath it so as not to arouse suspicion. This thing you are investigating appears to be a localized phenomenon.*"

"Then likely it's not related to the Pulse, unless it's something specific to Nehdi physiology. But I'll test for it anyway. I hope you don't mind my leaving you in the lurch like that."

"*Scientific curiosity is a powerful hunger,*" Rajhemda'la said sagaciously. Did McCoy only imagine he heard live *gagh* squirming in the background? *"Besides, your replacement, this Tuvok, is quite . . . efficient,"* she added with what might have been a giggle.

Satisfied that he'd done his diplomatic best, McCoy went to work.

It took him a while to familiarize himself with Payav medical equipment, particularly since what the Nehdi had available predated the Pulse by a decade or two and was not in the best condition. He wished Sulu hadn't had to leave so soon, and that he hadn't gotten trapped babysitting Rajhemda'la for the first few days, or he might have cadged some of the top-of-the-line equipment from *Excelsior*'s sickbay.

"Not the first time I've had to make do," he muttered, fiddling with the focus on what passed for an electron microscope in this time and place. That thought took him on a trip down Memory Lane to the hundreds of worlds and thousands of seemingly undecodable pathogens he had studied and, in some cases, cured in his career. A good thing, too, because suddenly what he was looking at under the microscope began to make sense in context.

"Now, what does this remind me of?" he asked of no one in particular as a sequence of peculiar-looking nucleotides swam across his field of vision. The terms "suppression of nucleotides" and "life prolongation" echoed in his ears, spoken in Jim's voice. McCoy's eyes blurred; he blinked and sat back away from the microscope. "Of course . . . Miri's planet . . ."

There the problem had been a group of scientists tampering with ways to make humans live virtually forever, aging on an average of one month per hundred years. Their serum had become contaminated with a virus which killed off the entire adult population, leaving only the children, children who were centuries old by the time *Enterprise* discovered them, responding to a distress beacon the adults had left behind hundreds of years before.

All of the humans in the landing party had contracted the

virus, and it had been up to McCoy to isolate the virus and develop a cure, all the while fighting the raging fever that was consuming him. Racing against time, he'd done the only thing he could: hoped that the formula he'd concocted was the right one, and injected himself.

Jim had never forgiven him for that one.

Just as he wasn't about to forgive Jim for running headlong into danger on the *Enterprise*-B.

Shaking those thoughts out of his head, McCoy focused on the situation at hand. Here he was facing the opposite problem from the life prolongation project on Miri's world. In this case it appeared as if someone had programmed a particular sequence of nucleotides—found, as nearly as he could tell by having run comparative samples, only in Payav of Nehdi ancestry—to overpopulate and destroy other cells. The result was that those who were infected aged rapidly, on the order of a decade per month, and died of old age while still nominally in early adulthood.

Well, at least now he knew what he was looking for. And having arrived at that conclusion, he discovered he was not alone.

Nehdi medical personnel were too overworked tending to the dying to lend him a hand. Just as well, since he always did his best work in solitude and quiet. But he found himself being observed by the large, liquid eyes of a rather small Payav.

"Dinpayav doctor," the little boy observed.

"That would be me. Dr. Leonard McCoy." He held out his hands in the Nehdi version of the traditional Payav greeting. "And you would be?"

"Chimeji elPrahno."

"Sorodel and Ejo's grandson. You weren't at the house when I arrived."

"School," the boy said. He seemed to be able to communicate with as few words as possible.

"Chimeji—that's a mouthful. Any objection if I call you Chimmy?"

The boy shrugged, his way of saying it didn't matter. McCoy guessed him to be about seven or eight years old in human terms. He was clearly curious about what the "Dinpayav doctor" was up to.

"Ever look into a microscope?" McCoy asked. The boy made a negative gesture. "Well, then, past time you did. Come on up here and have a peek."

From that day on he and Chimmy were inseparable. McCoy made sure the boy was protected from anything that could be a potential pathogen, mostly had him cleaning up and acting as a runner to the medical personnel in the tents, but he also showed him things as he went along. Just as Jim had trained Miri, he realized, seeing the hero worship in Chimmy's eyes. It was there wherever they were, either in the lab or in the evenings during dinner at his grandparents' house. The only time the boy made a fuss was when his grandmother packed him off for bed instead of letting him follow McCoy back to the lab for a late-night shift.

Chimmy's face was solemn, and he rarely spoke. On the third day he asked McCoy the question uppermost in his mind.

"My parents died. Will I die, too?"

McCoy let one hand rest on the small, bald head. "Not if I can help it, son."

"It's a type of progeria," he explained, watching the look of wonder on the boy's face as he studied the tissue samples under the microscope. "You see, many cells in your body replace themselves. New cells replicate, old ones die. That's what makes you grow, for one thing. But this disease disrupted that somehow, and that's why some of the cells are dying without being replaced. All we have to do is figure out why."

"Is that all?" Sorodel said from the doorway.

She managed to check in on McCoy at least once a day, and sometimes she was able to assist him for a few hours. He'd been impressed with her knowledge of basic medicine.

"Science and religion are one with us," she had explained. "And so many died in the wake of the Pulse that many of us have had to do two or even three jobs. Then, when we started to lose our young people, our Middle Generation . . ."

Today she was all business. "What have you found?" she asked as Chimmy silently beckoned her over to the microscope to see for herself.

"It's what we haven't found," McCoy said, trying not to sound too frustrated. "First we have to rule out what it isn't. Since every one of the victims was a child or adolescent when the Pulse hit, it's necessary to rule out anything in the combination of assaults on their immune systems while they were still growing which could have triggered a cascade."

Sorodel looked thoughtful. "What is the likelihood of that, Doctor?"

"Well, the good news is, this phenomenon hasn't evidenced itself in any other group of Payav . . . so far. If it hasn't in over twenty years, it's probably not going to. So my hunch is it's a local phenomenon, either environmental, genetic, or a combination of both. And I need to be as thorough as time allows."

CHAPTER
6

Time might allow, but rumor didn't. McCoy's departure from vosTraal had not gone unnoticed, and someone from the news media had been curious about where he was going and why. It wasn't long before the rumor that something was killing the Nehdi made its way to the ears of the press and, through them, to the councillors at the Summit.

It had taken them a twelveday to finalize the seating plan, rearrange living quarters, see to everyone's dietary needs, make certain every councillor had a chance to air his or her particular laundry list of grievances—in writing, per Raya's order—against the Federation, the Klingons, or both, and finally allow Spock to present the offer on the table: what would be entailed if the Payav voted "yes" on membership, and what would happen if they voted "no."

Not surprisingly, discussion of the latter alternative had taken up a great deal of time and energy. Only when the last of the fears regarding the possibility of intervention, interference, nannying, "keeping us dependent on your handouts," and even invasion and conquest had been tirelessly addressed down to the last jot and tittle had the councillors been prepared to proceed.

This day's meeting was to have been taken up with each of the councillors' making a brief speech outlining his or her reasons for or against joining the Federation. But Raya was still in the corridor making her way to the meeting room when the uproar assailed her.

"It's the resurgence of the old feud between the Nehdi and the Alangabi," someone was saying.

"Who?" someone else demanded. "Until today, I'd never heard of either of them."

"Not surprisingly. There can't be more than a few thousand members of each tribe. . . ."

"'Tribes'? They still refer to themselves as 'tribes'? Well, that explains it."

"Explains what? There were two laureates in the sciences from Ayanava. And you can't tell me you've never heard of the performance artist Rhilnam?"

"How do we know it even has anything to do with the two tribes?" a third party interjected. "None of this was talked about until the Dinpayav doctor arrived. How do we know it isn't a plot on the part of the Federation to keep us dependent on them? Very convenient, if you ask me!"

"And I suppose the dozens of dead even before the doctor arrived were prearranged as well?"

"Then it's a cover-up! We know there were several governments conducting similar experiments. . . ."

"What if the disease spreads to other regions?"

"What if there *is* no disease, just a ploy on the part of the Nehdi to qualify for more aid than their neighbors?"

"It could be the beginning of a pandemic. . . . All of our lives could be in danger!"

Deliberately, Raya walked away. She would make no comment, officially or unofficially. Let the reporters talk to the councillors and the councillors talk to the reporters in an endless loop. If it wasn't this it would be something else. She had more important things to do.

Entering the Summit chamber, she made her way to the head of the table. By now the entire room was abuzz with rumor. Raya looked to Spock and Azetbur, observing silently, and made a helpless gesture. As she reached for the gavel, Spock shook his head slightly.

"I would recommend you let them get it out of their system," he suggested. "When they have exhausted themselves, you can make an official statement."

Raya sighed. "You realize that could take days?"

"Indeed."

Raya continued to hold the gavel, but did not bring it down just yet. "I draw the line if they start throwing things," she said wryly.

"It's all over," Uhura reported to McCoy from a remote outpost in a region lush with tropical vegetation, exotic animals, and pristine rivers full of rapids and cataracts that she thought would make a wonderful tourist spot, as she intended to tell its people once she got them on the grid. *"Don't be surprised if—"*

"—if every time I leave the lab I'm accosted by reporters?" McCoy interjected. "Too late. They're as plentiful as mosquitoes in August."

It was a slight exaggeration. Perhaps a half dozen had braved the journey over the mountains on the bus to find out what the Dinpayav doctor knew and when he knew it, but what they lacked in numbers they made up for in persistence.

"Just what I need—reporters camped on my doorstep, being in the spotlight when I'm trying to get some work done! Pity you had to be so efficient in getting the global grid up and running."

"Well, I've still got a few more stops to make," Uhura said, ignoring the implication that she'd done it just to annoy him. *"What about you? Any progress on this mystery disease?"*

"I can tell you what it is," McCoy said. "Got the mechanism of action figured out—it performs really well under a microscope. As for what's causing it or how to stop it . . ."

The breakthrough had come that very afternoon.

"Tsk, tsk, tsk, will you look at that?" he'd said, and since he was hogging the microscope, Sorodel wasn't sure if McCoy was talking to her or to himself. "I've never seen a gene sequence literally unravel before my eyes before. Have a look at this."

As McCoy put another sample in the scope field, Sorodel did have a look. What she saw at first distinguished itself as a chain of molecules wrapped around itself like the fibers of a rope, loose at either end, but tightly wound at the center. As she watched, one end of a single sequence began to unwind until the two strands separated and floated apart. Within seconds, they had disintegrated, vanished into nothing, even as their companion twinned strands began to do the same. Sorodel stepped back suddenly, shaken by what she'd seen.

"There's your culprit," McCoy stated grimly. "Now it's just a matter of figuring out why it's doing that, and how to either stop it or reprogram that gene sequence to rewind itself."

"Oh, is that all?" Sorodel mused, catching some of his cynicism.

"Well, no one said it would be easy. Meanwhile, there are several ways to reverse the condition in those who've already developed it, but the damnable thing is, I can't figure out where it's coming from. If it is a gene mutation, it should have cropped up over millennia, not a couple of years, not without a big boost from something environmental. I'll need volunteers to check air samples, water, soil samples, vegetation. . . ."

Nothing would be accomplished in the *Zamestaad* that day. With much pounding of the gavel, Raya finally convinced them all to go home. There was no putting the genie of rumor back into the bottle, and she doubted that by now there was a single Payav on the grid who hadn't heard this one. Despairing of doing anything further with the councillors, she exerted her clout and called a press conference, demanding that every reporter and stringer in vosTraal meet with her at once.

"Are you attempting to censor us, *Jo'Zamestaad*?" one asked.

"I'm asking you to police yourselves!" she said, making sure the cameras were on her and the recorders were picking up every word. "What is accomplished, besides selling a few more downloads, by spreading panic and hysteria? Have you no pride in your world? Where is your dignity?

"Dr. McCoy went to Nehdi to help people. The disease existed long before he arrived. That your employers were too little interested in an obscure story in a remote backwater until now is no one's fault but their own. You will each of you see to it that the rumors are put to rest. The fact that this is a local phenomenon and there is no need to panic will be your lead story tonight. I give you fair warning: I will pull the license of every outlet that refuses. If it's censorship you want, you will have it!"

She stormed off without waiting for them to answer. Not that she expected them to have any answers, though she heard some muttering in her wake. The media were accustomed to *asking* questions, not answering them.

In the antechamber leading into the council room, Raya tried to calm herself. Just when she thought she had seen and heard everything from her fractious and unruly people, they managed to surprise her, and not in a positive way. Massaging her temples with her thumbs and breathing deeply, she put on an expression of serenity out of old practice and nodded to the guards at the doors to let her pass.

Spock had wisely led the Federation delegation back to their quarters for the day as soon as the *Zamestaad* had departed. The Klingons, however, were still there. Raya sighed inwardly, wondering how much controversy she could countenance.

She moved toward Azetbur and was about to apologize, but the chancellor's advisers had gathered in a tight knot around her and were engaged in a heated—if quiet, for Klingons—discussion. Raya could not have interrupted if she'd wanted to.

It occurred to her that she was alone in this room with a half-dozen Klingons and was not afraid. Was that a good thing, she wondered, or was she just too weary to care?

"*naDevvo' yIghoS!*" Azetbur said. "Leave us, the *Jo'Zamestaad* and me, all of you. There are too many voices in this room, and I need to concentrate."

"You should not be alone with any of them," Kra'aken muttered.

The chancellor dismissed this with an impatient gesture. "I have no reason to believe any here will harm me. Besides, she weighs no more than a child. With which of her four thumbs will she manage to break my neck?"

"Our people and theirs have a past," Kra'aken reminded her.

"That was a long time ago, it was not me, and no one is holding me responsible for it," Azetbur said tightly. "These people do not have the same sense of honor that we have, or they would not have invited us here. More likely they'd have blown us out of the sky as soon as we made orbit."

She regretted it the moment she said it, caught the glint of suspicion in Kra'aken's eye. There were many who thought her soft, and not only because she was a woman. Too friendly with outworlders, went the murmurs; not Klingon enough.

They would rather die on a Qo'noS gasping for air than do business with anyone who is not Klingon! Azetbur thought with something like disgust. *They will be the death of me yet. . . .*

"*naDevvo' yIghoS,*" she said again. "Go away. Wait outside the door if you want, but go."

"Madam Chancellor . . ."

"*bIjatlh 'e' yImev!*" Would the man never stop talking? "Shut up! Go. Question my orders again and I'll—"

Kra'aken gave the Klingon equivalent of a shrug, saluted, and turned smartly on his heel, drawing the rest of the entourage with him like a comet's tail.

When the door had closed behind them, Azetbur gave Raya a quizzical look and, in a surprising gesture, leaned down to pull off her boots, tilted her chair back, and put her feet up on the highly polished table.

Raya understood the gesture and, with a short, bemused laugh, kicked off her own practical shoes and did the same.

Not for the first time, Azetbur was struck by how fragile Payav seemed, with their reedlike necks and their startling hairlessness. She reminded herself that not all strength was in muscle—consider Andorians, for example—nor was all strength physical. Having studied this Raya elMora and her people before coming here, Azetbur had come to respect her for her sheer endurance, if nothing else.

CHAPTER
7

"I sometimes think," Raya said, pouring them each a cup of the local fermented beverage from the carafe at the center of the table, "that if policy were left to the women . . ."

"Perhaps," Azetbur said, raising her cup in a salute before sipping. "But then there is the tale of Magna the Magnificent, who began a war that lasted forty years because her husband's mother insulted her gown. . . ."

Raya wondered if the tale was true or just made up on the spot, but found herself giggling anyway. "Perhaps. And you'll note that half of my councillors are women."

Azetbur seemed to be doing a mental head count. "Also true. But surely you, *Jo'Zamestaad*, appreciate how often women in power have to act like men in order to retain that power?"

Raya touched the rim of her cup to Azetbur's and both women drank ceremonially. Then Raya said what she had been meaning to say from the very first day.

"Why are you here, Chancellor? I mean you, personally. Oh, I know, a Klingon presence was requested by the Federation because of Mestiko's proximity to the Empire; the situation on

Qo'noS suggested a study of Mestiko's plight might be helpful. But surely you could have done as President Ra-ghoratreii and sent a delegation. I am most interested in why the Chancellor of the Klingon Empire takes it upon herself to come in person."

"You do not trust me, *Jo'Zamestaad*," Azetbur answered by not answering. "And in your place, I would not trust me either. I could say I am here solely because of the situation on Qo'noS, but I doubt I would convince you. After all, we Klingons have the luxury, unlike you, of having years to prepare to either abandon our world or try to save it. But I wished to see what the Payav have done, and to learn from it."

Wisely, Raya waited, knowing there was more. A gesture inquired whether Azetbur wished to have her drink refreshed, and a nod from Azetbur indicated she did.

"I could point out, empirically, that my skills at diplomacy are a shade better than Kra'aken's."

This made Raya laugh again. Then Azetbur said something which surprised her.

"But the real reason is that I was curious about you. If you and I are to be 'neighbors'—inasmuch as, while our worlds are parsecs apart, nevertheless the universe is shrinking every day—I wanted to understand what you are like. What I discovered is that you and I have a great deal in common."

"I'm not sure I understand," Raya said, setting her cup down and rotating it idly among her four thumbs.

Azetbur found herself unconsciously doing the same, though she had only two thumbs. "There is a saying on my world. 'Some are born great, some achieve greatness, and some have greatness thrust upon them.' You did not wish to be *Jo'Zamestaad*," she said incisively.

"I most assuredly did not!" Raya blurted before she could stop herself. Was it only the drink? Why else had she taken such an instant liking to this Dinpayav, whose people had been less than honorable in their dealings with her own?

No, it was not the drink; it was the fact that Azetbur was right. What might she have become if there had never been a Pulse? A dozen alternatives coiled through Raya's head, all of them easier, less harrowing than the one which had indeed been thrust upon her. And yet, she had never stepped down, never willingly let another take her place. She had gone into exile and fought her way back to stand where she stood now. Why? Because she believed she and she alone knew what was best for her people, or because she was simply too stubborn to let go? When she emerged from her reverie, the look in Azetbur's eyes was knowing.

"Indeed. I at least had some forewarning. My father was grooming me to be his successor. Had things followed their usual course, I'd have had to be approved by the High Council, but when he was murdered . . ."

The memory was not recent, but the wounds still ached. Wisely, Raya said nothing. The more she could learn about this woman, the better.

"And had things followed their usual course, I might have begged off," Azetbur mused. "Accepted a lesser office, a diplomatic post, even an academic one, though I might have been assassinated anyway, lest I change my mind. I had thought I might marry someday, have children. Not that I necessarily had to do those things, but it might have been nice to have the option. As chancellor, it is impossible. Too many of my enemies would try to get to me through someone I cared for."

Here the paths diverge, Raya thought. *At least no one's tried to assassinate me. That's not how we do things. Send a leader into exile and pretend she's dead, yes, but have her killed outright? Not Payav.*

And now? she thought, studying the depths of the liquid in her cup and finding unsettling thoughts there. *I'm past hope of childbearing, and I've always questioned the wisdom of those who did have children in the immediate wake of the Pulse. If they had not, of course, the Payav would have gone extinct, and yet to bring a child into a world underground because the air outside was poisoned . . . in any event, it was not for me. Not then, not now.*

There was Theena, she reminded herself. But the little girl she had snatched off the street as the Pulse passed and raised as her own had always been wise beyond her years, and their relationship had always been more that of mentor and student than mother and daughter. Until Theena betrayed her trust by siding with Vykul and the Torye.

That thought was painful, and Raya set it aside.

When she and Cadi orMalan had been together in exile on Kazar, she'd thought they might marry, but he had stayed behind when she returned to Mestiko, not understanding her loyalty to the place. And what other man would tolerate the hours she kept, the work she did; and how could she expect him to go for weeks or months or even years without seeing her?

There was one man who might have, given that his own life was as fraught with responsibilities as hers. *Well,* Raya thought, *too little too late.*

She looked up to find Azetbur studying her in silence and wondered how long the silence had endured. She found herself wiggling her toes, and wondered if that, too, was only the drink.

"I will be blunt," Azetbur said, tilting her chair forward and swinging her feet back onto the floor. "I cannot tell you how tempted I am to say, 'Leave Mestiko to the Federation—they deserve each other.'"

Raya laughed nervously. "I wish to apologize for my people's bad manners."

"On the contrary." Azetbur's smile contained a hint of teeth. "I find them refreshing. I have had too many dealings with humans of late. They say one thing and mean another. And Vulcans! They either say nothing, or attempt to smother you in words. Oddly, I find myself preferring Payav."

Raya wasn't sure what to say to that, so she said nothing, suspecting Azetbur had more on her mind. She also managed to slide her feet onto the floor and try to remember her dignity.

"A meeting of minds never attempted before," Azetbur was musing. The carafe in the center of the table, meant to refresh half a dozen Summit members, was nearly empty. "Your people, mine, and the Federation, in the person of Spock, who attempted to bring my father to what was to have been the Khitomer Peace Accords. Do you know the story?"

Raya had a vague idea, but shook her head anyway, wanting to hear it from the Klingon point of view.

". . . and then," Azetbur concluded her narrative, "there is

Kirk. Or, perhaps better to say, there is no longer Kirk. Kirk, who restored my father's faith, and mine, but who is no longer with us. I miss him."

"I do, too," Raya heard herself say. "Over the past few days, I've found myself wondering if the negotiations would have gone differently if James were here. Spock is a gifted diplomat—"

"—but sometimes diplomacy needs to yield to the desire to knock heads together," Azetbur suggested dryly, and this time both women laughed. Then Azetbur drained her cup and went looking for her boots.

"We must find a way," she said, on her feet and completely sober regardless of how much of the unfamiliar liquor she had consumed, "to bring a little bit of Kirk back into the room the next time your councillors meet. As my father would say, 'Politics makes strange bedfellows.'"

Raya watched her depart. Whatever else had just happened in this room, she believed she had found in Azetbur someone from the Klingon side whom she could trust.

CHAPTER
8

Uhura's work was almost done. She'd been hopscotching back and forth from orbital stations to comm nodes on the ground, assisting local authorities in bringing Mestiko's entire comm grid in synch, and had just a few more locales to visit. Borrowing a small Federation-issue skimmer left behind by one of Dr. Lon's assistants at her last location, she was on her way to troubleshoot one last tangle of comm nodes that hadn't responded when "tickled" from orbit. While gadding about the planet renewing old acquaintances and seeing how well the recovery was progressing had been gratifying, she was looking forward to returning to vosTraal for some R & R, or perhaps investigating the famed hotsprings of Gelta province, which she understood were accepting visitors again.

Most of the problem sites she had needed to visit were in remote areas and, while the work was tedious, the countryside was varied, and signs of regeneration were everywhere, so very different from her last visit here.

The Payav she met along the way were for the most part friendly, grateful for her presence, because it meant they could watch the video feeds from vosTraal and follow the proceedings of the Summit. Occasionally she encountered Payav who had never met a Dinpayav before. Too polite to stare, they were nevertheless watchful, and Uhura made a point of holding impromptu tutorials while she worked, so that the locals would know exactly what she was doing and why.

It was at one site just on the other side of the hills separating Alangabi territory from Nehdi that she quite literally stumbled upon a group of young people who had transformed one of the relay stations into a kind of clubhouse.

They'd heard her skimmer set down outside and emerged from the bunkerlike structure to investigate. Uhura counted nine of them, six boys and three girls, all sporting the same tattoo of a flowering vine just below the left ear. Silent, they gathered around her in a loose circle and simply stared.

"Dinpayav," one of them said finally.

"Yes," Uhura said hopefully, giving them her best smile. "I'm here to—"

"We didn't do anything!" one of the girls shouted, and as if on some prearranged signal, they bolted as one, disappearing into the underbrush. With the sound of badly tuned engines— some sort of improvised dune buggy—and a cloud of dust, they were gone.

With a shrug of resignation—she really would have preferred to assure them she meant them no harm—Uhura retrieved her tricorder and cautiously scanned the relay station from the outside to determine that in fact it was empty. Inside she found it surprisingly neat, until she remembered that these kids had been born and had lived most of their lives underground. But they had disabled the comm grid, probably scrounging it for parts for their vehicles, and it took her the better part of an hour to set it to rights. She left the tricorder running in case someone decided to come back. That was how she noticed the peculiar readings.

Apparently the aboveground portion of the building was only a small part of it. What Uhura found next, hidden behind a bolted-shut door further hidden by utility shelves stacked with cartons of stem-bolts and coils of antique coaxial cable, set off alarms on more than her tricorder.

"Water," Ejo elPrahno said from his place at the head of the table, refilling his guest's glass unerringly despite his blindness. "Water that glows in the dark."

McCoy had brought them hopeful news: Several patients had responded well to the treatment, while a few more had at least stabilized. But he was no closer to figuring out what was causing the anomaly, and it was a weary McCoy who could barely keep his eyes open during dinner that evening. Sorodel was too polite to notice, but nothing escaped Ejo's observation.

"Chimeji," he said, as Sorodel brought more homemade biscuits straight from the oven and the boy immediately grabbed one in each hand. "Tell our guest, what is the greatest change in our society since the Pulse came?"

"Water," the boy said as solemnly as he could past a cheekful of biscuit.

"You have seen the stilt-houses," Ejo explained to a puzzled but intrigued McCoy. "And no doubt wondered why they were built in the desert."

"They do seem a little odd," McCoy admitted. He'd thought he was full until the biscuits arrived, but their enticing aroma changed his mind and, emulating Chimeji, he soon found himself with one in each hand.

"Before the Pulse, much of our land was marsh," Sorodel explained. "There was always enough water. But the Pulse changed everything, transforming our world into desert. We have since had to learn about such things as irrigation." She stopped, looking at her husband with great seriousness. "Ejo? You have seen something," she said.

"What does a blind man see?" he asked with a wry smile. "A river that glows in the dark. That is where, Dr. McCoy, you will find the cause of our affliction. I only wish I had seen it sooner. . . ."

There was, as it turned out, no river on Nehdi land that glowed in the dark, and McCoy filed Ejo's observation away as something from a mystic realm he did not fully understand.

When Uhura woke him in the middle of the night, the pieces began to fall into place.

"Leonard, you've got to see this for yourself."

"In my ample spare time," McCoy groused. "Until we can figure out what the hell's causing this mutation, all I'm doing is—"

"What if I told you I might have your answer?"

"Say again?"

"I'm no medical expert, but I think I'm looking at a roomful of documentation about medical experiments conducted on animals more than fifty years ago. There's one whole file on 'Accelerated Aging.'"

There was a long silence, so long that Uhura checked the frequency.

"Leonard, did you hear me?"

"Damn right I heard you. Where the hell are you? What are you waiting for? Hook me up and relay the stuff to me, can't you?"

"Even if I could, I wouldn't trust it to remain secure. The grid's still too compromised. If the media got hold of it, or—"

McCoy hadn't thought of that.

"Besides," Uhura added. *"It's all on paper."*

"Old-fashioned paper printouts . . ." McCoy mused with a kind of wonder in his voice. "Now, that's something I never thought I'd see."

Once more Uhura had had to go and retrieve him, flying low over the hills in the dead of night and spiriting him away in the tiny skimmer. What she'd found was exactly what she'd thought it was, and McCoy was as excited as she'd seen him since this mission began.

It would take a while to read through all of it, but the documentation was all here. The Alangabi government had been conducting bioweapons experiments—long before the Pulse and, according to the stacks of paper McCoy was rummaging through, only on lab animals. But some of their stored materials had disappeared—either lost or stolen—in the chaos immediately following the Pulse.

"And I'm guessing some of that got into the aquifer on this side of the mountains and leached into the underground water supply the Nehdi were dependent on during the nuclear winter," McCoy said.

"Is there enough material here to help?" Uhura asked, scarcely believing their good fortune.

"There should be. Pity it's all on paper; it'll take that much longer to read through, much less the inconvenience of transporting it out of here. Too bad none of Spock's ability to memorize data stuck in my brain. Anyhow, let's put it all together. Shouldn't take more than a couple of trips in the skimmer to get it out of here.

"It never ceases to amaze me," he went on, scooping files into what looked like a wastebasket he'd scrounged from under a table somewhere, "the capacity for otherwise intelligent beings to expend so much of their time and energy playing 'Gotcha!' with people they don't like. . . ."

Having filled the wastebasket, he went rummaging for something else, and came up with a storage box full of odds and ends so dusty they made him sneeze. There were a lot of files.

". . . Used to think it was just humans, until I got out into space and realized there's a pattern to the evolution of damn near every species except possibly the Halkans. Scratch and claw for survival for a few million years, then when things get peaceful and you have enough to eat and land to grow it on, you sit around the fire in the evenings thinking of ways to kill your neighbor. . . ."

"Leonard . . ." Uhura said quietly.

"I know, I know—I'm hurrying! Maybe if you gave me a hand instead of playing lookout in the middle of the night in a facility in the middle of nowhere that hasn't been occupied except by desert rats for at least a generation—"

The slide and click of an old-fashioned disruptor—the kind the Klingons had probably left behind during Traal's brief reign—shut him up. Hyperfocused on gathering as many bulky paper files as he could, he'd neither heard nor seen the return of the wild ones Uhura had frightened off earlier in the day. They filled the small bunker and had their weapons trained on both of them.

"Oh, damn!" McCoy muttered.

He'd been among the Nehdi long enough to know those weren't Nehdi tattoos. The twining red-and-blue thorny-vine below the left earlobe was a distinctly Alangabi design. There was something else disturbing about this group, too. None of them looked well.

Payav as a species, once you accepted the pallor and the hairlessness and the longer necks as a normal part of their body habitus, were for the most part beautiful, from both a medical and an aesthetic point of view. There was something fawnlike about them: large-eyed, graceful, innately gentle—until they started quarreling.

And until the Pulse, which brought many kinds of scarring—burns, blinding cataracts, frostbite, the long-term effects of hunger and lack of sunlight—one hadn't seen any deformities among these people. McCoy had never seen them this way—his first exposure to Mestiko was a couple of years after the Pulse hit—but he'd studied the records gathered by the Federation observation team before the pulsar was discovered. The Payav had been an eminent example of a case in which nature had gotten it right.

Not so these children—and that was really all they were. The eldest, a spindly male at the forefront who was obviously the leader, couldn't have been more than an adolescent on the cusp of adulthood. But in each of them, on the cursory glance McCoy allowed himself past the muzzles of outdated weapons pointed at him by a gaggle of unsteady adolescents, there was something *off*, something more than the effects of being born and raised in darkness and cold and inadequate nutrition. It wasn't even necessarily anything physical—a limp, a squint, a twisted limb—but some emotional darkness that made the good doctor profoundly uneasy.

Setting the storage box he'd been stuffing full of documents down on the floor beside the overflowing wastebasket, he tried his best grin and the old McCoy charm.

"My guess is y'all are wondering who we are and what we're

doing here," he began. "I don't suppose you'd believe me if I told you we're part of a cleanup crew that's—"

"Silence!" the tall spindly one said predictably. "Get away from those papers. Stand next to the female."

McCoy did as he was told. If he'd known how long he'd have to stand there. . . .

Mentally he assessed each of his captors' physical state. Prolonged malnutrition during the growing years for that one, some sort of chronic neuropathic skin condition for that one, poor diet and lack of sunlight for that one.

"What's the matter?" the spindly one said, noticing the scrutiny. "Don't like looking at us? Do we offend you? We're not as pretty as your Nehdi hosts over the mountains. Do you want to know why? It's because in the worst times they would not share their resources with us. They made us this way."

"Not so!" one of the females said suddenly. "What I heard was—"

"Lies!" one of the younger boys piped up. "Government lies, Nehdi lies!"

"Dear God . . ." McCoy said out of the side of his mouth, shifting his feet restlessly. "I'd rather they killed us outright than argued us to death. . . ."

"They're not going to kill us," Uhura said pragmatically. The youngsters were arguing so loudly they could talk underneath them, and if there hadn't been so many of them and they hadn't been blocking the only way out, some sort of escape could have been attempted. "They need us as bargaining chips. There are still reporters snooping around these parts. I repaired the relay station. If I could just get to the controls . . ."

She was standing quite still, centered, her eyes on the youngest male, who was probably no older than McCoy's newfound friend Chimeji, and who kept wiping his runny nose on his sleeve. At least the others hadn't trusted him with a weapon; all he had was a long stick. If she could charm him . . .

"And if they don't get what they want?" McCoy said a little too loudly.

"Let's not get caught up in 'ifs' right now . . ." Uhura started to say, but suddenly all nine of their captors seemed to be talking at once, in an obscure dialect that McCoy couldn't follow. A barely perceptible shake of her head told him Uhura couldn't understand it, either. But judging from the body language, including a great deal of gesticulating from one of the females, the gist of the conversation seemed to be "Oh, great! Just what we need, hostages! Can't we just burn the papers and send these two on their way? Who's going to believe Dinpayav, anyway?"

This was no doubt followed by, "It's not just the papers, you idiot. The very fact that these two are here means there'll be news crews as soon as we release them. They'll bring in research teams and run tests, and then we're doomed."

"Who's 'we'? This is something that happened in our *elors'* era. It's got nothing to do with us."

"Your *elor* or mine?" That was followed by a startled silence. "Yes, now you see the size of the problem. Our people did this. And even if it was a long time ago, people are dying now. We'll be blamed. We can't let these two leave here."

"So who's going to kill them? It won't be me, and I doubt it'll be you. Or did you plan to keep them and feed them for the rest of their lives?"

"Dear God!" McCoy interjected finally, and all nine pairs of eyes turned to him. "Look, I realize we've put y'all in a situation here, but either kill us and get it over with, or put us somewhere while you figure it out—"

"Leonard!" Uhura whispered. McCoy was suddenly grateful he wasn't close enough for her to kick him.

"—because I for one am not a young man, and it's past my bedtime and I need to sit down. We could also do with some food and water and maybe a hot bath after digging through these dusty old papers all night and—"

He'd pushed it too far. The leader made an impatient noise and waved his weapon at them again.

"Quiet! Get in the storage room. Both of you, now!"

Two of the others searched them and confiscated anything that could be used as a weapon or a means of communicating, including the comm unit Uhura had secreted in her boot while McCoy had been speechifying. There was barely enough time to see that the room they were being shoved into was about two meters square and full of gardening equipment and not much else before the door was slammed and locked behind them, plunging them into all but total darkness. A rim of light around the door and the murmur of voices told them their captors weren't going anywhere.

CHAPTER
9

"Can't say I blame them," McCoy said once the door had closed and locked between them and their captors. "Given their history with the Nehdi, the least this kind of information could do is heat up the old hostilities. But with the Summit meeting and the eyes of the quadrant on them—"

"Which is why we have to convince them we're not going to run to the media with this," Uhura said. The door had barely closed when she'd begun groping her way around the walls, looking for . . . well, she wasn't sure what, but she had to keep moving.

"Exactly. Although how we're supposed to do that from in here . . . All we want to do is work backwards from the data in those files to—ow!"

"What's the matter?"

"Tripped over something. Feels like a garden hoe. And is that . . . Oh, please tell me that's not manure!"

Uhura gritted her teeth to keep from snapping at him. "Look, why don't you stay still and let me do this before we end up bumping into each other?"

"No, dammit! You stand still. Go over by the door and try

your charms on them. God knows I've failed, but communication is your thing."

Uhura banged her palms on the door. "Hello? Can I talk to you for a minute? Someone? The last thing we want to do is start up old hostilities. We just want that information so we can help the people who are sick. Can't you let us out so we can talk?"

Her words were met by a loud banging from the other side.

"Be quiet in there!" It was the leader again. "We need to discuss this among ourselves. Someone will feed you in a little while, but only if you don't say another word."

With that, the murmuring on the other side began anew.

"They're just children . . ." Uhura said.

"Children with guns," McCoy pointed out, mindful of Miri and her friends. Uhura hadn't been in the landing party that time.

When the haranguing outside finally subsided and one of the females came in with food, Uhura deliberately did not look toward the light from the opening door. That way, she was able to retain her night vision and find an escape route.

"There's a draft from somewhere up there," she told McCoy once they were locked in again and the arguing outside resumed, though with less intensity. "Has to be an air vent, or even a window. I didn't have time to see when they tossed us in here, but I noticed it now. They have to get tired of arguing and sleep eventually."

"Good luck with that!" was McCoy's opinion.

"Actually," Uhura said, already moving while she ruminated, "it might be better to investigate this *while* they're arguing. That way if we make any noise, they won't hear us. . . ."

"And if they've posted a guard outside?"

"It would just be one of them. A kid. Are you saying we can't sneak up on and overpower a kid?"

"Who's 'we'?" McCoy demanded. "I can boost you up there, but you can't haul me up after you. I'm not going anywhere. Just go!"

"Just long enough to get back to the skimmer and alert the *Jo'Zamestaad*," Uhura promised. "You know I won't leave you here."

"Whatever," McCoy said. "Let's get on with this!"

There was in fact a window, neither locked nor barred, but half-open and just big enough for Uhura to crawl through. McCoy made a stirrup of his hands, and Uhura scrabbled up the earthen wall and pulled herself up by the window frame, cursing under her breath as she felt several nails break and realized her palms were full of splinters. But she got over and out to discover that, as they'd hoped, the window was at ground level and hidden by overgrown shrubbery. She was free.

"You okay?" she heard McCoy's voice below.

"I'm out," she said. "But—"

"Just go, willya?" he said, not giving her a chance to finish with *I don't want to leave you behind.* "These are Payav, remember? They won't kill me without arguing about it for at least another three days. I expect you to come rescue me before that."

"You know I will," she whispered, then brushed the dirt off her knees, looked around, and listened for a moment before slipping through the branches and out toward where she thought she remembered the road.

Amateurs, she thought gratefully. There had been no guard, and her little skimmer was right where she'd left it. She risked a short burst of power, just enough to let it roll down the incline for several hundred yards without another sound. Then she fiddled with the comm until she found a frequency she didn't think the Alangabi would use, and patched in to Raya elMora's personal transceiver.

Matters moved swiftly from there. Bouncing a signal off the nearest comm satellite, Uhura activated the relay station where the kids were holding McCoy, and it came to life. On a secure frequency, *Jo'Zamestaad* elMora came straight to the point.

"What is your name, Young One?" she demanded of the apparently Alangabi ringleader.

"S-Stenho etLaja, *J-Jo'Zamestaad,*" he stuttered, his cheeks suffusing such an uncharacteristic pink that several of his followers giggled.

"You do realize you're on the verge of causing an interstellar incident, do you not?"

"An inter—what? We are holding two Dinpayav intruders who were attempting to slander our people with accusations of germ warfare. We expected the *Jo'Zamestaad* to reward us, not accuse us of—"

"*One*," Raya couldn't resist. Something of James T. Kirk's best persuasive manner arose from her memory, and she used it. "*One 'intruder,' or should I say 'hostage'? You haven't even managed to do that much right.*"

This produced a flurry of activity in the relay station, and finally the youngsters, chagrined that they hadn't even noticed that one of their hostages had escaped, produced a sleepy-looking McCoy, hair and clothes rumpled, blinking in the unaccustomed light.

"*Are you all right, Doctor?*" Raya demanded.

"I suppose so," McCoy muttered, scratching his head. "Listen, the little I was able to read of that documentation we tried to confiscate—"

Raya cut him off. "—*you should not discuss on an open frequency, however secure. First we get you out of there, then we worry about—*"

"Forget me! You've got to find the source of the pathogen. My guess is that somewhere around here you'll find the experimental batches that the original scientists left behind. Then you can—"

"*Doctor, please shut up!*" Raya said tightly. "*Let me talk to Stenho again.*"

When the now obviously completely flummoxed young man returned to the screen, she scolded him the way a mother might a wayward adolescent.

"*Now, you listen to me, young man!*" Bless you, James! she thought, perversely enjoying the moment despite its seriousness. "*Commander Uhura has gotten the global comm grid back online, and I am* this close *to letting the news media descend on you. You will release Dr. McCoy at once and return him to the Nehdi. You will evacuate the relay center, because at the very least you are trespassing and at the very worst you are impeding an investigation into a catastrophic medical situation. Now, you and your friends have one minute exactly to evacuate the premises. Go! Shoo!*"

CHAPTER
10

"There," Cart etDeja said, pointing to the anomaly. From orbit, the river did indeed glow against the dark of the background readout. "Seepage into the aquifer that feeds the Nehdi irrigation system. Something in the pathogen makes it phosphoresce under spectral analysis. When we trace it backwards, we'll probably find a cache of long-forgotten Alangabi chemicals buried somewhere."

And so they did. Hidden within a concrete bunker not far from the relay center where McCoy had spent an uncomfortable night, the missing bioweapons material had been rather hastily hidden, sealed in what at the time were assumed to be damage-proof storage drums. But the years of intense cold following the Pulse, along with seismic activity in the region, had damaged the bunker, allowing the ice and snow in and corroding the temporary containers. Some had seeped into the water table and thence into the underground streams that supplied the Nehdi Valley with water.

The disturbing thing was that the bioweapons did not affect Alangabi, only Nehdi who had inherited a certain gene sequence, causing the mutations that resulted in premature aging and death. While the original experiments had been done only on animals and then abandoned, the intent was clear. Taken to their logical extreme, these experiments had been meant to produce a bioweapon to be used against the Nehdi.

"So all we have to do now is reverse the process," McCoy told Raya, trying to make it sound easy. "I've lost three more patients in the meantime, but with the added data, we should be able to put a stop to this. Now, can you do something to get rid of the reporters camped on my doorstep? It's a nuisance having to step on them every time I go outdoors."

"*I'll do my best, Doctor,*" Raya promised, remembering what it was she'd always admired about this man. "*I'll be there first thing tomorrow to . . . what is the term? 'Kick ass and take names'?*"

It wasn't quite that easy. Raya brought the Elders of the Alangabi to meet with Ejo and Sorodel on neutral ground and try to resolve centuries of enmity in a single morning. In an inspired move, she also brought representatives of the young people, the "wild ones," from both sides to attend the negotiations.

After several days of intensive talks (during which there were rumblings from vosTraal, where Spock, Azetbur, and the *Zamestaad* continued the Summit in Raya's absence, though some of her constituents were less than pleased to do so), the two sides reached a rapprochement.

The Alangabi agreed to clean up and destroy all traces of the experimental pathogen. In exchange, the Nehdi agreed to offer their medical expertise to heal those like the wild ones who had suffered so much during the aftermath of the Pulse.

Both tribes drafted anyone with even a smattering of scientific or medical background to read through the mountains of paperwork generated by the animal experiments in order to help the Dinpayav doctor McCoy refine his treatment regimens so that the pathogen would claim no more victims.

Sorodel, watching Chimeji play out under the sun, wiped tears from the corners of her eyes.

"So unnecessary!" she whispered to McCoy. "My daughter and son-in-law should have lived to see this day. So unnecessary . . ."

McCoy put a hand on her shoulder to comfort her. After all these people had been through, he could find no words that sufficed.

But Sorodel was an Elder, and hers was not the only loss among the Nehdi this day. Her people expected her to be strong, and so she would be. Silently clasping McCoy's hand where it rested on her shoulder, she looked toward the future in the person of her grandson, running free under Mestiko's sky, promising hope.

CHAPTER
11

Raya elMora hooked her four thumbs into the buckle of the shoulder harness and snapped it into place. Checking wind speed and direction, she began to set the shortest course back to vosTraal, then hesitated.

What was the rush?

To everyone's surprise, she had named Deman elKramo as deputy in her absence, and he would speak for her as first Spock, then Azetbur, presented their respective cases for Mestiko's admission to, or independence from, the Federation. The presentations, arguments and counterarguments, could be expected to last at least a week.

All Raya needed to do was to be present at the end in case a tie-breaking vote was needed.

Thanks to Commander Uhura, the global grid was up and running. Raya could listen to the proceedings and still take the leisurely route home.

As a teacher, a small eternity ago, she had traveled occasionally, saving up her salary and taking all the recommended tours to the historic places, gathering up memories, never knowing that in the blink of an eye many of those places would be either gone forever, or rendered uninhabitable without drastic alterations that would render them historic in an entirely different way.

As *Jo'Zamestaad*, every journey had been one of duty: formal tours to inspect the devastation and make decisions about who needed to be evacuated, who could stay, and under what circumstances. Later there were more inspections to see that the restorations were progressing as promised, that corruption and inertia were kept to a minimum, that people got what they needed.

Since things had been "going well"—that is, since she and her government had returned from exile—it seemed she hardly left vosTraal.

This afternoon, she would remedy that. If she set the skimmer for maximum speed, she could chase the sun around her world, and see vast swathes of it, good and bad, before nightfall. She had rations enough for several days, and if the *Jo'Zamestaad* herself couldn't sometimes bend the rules, who could?

She logged in a flight plan that would give her an ETA at vosTraal sometime tomorrow evening, and left a channel open to the Summit proceedings, where she could hear Spock's sober, reasoned tone laying out the terms under which Mestiko might join the Federation without losing any of its autonomy as a sovereign planet.

Raya deliberately left the channel on listen-only, not wanting to alert any one of her ministers as to her location or her availability. She did not wish to listen to the objections and reminders of unfinished business she knew would greet her if she let them know where to find her.

As she followed the sun, she somehow felt as if she was not alone.

It was difficult for her to admit even to herself how much she had been looking forward to seeing James again. Primarily, of course, she had been eager to show him how much progress her people had made since the last time he'd been here; but also, in light of that progress, she'd hoped, at last, to be able to take some time for herself, to capture some of what she'd sacrificed of a private life when the Pulse occurred.

Had she been out of her mind to even consider spending some of that private life in the company of Starfleet's living legend, James T. Kirk?

She knew from their years-long correspondence that he still harbored some guilt for his part in failing to stop the Pulse from ravaging Mestiko. She had hoped somehow to help him confront that guilt and begin to heal it.

At the very least she'd hoped to persuade him to stay a little longer on her world than protocol demanded, to linger for a while when the diplomatic mission was over. As her world emerged at last from its years-long nuclear winter into something resembling normalcy, she might have offered him a beach to walk on.

But now he was gone forever. The might-have-been brought tears to Raya's eyes. There had been times when she'd hated him, and said as much, times she'd accused him of not doing enough, until she'd realized that what he was in fact doing was helping her people to do for themselves.

In mourning him, she was mourning everyone she had lost. But was she losing sight of everything her people had done? Its evidence was all around her. Dashing away her tears, she smiled.

"Well, James?" she said aloud. "I think I've learned more from you than either of us ever realized."

The Mestiko of her youth was gone forever. But in its place was a pristine, beautiful world of forests and ice-fields and oceans and fields, of gleaming cities rising from ruins or places where there had never been cities before; and for all the many dead, there were as many living, giving birth, flourishing. It would never be the same, but that didn't mean it wasn't good.

Raya thought of the terrible ordeal she and her people had been through in the wake of disaster, and how it had in some ways strengthened them, and in other ways shown their vulnerabilities.

Not for the first time, she could not help wondering how her life, and all their lives, might have been different if the Pulse had never passed their world. Then again, what if the Federation hadn't been there to first mitigate the effects of the Pulse, and later help the Payav survive and restore their world?

What-ifs, Raya realized, were as dangerous as if-onlys, and she made up her mind at that moment to stop second-guessing herself. Somehow, she suspected, James would approve.

McCoy eased his weary bones down onto a stone bench in the quiet rear courtyard of the medical building. The oldest building in town, it had been built many centuries ago of native stone, on a rise above the valley so that there was no need for stilts. The inner courtyards had once been a maze of small gardens. Most were barren now, waiting to be replanted. Nevertheless, it was a peaceful place to spend the latter part of a long day.

It was early evening, and construction on the new housing across the plaza had ceased for the day, restoring the natural quiet. Some of the hospital staff were leaving work, some arriving for the night shift, and they nodded to the Dinpayav doctor without speaking, respecting the man and his solitude, particularly after what he'd been through recently. If there were no words sufficient to thank him for saving an entire generation of their young people, their respectful silence would have to suffice.

Off in the direction of the encircling hills, McCoy could hear birdsong. He wasn't versed enough in the local fauna to know if they were native species that had somehow survived, or some new hybrid species the locals would find as alien as he did. In any event, it occurred to him that he was enjoying the sound.

He was enjoying the view, too. For the first time, he noticed that the medical building had been positioned so that the morning sun graced the elaborate front entrance and the brilliance of the sunset flooded the inner courtyard.

And it was brilliant indeed. There were still some traces in the atmosphere of the noxious elements kicked up by the pulsar; McCoy supposed Spock or that young pup Tuvok could quote him the chemical breakdown to the last molecule, but he didn't care. Whatever the chemistry of it, the sunset was spectacular, and he intended to enjoy it on that level alone, thank you very much.

An odd thought struck him. This was the first time he could remember actually *enjoying* anything since . . . since Jim had died.

Oh, he'd gone through the motions, eating and sleeping when he needed to—knowing too well what the consequences would be if he didn't—getting out of bed when it was time to go back to work, putting one foot in front of the other to get where he had to go. And the work itself had been both challenging and meaningful. But he couldn't have described a single meal, or remember lacing his boots or told you whether his socks matched or if the weather on the walk over here had been warm or cold, clear or misty. None of it had mattered.

He'd known it wasn't healthy. How many people had he lost over the years? He knew the five stages of grief and could almost predict their duration each time someone he knew passed on. So many days for denial, so many more for anger, this many for bargaining, depression, and finally acceptance. But he'd gotten stuck somewhere in depression this time, a depression, oddly, colored by guilt.

Not the I-was-there-and-should-have-saved-him guilt that Scotty was going through—McCoy made a mental note to stay in touch with the grizzled engineer to make sure he didn't do anything dangerous—but more of an I-wasn't-there-and-should-have-been guilt.

Patently ridiculous, of course. He'd been invited—they all had been—to attend the commissioning of the *Enterprise*-B, but he'd been up to his ears in a research project, had growled something about dress uniforms and begged off. No one had really expected him to do otherwise.

But if he'd known he'd never see Jim Kirk again after that day . . .

You'd have done what, you old fool? he chided himself. *You don't have psychic powers or even that weird telepathic sense that Vulcans have that told Spock the* Intrepid *had been destroyed from parsecs away, so why don't you stop feeling sorry for yourself and . . .*

And enjoy the damn sunset, he decided, his shoulders

slumping. The fact that he'd even noticed that Mestiko had a sun, and that it set in Technicolor every evening, was, he supposed, a sign the depression was lifting. The final step would have to be acceptance. Yes, James T. Kirk really was dead, and there wasn't a damn thing anyone could do to bring him back.

So after a long day of squinting through a microscope—refusing to take the computer's word for the fact that the regen batches were uniform and free of artifacts—McCoy closed his eyes and felt the warming rays on his face, breathed in the clean air of a restored Mestiko the way he'd seen Payav do every time they emerged from an underground shelter, never again to take it for granted . . . and realized he was not alone.

Chimeji stood beside him, silent, not so much as letting his shadow fall over the old man's face to disrupt his enjoyment of the sunset.

"How do, Chimmy?" McCoy smiled in spite of himself. Until today, the kid had been the only thing on Mestiko to make him smile. "Whatcha got there?"

The boy's grubby fists cradled something small and dirt-covered as if it was incredibly precious.

"Treasure," he said in that blunt, shorthanded way of his, waiting for McCoy to hold his hands out so he could deposit his "treasure" there.

Rocks, McCoy thought at first when he took them. He was holding five uniform-sized roundish lumps, automatically brushing the dirt off them to see what was underneath. *Like all kids his age, Chimmy thinks he's found pirate treasure or a gold mine. Do I encourage him in his fantasy, take his mind off his dead parents, or . . . ?*

But the objects were too lightweight to be rocks. Hoping he wasn't holding the petrified scat of some long-dead animal, but intrigued in spite of himself, McCoy hauled himself up off the bench and motioned for Chimeji to accompany him inside. Back in the lab, he rinsed the dirt off the "rocks" and scowled.

"Well, I'll be damned! Could these be what I think they are?"

"Computer'd tell you," Chimeji suggested, his upturned face expectant.

McCoy looked down at the boy with renewed admiration.

"It might. But the records from back then aren't complete. We don't want to make any mistakes, get people's hopes up unnecessarily. Sometimes it's better to do things the old-fashioned way." Placing the objects reverently on a specimen tray, he dried his hands and hit the intercom. "Dr. elKanai, are you still on the premises?"

The medical center had a staff of experts in biologicals and herbs. Jana elKanai was not long in arriving. Her eyes widened when she saw what Chimeji had found. She picked the objects up gingerly and examined them for a moment without speaking.

"Could be . . ." she said carefully, as if trying not to get her own hopes up. "But even if they are, no guarantee they're viable, or that they'll germinate, or that the seedlings will survive any more than . . ."

She stopped herself, seeing the crestfallen look on Chimeji's face.

"Whatever happens, Young One," she assured him, "you've earned yourself a tattoo for finding these."

"Maybe not," the boy said, looking down at his feet.

"Ah," Jana said. "I can see I'm not being a good scientist. The first thing I should have asked you is where you found them."

Something there was about small boys and construction projects which spanned solar systems and species. Not only did the Nehdi need new homes and shops and offices to replace those damaged and left fallow following the Pulse, but new housing was being built to accommodate the arriving medical and environmental workers, and new construction was everywhere. The soil had finally warmed enough for large earthmovers to dig deep excavations, well below the former frostline, for the foundation of more-than-temporary shelters. And the local kids couldn't stay away.

Playing near the excavation no matter how many times the workers chased him away, Chimeji had apparently found some seedpods buried in the softening permafrost. He didn't have to say a word. Jana knew.

"Your *elor* will not know whether to scold you or reward you," she suggested.

The boy shrugged. "Probably both."

"So are these what I think they are?" McCoy interjected, strangely excited.

"Indeed they are," Jana concurred. "Whether they've been dormant for centuries or only since the Pulse, they are in fact the seeds of a *noggik* tree. The scanners should tell us how old they are and whether or not they're the original strain and not a more recent hybrid. Beyond that, we can only hope."

As she proceeded to scan the seedpods, McCoy couldn't help noticing the expression on Chimeji's face, something he hadn't seen before in the brief time he'd known the boy. Hope, indeed.

There's a lesson here, he told himself, *about life, death, things of that nature. This youngster's lost a lot more than you have, and yet he can find hope in a little thing like a handful of seed pods. The young heal faster, but still . . .*

"Are they, are they?" Chimeji could barely contain his excitement as the scanner worked its magic. A grin as wide as he could make it without showing any teeth lit up his face. McCoy squeezed his shoulder affectionately.

"Whether they are or not, there's enough dirt on your neck, youngster, to grow a forest of *noggik* trees. . . ."

Was this acceptance, the final stage of grief? he wondered. It no longer felt like depression, anyway.

Dammit, Jim! he thought, watching Jana and Chimeji clasp hands as the scanner reading showed that, yes, the seed pods dated to around forty years before the Pulse, and that three of them showed 90 percent viability and the other two 40 and 30 percent, respectively. He found himself sharing their delight vicariously. *Chekov's wrong, and so's Sulu. Heroes die all the time, usually at a greater rate than us ordinary mortals. You did this deliberately, left us here to mourn you . . .*

. . . or to carry on your mission, the way Raya's doing, the way the entire population of Mestiko is doing, even as they're working at cross-purposes the way Spock and I used to.

Used to? he asked himself. It was still going on, probably would for the rest of their lives, despite their once having shared the same brain.

And yet they expected the Payav to behave themselves,

make nice for the visiting diplomats, and decide with a single voice whether or not to join the Federation.

In any event, he was not a diplomat, and he'd leave it to Spock and the other ambassadors. And it was past time he stopped feeling sorry for himself. Whether or not Mestiko elected to become a member of the Federation, there was good work being done here, and more good work to do. McCoy found himself grinning for the first time since he could remember, reminding himself just in time not to show any teeth.

As a wise man once said, there were always possibilities.

ACKNOWLEDGMENTS

Dayton Ward & Kevin Dilmore:

Many thanks to editor Keith R.A. DeCandido, for inviting us to participate in the development of *Star Trek: Mere Anarchy*, and trusting us to come up with the initial concept intended to drive all six books. It was an exciting opportunity, and one we relished.

Thanks also are due to our fellow writers on the series: Mike W. Barr, Dave Galanter, Christopher L. Bennett, the incomparable Howie Weinstein, and one of our favorite "old school" *Star Trek* novelists, Margaret Wander Bonanno. Developing the series with this collection of talented writers was far more fun than any job has a right to be, as evidenced by the trunk-load of e-mail we all exchanged in the weeks before the first word of story was actually written. The spirit of collaboration permeating every moment of this project was a reward all its own.

As always, we save our final thanks for our wives, Michi and Michelle, who continue to support us and our writing, as well as everything that comes with it, not the least of which is remaining tolerant of two boneheads who have yet to discover the secret of actually acting like . . . you know . . . adults. We love you, ladies!

Mike W. Barr:

Sometime in the 1980s, the members of KISS released solo albums, each one dedicated to the other three members of the group. By the second album, you pretty much figured out what was going on.

The acknowledgments for each book of *Mere Anarchy* are going to read a lot like that. But why not? Though each individual eBook bears the unique stamp of its writer, the overall structure and many of the bits and the characters were worked out in mass e-mail exchanges that were as funny as they were occasionally infuriating. The end results are the products of a team, not a committee, and I thank the rest of "the usual gang of idiots" who helped make Book 2 what it is: Dayton Ward and Kevin Dilmore, Dave Galanter, Christopher L. Bennett, Margaret Wander Bonanno (the other MWB), and Howard Weinstein. (Collaborating with Howard was a rush for me as he wrote one of the *Star Trek* animateds, "The Pirates of Orion," and thus actually worked with Shatner, Nimoy, and Kelley; how cool is that?) Either we all deserve special commendations for putting up with editor Keith DeCandido, or he deserves a special commendation for putting up with us. Probably both— commendations all around!

In writing this story I sometimes wondered how I would have felt if, at 9:30 PM on September 8, 1966, having just seen the premiere of *Star Trek*, I had been told that four decades later I would be contributing to a story designed to commemorate the fortieth anniversary of that series. That will never be known, but I think my younger self would have been amazed and pleased. Over the years *Star Trek* has been a source of entertainment, inspiration, and sometimes even income, and I have always tried to do my best by the *Enterprise* crew and the examples of Gene Roddenberry and Gene L. Coon. At its worst—which it sinks to no more often than any other American television production—*Star Trek* is still an agreeable visit with old friends. At its best—which it achieves no less often that any other American television production—*Star Trek* entertains, lifts the spirit, lightens the heart, and provides that sense of redemption without which no creative endeavor can ever aspire to the title of Art.

It can never be known how I would have felt back in 1966. But I do know how I feel today.

To quote James T. Kirk from *Star Trek II:* "I feel young."

Dave Galantar:

I think it goes without saying, if you've read the other authors' acknowledgments in this series, that the writers collectively had a blast in discussing and planning their respective works with one another. I so enjoyed the wit and intelligence of them all: Dayton Ward and Kevin Dilmore, Mike W. Barr, Christopher L. Bennett, Howie Weinstein, and Margaret Wander Bonanno. Working with these folks has been one of the most rewarding experiences of my writing career, and I'd not have missed it for the world.

Which leads me to especially thank Keith R.A. DeCandido for having the crazy notion to bring us all together for this most enjoyable of projects.

Thanks as well to my friends and my dad for being understanding about deadlines, and to my brother Josh for his last-minute proofreading skills. Any typos are his fault, you know. If you e-mail me with complaints about them, I'm just forwarding them to him, be warned.

Last, but most important, thanks to the folks who forty years ago brought us what would become the legacy of *Star Trek:* Gene Roddenberry, Gene L. Coon, D.C. Fontana, Bill Shatner, Leonard Nimoy, DeForest Kelley, James Doohan, George Takei, Nichelle Nichols, Walter Koenig, and Majel Barrett. I could go on with a list of names that would greatly extend the length of this book—so many helped to build the mythos of *Star Trek*—but their names are writ on the episodes we can forever watch, and remember, and love. Thanks to all of them, and the casts and crews of all past and future *Star Trek* shows for reminding us that "the human adventure is just beginning."

Christoper L. Bennett:

If you've read the acknowledgments above, you know that each of my illustrious predecessors has acknowledged the contributions of the whole group and the importance of the collaborative process in the creation of this series. In that spirit, let me just say:

I did it all myself! It was me, all me! That whole pulsar thing? My idea, completely! I've been carrying everyone else this whole time!

Of course, I'm just kidding, in the spirit of often boisterous fun that's characterized this whole project. This story wouldn't have existed if Keith R.A. DeCandido hadn't come up with the idea of a mini-series to celebrate *Star Trek*'s fortieth anniversary and assembled this team to write it. Thanks to him for picking me for the team and for giving me the opportunity to work alongside legends like Mike Barr, Howie Weinstein, and Margaret Wander Bonanno . . . not to mention my fellow young upstarts Dayton Ward and Kevin Dilmore, plus Dave Galanter, who's somewhere in between the generations (it's hard to pin him down about himself because he won't stop going on about the monkeys).

A number of specific elements in *The Darkness Drops Again* were conceived in our group e-mail exchanges and snapped up by me. Mike created Dr. Lon and suggested his story arc through the saga. Dave and Dayton (among others) proposed looking into the refugee side of the story. Kevin found the solar-system simulator that helped me figure out the gravitational effects of the pulsar on Hertex's planets. Howie proposed the character that became Asal Janto and planted the seed for the idea of her misguided push for a radiation shield. Keith came up with the terms used by the mar-Atyya and the name of the system's star, among other terminology. And other ideas are too much a product of the gestalt to pin down to any one person.

The attributes of the Kazarites and Zaranites were described by Robert Fletcher in his costume notes for *Star Trek: The Motion Picture*. The customizable *TMP*-era shuttles with their "plug-in" modules come from a design sketch done for the movie by Andrew Probert. Minara is from "The Empath" by Joyce Muskat, and Beta Niobe is from "All Our Yesterdays" by Jean Lissette Aroeste. The *Wraith* stealth shuttle is from *Star Trek: Traitor Winds* by L.A. Graf. Mr. Leslie was played by Eddie Paskey and appeared in dozens of *TOS* episodes. Captain Terrell (the late, great Paul Winfield) comes from *Star Trek II: The Wrath of Khan*. Admiral Morrow (Robert Hooks) comes from *Star Trek III: The Search for Spock*. And young Ensign T'Lara will grow up to become Admiral T'Lara (Deborah Strang) from *Deep Space Nine:* "Rules of Engagement."

Well, this has been fun. Let's do it again for the fiftieth anniversary!

Howard Weinstein:

This is my first time involved in a project with this many writers kibitzing together—a veritable writing orgy!

However, as much as we hope our readers enjoy these stories, you'll never know just how much fun we had writing them for you. Why? Because you'll never get to read the loony e-mail exchanges we had during the process (unless Keith decides to include them in a future "Special Edition").

Like most writers, I'm accustomed to working alone. Remember, many of us became writers in the first place because we're socially maladroit. So this was a welcome change of pace.

It was a great pleasure working alongside and being inspired by my talented *Mere Anarchy* colleagues. Thanks to Kevin Dilmore and Dayton Ward, Mike W. Barr, Dave Galanter, Christopher L. Bennett, and Margaret Wander Bonanno for the honor of their company.

Thanks to Our Glorious Editor (O.G.E.) Keith R.A. De-Candido for inviting us to play together.

And on a personal note, thanks to all the devoted fans who have kept *Star Trek* alive, and given me the lucky opportunity to write these for more than thirty years.

Margaret Wander Bonanno:

With thanks to Keith R.A. DeCandido for inviting me along for the ride. Thanks to the Boyz—Dayton, Kevin, Mike, Dave, Christopher, and Howie—for making the ride so much fun.

ABOUT THE AUTHORS

MIKE W. BARR has contributed to some of pop culture's most enduring series, including *Sherlock Holmes*, *Ellery Queen*, *Star Trek*, *Star Wars*, *Doc Savage*, *The Shadow*, *Batman*, and *The Simpsons*. He's also created some, including the comic book series *Camelot 3000*, *Batman and the Outsiders*, *The Maze Agency*, and *Mantra*. In 2003 he penned the *Star Trek* novel *Gemini* and is writing another due in 2010, as well as an original science fiction novel. His book on science fiction comic books of the Silver Age, *The Silver Age Sci-Fi Companion*, was published by TwoMorrows. He is marketing a fantasy novel and writing a tie-in book for one of this summer's hottest movies. He lives in a house with too many cats and not enough books.

CHRISTOPHER L. BENNETT is the author of *Star Trek: Ex Machina*, the critically acclaimed follow-up to the events and character threads of *Star Trek: The Motion Picture*. *The Darkness Drops Again* marks his return to the post-*TMP* milieu. His other *Star Trek* fiction includes the *Titan* novels *Orion's Hounds* and *Over a Torrent Sea*, the

Next Generation novels *The Buried Age* and *Greater Than the Sum*, the *Voyager* short novel *Places of Exile* in *Myriad Universes: Infinity's Prism*, and the *Corps of Engineers* novella *Aftermath* in the collection of the same title. He also has stories in all four *Star Trek* anniversary anthologies to date and in the *Mirror Universe: Shards and Shadows* anthology. His other works include two original novelettes in *Analog Science Fiction and Fact* and the novels *X-Men: Watchers on the Walls* and *Spider-Man: Drowned in Thunder*. More information and original fiction can be found at http://home.fuse.net/ChristopherLBennett.

MARGARET WANDER BONANNO sold her first novel in 1978, at a time when "serious women's fiction" was not an oxymoron. Characterized by one reviewer as "the new Mary Gordon," she followed this first mainstream novel with two more, before the recession of '82 changed the face of U.S. publishing forever and she, along with several hundred other midlist writers, found herself needing to rethink her career. A *Star Trek* fan "from the time of the beginning," Margaret recalibrated her style and wrote first one, then a second *Trek* novel entirely on spec. That second manuscript became *Dwellers in the Crucible*, which was followed by *Strangers from the Sky*. Following a bit of strangeness that resulted in ninety-three percent of *Probe's* being written by someone else, Margaret segued into straight s/f with two trilogies, *The Others* and *Preternatural*, and with Nichelle Nichols co-authored *Saturn's Child*. A bit of pseudonymous fiction here, another mainstream novel there, a bio, ghostwriting, and book doctoring, oh my, and Margaret was welcomed back to Pocket Books when Marco Palmieri invited her to participate in the *Lost Era* series with *Catalyst of Sorrows*. Most recently there has been the challenge and delight exploring the character of Christopher Pike in *Burning Dreams*. A native New Yorker, Margaret currently lives on the Left Coast, where she dabbles in *bonsai* and has found a beach to walk on and a Romulan to walk with her. She has two adult children, and is the co-founder of Van Wander Press (www.vanwanderpress.com). Please visit her website at www.margaretwanderbonanno.com.

KEITH R.A. DECANDIDO (editor) co-developed the *Star Trek: Starfleet Corps of Engineers* eBook series, and was the editor responsible for the monthly *Star Trek* eBook line that ran from 2000 to 2008, which included not just the *Corps of Engineers*, but also the anniversary miniseries *Mere Anarchy* (reprinted in this volume) and *The Next Generation: Slings and Arrows*. Keith has also assembled three *Star Trek* anthologies—*New Frontier: No Limits* (with Peter David), *Tales of the Dominion War*, and *Tales from the Captain's Table*—as well as a dozen other anthologies, most recently *Doctor Who: Short Trips: The Quality of Leadership*. On the writing side of the ledger, Keith has penned sixteen novels, twelve novellas, seven short stories, and five comic books in the *Trek* universe, covering all five TV shows, as well as several prose-only and cross-series tales. Learn more at his official web site at DeCandido.net, or read his inane ramblings at kradical .livejournal.com.

KEVIN DILMORE's solo story "The Road to Edos" was published as part of the *Star Trek: New Frontier* anthology *No Limits*, and he was a regular writer for *Star Trek Communicator*. With Dayton Ward, his work includes stories for the *Star Trek: Tales of the Dominion War*, *Star Trek: Constellations*, *Star Trek: Mirror Universe: Shards and Shadows*, and *Star Trek: Seven Deadly Sins* anthologies, the *Star Trek: The Next Generation* novels *A Time to Sow* and *A Time to Harvest*, the *Mirror Universe* short novel *Age of the Empress* (in collaboration with Mike Sussman), ten novellas in the *Star Trek: Starfleet Corps of Engineers* series, the *Star Trek: Vanguard* novels *Summon the Thunder* and *Open Secrets*, and *The 4400: Wetworks*. A graduate of the University of Kansas, Kevin currently works for Hallmark Cards in Kansas City, Missouri.

DAVE GALANTER has authored various *Star Trek* projects, among them the *Voyager* novel *Battle Lines*, the *Next Generation* duology *Maximum Warp*, the *S.C.E.* eBooks *Ambush* and *Bitter Medicine*, short stories in *Tales of the Dominion War* ("Eleven Hours Out") and *Constellations* ("The Leader"), and the forthcoming Original Series novel *Troublesome Minds*. His not-so-secret Fortress of Solitude is in Michigan, from where he pretends to have a hand in managing the message board Web sites he co-owns: ComicBoards.com, a comic book discussion site, and TVShowBoards.com, a similar site dedicated to television and movies. He also edits and is the main contributor to his own blogsite, SnarkBait.com, on which he babbles about philosophy and politics. Dave spends his non-day-job time with family and friends, or burying himself in other writing projects. He enjoys feedback on his writing, positive or negative, and would appreciate seeing any comments you have on his work. Feel free to email him at dave@comicboards.com.

DAYTON WARD. Author. Trekkie. Writing his stories and searching for a way to tap into the hidden nerdity that all humans have. Then, an accidental overdose of Mountain Dew altered his body chemistry, and now when Dayton Ward grows excited or just downright geeky, a startling metamorphosis occurs. Driven by outlandish ideas and a pronounced lack of sleep, he is pursued by fans, editors, his wife and kids, as well as funny men in bright uniforms wielding tazers, straitjackets, and medication. In addition to the numerous credits he shares with friend and co-writer Kevin Dilmore, Dayton is the author of the *Star Trek* novel *In the Name of Honor* and the science fiction novels *The Last World War* and *The Genesis Protocol*, as well as short stories that have appeared in the first three *Star Trek: Strange New Worlds* anthologies, the Yard Dog Press anthology *Houston, We've Got Bubbas*, *Kansas City Voices* Magazine and the *Star Trek: New Frontier* anthology *No Limits*. Dayton is believed to be working on his next novel, and he must let the world think that he is working on it, until he can find a way to control his gambling habit and win back the advance his editor already paid him. Though he currently lives in Kansas City with his wife and two daughters, Dayton is a Florida native and still maintains a torrid long-distance romance with his beloved Tampa Bay Buccaneers. Visit him on the web at www.daytonward.com.

Print publication of *The Blood-Dimmed Tide* marks thirty-five years since **HOWARD WEINSTEIN** sold his first story at age nineteen (the 1974 animated *Star Trek* episode "The Pirates of Orion"). Over the years, he's written a half-dozen *Star Trek* novels, three *V* novels, and sixty-odd *Star Trek* comics. Recent contributions to *Star Trek* short story anthologies are "Safe Harbors" in *Tales of the Dominion War* and "Official Record" in the original-series fortieth-anniversary collection *Constellations*. His nonfiction work includes the essay "Being Better" in *Boarding the Enterprise*, a fortieth-anniversary celebration of *Star Trek*'s legacy from BenBella Books. Howard has also written *Puppy Kisses Are Good for the Soul & Other Important Lessons You & Your Dog Can Teach Each Other* and a biography of New York Yankees baseball star Mickey Mantle. His numerous articles and columns have appeared in the *New York Times*, *Baltimore Sun*, *Newsday*, and *Starlog Magazine*. A displaced New Yorker, Howard lives in Maryland with his wife, Susan, and their two cute Welsh Corgis, Mickey and Callie. Howard also runs Day-One Dog Training, helping dog owners get the most enjoyment from life with their canine companions.